Winter of the Comet

GORDON JOHN THOMSON

DEDICATION

For my son Ken Thomson, who loves the world of the theatre just as much as Molly.

Winter of the Comet

In the cold winter of 1664, the Thames has frozen over, and a great comet has appeared in the skies above the city of London. The comet seems a portent of disaster because England is in a deeply troubled and divided state. The King, Charles II, had been welcomed back as a saviour four years before, but is now resented by increasing numbers of his own people. And war too is looming with the Dutch, England's great seagoing trade rivals...

Molly Titchen is a precocious 16-year-old orange seller at the new King's theatre in Drury Lane who dreams of becoming an actress, and strutting the stage in breeches parts. Yet being an actress in the King's company seems to be a dangerous choice of profession at present as a succession of young actresses die in mysterious circumstances. The leader of the company, Sir Thomas Killigrew, asks a wealthy young physician and merchant, Henry Raven, to investigate the deaths of the actresses.

Then a masked man threatens the life of the King, and Raven finds himself also asked to hunt this madman who has a wicked plan for London in mind...

Set against the lively and pulsating world of Restoration London, with its bear-baiting and dog-fighting pits, its taverns and bawdy houses, its libertines and Puritans, its fops and society beauties, this historical mystery thriller is full of mystery, murder, suspense and romance...

CONTENTS

PROLOGUE

Friday, 9th December 1664

Molly Titchen felt a hand snake up under her petticoats, slide up the length of her silk stockings, and squeeze her knee hard.

'Ye shall find no oranges up there, sir,' she declared primly, stepping back and extricating herself nimbly from the man's grip.

The man, a mere shopkeeper from his dress, did not seem put out by her slippery behaviour. 'I might find a much better treasure up there, though, my sweet dumpling,' he said with a toothy leer.

Molly was not sure that she cared to be called a dumpling. "Dumpling" did imply generous womanly curves, of course, which was well enough in its way. Yet it also perhaps implied "fat", which certainly did not suit her...

Seeing that the man was still leering at her from the pit, and that he had his podgy white hand temptingly within reach on the edge of the stage, Molly stamped lightly on his fingers (just enough to hurt them, but certainly not enough to break them – she was no heartless strumpet after all.) The man did then yelp very satisfactorily, much to the amusement of the fellow's companions.

As usual, the King's theatre in Bridges Street was packed to the rafters, with a clamorous audience of seven hundred souls squeezed onto the green baize-covered benches that sloped gently back from the stage. Molly was one of the line of girl orange sellers who stood at the front of the stage before the performance began, selling the delicious golden fruit from their baskets at tuppence each.

Normally the girls plied their trade at the front of the pit, but for the last few minutes before the play started, they were allowed to ascend the stage and make a last bold push for customers before the play began. On stage, lit by blazing chandeliers and in full view of the crowd, they were invariably subjected to brazen attention and saucy wit from the audience - in fact, receiving quite as many lewd remarks and whistles as did the most beautiful

1

actresses during the play itself. Yet Molly and her six companions did not mind this ribaldry in the slightest. Since the orange sellers were paid according to the number of oranges and other fruit sold, there was always a severe contest between the girls for custom – and success in this little war depended not only on how the girls compared in voluptuousness, but also at their ability to flirt with the audience and respond to their comments with equally saucy ripostes.

Molly's friend Nell stood next to her in line as usual, smiling amiably at her out of the corner of her eye. Despite their close friendship, though, there was always a strong element of personal competition between Nell and Molly to see who could sell the most oranges in a week, and neither was prepared to show the other any favours when it came to this cutthroat business.

The pit was inevitably populated by the lowest ranks of society – at least the lowest ranks that could afford the shilling to go to the theatre anyway - shopkeepers and tradesmen and the like – therefore Molly was well used to low class banter and coarse behaviour from them. Yet the behaviour from the private boxes was hardly any better, even though these were ostensibly occupied by gentlemen and court gallants. The looks and comments that the orange sellers received from the boxes were often as earthy and vulgar as any from the tradesmen in the pit.

Molly had always found that the most modest and gentlemanly behaviour in the audience came from the upper galleries, which were the seating choice of wealthier merchants and professional men, artists and lawyers - gentlemen apparently with a discerning taste for drama, and with infinitely better manners than either the riffraff from the pit or the spoiled upper classes yawning indulgently in their private boxes.

Approaching the start of the play, the noise in the theatre became ever more deafening...

Molly became aware that Mary Meggs was watching the orange girls from the back of the pit and had her evil eye on her in particular, as if she'd noticed that little stamp on one of the theatre's patrons. Mistress Meggs – otherwise known to her girls as "Orange Mary" – ran her orange sellers with all the discipline of the New Model Army, and certainly did not brook rebellions from any of her foot-soldiers, no matter how trivial.

Molly smiled innocently at her in return. It was essential for all the orange girls to keep on the fair weather side of Mistress Meggs, of course, otherwise they would be booted out of the stage door in an instant. Out on the streets of Covent Garden, there were a thousand pretty girls who would dearly like to take their places. And Molly could not bear the thought of losing this job in the theatre because it gave her access to a strange and brilliant new world...

She loved working here at the King's theatre – every intoxicating moment. She loved the heady atmosphere of the theatre itself, the stage craft that could create such spellbinding illusions, with its ropes to fly in angels, and its movable scenery and mysterious trap-doors that allowed figures to arise from the abyss like magic. And, of course, the impossibly handsome actors and beautiful actresses added their own physical perfection to proceedings – even though this was very much illusion too since few of them (apart from Molly's special actress friend Sarah) looked quite so fine close up as they did on stage. In the theatre, illusion was everything - in an instant, Molly found that her mind could easily be transported by the grandness of the dialogue and costumes to the imagined mountains of Sicily or the streets of Madrid, or wherever the play happened to be set. Even when the play was set in the more familiar territory of the Strand or Spring Gardens, or the new pleasure gardens at Fox Hall, the imagined world of the playwright always seemed far more enticing to her than the real world.

Molly even loved the audience and their antics: fops complacently combing their fine new curled wigs as they ogled the actresses, the heckling of gentlemen wits who did their best to make the actors forget their lines, the chatter of white-bosomed court ladies competing with the flutter of their painted fans and the rustling of their silk gowns. The theatre seemed constantly alive with the whispers of romantic assignations and gossip, the latest scandals spreading from here to dinner tables and coffee houses, and then all over London.

If truth be known, Molly even liked the regular brawls and fights that erupted in the audience, if not the occasional evil language and overly savage blows. The only thing she actively disliked about the theatre was the unpleasant atmosphere in summer – the packed hall could be suffocating on hot days, and ripe with the overpowering smell of sweat, powder and heady perfume. In winter, though, the relative warmth of the theatre was a welcome escape for her from her freezing lodgings in a high garret in Coal Hole Lane.

Molly saw from the restive mood of the audience that it must be nearly a half hour past three o'clock and therefore finally time for the play to begin. Today's play was a new one to her, a bawdy comedy written by a young novice playwright George Etherege, and entitled *The Comical Revenge, or Love in a Tub*. Her friend Nell – two years younger than her yet precocious far beyond her fourteen years – had told Molly that the play was not a new one, though, but had been put on at the Duke's theatre last spring to great public acclaim.

Molly wished she could be backstage in one of the tiring rooms at this very moment as the actors and actresses checked their costumes and their painted faces. Soon they would be going down to the green room where they would wait for their cue. How Molly longed to be one of their company, to paint her own face with vivid greasepaint and appear on this stage as a queen or an Amazon, or – best of all - a lover in disguise as a page. What she would give to stride around this stage in men's breeches and show off her fine legs! That would certainly give that low man in the pit something proper to ogle. She noticed guiltily that he was still nursing his injured fingers, which did prompt a mild attack of conscience on her part, and a brief pause in her enticing daydream of herself as an actress...

Molly glanced up from her disturbed reverie and saw that the King's box was empty tonight, which was disappointing. When he was in attendance, the King did often lean over the edge of his private box and give her a particularly knowing smile – although her friend Nell was equally sure that those admiring looks were intended for *her*, and her alone.

But Molly's disappointment at the lack of a Royal presence was mitigated by the clear attention she was getting from a private box on the opposite side of the theatre, where three gentlemen sat engaged in apparently agreeable discourse.

All handsome young men, as far she could see from here in the candlelight, although, if she had to choose between them, then she preferred the looks of the fair-haired and particularly youthful-looking gentleman on the right of the group. All three were wearing their own hair rather than wigs, she noted, therefore not quite in tune with the latest fashion set by the King. But impressive manly heads of hair for all that, Molly had to admit.

The second man, on the left of the group, was someone she vaguely recognized from somewhere. His shoulder-length brown hair curled strikingly over his lace collar, and he had a haughty beauty that was difficult to forget. She remembered now where she'd seen those handsome curls and that striking jaw. Last month, at a performance of Mr Dryden's play *The Wild Gallant*, Molly was sure that the very same man had been sitting in the Royal box, making small talk with the King himself.

Molly's attention finally rested on the third gentleman, the one in the middle. If she was being critical, then this dark-haired gentleman was not quite to her taste, and, with his long nose and square jaw, certainly did not compare for manly beauty with his two companions. He seemed a little gloomy and stern, with something of the look of a puritan about him despite his long curling hair, as if he was reluctant to indulge in something as frivolous as a play. Yet Molly could have sworn that even he had been giving her admiring looks from time to time...

*

Henry Raven (the gloomy-looking gentleman in the middle) had indeed noticed the tall orange girl standing in the middle of the row of tempting beauties on stage. The orange sellers were selected of course for their beauty, sparkle and sauciness, but, even compared to her pulchritudinous fellows, this girl seemed especially gifted in those areas, particularly the sauciness.

His friend Anthony Mawdsley had caught the direction of his eyes and laughed out loud. 'Ah, Henry. I am disappointed at your sudden devotion to a mere orange girl. I had thought that a Fellow of the Royal Society would find higher objects for his passion. And that even if he did succumb occasionally to baser thoughts, he would at least employ them in the admiration of a white-skinned, big-bosomed, long-legged actress, rather than a simple orange seller.'

Raven smiled back and feigned puzzlement. 'And which of these maids is the object of my supposed devotion, Anthony?'

Mawdsley chuckled. 'Why, the bold strumpet in the middle of the row, of course, flaunting her charms to all and sundry.'

'By God's blest mother! - they are all doing that,' intervened Adam Strange. 'But, for myself, I do prefer the charms of the Amazon with the tawny hair to your lady's left, Henry. I would wager that she knows some enchanting bed tricks.'

Raven decided to change the subject. His friends were practised womanisers, and therefore full of mockery for his own more reticent behaviour with women. 'Do you know anything about this play, or its author, Anthony?' Raven was an infrequent theatregoer, whereas his friends were hopelessly addicted to the stage. Especially his lawyer friend Strange, who went two or three times a week, although Mawdsley too was a passionate follower of the theatre, despite the pressures on his time of working as the chief secretary to the Lord Chancellor of England.

Raven did wonder how on earth these theatre companies managed to put on so many different plays in a nine-month season – usually at least fifty in number - although many were revivals, of course, of Ben Jonson, or Beaumont and Fletcher, or translations of Molière and other foreigners. The actors rehearsed the plays in the morning, and performed them in the afternoon, six days a week. And even this hectic schedule did not count any special evening performances given for the King in the Cockpit in Whitehall Palace.

Mawdsley quickly proved his intimate knowledge of the theatre – Raven even suspected that Anthony might have some ambitions as a playwright himself, despite his political devotion to the cause of the King. 'I haven't seen this play before. But I dare say that *Love in a Tub* will turn out to be precisely what you would expect from the title. I do know that Etherege has dedicated the play to the King's naughty boy, Lord Buckhurst, therefore we must expect the worst. It will be full of wild living, exuberant and vital characters, a rich lusty widow jousting no doubt with a spendthrift hero, and a plot mixing realism and heroism, fantasy and ridicule. Etherege clearly wants to write plays that celebrate the end of Cromwell's puritan England,

and the replacement of those puritan values with his own libertine's manifesto.'

Raven was a little dismayed to hear whom the play had been dedicated to. Buckhurst was one of the King's favourite drinking companions, and not a man noted for his reserve or sobriety. Raven could not understand the King's apparent devotion to the man, whom he considered a reprobate of the worst kind. Many people agreed with that view of Lord Buckhurst, of course – especially after he and his friend Charles Sedley had been arrested over an infamous incident last year in the Cock Inn in Bow Street, very near to Covent Garden. Inflamed with strong liquor, Sedley had stripped naked on the balcony of the inn, then gave the crowd in the coach yard below a jolly pantomime of lust and buggery, preaching a mock sermon in which he had conflated priest, quack and pimp. Raven had happened to be passing the inn at the time and had watched this unsavoury balcony performance with dismay, knowing that this man was one of the King's truest friends. Sedley had boasted to the men below at the end of his sermon, 'Good sirs, I have to sell you such a powder as will make all the cunts in town run after you,' before exposing his manhood with vulgar ostentation and washing it in a glass of wine in which the efficacious powder had supposedly been dissolved. A riot among the more devout and puritan citizens of Covent Garden had resulted...

Raven noticed the orange girls finally leaving the front of the stage, so the play was clearly ready to start. 'If this play be written by a friend of Buckhurst and Sedley, 'tis not likely to be heroic drama, that much is certain,' he commented dryly...

*

After two hours, *The Comical Revenge, or Love in a Tub* was over, and had received a tumultuous ovation.

Molly had changed out of her fine orange seller's gown (which was the property of the theatre) into her own poorer clothes, and now stood in the wings offstage as the audience dispersed, still clutching her sides with laughter - if slightly shocked laughter at the brazenness of what she'd just witnessed. The play had been full of the crude armoury of bawdy and bodily jokes, replete with buffoonery and burlesque. Comedies had been getting ever more risqué and daring since the King had allowed theatres to open again four years ago, and the playwrights seemed determined to make as much use as they could of this sudden freedom to shock and amuse.

What shocked Molly so much were not simply the words that Master Etherege had put into the players' voices, but that the actresses too seemed to revel in saying such naughty things. Some of the most talented actresses of the company, Mary Pettican, Anne Carey and Jane Golightly, had appeared in the play and entered into the bawdy goings-on with abandon. And even Sarah too had been unrecognizable in her role of a fat and vulgar maid with a tendency to get her words mixed with hilarious results...

Sarah Lusted was Molly's particular friend among the actresses, a beautiful peach-skinned girl from the village of Islington. It was she who had helped Molly find a job here two years ago as an orange seller, and they had been fast friends ever since. And it was Sarah who had taught her to read properly over these last two years, and lent her books that had opened up a whole new world of learning and ideas for a poor orphaned girl from Coal Hole Lane. Sarah had originally been an orange seller too - if a very ladylike one - before attracting the eye of Sir Thomas Killigrew himself and being soon elevated into the role of actress. So far she had still only embraced relatively minor and uninteresting parts, but today she had played the part of the fat and stupid maid with comic aplomb and threatened occasionally to steal the show from the true stars of the play - Mary Pettican as the lusty widow, and Anne Carey as her devious rival.

Mary Pettican was the leading light of the company and a great favourite of Sir Thomas, with whom she was rumoured (at least according to Molly's friend Nell) to be intimate, hence her elevation to the best roles. Yet, in Molly's honest opinion, Mistress Pettican justly deserved her top billing in the company on her acting ability alone – today she had played the lusty widow in the play to perfection, and eventually seen off the competition from Sarah and the others.

Molly did not know any of the other actresses in the company as well as Sarah, but Jane Golightly - who had played a society beauty in *The Comical Revenge* - seemed a sweet, shy girl, while Anne Carey – who was Jane's complete opposite in every respect except physical beauty - was undoubtedly a vicious gossip, and as devious a person in real life as the one she had been playing.

As the pit and the galleries slowly emptied, Molly set off upstairs to the tiring rooms to help Sarah change out of her costume. Most of the cast were still at the side of the stage, and embracing each other with high spirits after the success of their performance. Sarah was not with them, though. As she had left the stage hurriedly five minutes ago, she had begged Molly to follow her quickly up to the actresses' tiring room to help her out of her imprisoning costume, as her normal dresser had eaten something that disagreed with her and had gone home. Molly had not been prepared to risk Mistress Meggs' wrath, though, so had first gone to ask her permission to help Sarah disrobe: normally the orange girls were not allowed to fraternize or mix with the actresses, and especially not after performances.

But Sarah certainly needed some special help today to undress from her cumbersome costume and padding. For the part of the maid in Etherege's play, she had been padded with huge false breasts and an equally vast pair of false buttocks, which had made both her and Molly erupt with the giggles when they had encountered each other briefly before the play. Sarah must be desperate to get out of this hot and uncomfortable costume by now (particularly since the constraints of the costume made it impossible to piss) so Molly decided that perhaps she'd better hurry even faster to her friend's rescue.

Molly climbed the creaking oak stairs as fast as the dim lighting would permit, and reached the narrow gallery that led to the main tiring room. A woman was just leaving the tiring room as Molly reached the other end of the gallery. Molly did not recognize her, so wondered naturally who she was. From twenty paces, this dark-haired lady appeared in profile to be a beautiful and voluptuous young woman in red silk. Molly had time to note the stylish sleeves of her gown, tied with ribbons into a series of puffs as *virago* sleeves, and the modest square-shaped neckline. Her height was certainly exceptional, and her hair was drawn back from her forehead with side partings on both sides of the head, and curls hanging from them. As the woman turned her head, Molly saw that she was wearing a small knot of hair halfway up the back of her head, a delightful detail which Molly rather envied.

Molly had presumed by now that the stranger must be an actress and member of the company. Yet Molly had thought she knew all the actresses of the King's company tolerably well by sight now, so was curious to know who this unfamiliar lady was. But with a rustle of silk, the dark lady vanished down the staircase at the other end of the gallery before Molly could get close to her. Molly wondered if she was perhaps a visiting actress from the rival Duke's company, without a role today, come to jaw with her acting friends after the performance.

Molly found Sarah alone in the tiring room, the other actresses still not having returned from their triumph on stage. Sarah was sitting in front of the mirror, still dressed in the fat maid's outfit, of course, and with her face ludicrously made up with fat red painted cheeks and false eyebrows, blackened with burnt cork. It seemed a pity in Molly's opinion to conceal Sarah's beauty under all that paint and padding, although Molly – equally beautiful, if nothing like so ladylike - would have loved to try such a vulgar role herself.

'Who was that wondrous-fine lady who just departed, Sarah?' Molly asked her, putting her hands on Sarah's shoulders and beginning to unlace the back of her serving maid's dress.

Sarah made no reply but continued to stare in silence at the mirror.

Molly was disturbed that she might have offended her friend over something because she had seemed in good spirits just five minutes before as she had walked off stage. Sarah was twenty years old and therefore Molly's elder and better by four years. She was an orphan too, like Molly, but, unlike her friend, Sarah had been raised in the home of a respectable yeoman dairy farmer in the handsome hilltop village of Islington where she had acquired her genteel country nature and manners. Molly, on the other hand, had been brought up by a bawdy house madam in a dingy alley of Whetstone Park, behind Lincoln's Inn Fields.

So she and Sarah were scarcely equals in anything, if truth be known, although it was sad that Sarah's adoptive family had disowned her completely when she had chosen to work in the theatre, which they equated well nigh with a bawdy house. It was perhaps because of that rejection by her family that Sarah had treated young Molly from the beginning of their acquaintanceship like a friend and equal, not as a skivvy to be browbeaten and abused. So, although she scarcely had reason to doubt her friend's constancy, Molly was always slightly fearful of losing that special friendship.

Then Molly forgot her own worries entirely as she looked at Sarah's face in the polished metal mirror and saw with shock the glassy, staring eyes of her friend...

Molly had lived too long on the streets of London not to know death when she saw it. 'Oh, my sweet Lord!' she said simply, as the tears began to flow.

CHAPTER 1

Friday, 9ᵗʰ December 1664

Claiming pressure of his legal work, Adam Strange had made a dash for the exit as soon as the play had come to a close, so that Raven and his friend Mawdsley had been left to enjoy the comforts of their private box on their own for a few minutes while the other patrons of the theatre filed out noisily into the snowy December night.

Raven had been looking around the pit and the stage below, hoping to catch a glimpse of his favourite orange seller. But she had disappeared very adroitly from view, and the only people now visible below were cleaning drudges, clearing the theatre of the waste and detritus left behind by the recently departed audience.

Raven heard a discreet knock at the door of their box, and opened it to find a middle-aged man standing there in a visible state of distress. Despite the dimness of the candlelight in the corridor, Raven recognized the man immediately from his distinctive appearance as Sir Thomas Killigrew, the witty leader of the King's company.

Raven was not well acquainted with this gentleman yet had met him several times at court over the last four years. These meetings had been brief ones only, though, since Raven had formed no particular rapport with the man that might have encouraged him to seek a deeper acquaintance. Sir Thomas, a playwright and former courtier of the King's late father, Charles I, belonged to a different level of society than that which Raven normally encountered in his business and professional life, and certainly a racier one than he was comfortable with. Yet his friend Mawdsley knew Sir Thomas tolerably well through their mutual connection to the King and Whitehall Palace, so Raven assumed that Sir Thomas must be here to give his greetings to his friend rather than to him.

And Sir Thomas did indeed address Mawdsley first with a polite greeting, which seemed initially to confirm Raven's expectation. Yet it turned out, surprisingly, that Killigrew's principal business was in fact with Henry Raven rather than his friend...

Sir Thomas's long white hair was in slight disarray and his long velvet coat and breeches seemed a little dishevelled as if he'd been running up stairs. 'Mr Raven, forgive this interruption. But I have a favour to ask. You have been pointed out to me in the past as a physician, sir, as well as a man of business. Is that true, sir?'

Raven was a little wary of answering the man directly. Killigrew was well known as a man of biting wit and a practical joker - in fact, some called him the King's personal fool and jester. Given that Royal connection, it did seem that Killigrew had the power to mock and revile even the most prominent in society without any fear of penalty. Raven had to wonder whether he was now about to become the butt of one of Sir Thomas's infamous japes, perhaps because of his own sober reputation and well-known obsession with the study of natural philosophy. Or perhaps even at the behest of his friends tonight, who were equally addicted to practical jokes...

But a glance at his friend Mawdsley indicated that this must be a serious question from Sir Thomas, and not one asked in jest. 'I studied medicine at Cambridge, Sir Thomas, and I am a Fellow of the College of Physicians,' Raven finally admitted, 'but I later became interested in business and trade so I have never practised as a working physician. Yet I have maintained my interest in medicine by undertaking research into the ailments and diseases that afflict mankind.'

Killigrew seemed a little disappointed with Raven's answer, but finally made up his mind. 'No matter, sir, that you are not a working physician. There is no one else at hand in the theatre who is better qualified to help. I would ask that you make haste with me to the tiring room. One of my dear young actresses has met a strange fate. Can you come at once, sir?'

Raven looked across at his friend Mawdsley, who said, 'Shall I join you, Henry?'

Sir Thomas nodded vigorously. 'By all means, Mr Mawdsley. Perhaps you can be off assistance too, with your clever lawyer's mind.'

Raven slapped Mawdsley lightly on the back, still not completely convinced that this was not an elaborate hoax to make a fool of him. 'Then it seems you must come too, Anthony. You would not wish to miss such a mystery as this seems to be.'

*

'She seems but to be sleeping,' said Sir Thomas in wonder.

'Nay, she is certainly dead,' Raven answered dryly, choosing to take his words literally. Raven had finally accepted the seriousness of the situation. Even such a joker as Sir Thomas Killigrew could hardly produce a corpse at will for the purpose of making mockery of someone.

After making sure that there truly was no breath left in the poor lady's body, Raven and Mawdsley had personally carried the corpse of Mistress Lusted from the tiring room to a nearby private chamber which contained a bed used by Sir Thomas to rest during breaks from rehearsals, and before performances. There, in the small oak panelled room, with a fire burning cheerfully in the hearth to ward off the December cold, a young maid had tenderly removed the ridiculous costume the actress had been wearing, and gently cleaned the paint from her face with a basin of warm water to reveal her perfect features and lily-white skin.

With a sheet now laid over her, leaving only her pale white face and golden hair exposed, Mistress Lusted did indeed seem to be merely sleeping. Raven had watched her performance on stage barely one hour before, and had not realized that this had been a beautiful slender young woman taking the part of the fat and comic old maid, so perfect had been her rendition.

'I suppose that I must report this immediately to the coroner,' Sir Thomas said, still all of a fluster. 'Is that not my duty?'

'You are quite correct that the coroner should be informed officially when there has been an unexplained death like this. But I doubt there is any pressing need of that tonight, Sir Thomas,' Raven reassured him. 'In fact I am well acquainted with the city coroner, so I will inform him personally on the morrow of this sad event, if you wish.'

Killigrew nodded gratefully. 'But what did she die of, sir?' Sir Thomas asked worriedly. 'Could it be the plague?' The gentleman manager gulped in distress at that dismal thought. 'I have heard reports that the plague has returned to the Turks' infidel empire and is spreading westwards to the civilized world.'

Raven knew that Killigrew had been a great traveller during his years of exile during the Interregnum, and still had many contacts in Europe, so was perhaps speaking from personal knowledge of someone who had just returned from the East. In fact Killigrew had been such a great traveller as a young man that it was said that he had written each of his most famous plays in a different city: *Thomaso, or The Wanderer*, which Raven had seen performed here only recently, had been written in Madrid, for example.

Raven reflected a little more on what he knew of this witty if unpredictable gentleman. Killigrew was a devoted Royalist and Roman Catholic, and had willingly followed the young Prince Charles into exile nearly twenty years before. In those years of exile, Killigrew had sojourned in Paris, Geneva, and Rome, and had later been appointed as Charles' diplomatic representative in Venice, where there had been many reports of his debauchery. Killigrew's devotion to his monarch had paid off handsomely four years ago on the Restoration when, along with Sir William Davenant, he had been given a royal warrant to form a theatre company and to revive English drama. Killigrew had beaten Davenant to a debut at Gibbon's Tennis Court in Clare Market, with the new King's company. Later, they had played for a time at the old Red Bull Theatre, but last year the company had moved to this newly built King's theatre in Bridges Street, just off Drury Lane.

Raven frowned as he considered this news of the plague. 'Yes, I have heard these reports from foreign lands too.' He regarded the pale corpse on the bed. 'But rest assured, Sir Thomas, this is no case of the plague. In fact, I know not for certain how this poor creature died...'

Despite this reassurance, though, Killigrew would not be denied his worries about the plague. 'Yet there is a comet in the heavens at present, and that is always a harbinger of death and disaster, is it not?'

'There is indeed a comet, Sir Thomas...' Using his six-inch telescope, Raven had seen the comet with his own eyes only the night before from the backyard of his house in St Martin's Lane, and it had certainly been a splendid sight, located near the first magnitude star Aldebaran in the constellation of Taurus, and displaying a distinctive tail and fine bright head. The comet had first been observed last month in Spain and had brightened considerably since then so had to be approaching the Earth even more closely. As he'd made his regular observations of its declination and right ascension last night, Raven had wondered about the path of a comet and whether it could really conform to a mathematical curve of some description, like the planets, as his friend at the Royal Society, Robert Hooke, suspected. Mr Hooke, the Curator of Experiments at the society, thought that some mysterious force emanated from the Sun and controlled the motions of both the planets and strange objects like comets. Yet Raven could hardly countenance such a notion, which sounded almost like magic or sorcery. One thing Raven was certain about, though, was that comets had nothing to do with earthly disasters — not unless one of these objects should strike the earth itself, of course, which seemed an even more fanciful notion.

He spoke up again. 'But as for a comet being a harbinger of death, that is mere superstition, Sir Thomas. It has been known since the time of the great Danish astronomer Tycho Brahe in the last century that comets are part of the solar system and lie well outside the influence of the Earth. They can have nothing to do with our affairs here. '

Sir Thomas had clearly never heard of Tycho Brahe and was still not completely reassured that some malevolent influence was not at work here. 'Then poison? Could she have been poisoned?'

The young maid turned from her kneeling position by the bed, and gasped aloud at this suggestion. Yet it did not seem so much a gasp of surprise to Raven, as one of agreement and vindication. Raven suddenly realized with surprise the identity of this young maiden, as her face came clearly into his view. She was no longer in her orange seller's costume, but dressed instead in a plain dark dress of homespun material with a prim high neck, and a white coif modestly covering her dark hair, like a servant girl. Yet this was undoubtedly the same tall girl who had attracted his attention on stage before the play.

Raven glanced at her briefly – and caught a hint of recognition in return – before speaking to Sir Thomas again. 'I know of no poison that could kill like this and leave not a mark behind, or even a sign of physical distress. It's almost as if the angels had simply arrived and spirited this poor lady's soul away.'

The maid coughed disbelievingly. 'And is talk of angels not superstition too, sir?'

Sir Thomas silenced her with an apologetic glance at Raven. 'Sssh! Be silent, girl. No one needs to hear your opinions, especially not a gifted man of philosophy and business like Mr Raven here, who is perfectly capable of making his own deliberations in this matter.'

Mawdsley finally stepped forward from the shadows. Raven could see that he was taken with this girl too because he spoke to her with extreme gentleness. 'What is your name, Mistress?'

The girl looked up at him gratefully for the polite form of his address. She stood up and gave a little curtsey. 'Molly, sir. Molly Titchen.'

'So, Molly, it was you who found Mistress Lusted in this pitiable state in the tiring room?'

'It was, sir.'

Mawdsley frowned. 'Why were you there? Are you not one of the orange sellers?'

'I am, sir. But Mistress Lusted is –' her face fell – '*was* a friend, and she asked me to come to the tiring room after the play and help her disrobe from this cumbersome costume. I had the permission of Mistress Meggs to go backstage,' she said in an apologetic aside to Sir Thomas.

Mawdsley leaned forward to look at the body on the bed again. 'Was there no one else there in the tiring chamber to see what happened?'

'No. The other players had not yet returned to disrobe.' Molly hesitated. 'But I did see a lady leaving the tiring room as I was arriving.'

Mawdsley exchanged a significant look with Sir Thomas. 'Did you know this lady, Mistress?'

The girl hesitated slightly. 'No, sir, I did not recognize her. But she looked like an actress, with her low-cut gown and her distinctive hair style.'

Raven intervened again. 'There is no need to go searching for culprits in this matter, Sir Thomas. I believe this to be an entirely natural death, if a perplexing one. I have examined Mistress Lusted's body in detail, and can see nothing external that might explain it. Therefore I believe that the lady must have had some defect of the heart, perhaps a weakness in the ventricle or the valves. We are only just beginning to understand the workings of the heart, but from my own study of animal hearts, I know well that malformations of the mitral and tricuspid valves are common and can cause sudden death for no apparent reason.'

'Yet Mistress Lusted was young and in perfect health, sir – hale and hearty always,' Molly piped up testily.

'She may have appeared so,' Raven assured her, 'but external appearances can be deceptive. Hearts can work perfectly for many years, and then – for no apparent reason – seize and stop. Even in a lady as young as this.'

The girl was unwilling to concede her point. 'You say there is no mark on her, sir. But there is – I saw it clearly as I was washing her face. You can see it too, sir, I am sure, even in this light.'

'Show me, then,' Raven said with slight irritation, not liking to be corrected.

Molly pointed to her friend with a long fine index finger. 'Regard her neck, sir.'

Raven bent down to peer at Mistress Lusted's swanlike neck. 'You mean that tiny pinprick of dried blood?'

'Yes, indeed.'

Raven had not noticed that blemish before – this girl must have good eyes – but he shook his head in denial. 'That is merely a fleabite. No poison that I know could penetrate such a pinprick of a wound, if that's what you're suggesting. Nor cause such a quick and peaceful death...'

Molly bit her lip with exasperation. 'How can you be so sure, sir? Sarah herself once told me that physicians understand almost nothing about the workings of the body – why our blood must journey to the lungs, how we use our nourishment to stay alive, what the source of our intelligence and humanity is. Although she said that some suspect now that the *brain* might be where our intelligence rises, not in the heart or the liver as the Ancients thought...'

Raven was taken aback by this girl's obvious cleverness. Raven had just bought a new book written by the eminent Oxford physician Thomas Willis – *Cerebri Anatome*, concerning the anatomy of the brain -

in which Willis had made precisely that bold claim - that it was the brain that was the chief seat of the rational soul in man, the chief mover in the animal machine. After reading the book and studying the complex anatomy of the cerebrum depicted within its pages, Raven had become convinced that Willis must be right. Yet how was it that a mere orange seller could express such unexpectedly complex thoughts about the nature of human intelligence? These girls were usually common strumpets of the most silly and obvious kind...

'Then your friend was a wise young lady because all of that is true,' Raven finally admitted. 'Our ignorance of the workings of our own bodies is still woeful, and we are even more ignorant of the animating spirit that gives us life and movement.'

Sir Thomas waved Molly impatiently towards the door. 'Perhaps you should leave us now, and allow us to escape from your inane chatter, girl.' He relented a little at the look of dejection on her face. 'I thank you for your kind attention to poor Mistress Lusted, Molly, but we gentlemen will deal with her now.'

Molly went, but only with great reluctance. She gave Raven and Mawdsley a token bow of acknowledgement before leaving, but her eyes were hostile.

'Mistress Titchen is a surprisingly sharp thinker for one so young,' Mawdsley suggested, after Molly had gone.

Raven agreed with that sentiment, but discreetly said nothing.

Sir Thomas, on the other hand, laughed coarsely. '*Mistress Titchen*! A deep thinker? I hardly think so, gentlemen. That girl was brought up in the infamous bawdy house in Whetstone Park run by Madam Celia Hornett, good sirs, so scarcely deserves such respect as you choose to give her.'

Raven felt obliged to defend her. 'I would disagree in turn, Sir Thomas. She does deserve our respect. We do not choose where we are brought up, after all. And that girl clearly has a good head on her shoulders for one of lowly birth and with so little education.'

'Well, if she has, it will do her no good as an orange seller in the theatre. Our patrons are rather less interested in the good head on her shoulders than they are in the size and shape of her titties,' Killigrew pronounced dryly. He clapped his hands together sharply, as if he had just been relieved of an awkward burden. 'But back to this morbid affair, good sirs. I will send word to the local ward constable of these sad events in the morning. And I will be very obliged if you will inform the coroner accordingly. In the meantime, Mistress Lusted can lie here so that her fellow players can come and see her, and make their farewells to her. 'Tis a tragedy in one so young. But I am content to accept your view, Mr Raven, that nothing untoward has gone on here tonight, and that Mistress Lusted is a sad victim of her own mortality and bodily weakness, nothing more.' Sir Thomas contrived to appear a sweet old man with these more sympathetic statements, Raven thought, yet he remained unconvincing in this guise - someone merely playing a kindly part for a change. Mawdsley had told Raven some interesting stories about this gentleman that contradicted any benign view.

Even though Killigrew was a married man well past his fiftieth year, he still apparently had a taste for bedding saucy and nubile ladies. Raven wondered just how many of the actresses of this company had been forced to audition in this very chamber, in a role earthier and more physical than any they would essay on the stage. It was a sad thought, but perhaps Mistress Lusted herself had already enjoyed some familiarity with that bed where she now lay in solemn state.

Mawdsley had even suggested that Sir Thomas had a predilection for pretty boys too – particularly pretty boys dressed as ladies, if the even saucier rumours about him were true. Until the puritans had banned the performing of plays after the Civil War, the world of the theatre had been used to boys playing the parts of ladies, of course. The restoration of the monarchy four years ago had not only brought back the theatre to England, but new innovations too, one of which was the arrival of real flesh-and-blood women to play the female roles. Yet not everyone was happy to see the beautiful boy actors, in their fine gowns and silk stockings and high wigs, replaced in their portrayal of ladies by the real thing. And perhaps Sir Thomas Killigrew might be one of that regretful number, if the salacious rumours were true...

Yet even a sober and serious man like Raven had to admit that the pretty boy actors had been a wonderful thing to behold. Several years ago, Raven had seen the famous Edward Kynaston play the part of the Duke's sister in *The Loyall Subject,* and found him on stage to be the loveliest looking lady he ever saw in his life. Only a low husky voice had betrayed that this beautiful lady might be concealing something unexpected between her legs - like a pillicock...

*

A little after nine o'clock, Raven and Mawdsley walked back home together at a leisurely pace down the Strand. Despite the intense cold, they both had preferred to walk home after their evening engagement rather than taking a carriage or a sedan chair. It gave them the opportunity to talk in peace, and was convenient enough for both gentlemen since Mawdsley's route to his home in Axe Yard, Westminster, took him past the bottom of St Martin's Lane where Raven resided.

The Strand was the busiest street in the capital, if no better lit than anywhere else in the kingdom. But tonight was a clear starlit winter's evening so that the snowy street was easy to negotiate for once, especially with burning brush torches lighting the way outside the great mansions on the south side of the Strand. The riverside had long been dominated by these great mansions of England's mightiest families – the Savoy Palace, now the seat of the Bishop of London, Somerset House, Arundel House – although all these mansions were in decline now, as were the families who owned them.

Until recently the north side of the Strand had remained a private country estate owned by the Earl of Bedford. But as the population of the city expanded, and the wealthy business and merchant classes found themselves anxious to escape from the confines of the city walls to more elegant and fashionable surroundings, this area - bounded by Drury Lane, Long Acre, St Martin's Lane and the Strand - had been built over in the years before the Civil War with vast terraces of elegant homes. The piazza in Covent Garden was the crowning feature of this ambitious building programme, although the Bedford family had still held on to Bedford House and a large walled garden that extended all the way between the Strand and the piazza.

Yet, for all the affluence of Covent Garden and the Strand, these streets were still in close proximity to the slum areas of St Giles and Moorfields, therefore dangerous to walk, particularly at night, being the haunt of cutpurses and assassins, deceiving whores and footpads. Raven carried a sword when walking the streets, of course, as did most gentlemen. But unlike most gentlemen, Raven knew how to use his to defend himself against ruffians.

Yet they would be hardy footpads who would venture to roam these streets tonight, Raven decided, as his tall wooden heels slipped on the frozen rutted ground. He was wrapped up in his thickest cloak, woollen knee-length coat and heavy Rhinegrave breeches, yet the fierce cold still penetrated to his skin.

'By God's lid, 'tis cold!' Mawdsley exclaimed, agreeing with his friend's unspoken thought. 'The winters seem to grow ever more dire, do they not? The river is already beginning to freeze over solid, although we are scarce into December. I remember no such severe winters when I was a boy in Streatham.'

'Nor I,' Raven agreed. 'The sun seems as bright as ever on midsummer's day, yet perhaps it is going into a slow decline and the Earth will now grow ever colder until there are no more summers at all.'

Mawdsley looked alarmed. 'Is this a serious proposition you make, Henry?'

Raven grimaced. 'My friend Robert Hooke at the Royal Society believes it could be. No one knows the source of the Sun's great heat, after all, so how can we predict how long its life-giving warmth will endure?'

'Then we shall soon be wearing thick winter drawers all year long.'

Raven nodded wryly. 'Ay, that we may.' He smiled. 'And perhaps ladies will not be able to show quite so much of their white bosoms in public, which would be even more of a pity.'

Mawdsley laughed too. 'That would truly be a pity.' He cocked an eye at his friend. 'You recognized that maid who found Mistress Lusted, of course, Henry?'

'How could I not when I am so enamoured of her? ' Raven laughed. 'You seemed rather more enamoured of her yourself, though, Anthony.'

'Unlike you, Henry, I choose not to deny it. Mistress Molly Titchen is a very fetching girl. And as you said, she has a fine head on her shoulders for an orange seller, which makes her far more interesting to me than a common troll.' Mawdsley frowned. 'That was a sad business tonight, though, was it not? Do you really believe her actress friend, Mistress Lusted, died of natural causes?'

'I do.'

'You give no credence at all to Molly's notion that she was poisoned through that small wound on her neck?'

'None at all.' Raven grunted cynically, his breath rising like thick white mist in the frozen air. 'God's bread! Why would anyone poison an actress?'

Mawdsley strode on, his feet crunching on the frozen snow. 'I cannot say. Another actress perhaps? A deadly rival?'

Raven snorted loudly at that suggestion. 'If she did, then this rival actress knows of a quick-acting poison that I have never encountered before.'

Mawdsley raised his eyebrows. 'Would that be difficult, though? You are many fine things, Henry, but you are no alchemist, are you?'

With gloved hands, Raven tightened his lace cravat which felt as stiff as leather in the fierce cold. ''Tis true that I have wasted none of my time foolishly pursuing the Elixir of Life, nor the Philosopher's Stone for turning base metal to gold. Yet I know enough of alchemy to pass muster, Anthony. I am familiar with the common poisons like hemlock and monkshood. I have made experiment with iron and mercury, with Epsom water, flowers of sulphur, hagiox and laudanum, resin of jalop, and sal ammoniac. Many substances can kill, but I know of none that can enter the body through a tiny fleabite and then render the victim inert within seconds.'

They had reached the crossroads at Charing Cross at the end of the Strand by now where several roads met, including the way south into Whitehall Palace. The cross – the last of the Eleanor Crosses built four centuries before by Edward I to mourn the loss of his beloved queen –

was no longer there, though, but had been taken away during the reign of the Lord Protector after the Caen stonework had fallen into a dangerous state of disrepair.

Yet even without that stone cross in the middle of the road, this was still a significant place in English life. Just four years ago, there had been evil scenes here that Raven had personally witnessed with distaste and horror. It was one of many things that he held against his monarch in consequence, even though he had never discussed such feelings with his Royalist friend Mawdsley who had no such similar doubts about the King's conduct.

Although the King, on his restoration to the throne, had mainly listened to the wise counsel that had proposed forgiveness and reconciliation towards his old Parliamentarian foes, he had not been able to extend that forgiveness to the men who had signed his father's death warrant. Colonel Thomas Harrison and the seven other living men who had committed this crime – the regicides – had been executed here at Charing Cross only four years ago in a most barbaric manner – hanged, then taken down alive to have their bowels removed with red-hot tongs, their hearts ripped from their chests and their severed heads displayed for the baying crowd to mock.

Raven had been in the crowd that day, even though the spectacle had sickened him to his stomach. Overcome by the awfulness of the occasion, he had stayed only because he had never seen men display such steadfastness and bravery in the face of this awful punishment as Harrison and his companions did that day. This barbarous execution had been a Pyrrhic victory for the King – made even worse perhaps by the decision a few months later to unearth the bodies of the four men already dead who had signed the old King's death warrant, including Cromwell himself. Their rotting corpses had been dragged to the Old Bailey and put on "trial", sentenced to death, then dismembered at Tyburn before a jeering mob. Their heads were arrayed still in grisly fashion on the wall spikes of Westminster Hall, the Lord Protector's dour features still easily recognizable...

Raven tried to forget these unpalatable things, as he took leave of his friend. His home was not two hundred yards to the north along St Martin's Lane, while Mawdsley's route home took him south through the Holbein Gate of Whitehall Palace and into King Street beyond.

This crossroads at Charing Cross marked the western edge of London, although not perhaps for much longer. The Lord Chancellor, the Earl of Clarendon, was presently building himself a fine new mansion – reputedly at the cost of forty thousand pounds - in the country lane that led from Piccadilly Hall to Hyde Park, and Raven had heard that there were also plans to build some grand new houses on St

James's Fields opposite the palace, where the annual summer fair was presently held every May, and turned those meadows for a few days into a merry carnival of a place, filled with booths and stalls, and populated by milling crowds of mountebanks and jugglers, pedlars, musicians and saucy maids. On a fearsome mid-winter's night, though, with the wind whistling across those wintry open fields, there was nothing to relieve the bleakness of this snowy scene, apart from the flickering light from torches at the entrance gate to St James's Palace, and from those spaced along the line of gravel that formed the King's Pell Mell ground. This French ball game, in which the ball was struck with a mallet to pass through a series of iron rings, had been played here on this strip of ground next to St James's Palace since the time of the King's grandfather. But since the recent return to England of so many courtiers who had developed a passion for this game while living in exile in France, the sport had now become a highly fashionable one among the King's inner circle.

Mawdsley seemed to realise what Raven was thinking, and pointed to the lights of St James's Palace. 'Did you know, Henry, that there was originally a house for leper women on that spot? And that the annual May fair was instituted for their benefit? But King Henry decided that the leper house would make a perfect hunting lodge for him, so had the leprous maids evicted elsewhere. And eventually the hunting lodge became a palace, though it has now become more of a royal maternity home than anything else. Both the King and the Duke of York were born there...'

'Yes, I know that well, Anthony,' Raven said bluntly, anxious to be on his way, now that his hands and feet felt close to freezing solid. 'Shall we meet tomorrow morning at Jonathan's Coffee-House as usual, where we can continue this conversation in the warm?'

'Yes, I shall endeavour to be there so that thou canst boast to me of thy latest business dealings, as thou art usually inclined to do.' Mawdsley said jokingly. Yet behind the bantering tone, he seemed reluctant to leave his friend immediately, as if he had something rather more serious he wished to say.

'What ails thee, Atlas?' Raven inquired. 'You suddenly look like a man carrying the weight of the world on your shoulders.'

Mawdsley sighed. 'I feel like Atlas, indeed.'

Raven regarded his friend with concern – clearly the business of government, once such a joy for him, was becoming a more tiresome burden for him these days. 'It's not the bone-ache that afflicts thee, is it, Anthony?' he said, only half in jest.

Mawdsley laughed humourlessly. 'The chance of catching the pox would be a fine thing. I have little time for pleasure at the moment, and none at all for whoring.'

'Well, then, what is the matter?' Raven inquired, studying his friend's face with concern. Mawdsley was the second son of a wealthy Royalist family who held a large estate near the village of Streatham, south of London in the green Surrey countryside, on the main coach road to Croydon and East Grinstead. Raven had first met him at Trinity College, Cambridge where they had both been students during the Protectorate – Mawdsley studying the law, and Raven medicine and natural philosophy - and they had soon become fast friends despite their divergent politics. Mawdsley's family had secretly supported Charles' court in exile with vast sums of money, so that they had prospered even more on the King's return to England, being given even more land and titles. Despite being only eight-and-twenty, Mawdsley had soon won the coveted job of Chief Secretary to the Lord Chancellor yet, in truth, this appointment had as much to do with his fierce natural intelligence as with his family connections.

His master, the Lord Chancellor, had also enjoyed a sudden change in fortune with the Restoration, of course. Once plain Mr Edward Hyde, a mere advisor to Prince Charles in exile, he had been raised four years ago to the peerage as Baron Hyde of Hindon in the County of Wiltshire, and the following year his rank and titles increased even further to Viscount Cornbury and the 1st Earl of Clarendon. He had become even closer to the royal family through the recent marriage of his daughter Anne to the King's brother James, Duke of York, although this was not a match that the King himself had apparently wished to see.

Mawdsley was troubled, as he stood at the crossroads, his breath hanging white in the air like hoar frost. 'There are difficult times ahead for us all, Henry. The King was welcomed back like a saviour four years ago but is now reviled everywhere by his people...'

Raven shrugged his broad shoulders. 'Is that not due in part to his heavy-handed actions against dissenters and men of conscience? I believe the Act of Uniformity was a grave error of judgement, Anthony, with its insistence that all ministers of the Church must be ordained by a bishop, must agree to the Thirty-Nine Articles of the Church of England, and also use the Common Prayer Book. What is this pressing need that the King feels for us all to conform so rigidly to his will?'

Mawdsley looked up sharply, his fine features outlined against the line of torches burning outside Northumberland House. 'The King fears that religious dissenters are at heart rebels and anti-monarchists. He worries that if he allows his people too much freedom, then it will eventually stoke the fires of dissent and prompt another civil war. He does not wish to relive the agonies of his father.'

'Yet repression might provoke dissent much more rapidly than a little tolerance and understanding ever would, Anthony,' Raven said caustically.

'Perhaps the Act could have been applied with more tact and discretion,' Mawdsley admitted. 'The King has certainly made many enemies among these Anabaptists, Fifth Monarchists and Quakers, who now wish him nothing but harm.'

'And not those gentlemen alone. Many ordinary and devout men, who would normally support the King strongly, resent the new taxes he has imposed – particularly this damned Hearth Tax, which is mere robbery under a fine-sounding name.'

'We must have revenue to pay for our army and navy,' Mawdsley complained. 'Your comet may not be a portent of the plague, Henry, but it seems to be a fitting portent for war…'

Raven frowned. 'War?'

Mawdsley looked surprised. 'You must know, Henry…all-out war with the Dutch appears inevitable now. They are an ambitious nation very like ourselves, a seafaring people anxious to secure control of trading routes and to find permanent overseas possessions. Our rivalry grows now to breaking point.' He sighed. 'In fact we are already at war, in everything but name, attacking each other's ships on the high seas at will.'

Raven nodded sagely. 'Then I can understand your gloomy demeanour, Anthony, when you have so many pressing problems to attend to. I suggest you get to your bed. Perhaps things will look more tractable in the morning.'

Mawdsley finally raised a weak smile of farewell. 'Somehow I doubt that very much, Henry…' He called out again as he departed. 'Remember thou art invited with Adam to the palace on Wednesday, Henry, to see another play by the King's company. A more decorous play than tonight's offering, ye shall be pleased to learn. Be there early. I shall be most offended if you decline to attend…'

*

Raven's housekeeper, Dora Bagwell, was waiting at the door of his house to let him in, having been watching the street from the first floor sitting room for signs of his expected return.

Raven bustled into the warmth of the main entrance hall, desperate now to escape from the fierce cold. 'You need not have stayed up, Dora,' Raven informed her with a wry look, as he noticed how she was shivering in her thin bodice.

Raven's household was a small one for such a wealthy man – apart from himself as master of the house, there were only three other souls, of which Dora was the dominating presence. He had known the kindly if gruff Dora in Dorset since he was a child, and, after she'd been sadly widowed last year, she had volunteered to leave his country home establishment near Bridport in Dorset, to look after her young bachelor master in his London townhouse.

Many people wondered why Henry Raven was still a bachelor at his age, his family in particular. Although a man of natural tastes where it came to women, Raven was not adept at insinuating himself with those women that he liked, and even worse at repelling those that he did not. Therefore he tended to a wary disposition when it came to his relations with the opposite sex, and presently dedicated far more of his time to his business affairs and to the study of natural philosophy than to the pursuit of a female companion for life. This complacent attitude perplexed his sisters Catherine and Mary considerably, who were always pressing him in their letters from Dorset to find a respectable wife.

Dora clucked at him now in her best Mother Hen fashion. 'I did not stay up specially. I was washing bed linen in the scullery this evening anyway, Master, while it was still warm in there. Then I did a bit of sewing in the sitting room upstairs.'

As she took his discarded cloak from him, then his broad-brimmed hat and black camlott coat with silver buttons, Raven studied her plain round face with concern and wondered whether she was truly happy here in this crowded smoky city – so different from the green hills and dales and heaths of her native Dorset. Her husband Nathaniel had been a fine man and a loyal servant of the Raven family in Dorset for thirty years, and his death had been a great blow to Dora. Last summer, childless, and finally alone, she had declared her wish to move to London and get away from the constant reminders of her sad loss. But now Raven suspected that she was missing the pleasures of a country life, and the society of her surviving sister and her old servant friends.

Dora pulled her shawl tightly around her. 'Please do not bar the door yet, Master. Martin remains abroad tonight – I believe he has been paying close attention to the new maidservant at the next corner house.' Martin Gibney, an amiable young man, only a year or two younger than Raven himself, had been Raven's personal manservant since his student days in Cambridge.

Raven turned his back to the crackling fire and felt the heat soaking through his baggy Rhinegrave breeches. 'I had thought that Martin was interested in your own sweet little Katie.'

Kate Soule was the last member of Raven's small household. She was a distant kinswoman of Dora's from Dorset – a demure little thing, just fifteen, blue-eyed and golden-haired, if perilously thin, who'd recently arrived as a replacement kitchen maid. Raven suspected that Dora had brought her here as much for her own company as for help with all the domestic chores in such a large house.

'Perhaps he has been rebuffed by her,' Dora declared primly. Relations between Martin and Dora were not always of the best because of Martin's sometimes superior manner with her, which was not something that she appreciated. Yet, on the whole, it was a happy and well-ordered household, as well as being close to both a clean water well and to the local pond, which was a great blessing for those among the household required to fetch water.

Raven's home in St Martin's Lane was not an old house – in fact, barely five-and-twenty years old – yet it felt more established than that. It was a well-constructed if unexceptional town house, four stories of solid red-brick, but of exceedingly narrow frontage, reflecting the builder's intention to cram as many houses as possible onto this desirable new West End street. Although the tradesmen's houses and coach yards that had recently been built on the other side of the street now partly blocked the view of open countryside to the north and west, it was still possible in summer to see sheep grazing on distant Primrose Hill, fields dotted with apple orchards and hayricks, and, across those fields, the untouched rural hamlets at Tyburn, Paddington and Kensington. Yet not perhaps for much longer, given all the plans for expanding the city westwards to St James's Fields and beyond.

Even with the threat to his view of open countryside, Raven still found this townhouse greatly to his liking. The roof had fashionable Dutch gables, and a quiet courtyard at the rear, with a privy and outhouse. Raven slept in comfortable if lonely splendour in a giant four-poster bed on the second floor. The ground floor was laid with fine black and white mosaic marble in the Dutch style, and held all the finest furniture he possessed – inlaid French cabinets and finely crafted oak tables and chairs. Yet the upper floors of the house were truly to Raven's liking more - the creaking timber floors reminded him of his childhood home in Dorset, and the rooms were filled with the treasured family possessions he'd brought with him when he moved to London.

Henry Raven was one of those fortunate people who had never had to worry about money, or where his next meal would come from. His mother had been the daughter of an earl, and his father, Thomas Raven, had been one of the largest landowners in Dorset. But Henry had nevertheless endured his share of unhappiness in his six-and-twenty years of life.

His father, Thomas, a dour man of principle, had taken the Parliamentarian side in the Civil War and died twenty years ago in the bloody carnage at Marston Moor, so that Henry barely remembered him. The Raven family had been rewarded by Cromwell for their loyalty during the war and through the Interregnum that followed, even though his mother had not lived long past her fortieth year to enjoy this acclimation. Henry – the only son – had inherited everything at the tender age of nineteen.

Now that the Royalists had returned to power, aided by many former Parliamentarians who had judiciously changed sides after Cromwell's death, Henry had long been expecting to see his possession of his estate near Bridport in Dorset challenged by the new power in the land. So far, though – perhaps because the land had been in his family's hands for many generations – no Royalist had yet appeared to lay any dubious claim to Henry Raven's estate or wealth.

Unlike his father, Henry Raven was far more interested in natural philosophy and business than in politics, which was why he had been able to make close friendships and alliances even with devout Royalists like Anthony Mawdsley. And Henry had to concede that Mawdsley's friendship might perhaps be one more reason why he had enjoyed a relatively trouble free existence under the new regime, even though his father had been so close to the Lord Protector.

'Why are so you so late, Master?' Dora wanted to know. 'I had a mutton stew waiting for you in the pot but 'tis long since gone cold.'

Raven nodded at his trusty old pointer dogs lying by the fire. 'I am not hungry, Dora. So fret not. Give it to the hounds, if ye will. I dare say they will not turn their noses up at it, cold or not.' He went on and told Dora of the sad turn of events at the playhouse that had delayed his return.

Dora looked woeful at the news. 'Oh, poor dear thing. To die so young and in such distressing circumstance.'

Raven continued to warm himself by the fire. 'Ay, 'tis a pity to see anyone so young meet their maker.'

Dora hesitated. 'Before I retire, can I at least bring you a hot brewed drink to warm your innards, Master?'

Raven, having warmed his backside enough by now – to the point in fact where it felt like his Rhinegraves might be about to burst into flame – finally eased himself onto the settle by the fire. 'Yes, if you will, Dora. Bring me a cup of the China drink, if we have any leaf left in the house.'

'We do have,' Dora confirmed with pleasure. 'I shall make it at once.'

Raven was now quite addicted to this new *cha* drink from China, despite its exorbitant price – ten times or more the price of coffee.

Sitting by the fire while he waited for his tea to be brought, Raven allowed his mind to dwell on what had happened at the King's theatre this evening. It had indeed been a strange turn of events.

Yet the most striking thing of note for Henry Raven had been the behaviour and deportment of that orange seller girl. She seemed a remarkably self-possessed young thing for such a lowly creature, as well as unsettlingly handsome, and she had certainly intrigued him.

Raven decided that he would like to meet her again and find out if she truly was as interesting as she appeared on the surface.

CHAPTER 2

Friday, 9th December 1664

Celia Hornett smiled invitingly, unwittingly revealing her missing side teeth, as she answered the discreet knock at the back door of her establishment and recognized a familiar customer, stamping his feet together for warmth in the snow-covered yard.

'Welcome, Sir William,' she said as she stood aside to let him in. 'My girls are always pleased to see you, good sir. 'Tis kind of you indeed to come out on such a wicked cold night as this. Which of my girls would be your pleasure tonight?'

Sitting by the fire in the snug parlour near the entrance, Molly examined this new visitor with suspicion as he appeared in the corridor outside. "Sir William" – whether that be his true name or no – was a wicked-looking middle-aged rogue with a violent red complexion, and an absurd curled black wig. This "gentleman" was clearly a dedicated follower of fashion, though – his coat was an open doublet in the latest shrunken style, with sleeves reaching only to the elbows, and ending high above the waist. He had taken the fashion for full baggy breeches to its ridiculous limit too, so that the ones he was wearing looked like wide skirts and were gathered below the knees with absurd lace frill *canions*. Molly had heard that some gentlemen were now even wearing full skirts over their breeches, the so-called petticoat breeches.

Sir William glanced casually into the parlour and sniffed curiously when he saw Molly in her seat by the fire. Molly ignored him and turned her face to the fire. Even if he had been handsome, Molly would still not have given him her attention willingly. Middle-aged men who wore preposterous breeches like that were hardly to her liking.

The rake kicked some of the snow off his boots and turned his eyes back to Celia with seeming reluctance. 'I believe, Madam, that I would like the company of Mistress Marion tonight.'

Then I pity poor Marion! thought Molly angrily.

'I believe she is free so I shall fetch her at once, Sir William.' Celia had no similar qualms about Marion's fate tonight, it seemed, and scuttled up the stairs to fetch her.

Sir William came into the tiny parlour without invitation, and warmed himself at the fire, holding his sword clumsily out of the way. It did not seem likely to Molly that this weapon would ever find much real use, Sir William being such an overweight lump of lard, and one unlikely to know one end of a sword from t'other. The man looked at her sideways and tried to engage her in conversation. 'A fierce cold night,' he said indulgently.

Molly reluctantly got to her feet and curtsied briefly. 'It is indeed, sir,' she answered deferentially.

Celia returned presently with the clearly reluctant Marion - a clear-skinned, blue-eyed girl from Kent – in tow. Sir William, casting a lascivious eye briefly in Molly's direction, seemed disposed for a moment to change his mind about his choice of lady. But despite this slight air of confusion and uncertainty that prevailed for a few moments, Celia soon managed to pack a reluctant Marion and her paramour up the stairs.

Despite the penetrating cold, Celia's bawdy house, located in one of the alleys of Whetstone Park behind Lincoln's Inn Fields, was still doing a brisk trade on this late Friday evening. Molly had seen five gentlemen arrive in the few minutes that she had been here visiting.

'The Lord help that poor dear!' Celia commented to Molly on her return to the parlour. 'That man truly has a bestial nature. Marion will likely have a severely sore bum in the morning after "Sir William" has finished with her.'

'Why let him in, then?' asked Molly coldly.

'It would not be politic of me to exclude him. If I began such a policy of exclusion, where would it end?' Mistress Hornett sighed, then relaxed in her straight-backed chair by the fire. 'I presume from that remark that you have no intention to come back here to work, then, Molly?' she suggested resignedly.

'No...*Mother*...' Molly got the word out only with the greatest difficulty. It was hard for her to use that form of address now on such a contrary and unfathomable creature as Celia.

Celia sniffed coolly. 'I am glad to hear that unfamiliar word again. I was fair wondering if I would ever hear myself called by that name again.' She frowned, and there was a look almost of hurt in her eyes. 'I have not seen thee these three months. Have I really done something so ill to offend you, Molly? Am I truly such a harpy in your eyes now that you cannot bear to visit me?'

Molly wanted to say no, but could not find the words of clear denial, still uncertain of this woman's true nature. As a babe in arms, Molly had survived a house fire in Bartlett's Passage, just off Fetter Lane, that had killed her real mother and father in their modest draper's shop. Mistress Hornett, who was no blood relative, but lived nearby at the time, had taken the orphaned baby girl in charge when no other relative came forward to claim her. Celia had always treated her charge well as a child, if not perhaps with the genuine warmth and affection of a true mother.

Molly took her seat by the fire again and smoothed down her skirts. 'Was it always your intention that I would finally work in your house? Is that truly why you took me in as a babe? Is that why you taught me to talk genteel, and to smile and simper at all your gentlemen callers? Did you see a profit for yourself in time?'

Celia gazed back at her in perplexity from her seat on the other side of the fire. 'No, that was not my intention – I thought I was merely being kind to a child in need, and teaching her the things she needed to learn to survive in a harsh world. But remark this – I am not ashamed of what I do. And this trade fed and clothed thee for fifteen years, Molly, so please do not look down your nose too much at it.'

Molly raised her eyebrows. 'Trade? You call it a "trade"?'

'A profession, then, if you will. The world's oldest, I am sure.'

Molly regarded her surrogate mother with misgivings, but had to concede that despite her dubious "trade" she was still a fine figure of a woman at the advanced age of seven-and-thirty. Her hair remained dark and lustrous, her skin smooth and creamy, and her bosom impressive and maidenly. But then she had never been able to bear children of her own, which perhaps had helped her retain some physical aspects of her youth, and made her perfect for her chosen "trade". As the proprietor of a bawdy house, she had long since personally retired from the rough and tumble of the work bed, and had turned herself into a wealthy woman of business since opening up this particular house four years ago. She had certainly progressed a long way from her own impoverished background as a simple country girl from the Thames-side village of Deptford, Molly had to admit, therefore deserved some measure of respect for that. Yet Molly still felt the urge to ruffle her feathers a little. 'Hah! You give yourself airs, Mother, and deceive yourself, if you truly believe this to be a trade like any other. I for one have no further desire to barter my body to all and sundry, Mother.'

Celia sighed as she looked into the fire. 'Men have a carnal nature, Molly, and women have been blessed with the skills and arts to satisfy their appetites. In return, we can gain much reward and security for ourselves, if we play the game of Venus skilfully enough. Not all of the men folk who come here are depraved oafs like Sir William. Some of my girls have found themselves comfortable billets with nice gentlemen. A few have even acquired a wedding ring, and one a title. Even you might have done so well, if you had chosen to stay here, and were not so contrary in your moods. Stabbing one of my customers was not called for...'

Molly bristled with anger. 'That man wanted to do severely unnatural things to me! Was I supposed to submit meekly to having my bum flayed alive?' Her anger subsided, yet she was still resentful. 'In any case I hardly touched that male varlet – I merely nicked his manhood.'

Celia bit back a smile. 'The marks on your bum would soon have faded, Molly, while you caused that gentleman so much fear that he may never do the deed again. We have to take the rough with the smooth – that is the nature of a woman's bargain with life. I make no excuses for my life, Molly. What truly is the difference between the services my girls offer, and those offered by Lady Castlemaine?'

Madame Barbara Palmer, now Lady Castlemaine, was the King's kept woman, his *Maitresse en titre*, as everyone in London knew. The King even maintained her openly in her own private apartments in Whitehall Palace, a cosy arrangement to which Queen Catherine was simply expected to turn a blind eye. Molly wondered why she put up with this affront to her dignity and respect, but then perhaps the King's Portuguese queen had even less freedom in these matters than ordinary folk.

Molly said nothing in response, though, so Celia briskly changed the subject. 'How goes it at the theatre, Molly? Dost thou dream still of becoming an actress?'

'Why does that notion amuse you so, Mother?'

Celia warmed herself complacently at the fire. 'Because you mercilessly abuse my trade, Molly, yet wish to embrace a profession equally unrespectable. If you want to progress from orange seller to actress, you will certainly have to bed that old goat Sir Thomas Killigrew, or at least one of his underlings. He has a wealthy Dutch wife, so they say, and three young children, yet he seems to give little thought to them.'

Molly regarded her coolly. 'Perhaps I would be prepared to do that. If I have to sell myself to progress in life, then I would prefer that it was to some individual wealthy gentleman who could do me some genuine good.'

'Then a word of advice, Molly. Sir Thomas likes to untie a virgin knot wherever possible, and then make the rest malleable with his tiny horn. So a little playacting on your part - to make him believe that he is the one who broke the glass of your virginity - would help to seal such a bargain.'

''Tis easy enough to play the virgin, Mother, at my age – although not at yours,' Molly snapped.

Celia laughed at her daughter's barbed insult and relented a little in her harsh tone. 'You seem a little thin and out of sorts, Molly. Are you eating enough? Do you need money? Selling oranges alone cannot keep you in food and shelter.' Celia went to her fat embroidered purse and counted out five shillings in pence. 'Here, take this, Molly. It will tide you over until you are ready to make your impressive stage debut as an Amazon.'

Molly ignored the mockery in her voice, and leaned over and reluctantly took the money. The need to borrow some money had in truth been her main reason for coming here tonight after the theatre had closed.

Celia had noticed Molly's red eyes as she came closer. 'Hast thou been weeping tonight, child?'

Molly saw no reason to deny it. 'I have, Mother.'

Celia displayed a look of genuine motherly concern for the first time this evening. 'Tell me why, sweetheart.'

Molly twisted her face. 'A friend died tonight. One of the actresses at the King's theatre - a Mistress Lusted. I am very distressed - she was always so kind and obliging to me.'

'I know this lady – I have seen her perform. Mistress Lusted was but a young woman,' Celia observed in wonder. ''Tis sad news indeed. But perhaps it means a vacant position for an actress in the company,' she added unfeelingly. 'How did this poor lady die?'

Molly regarded Celia uneasily. 'I believe she was poisoned by a jealous rival, another actress in the company.'

'Surely not,' Celia scoffed. 'Are there really such evil people among these players?'

Molly maintained her impassive expression. 'Perhaps not,' she admitted reluctantly after a long pause. 'I cannot be certain at present. But if there are such people in that theatre, I intend to discover the truth about them...'

*

Through the deserted snowbound streets south of Lincoln's Inn Fields, Molly walked back to her lodgings near Drury Lane as fast as her tired legs could carry her.

The cold was a frightening thing: tonight it seemed to Molly almost as if the city of London had been cut away from the rest of the world and set down by God's implacable hand in some remote arctic region entombed in an icy world of eternal night. Even with her thick woollen cloak and several layers of petticoats under her skirt, Molly felt naked and exposed to the wind's icy blast. A few minutes outside in this cold might be enough to kill even a healthy person, Molly thought, so she tried to move even faster on her way to her destination in Coal Hole Lane. Desperate to get home and out of this hideous weather, she took a shortcut that she would normally have rather avoided because it was frequented by villains and cutthroats. She told herself, though, that even robbers and vagabonds would not choose to be abroad on such a night as this, therefore the risks of being accosted must be much less than normal.

Her short route took her down the dark alleyway at the side of the Duke's house in Portugal Row, which was well known as the particular haunt of thieves and footpads. This building was the city's alternative theatre venue to the one where she worked - owned and managed by Sir Thomas Killigrew's great theatre rival, Sir William Davenant - but located in a less salubrious area than Covent Garden. The side of the building was in almost complete darkness, with today's performance long since finished, but, ahead, Molly could discern a light in the alleyway, which soon resolved itself into the weak and flickering glow of a lantern. As Molly drew closer, the light from the lantern enabled her to see that there were two people conversing in whispers near the side door of the theatre, one a gentleman from his lavish wig and fine clothes, and the other an elegant young woman of style. Molly noted the exceptional height of the woman, who seemed three inches taller than the man by her side.

Molly thought it perplexing that anyone would choose to converse here in this terrible cold so she approached the two cautiously, not quite sure that this pair were not footpads in disguise, setting a clever trap for some unsuspecting passer-by. Yet that did not seem likely given the sumptuousness of their costumes. Then something about the woman's costume in particular excited Molly's interest. From a few paces, Molly noted the line of pretty *virago* sleeves showing through her heavy brocade cloak, while the laced red silk bodice had a modest square neckline...

Molly wondered why this costume looked so familiar...

With a rush of inspiration, Molly was suddenly convinced that this must be the very same dark lady she had seen leaving the tiring room in the King's theatre a few hours earlier. She had not seen enough of the lady's face to remember her features with any certainty, nor was the view of her face now sufficient to excite any recognition, yet Molly had an unerringly good eye for costume, and was sure this was the very same gown.

Molly approached the two warily, hoping perhaps to overhear a little of their whispered conversation, or at least to get a closer look at the woman's face. From finding this well-dressed lady here, Molly thought that perhaps her first intuition about the woman had been a good one, and that she might indeed be an actress with the Duke's company.

Yet Molly also reminded herself that she knew no definite ill against this woman. She had simply seen her leaving the tiring room, and perhaps there was no more to it than that. This tall dark lady might be – nay, probably was - entirely innocent of anything to do with Sarah's untimely death. That gentleman, Mr Raven – the gloomy philosopher - had been sure that Sarah had died of a natural defect of the heart, and although Molly had not liked his looks much, she had to admit to a grudging respect for his gentlemanly demeanour, and for his thoughtful opinion.

Yet, if that were the case, and Sarah had merely suffered a natural affliction, why had this dark lady, a visitor to the theatre, not raised the alarm? She must have seen that Sarah was dead. But Molly had to remind herself that it had also taken *her* a few seconds to discover the awful truth, so perhaps it was entirely possible that a stranger could have passed through the tiring room without realizing that the woman sitting in quiet contemplation at the mirror was in reality deceased…

Yet that still did not explain what the woman had been doing there in the first place, or why she had been leaving with such apparent secrecy…

Molly was within ten paces of the couple now. The gentleman's back was to Molly, while the tall dark lady had moved inconveniently out of her line of sight so that her face was mostly obscured now by her companion's broad head and wig. Molly could see nothing of his face either, yet he seemed a young man from the frizzed and crimped style of his elaborate French wig, falling to the shoulders from a centre parting, and divided into three distinct parts. Molly saw that the folds of hair hanging in front were tied at the end with distinctive green bows, which no elderly man would dare to do, even if he had the temerity to adopt this strange new male French fashion for wearing wigs.

Suddenly the dark lady gasped as she finally became aware of Molly's presence and the stealthy manner of her approach. She whispered something urgently to her companion who turned abruptly and, without warning, lashed out violently at Molly with his short sword, hitting her ferociously on the side of the head with the flat of the blade.

The world spun around alarmingly and then went completely black for a few seconds. When Molly came to, she found herself lying on her back on the frozen ground in the icy alleyway, with her wounded head aching and tender.

But of her assailant and his woman companion, there was not a sign.

*

Despite feeling sick and light-headed, Molly managed to climb unsteadily to her feet and totter home the near quarter-mile to her lodging house in Coal Hole Lane, and then ascend the three flights of creaking stairs to her tiny garret.

Her head was clearing a little by this time, but still not sufficiently to understand why that bewigged man had struck out at her so deliberately. Yet the only sensible conclusion was that the couple were up to no good in that alleyway, and did not want to be identified.

Had the woman perhaps recognized her as the person who had seen her leaving the tiring room in the King's theatre earlier this evening? Was that why she had been assaulted so cruelly? Yet Molly herself doubted this could be true - the woman would have to possess eyes in the back of her head to have even seen her in the King's theatre, ne'er mind recognize her. And tonight, in the alleyway at the side of the Duke's theatre, Molly's face had been mostly covered with the hood of her cloak, as well as being in near darkness, thus making recognition doubly impossible.

So Molly was quietly convinced that she had been assaulted at random – these two simply did not want to be seen together by anyone, therefore were up to something devious. But that did not make them murderous conspirators with certainty. Perhaps this was simply an illicit liaison of some sort between a married man and woman, whose accidental discovery by a passer-by had made the man act blindly and impetuously.

Yet, regardless of the depth and intent of their complicity, Molly knew she would struggle to identify these two again – not unless the man was obligingly wearing the same wig with the green bows anyway, and the woman her distinctive gown in red silk.

Molly found her lodging room empty and bitter cold. Lighting a candle with her tinder box did not make it seem any warmer or more welcoming.

Amy, the girl who shared this tiny garret room with her, had not yet returned either, even though it was close to midnight. It worried Molly that Amy might still be working on the streets in such fearsome cold weather. Amy Leatherbarrow came from the village of Dartford in Kent, but had been working in Celia's bawdy house earlier this year when a reluctant Molly had also been inducted briefly, at Celia's persuasion, into the timeless profession of troll.

By chance, they had quitted work at the bawdy house at the same time – Molly because she wanted to escape such employment altogether after her experience with the stick-wielding gentleman - while Amy, who had no similar moral compunctions about her way of life, was more of an opportunist who had left Celia's house with the pragmatic hope of keeping all of her earnings for herself. But finding reliable and lucrative custom beyond the doors of a bawdy house was a much more difficult business for Amy than she had expected, and the last months had been hard and salutary ones indeed for young Mistress Leatherbarrow.

Yet at heart, despite her promiscuous and mercenary nature, she was a good-natured girl and Molly certainly did not want any harm to come to her.

Molly felt the side of her head, and discovered no signs of blood fortunately, but instead a bump the size of a goose egg. She found a basin of dirty water left over from this morning on the bedside table, now covered with a surface layer of ice with no fire in the room. After taking off her outer dress and petticoats, Molly did her best to clean her face with what liquid water she could recover from the bowl.

Then leaving on her stockings and underbodice, she pulled on her nightgown over her head and dived into the single icy bed. Her shivering was so violent and uncontrolled at first that it felt likely to rattle her old wooden trestle bed to pieces. The cold was so penetrating on this December night that ice crystals had almost eclipsed the small thick panes of glass in the solitary window, while the usual damp patches on the plaster walls had turned to a ghostly shade of white. Tonight, even with a bedside candle burning brightly, this room did seem like a cavern hollowed in the ice rather then a garret room in a seedy lodging house in Coal Hole Lane. With the candle extinguished, it felt even colder and bleaker.

Despite the intensity of the cold, and the throbbing pain in her head, Molly's tiredness soon overcame even these obstacles and she began to drift off finally into a deep sleep. That was until she heard a key rattle in the lock of the door, and a figure appear in the rectangle of faint light at the doorway.

Molly stirred and quickly lighted the candle by the bed again to check that this was indeed Amy finally returning. She was reassured to find that it was. Surprisingly Amy was in good spirits, and had obviously been with an amenable gentleman tonight.

'Good evening to you, Molly,' she whispered. 'I saw thee at the King's house this afternoon, by the way, just before the play began. That orange seller costume looks most becoming on you. I waved at you, but you obviously could not see me.' She giggled, despite her shivers. 'But 'tis not surprising you failed to spot me - at the time, you only had eyes for three well-proportioned gents in their own private box, I believe.'

Molly had certainly not seen Amy in the audience at the theatre, but then her attention had truly been elsewhere, even if she was not prepared to admit it. 'And where were you, Amy?'

Amy smiled. 'I was up in the gallery with a beau – a very respectable gentleman, a ship's mate.'

'Handsome?'

'Well, not exactly handsome. But he has *some* hair still, and a few teeth left, if a little black. But I believe Mr Buck is handsome enough for a man of fifty. After the theatre, he took me to his nice warm lodging in Duck Lane where we lay on a rug before a roaring fire.'

Molly gasped. 'But fifty, Amy! Could he still do the deed?'

'Oh yes, most gratifyingly. In any case I prefer the older ones, Molly. So should you, if you had any sense. Old men have much better manners than these young fops and rakes.'

Amy had stripped naked by now, and quickly replaced her nice blue dress with several layers of coarse old nightgowns. Then she slipped into bed alongside Molly.

Molly had stopped shivering by now, but was forced to resume her shakes when this little block of ice clung to her for warmth.

'Brrrr! Can I huddle up close to you, Molly. If I don't, I might not survive the night.'

'Course you can, Amy,' Molly said, snuggling up to her in return, and gritting her teeth as Amy's frozen fingers touched her warm back.

CHAPTER 3

Saturday, 10th December 1664

Taking the wintry morning air in St James's Park, Madam Barbara Palmer (now recently elevated to the title of Lady Castlemaine as a result of her wealthy husband's promotion to the peerage as Earl of Castlemaine in Ireland) was increasingly discontented with life for several reasons. One of these discontents concerned the frigid weather, of course, which had made it so difficult to walk abroad and take the air this week. Yet, after a week of being cooped indoors, Barbara had been determined on this Saturday morning to take a turn in the park at the back of Whitehall Palace, despite the intensity of the cold. Lady Castlemaine was not a person much driven to take note of God's handiwork, being even in her own estimation a more superficial and shallow creature than those normally entranced by nature. Yet even she had to admit, as she promenaded up and down, that the park was truly a wondrous sight in the chill morning air, with the long straight formal lake frozen over with a thick skin of blue ice and layered in curtains of mist, while the straight formal lines of bare-branched trees were decorated with a rime of frost so heavy that they seemed to have been painted with white plaster.

A further source of discontent to Barbara on this cold morning was that her personal maid Henrietta, who had accompanied her on her walk around the park, was chattering some nonsense in her ear about the infamous comet. It seemed that one of the older gentlemen of the King's bedchamber, Sir Richard Clague, had offered to show her this wondrous stellar object late last night with the King's own telescope. But a diverted Barbara was scarcely listening to the rest of Henrietta's idle twittering.

'…I wanted to retire for the night but Sir Richard insisted on taking me to the Privy Garden where the King keeps his immensely long telescope, and showing me the location of the blazing star. It lies now in the Whale's mouth, he said, although I saw no whale at all, Ma'am. But now it moves ever closer to the star Aldebaran - or some such name - in the constellation of the bull. I could not truly make out any aspect of a bull either in the sky, despite Sir Richard's vigorous prompting, yet the comet itself was a most fearful sight in the telescope, looking like a brush besom stretched towards Orion's head...the number of stars visible beyond it was quite extraordinary, like clusters of jewels...'

Only half-listening to this unending verbal assault on her eardrums, Barbara decided complacently that Sir Richard clearly had designs on Henrietta's presumed chastity. But she did not resent the old goat for trying, for Henrietta was a handsome young thing, if entirely mindless, while Sir Richard's wife was a dreadful old crone of forty with a face like a hangman. In truth, Lady Castlemaine had rather more pressing problems of her own to concern her this morning than protecting her maid from the attentions of a concupiscent old goat, in particular her own reputation in the country. She knew that many citizens of the King considered her a witch and a whore, and hated her most of all among the King's close circle of courtiers. England's more Republican-minded citizens considered these courtiers to be a group of decadent and pampered rogues, who lived the high life in the King's protective shadow and who outraged the delicate sensibilities of England's masses with their base antics and lack of propriety. This hatred of the King's closest circle seemed to be growing ever more dangerous and brazen. Only a few weeks ago, a note had been pinned to Castlemaine's door in Oxford where she had been staying with the King, inscribed with the Latin quotation *"Hanc Caesare pressam a fluctu defendit onus"*. Barbara had no idea at the time what that meant, her knowledge of Latin being inadequate at best, yet had understood all too well the mock translation which had been appended below by some foul-mouthed wag.

"The reason why she is not ducked,
Because by Caesar, she is f..."

The outraged King had offered £1000 for information about the scurrilous author of this offensive note, but no one had come forward in response, not even for such an extravagant reward as that. Barbara had at first been more amused than outraged by the doggerel verse, but now she regretted it more - it was perhaps one more worrying sign of the people turning increasingly against the King and his court.

Yet Barbara's greatest reason for discontent today was not truly concerned with the tiresome opinions of the King's enemies, but more to do with her own faltering hold on the King's loyalty and patronage. She could not dismiss from her mind the thought that he seemed less enamoured of her these days, despite the wondrous sexual heights that she could still occasionally elevate him to. Perhaps it was simply a case of over familiarity, which she might overcome in time with the help of some new erotic tricks or costumes in the bedchamber. She hoped that the special entertainment she had organized for Charles in one week's time would reinvigorate their relationship. It was to be a special magic show with much erotic appeal, and therefore perfect for the King's sensual tastes. The last time she had put on such a show for him, Charles had been insatiable afterwards in bed, and Barbara could only hope that the forthcoming show by the famous Madam von Kladowitz of Vienna would provoke a similar response from him.

She tried to tell herself that her hold on the King was still unshakable and eternal despite his occasional dalliances with other women. She reminded herself that she had given birth to yet another child by him this year, and that the King seemed to dote on that daughter as much as he did with all their other children, while his plain and dowdy Portuguese queen remained childless, despite all of the King's best attempts to get her with child. He had even taken his Portuguese mare this summer to partake of the health-giving waters at Tunbridge and Bath, but – gratifyingly - all to no avail...

No, the Queen was certainly not a problem to worry her, Barbara decided complacently. Her most potent problem was that a new young rival for the King's affections had arrived at court. This was that scheming little minx, Mistress Frances Stuart, a girl all silly innocence on the surface, building sky-high card castles in the Queen's apartments with wide-eyed charm, and showing off her gartered legs to the King at every opportunity. Yet beneath that vacuous charm was a shrewd and worthy opponent in Barbara's opinion.

Somehow Lady Castlemaine knew she would have to come up with a plan to deal with this brazen rival. The best distraction for Mistress Stuart, of course, would be to find some handsome courtier for her to fall in love with...

Barbara's mind was still dwelling agreeably on this obvious solution to her problem when a giant masked man suddenly leapt out from behind the frosted trunk of a lime tree and confronted her angrily. Both Barbara and her maid gasped in fright at this masked and cloaked apparition, immensely tall and dressed all in black, who blocked their way ahead on the gravel path.

Yet Barbara was made of stern stuff and soon recovered her poise. 'What do ye mean by this outrage, rogue? Ye shall hang for this when the King's men hear of it! Stand aside, and let us pass, or else!'

The masked giant snarled at her like an animal and Barbara was forced to retreat, while Henrietta whimpered with fear at her side. The assailant was so well concealed by his moulded paper mask and cavalier's hat that Barbara could see nothing of his face, apart from a pair of piercing brown eyes. The man took a sealed letter from beneath his cloak and, putting his masked face close to hers, forced Barbara to take it from his gauntleted hand. 'Whore of Babylon! Take this epistle to your papist master. Tell him to devour its contents carefully and then to reflect on its sombre message. Bid him look tonight with his Dutch glass in the constellation of Taurus for the warning that issues presently from the sky, because it spells his end. Tell him this, lady! "When beggars die, there are no comets seen. But the heavens themselves blaze forth the death of princes"...'

With that, the spectre turned on his heels and was gone, a tall sinister black figure disappearing quickly among the dense, leafless rows of lime trees, before Barbara could say anything more.

*

The central courtyard of the Royal Exchange was filled with such a swelling, seething mass of humanity this morning that it was difficult to make out the stone cobbles beneath all their collective feet. As on most busy mornings in this great temple to commerce, the courtyard was crowded so intensely that a gentleman or lady could easily afford the luxury of fainting here without ever having to worry about the likelihood of hitting the cold hard ground.

Yet the mad rush of people in this place was scarce a surprise, Henry Raven thought, given that it was the best source of foreign and commercial news in London. Even the severe cold this frosty morning had not inhibited the visiting merchants and traders one whit, since the central square seemed quite as congested as it would be on a midsummer's morn. Each group of merchants had their own regular meeting point in the courtyard, while the upper floors arranged around it contained the finest shops in all England - apothecaries, armourers, milliners, booksellers, and goldsmiths. Anything of fine quality could be bought here - furs from the Baltic and the remote northern wildernesses of the Americas, fine coloured glass from Bohemia and Venice, Baroque furniture from France, lutes and viols and spinets from Italy, painted porcelain dishes and bowls from China. Even rarer articles were available too on occasion – lacquer work and bronze articles brought from Japan by the Dutch who were the only Europeans allowed access to these peculiar foreigners' remote islands. The imminent threat of war with the Dutch had not dampened trade so far across the North Sea, Raven was glad to see. When there was money to be made, both the English and the Dutch were prepared to overlook their mutual dislike and distrust of each other, in order to keep trading.

In the central courtyard of the Exchange, merchants haggled over the prices of tobacco leaf from the colony of Virginia, rare plants and bulbs from the Ottoman Empire, silks, satins and brocade from Flanders and Spain, and more prosaic trading materials too - timber, grain and wool. A new delivery of China tea was selling among the dealers for ten pounds a pound, so that the lucky owners of that cargo, presently lying in the holds of an East Indiaman at Deptford, were probably rich enough now to retire, if they so wished.

Raven's visit here today, in company with his manservant Martin Gibney, was concerned with one of the more common materials of trade – namely coal. Recently Raven had acquired two shallow drift coal mines in the North of England, and had purchased two large Whitby colliers to deliver the coals from Newcastle to ports all over Europe – to Antwerp and London, and even to the Baltic and Russia. England now produced four-fifths of all the coal used in the world, and with the winters growing ever colder in recent years, the price of coal was rising to very profitable levels. English coal was burning in hearths and furnaces and kilns all over Northern Europe now, helping to drive workshops and to stave off this terrible winter cold better than any wood fire ever could.

By eleven o'clock, Raven had arranged for the sale of nearly a hundred tons of his finest coal to suitable buyers and was mentally counting the profit on these transactions with quiet satisfaction. Raven had visited Newcastle in the autumn to oversee the management of his mines, and had been shocked to discover the backbreaking nature of the work, and the squalor and degradation of the conditions in which the miners lived. Although he wanted to make a profit, he had no desire to exploit his fellow men and cause them unnecessary misery, so was determined to make beneficial changes to the working practices, and to the living conditions, of his miners. Yet his manager, Alexander Hicks, a young Northern man of brutal manners, had been resistant to such talk so Raven could see that he would have to replace him in time with someone more pliable to his will. Raven had no firm replacement in mind as yet because the job was certainly a demanding one that could not be done by any common man. Yet he had been giving some thought to the radical idea of offering this job to his own manservant Martin Gibney, and had even discussed the possibility with his friend Mawdsley, whose forthright opinions he always valued...

Raven glanced affectionately at his manservant by his side, and reflected that Martin's intellectual capabilities were quite as well developed as his own despite their very different stations in life. Henry Raven was one of those few rich men who could acknowledge with honesty that his own satisfactory situation in life had much more to do with an accident of birth than with any particular virtues or intelligence that he might possess. He had to concede that, had he been born in

Martin's poor situation, he too would have probably been restricted to being a mere manservant or drudge for the rest of his life.

In Henry Raven's view, it was wrong to always judge men simply by their station in life; sometimes one had to look beneath the external trappings to see the true potential of a person. In Martin's case he saw enormous potential. Last night Raven had been struck equally by the cleverness of that orange girl Molly, so perhaps in future he should be less surprised at the virtues of the underprivileged and uneducated, who were often in their poor situation through no fault of their own. He debated with himself now whether it was time to make a radical choice and give Martin finally the opportunity to show his true worth...

'Are you ready to return home now, Master, or do we need to stay further here?' Martin now asked.

Considering he had not returned to his home until the early hours, Martin looked remarkably fresh-faced and sober this morning. Raven wondered whether he was really courting the new maidservant in the nearby corner house in St Martin's Lane, as Dora claimed. Personally he doubted it – Raven had seen the way that Martin looked at young Kate Soule on the sly, and was convinced his ambitions lay in that direction still. True, Katie was such a shy young maid that it was difficult to believe she might be ready for marriage, yet many girls married at the age of fifteen. Wealthy girls were often betrothed by their noble families much younger even than that.

'You can walk home now, Martin,' Raven told him, 'and take the ledgers with you. I plan to meet Mr Mawdsley in the coffee house across the way, and I shall probably be there some time, so there is no point in you staying.'

Martin frowned and lowered his voice to a whisper. 'Then a warning before I go, Master. Do not look around sharply, but I have observed a youth watching you with keen interest as you were arranging your affairs. He may be a cutpurse who has selected you as his victim.'

Raven nodded, then waited his chance to turn his head naturally. He spotted this young man that Martin meant at once – a well-dressed youth of sixteen years or so with long dark curling hair, a pert pretty face and slender body.

Raven laughed. 'I believe I can stifle my fear in the face of such a terror as that, and defend myself capably against him, if I have to, Martin.'

Martin flushed. 'If I am wrong, then forgive me, Master. But you should be cautious. I have heard reports that many gentlemen have been robbed in the city in recent months by just such a well-presented youth as this...'

*

A few minutes later Raven sat at a table beside a crackling log fire and reflected that there were quite as many business dealings going on now here in Jonathan's Coffeehouse as there had been earlier in the Royal Exchange.

This was no great surprise, though, since stockbrokers had recently been banned from trading in the Royal Exchange due to their rude and hectoring manners, so had been forced instead to re-locate to the nearby coffee houses in Cornhill and Threadneedle Street to expedite their business, an arrangement which certainly suited the proprietors of those establishments.

Coffeehouses were but a recent addition to the London scene: in fact the first had opened barely ten years before in St Michael's Alley, Cornhill. The proprietor of that coffeehouse was a man called Pasqua Rosée, the Armenian servant of a trader in Turkish goods named Daniel Edwards, who had imported the coffee and assisted Rosée in setting up the establishment.

Raven knew Edwards moderately well but chose not to patronize his establishment, preferring the quieter and more refined atmosphere of Jonathan's Coffeehouse, which, being almost directly opposite the Exchange in Cornhill, had benefited most directly from this banishment of the stockbrokers.

Yet these London coffeehouses were much more than simply places of business for stockbrokers, being open to all levels of society and allowing a surprising degree of free speech and the dissemination of radical ideas, which was something Raven heartily approved of. As a result coffeehouses had however become associated with the followers of social equality and republicanism in particular, which did not endear such premises to the King, according to Mawdsley, who was consequently trying to find ways to control and monitor such subversive activities.

Raven sat at one end of a long communal trestle table near the fire, while at the other a half-dozen well fed gentlemen stockbrokers argued and swore, their end of the table strewn with papers and writing implements. Coffeepots were ranged at an open fire, above a hanging cauldron of boiling water. The only women present in the establishment were of course serving wenches, who sat separated from the customers in a canopied booth, from which they served coffee on request in tall stoneware cups. Raven did regret that coffeehouses in this city, unlike those on the Continent, had not extended their liberal thinking so far as to contemplate opening their premises to lady customers.

Raven looked at the frosty pewter-coloured sky outside and, despite the lack of sun to guide him, judged from the recent sound of the bells from St Mary-Le-Bow that it was at least a quarter hour after eleven o'clock by now. How much more convenient it would be to have a portable accurate timepiece to fix the time, he decided irritably, rather than relying on judgement and the nearest church clock. Yet so far, man's ingenuity had failed miserably to deliver in regard to this "timeless" problem. Raven smiled to himself faintly at his own unspoken witticism.

Raven had recently formed the sanguine hope, though, that a solution might finally be at hand. Raven's friend at the Royal Society, Robert Hooke, had let him know earlier this year that he had come up with a workable solution for a portable timepiece using a small coiled iron spring to drive, what he called, an anchor escapement. Yet now it seemed that Raven's optimism had been misplaced and that society would still have to wait a few years more before this wondrous timepiece was available. Hooke had recently held a meeting with certain senior figures at the Royal Society - Robert Boyle, Sir Robert Moray and Lord Brouncker - to agree terms under which Hooke would agree to divulge the technical secrets of his watch and permit others to manufacture them. Yet these worthy gentlemen had only been prepared to offer Hooke a fourteen-year patent, which he considered woefully insufficient reward for his efforts and ingenuity (a view with which Henry Raven was entirely in accord.) Hooke had therefore not been minded to continue with the discussions. It was particularly frustrating to Raven that such a boon for mankind – the manufacture of accurate portable timepieces – should be delayed by such unseemly haggling over money, and unseemly treatment of the inventor...

Raven gave up his idle reflections on portable timepieces for the present and wondered instead what had become of his friend Mawdsley, whom he had arranged to meet here as usual at eleven o'clock. But, even a quarter hour later than this, there was no sign of Mawdsley appearing so Raven decided with disappointment that he might not be coming after all. Perhaps he had been detained by the pressing business of his monarch? Raven suspected that Mawdsley was now very close to the centre of power in the Privy Council, and had become a familiar and indispensable figure even to the King, therefore his time was hardly his own any more.

Yet although Mawdsley had not put in an appearance this morning at Jonathan's Coffeehouse, Raven now recognized one new arrival in the establishment. This was the same pretty youth whom Martin had pointed out to him in the Royal Exchange earlier. So, despite his doubts and his mockery, Raven was forced to conclude that there might be something to Martin's suspicions after all.

Yet Raven was even more surprised when, after moving around the room apparently looking for a suitable vacant seat, the youth brazenly appeared opposite him and looked him in the eye. 'May I sit here, sir,' the boy requested gruffly, indicating the vacant place opposite.

There were plenty of vacant places on the other benches to choose from so clearly the boy had an ulterior motive in mind. Yet Raven could not believe his motive was thievery or deceit – this boy looked far too genteel and refined for that.

Raven smiled and nodded. 'Of course, sir.'

The boy introduced himself as he sat down. 'I am Master John Goodricke, sir.'

'Henry Raven, sir. At your service,' Raven responded, observing the boy in more detail. Close up, he was a handsome creature, with long dark curling hair and cornflower blue eyes. Yet he seemed masculine enough for all that, despite his pale pink cheeks being unmarked by any trace of beard. His velvet coat and breeches were new and expensive, and overly formal for a boy of his age to wear, unless he was the son of an aristocrat.

Goodricke's face was grave. 'Yes, I know your name, sir. I saw you at the play at the King's house last night where an acquaintance pointed you out to me and mentioned your illustrious name. I happened by chance to see you over at the Royal Exchange earlier this morning and followed you over here.'

Raven waited for a moment to reply. 'Then this meeting is no accident and you clearly have business with me, sir. May I inquire what sort of business?'

The boy's dignified manner and deep voice made him appear rather older than his fresh cheeks might suggest. 'I have some connection with the King's theatre, and I know many of the company well, being a regular patron. I wish to know about the fate of Mistress Lusted, the actress who sadly died last night. I believe you had occasion to examine her body not long after she was found dead in the tiring room.'

Of all the possible subjects for discussion he might have expected to hear from this young man, Raven had certainly not been expecting *this* particular one, although in truth he had been at a loss up to now to understand just what this youth's business with him might be. He had to wonder at the source of Mr Goodricke's information. Could this pretty youth be acquainted with Sir Thomas Killigrew, or, failing that – an even unlikelier possibility - with the orange girl, Molly? Otherwise it was difficult to explain his intimate knowledge of what had gone on in that tiring room yesterday evening. 'What is Mistress Lusted to you, sir? And who told you that I had attended to Mistress Lusted's body last night?' he asked suspiciously.

Goodricke hesitated. 'As to the latter question, the death of Mistress Lusted was soon common knowledge among the theatre company, as was your involvement. As for the first question, Sarah was a close friend and confidante of mine.'

Raven narrowed his eyes in perplexity. Could this boy have been Mistress Lusted's lover, despite his apparent youth? Or was he perhaps an actor himself who had worked with Mistress Lusted?

Goodricke frowned intently. 'I have heard that you believe that she died from a natural cause. But are you truly certain of that, sir?'

It seemed that here was someone else apart from the orange girl Molly who had some suspicions about the manner of the actress's death. Raven phrased his answer with deliberate care, as if he was giving testimony in a court. 'I visited the city coroner this morning to inform him of last night's sad event, and told him that I did not know the precise cause of Mistress Lusted's death but that I believed it to be due to a natural heart defect. Yet, without a full examination of the body, I also admitted to him that I could not be absolutely certain of it. The coroner agreed with me that it seemed an unnecessary imposition on the young lady's family to carry out a full post mortem examination of the cadaver when there was no evidence of any external injury.' Raven remembered with slight misgivings the pinprick of blood on Mistress Lusted's neck that had been observed by Molly Titchen, and wondered whether he should perhaps have told the coroner of that slight anomaly.

Goodricke seemed to accept Raven's pronouncement with good grace. 'Then I thank you for your time and will not trouble you further, sir.'

Raven now wanted to ask him a few questions in return, such as who he was, and what his "connection" with the theatre might truly be. 'Master Goodricke, may I have a little more of your time...'

But the boy stood up, bowed awkwardly and was off before Raven could get out another word.

Raven thought him a most peculiar young fellow, but did not choose to pursue him.

*

Whitehall Palace was a name that suggested architectural grandeur, but the reality was in fact an undistinguished sprawl of separate buildings with no cohesion of style at all, or even practicality of use, having been added to arbitrarily by different monarchs over many generations. The best of this muddled mess of styles was the elegant Renaissance Banqueting House of Inigo Jones built in King James's time, yet the palace was littered with a far greater number of indeterminate and unappealing buildings, with old timbered gables and Dutch-style hipped roofs that went back to the Tudors. The palace even had a narrow and dirty public right of way that snaked behind the Banqueting House, across the Great Court, and then led finally between the tiled and thatched roofs of the various palace buildings lining the river. Even the approach to the palace from the river was normally an unedifying one - Whitehall Stairs was a mere wooden landing stage with a gallery above called a "bridge" that ran far out into the murky waters of the Thames. The jagged mounds of ice presently choking the frozen river had at least added an unusual degree of arctic grandeur to the scene.

From Whitehall Stairs, the full impressive sweep of the icebound river could be glimpsed as it turned east towards the city. Yet the most striking visible features of the riverside were still the old decaying mansions of those formerly powerful political families of old – Essex House, Arundel House, and Somerset House – timely reminders to the ambitious Whitehall courtiers of the present of the inevitable ebb and flow of political power.

In the Presence Chamber of the palace, the burning logs in the fireplace had been heaped up to a hopeful level, yet the resulting substantial fire was still making little impact on the cold in this dour chamber. This room had none of the personal charm or decoration of the King's more private chambers, Anthony Mawdsley thought, but was all grey stone and black wood, with tiny latticed windows that let in so little light that, regardless of the quality of the day outside, the brass sconces invariably had to be lit at all hours.

Mawdsley had been summoned here urgently, with his master Lord Clarendon, to a private meeting with the King, and so had been forced to forego his regular Saturday morning visit to Jonathan's Coffeehouse in Cornhill. At first he thought there must have been some new escalation in the conflict with the Dutch to merit this unscheduled meeting – perhaps a fresh report from one of the King's ambassadors in Europe - yet that did not seem to be the case. On entering the Presence Chamber, Mawdsley had been surprised to find Lady Castlemaine here, which was unusual to say the least, since she had never attended any of their political discussions with the King before. But he was soon apprised of her reason for her being here when the King told them of the unpleasant incident that had happened in the park a few minutes before. Mawdsley now waited to discover the contents of the letter she had been given with interest, but was resigned to the probability that it was yet another rude and vulgar message directed against the King's whore. Such sentiments and opinions were becoming commonplace among the population now, and being openly voiced in coffeehouses and taverns and ale-houses all over London.

The King, resplendent in a knee-length coat of purple velvet with a scarlet sash, passed the opened letter over to Clarendon and asked him in sonorous tones to read it aloud, even though he had clearly already perused its contents.

From the stiff and affronted look on his monarch's face, Mawdsley wondered whether the contents of the letter might be even more personal than he imagined.

Lady Castlemaine seemed less concerned, though, sitting complacently at a hard oak bench besides the fire and warming her beautiful face and hands, careless of the sparks striking her fine green satin skirt, as Lord Clarendon began to read out the missive from the madman in the park.

"To Charles Stuart

Sire, I have placed this letter in the hand of your whore…" - here Clarendon paused awkwardly in mid-sentence as he saw the King flinch, even though Castlemaine herself remained quite unperturbed by the term – *"…because she seems the most fitting person to deliver this message to you. As a jewel of gold in a swine's snout, so is a fair woman which is without discretion…"* Mawdsley saw with amusement that Lady Castlemaine did not even flinch at being likened to something stuck in a swine's snout.

"…Being mortal men, the days of our lives are all numbered, but I intend that yours shall be severely so. I have seen the ungodly in great power in this land, and flourishing like a green bay-tree, but now finally it is time to cut down these wicked branches that infest this country, and for you, sire, to repay so many debts you owe this nation.

These debts you owe the English people are many and severe, but chief among them is your part in the sordid death of Colonel Thomas Harrison and his fellows. For that infamous deed alone, you must forfeit your right to life and Christian compassion. As I watched Colonel Harrison and his fellow citizens being butchered on that scaffold at Charing Cross four years ago in a mockery of justice, I felt overwhelming shame of my fellow men and wanted to cry at that clamorous baying mob from my heart: Is this nothing to you, all ye that pass by? Behold these men's suffering, and see if there be any sorrow like unto their sorrow!

The Bible says that whoso sheddeth man's blood, by man shall his blood be shed. And I vow to make that fate come true for you, sire. We have all been warned by the greatest authority not to put our trust in princes, and the nation – even I myself - should have minded that advice carefully before taking you back into the fold. But even the complacent fools amongst your own fawning courtiers must regret that decision now, given the repression and violence you practise against your own people.

Pride goeth before destruction, sire, and a haughty spirit before a fall, therefore your fall shall indeed be precipitous and complete.

So this I now promise ye, Charles Stuart. Ye shall die horribly ere this new comet leaves the heavens. And that hand of retribution will come from one among your most trusted circle. You too will understand before you die what it is to fear everyone around you.

If I fail in this promise, sire, then even worse misery shall haunt your days. I will see that plague and fire and all manner of pestilence rain down on this Sodom of a kingdom until nothing remains of your miserable works.

Your formerly obedient servant"

Lord Clarendon sniffed as he came to the end. 'He signs himself the *Harbinger of Death*. Clearly he is a madman.'

The King seemed more dispirited than angry at the hateful tone of the letter. 'Perhaps so. But God's bread! It makes me spit blood that such a man should be allowed to roam free on the streets of my kingdom, and to voice such despicable thoughts! I want this man found, Edward, and I want him punished for his disrespectful behaviour and his evil threats towards Lady Castlemaine. This madman decries the fate of Colonel Harrison, but I shall want to see him suffer a punishment of his own, and one just as severe. Is that clear?'

'Perfectly, sire.' Clarendon glanced at Mawdsley, hoping for some inspiration from him.

Mawdsley felt obliged by that meaningful glance to say something. 'I wonder why…'

The King looked at Lord Clarendon's young protégé with interest, his dark eyes flaring into life. 'Yes, speak up, Mr Mawdsley. Do not be shy of giving us your worthy opinions.'

Mawdsley continued hesitantly. 'Your majesty, I wonder why this mad gentleman has taken four years to become so outraged at the manner of Colonel Harrison's death.'

The King nodded thoughtfully. 'Ay, a good point.'

Mawdsley waited to make sure the King had nothing more to add, before proceeding further with his own hypothesis. 'It suggests that this person was perhaps in no position to make a protest before. Perhaps he was in prison…'

The King guffawed loudly. 'Or in Bedlam Hospital!'

Mawdsley nodded agreement. 'Or perhaps he was abroad in exile…'

Lord Clarendon breathed out heavily, the plumpness of his cheeks outlined by the firelight behind him. For a man in late middle age, Mawdsley's master still had an enviably thick head of curling red hair, which had allowed him to avoid following the King's example in wearing a lavish wig to conceal his own cropped and greying hair. 'Yes, of course.'

Mawdsley turned to the Lord Chancellor. 'May I see the letter, my Lord? Perhaps the writing may give some indication of the true nature of this man.'

'I would have thought the depraved nature of his character to be obvious,' Clarendon said tartly, but he seemed glad enough to hand the offending letter over to Mawdsley, who accepted it gingerly in turn as if it might be tainted with the pox. He examined the wax seal in detail before finally looking up at the King. 'This seal is quite distinctive, sire –

with these three oak leaves – and could be a family crest of some sort. With some diligent investigation, we may be able to identify it.'

The King was impressed by this rapid insight. 'Really, Mr Mawdsley? That would be most useful, if you could.'

Mawdsley was a little embarrassed at raising the King's expectations on such a flimsy hope. 'I cannot promise success in this matter, sire. Yet I can promise that I will leave no stone unturned in my search for the writer of this wicked letter.'

The King exclaimed aloud. 'Ay, I am sure that you will apply great exertions to this matter, Mr Mawdsley.' He began to make a growling noise in his throat. 'But when you mention a family crest, are you suggesting that this message could have been sent by someone belonging to a noble family?'

Mawdsley retreated a little in the face of the King's anger. 'The wax is a little smudged so I may be wrong about the seal, your majesty. Yet it is worth investigating the possibility that this man has some important family connections, if I can determine which family it might be. It may help us run this man to earth before he has a chance to do any damage to your illustrious person.'

The King frowned, his expression emphasizing the size of his impressive Roman nose, and his dark brooding face beneath his curled wig. 'Do you really think this individual is a danger to me, or to Lady Castlemaine?'

Clarendon interrupted, his voice sounding thin and reedy after Mawdsley's own more mellifluous tones. 'Not to Lady Castlemaine, perhaps, since he could already have done her harm in the park,' he pointed out. 'Yet he could be a real danger to you. You still conduct your public affairs with disarming informality, sire, if I may say so. You walk in the park alone sometimes, and even in the street or at the theatre. Perhaps you need to be a little more circumspect in your behaviour until this man is apprehended.'

The King grunted dismissively. 'I shall not hide away like a child. I must be seen by my subjects.'

'Bravo,' declared Lady Castlemaine, getting to her feet, and taking his arm affectionately. 'That is why you are a king, Charles, while the rest of us must simply gaze on in admiration, prostrate at your feet.'

The King laughed and squeezed her arm in return, his good mood instantly restored by this compliant and sensual woman.

She might indeed be a shameless whore, Mawdsley thought, yet her beauty truly was something wondrous to behold...

CHAPTER 4

The Lord's Day, 11th December 1664

Raven was glad to finally escape from the communion service this morning, after that interminable sermon by Mr Jenkins, the parson of St Martin-in-the-fields. The church, built over a hundred years ago by Henry VIII, was no longer "in the fields" these days, of course, yet that appellation had nevertheless remained even though the building was now surrounded by an increasing number of new dwellings that had engulfed it like a muddy tide of flotsam and jetsam. Today the interior of the church had been quite as cold as the outside, and the parson's long-winded and prolix sermon had been nearly drowned by the cacophony of coughs, sneezes and unpleasant hawking noises being made by the shivering red-nosed congregation.

During the endless service, Raven had reflected at length on the long diatribe from the pulpit, and, more especially, on the inconstant character of the man making it. Mr Josiah Jenkins had been a parson of a distinctly non-conformist hue until three years ago but, seeing his livelihood in peril after the Restoration and the Act of Uniformity, had shown himself to be one of those pliable creatures all too willing to sacrifice their principles in the cause of security of tenure. In fact, judging from the strident tenor of his speech this morning, Mr Jenkins seemed well on his way to becoming a papist, as many people suspected the King to be - in private at least. Clearly Mr Jenkins was prepared to be whatever the state and the new Royal establishment wanted him to be.

Raven's own views on religion were more modest and unassuming than those of the fiery young parson who had castigated the presumed sins of his congregation with such mock-Catholic zeal today. Henry Raven truly attended church more out of habit than because of any great belief in the sacraments and the edicts of Christianity. Yet, despite

52

being a student of natural philosophy, and a man of a most rational turn of mind, he nevertheless did find comfort in the notion of a beneficent creator, and in particular of one who supposedly took a keen interest in the moral affairs of men.

Emerging from that sobering experience of morning communion into the hard light of day, Raven was not minded to return home just yet despite the bracing cold, and so, on impulse, turned south instead of north as he left the church. His first thought was to walk to Axe Yard in Westminster to meet with Mawdsley, yet, after reaching Charing Cross, Raven decided not to proceed with that plan in the end, aware of how little free time Mawdsley had these days for social intercourse, even on the Lord's Day. With a different destination now firmly in mind, Raven headed east instead along the Strand, past Bedford House and Exeter House, before turning eventually north again into the wide thoroughfare of Bow Street. It was an odd day to choose to walk for pleasure, he had to concede. Snow lay heaped in giant mounds all along the frozen rutted streets while the overhanging eaves of the tall houses were now decorated with icicles of monstrous length and girth. There truly seemed no relief in sight from this savage cold, which seeped into every nook and cranny of a timbered house - and into every nook and cranny of a man's body and soul too.

Bow Street had been laid out thirty years before, together with Covent Garden and the rest of the Bedford estate, and was a much sought after address for wealthy and powerful gentlemen. Oliver Cromwell himself had moved to this new street to live in the year '45, when he had hoped to retreat a little from public life after his military exertions and triumphs during the war, before realizing from the antics and corruption of the Rump Parliament that the country would soon slip back into anarchy without his strong leadership. Raven truly believed that Cromwell was a man of principle who had always acted in the country's best interests throughout his life, rather than his own, yet it occurred to him that even a man with as little personal vanity as Cromwell must have felt some stirring of pride and self-satisfaction when he had gone on to dismiss the Rump and to take the exalted title of Lord Protector of England.

At least Cromwell had not been seduced by power sufficiently to take the title of King, as many of his followers had later suggested he should. On the whole Raven still thought the Lord Protector a great man, and his soul burned with some considerable resentment that the withered head of such a noble Englishman as he should still be displayed to suffer dismal mockery on an iron spike at Westminster Hall...

Raven's destination today was not the former home of Cromwell, though, but a more modest four-storey townhouse at the unfashionable end of Bow Street that had recently been rented by his friend Adam Strange. Raven had not seen Adam since he had dashed out of the King's house immediately at the end of the play on Friday evening, and was curious to know whether Adam had heard any rumours, or anything noteworthy, pertaining to the strange death of the actress Mistress Lusted. For some reason, the matter of that woman's death was beginning to worry Raven in retrospect – perhaps as a result of his conversation yesterday with that odd youth Mr Goodricke - and he did wonder if he should not have given it more of his time and attention. Perhaps young Molly Titchen had been right to have some concerns about her friend's unexpected demise, although Raven could still see no feasible reason why anyone should want to murder such a woman. Strange was a barrister by trade, a member of the Middle Temple Inns of Court, and had defended some clients accused of heinous acts of murder already in his short career, therefore had some experience in the matter of investigating sudden unexplained death.

Adam's new housekeeper, Mistress Bilby, answered Raven's loud confident knock at the tall front door. She was a severe-looking woman who had joined Adam's household but a few months previously. She was still young, or at least under thirty – a widow according to Adam - but also tall, dark and brooding, and Raven had always felt oddly intimidated by her calculating appraisal and sombre manner, which had not softened at all towards him during these first few months of her employment. She recognized him as a regular visitor and friend of her master, however, and acknowledged him with cold politeness by name, before inviting him with her usual grim and unsmiling visage into the ground floor parlour, where Strange sat at a table with his back to a roaring log fire, scribbling a letter in an engrossed fashion.

Yet he put down his quill pen and set aside his ink well willingly enough, when he saw who his visitor was. Springing instantly to his feet to welcome Raven, he said, 'Thank Jesu you've come, Henry, even though I wasn't expecting a visit from you on such a bitter day! I have had quite enough of work for one morning and your visit gives me the perfect excuse to desist. Sit yourself down, while Mistress Bilby brings us some venison stew and a couple of veal pies to fill our bellies.'

The stern Mistress Bilby said nothing in response, but took that as her instruction and went off to the kitchen at the back of the house. For a young and still inexperienced lawyer, and a single man at that, Strange somehow managed to maintain a sizeable household that included two other servants – a sturdy young manservant called Will, and a young girl, Hannah - in addition to the gloomy Mistress Bilby. And the weekly rent on this house must also be a considerable sum for a young and impecunious lawyer to find, Raven surmised, as he wondered how Adam managed to stretch his limited income so far. Perhaps the law paid much better than he imagined, though, or else Adam had come into some new source of income that Raven had not heard about, though neither possibility seemed likely. Yet Adam had mentioned recently that he did expect a possible improvement in his fortunes soon, courtesy of an inheritance from a distant family connection, therefore Raven did wonder if his friend might not be borrowing against that future expectation to maintain his present household.

Raven slumped down in a sturdy high-backed chair on one side of the fire. 'I appreciate the kind offer but I will not join you in your meal, Adam, as I suffer a little today from the colic.'

Strange sat down on the oak settle opposite and gave Raven a sweet smile in return. 'No matter, Henry – your sore belly will mean all the more for me.'

Raven leaned back against the chair rest and regarded his friend with quiet affection. Strange had been the third member of his close student triumvirate at Trinity College, Cambridge during the Protectorate, together with Mawdsley, of course. Strange had a similar background to Mawdsley, if one not quite so grand, being the second son of a moderately wealthy land-owning family from Warwickshire with Royalist sympathies. The Interregnum and subsequent Restoration had not turned out so fortuitously for Adam and his family as it had for Mawdsley, though. After Strange's father had died fighting on the King's side at Naseby, Cromwell had stripped the Strange family of their estate and handed it over to one of his greatest supporters, a fellow general in the new Model Army, Sir Daniel Somerton. By rights the Strange family should have expected to be able to reassert their claim to their estate in Warwickshire after the Restoration, and this would no doubt have happened in the fullness of time, had it not been that Somerton, with impeccable timing, had switched loyalties just before the return of the King in the summer of '60, the unwritten price of his support being that he should keep the lands he had purloined during the Interregnum.

The King apparently thought more of rewarding Somerton for his last minute change of tack than of making recompense to the family of one of his father's long dead allies, so it seemed unlikely now that Strange would ever regain his estate. It was as well, then, that Strange had made a career for himself as a barrister, and one that was apparently making him enough for a comfortable living. Adam had suffered more bad news a year ago when his only surviving brother Titus had died in Vienna of the plague. Titus, the eldest son, had inherited their mother's lesser fortune so Adam had travelled to the Continent to try and recover what might be left of it after his brother's death. But it seemed that his brother had led a profligate, dissolute life in Vienna, and Adam had found nothing there but more despair, and more debts that needed to be paid off.

Raven studied his friend's face, which looked even more handsome than usual when highlighted by the lambent firelight. Strange had changed little in the five years since he had left Cambridge, and he remained tall, fair-haired and eternally youthful. He was not perhaps as classically handsome as Mawdsley, but women, young and old, still admired his boyish good looks and his charm. Despite the disappointments of losing his family's estate, he had no appearance of bitterness in his face, merely one of steely determination to prosper by some other means.

Raven had to admit to himself that he had certainly been the least handsome of the three student friends, if perhaps physically stronger and more muscular in build. He wondered idly why he had chosen to cultivate the friendship of two young men at university who were so much better endowed with physical beauty than himself. But being a man of modest temperament, he truly held no resentment against his friends for the manly beauty with which nature had kindly endowed them.

'Did you have any special purpose in calling today?' Strange asked curiously. 'You seldom call here on the Lord's Day.'

'It was really only to remind you that Mawdsley has invited both of us as his guests to the palace on Wednesday afternoon to see a special performance of a play in the Great Hall.'

Strange gave him an arch look in return. 'Our friend Mawdsley must now have considerable influence at court if he can get invitations for two such disreputable and unimportant people as you and I to join the King's private entertainments,' he observed dryly. 'Although I am surprised that a man with your political sympathies should be so willing to toady in front of the King,' he added with slight maliciousness.

'I have no intention of toadying,' Raven declared with a ghost of a smile. 'And what mean you about my political sympathies?'

Strange laughed. 'Oh, for all your protestations that you are only interested in business and the study of natural philosophy, do not try and deny that at heart you are a devout Republican, Henry.'

Raven was uneasy. 'What I hold dear, Adam, is a united and peaceful England. I care not truly if it is a monarchy or a republic, only that its citizens are treated fairly and honourably and given a chance to prosper in life through their own efforts.' He sighed. 'I never want to see this country riven by another civil war, ye can be sure of that.'

Strange looked as if he were about to say something more, but then relented, given the serious look on Raven's face.

Raven looked at the legal papers scattered about on the tabletop at which Adam had been working, and wondered whether these documents might have something to do with this possible change in his fortunes that Adam had mentioned to him a few weeks before. Although Strange had no realistic expectation of ever recovering his own family's estate – not while Sir Daniel Somerton and his descendants were alive anyway - it seemed that Adam was the only surviving kinsman to another wealthy Warwickshire landowner, his distant cousin Sir Oliver Runnalls. Runnalls was an elderly man close to death, and one moreover who had no other living relative as far as Strange could determine.

Adam had been making subtle enquiries with Sir Oliver's solicitor concerning the will and testament of this old gentleman, and whether he, as his closest living relative, might expect to prosper from it.

Yet when Raven put the question to Adam about the papers on his table, and whether they related to the will of Sir Oliver Runnalls, Strange's face fell immediately. 'No, these papers are nothing to do with that. As for Sir Oliver's will, his lawyer, Mr Wadsworth, will tell me nothing of its likely contents, so it seems I must simply wait for Sir Oliver to die and then discover my fate.' Strange smiled sheepishly. 'I suppose it does not become me to wish for another man's death, especially a kinsman, when I have so few to celebrate as it is. But it is difficult not to be avaricious in these circumstances, Henry. Sir Oliver's estate comes with ten thousand acres of Warwickshire fields and woods, three entire villages, and a house that quite puts Hampton Court to shame.'

Raven laughed at his friend's brazen ambition. 'Then I hope Sir Oliver does not disappoint you in the end, Adam.'

'Nor I.' Strange smiled back as Mistress Bilby returned with a wooden tray filled with steaming wooden bowls of stew, and trenchers of bread.

After she had served the food to her master and withdrawn again to the kitchen, Raven nodded in the direction of the passageway. 'Mistress Bilby is an efficient keeper of your house, Adam, but why did ye not hire a maid with a sunnier disposition? 'Tis like living with a thundercloud, when that woman is in the room. It would drive me to severely morbid thoughts if I had such a dark and brooding woman around me all the time.'

'Nay, you may keep your Mistress Bagwell, Henry. I would not swap Mistress Bilby for a thousand of your Bagwells...' - Strange laughed roguishly – 'despite her interesting name.'

Adam began to eat ravenously while Raven changed the subject abruptly to that of the death of the actress in the King's house on Friday evening.

It seemed that Strange had heard nothing at all of this story so Raven had to tell him everything he knew. Strange had many questions to put, with his keen lawyer's mind, but in the end he too discounted the possibility that the actress had been murdered.

Strange was particularly interested, though, in the identity of the person who had discovered the body of the actress in the tiring room. He gave Raven a knowing look. 'Ah, so this Molly Titchen is the very same orange girl whom you were ogling so shamelessly before the play.'

Raven smiled. 'Sometimes, Adam, I believe you listen too attentively to the nonsense that our friend Mawdsley spouts.'

Strange narrowed his eyes, trying not to smile in return. 'You completely deny any interest in this strumpet, then, Henry?'

Raven grunted. 'I do not deny that I took notice of her before the play – as did both you and Mawdsley. She is a fine-looking girl. When I conversed with her later, I confess I was surprised by her obvious intelligence. I suspect also she may know something about this business she is not telling us.'

Adam raised an eyebrow. 'You think she plays games of some sort?'

'I would not go so far as that. But perhaps she does have some intimations as to the identity of the woman she saw leaving the tiring room. Perhaps she intends to find this woman herself and discover what this dark lady's business was. Yet if she is practising some deceitful game of this sort –' Raven shook his head in puzzlement as he began to doubt his own premise – 'what could a girl like that possibly hope to achieve by it?'

'Perhaps she is intending to blackmail this dark lady?' suggested Strange thoughtfully.

Raven gave a sceptical grunt. 'I hardly think so, Adam. Mistress Titchen does not seem such a hard and scheming girl as that.'

Strange nodded sagely. 'Ah, ye find it hard to believe that a girl with a pretty face and fine bubbies might also have a devious and calculating mind.'

Raven sighed ruefully. 'Ay, I suppose that I do.'

Strange sniffed. 'Many men make that same mistake, Henry. Yet we underestimate women at our peril, my friend. The one thing I have learned to expect from the female sex is to be eternally surprised by them. They are never quite what you would expect from the outside – not even those with prim and proper external shells.'

Raven laughed at his mock seriousness. 'What? Not even your Mistress Bilby?'

Strange smiled mysteriously. 'Not even my Mistress Bilby. Ye might be surprised at what passions and desires go on in the head of a woman like Mistress Bilby. 'Tis perhaps as well that you cannot divine female minds, Henry, otherwise what shocks to your complacent system might result...'

*

Without the clamour and bodily exertions of an audience to stir any warmth into the interior of the building, the King's theatre was as cold as the grave on this Lord's Day. Molly Titchen, standing just offstage, was in a sombre mood today, and had been so since yesterday forenoon when she had come to the theatre to witness Sarah's body being taken away by cart in a cheap pine coffin, destined for burial in the nearby village of Islington.

Molly had been glad to see that Sarah's adoptive parents, the Lusteds, had forgiven their daughter her bold and inexplicable decision to work in the theatre, and had travelled in person from the country by cart to collect her body and possessions. They seemed a simple and modest couple to Molly, comporting themselves with quiet dignity despite clearly being uneasy among the noise and distractions and pestering rogues of this teeming city. Despite the icy grip of winter on the surrounding countryside, and the legions of hungry birds foraging vainly in the snow, Molly had earlier that morning found a sprig of green holly, still with untouched berries, growing in a hedgerow near Lincoln's Inn Fields. With a tearful gesture, she had hurriedly laid her green prize on top of Sarah's simple coffin as the Lusteds' muddied and shaggy old mare had finally pulled the cart away down Bridges Street with its sad burden. The farmer's wife, Mistress Lusted, a clear-eyed grey-haired woman of forty, had bowed her thanks to Molly as she followed after the cart on the beginning of its dismal journey north across the fields to Islington. With only the lightest of loads from the makeshift coffin and Sarah's slender body, the cart had rattled and bumped alarmingly as its wooden wheels slipped and turned over the frozen ruts and wheel tracks.

Now, a day later, Molly was still suffering severe melancholy (as well as some residual pain in her head from that sword blow administered to her on Friday night) as she stood quietly in the wings of the stage, listening to the actors going through a reading of *Twelfth Night* by the late Master Will Shakespeare. These old plays were less boisterous examples of the playwright's art than the modern ones, Molly thought, yet these wordsmiths of Queen Bess's time had a wonderful turn of phrase to make up for the slower pace and more serious nature of their plots.

Not that *Twelfth Night* was too serious a work, being the story of a shipwrecked girl, Voila, who, in looking for her lost twin brother in the foreign land of Illyria, had taken on the guise of a man to protect herself. In that guise of Cesario, she soon fell for the handsome Duke Orsino, who was already enamoured of the wealthy if silly Countess Olivia, who then in turn suffered an attack of Cupid's darts for Viola in her male guise as Orsino's emissary. The whole play thus formed an entertaining if unlikely love triangle, with much confusion of identities and consequent sexual innuendo.

Despite her dark mood, Molly soon found her spirits lifted by the witty language of the play, with Mary Pettican excelling in her role as the flighty Olivia, while the handsome young actor Miles Brammer (whose fine features and long slender limbs Molly had long formed an admiration of her own for, when displayed on stage) played Duke Orsino with authority and panache. Yet the person who had drawn Molly's admiration most during the rehearsal was the new girl Jane Golightly, who was playing Viola/Cesario with believable conviction. Rather to Molly's surprise, the pretty fair-haired Mistress Golightly did move and sound like a convincing man in the guise of Cesario, even though she was still dressed for the rehearsal in her own skirts and petticoats.

It was highly unusual for the theatre company to have to practise like this on the Lord's Day: normally this was as much a day of rest for actors – and orange sellers - as it was for everyone else. But it seemed that the King (being deprived of alternative entertainment this week) had requested a special performance by the company in the Grand Hall at Whitehall Palace on Wednesday evening, and the eternally grateful Sir Thomas was never prepared to say no to his noble patron. Sir Thomas had picked on *Twelfth Night* as the best play to perform because the company was so familiar with it that they could have attempted it even without rehearsal. Yet perfectionist that he was, Sir Thomas had nevertheless called in the company to run through the play today in preparation for Wednesday's special performance.

Molly truly had no reason to be here at all, though, except that it was slightly warmer in the King's theatre than in her flea-ridden lodgings in Coal Hole Lane. And even without that extra incentive, the fact was that Molly took such pleasure from watching the actors perform that she always came to watch rehearsals whenever she could. Luckily the elderly Janus who guarded the doors of the theatre was a man who seemed to want to curry favour with her, and was therefore prepared to look the other way and let her in whenever she asked. Molly knew perfectly well why, of course, but had no intention of indulging this toothless old man in return for his consideration with so much as a kiss. Not unless she absolutely had to, anyway...

Molly was so engrossed in listening to the dialogue of the closing scene of the play that she failed to notice a threatening and bulky figure stealing up to her from behind, until it was too late. Molly was aware only of a sudden whirlwind of noise behind her, then found herself pressed against a plaster wall with Mistress Meggs pinching her painfully on the bridge of her nose with a muscular finger and thumb.

Mistress Meggs finally released her tight grip on Molly's nose after what seemed like five minutes of agony. Thankfully, the older woman did not appreciate how close she had just come to having her front teeth removed by Molly's fierce right fist, when Molly's forbearance had been tested to such a degree. 'By what right are you here, Molly Titchen, may I ask?' she muttered balefully. 'I gave you no permission to be in the theatre today. And neither did anyone else, I am sure...'

Molly's mind raced as she tried to invent a plausible reason for being here - other than being cold anyway. It occurred to her to ask why Mistress Meggs herself was here today, but she decided that such a provocative and saucy riposte was unlikely to further her case with this difficult woman.

But an unlikely saviour came to her rescue when Sir Thomas Killigrew himself suddenly appeared magisterially at Mistress Meggs' side. ''Twas I who asked her to be here, Mistress,' he explained in his mellow actor's voice. 'To fetch us hot food when we need it, and perhaps also to help with the costumes should any of the actors wish to try their fit today. I am sorry I did not ask you earlier, when I know that Molly works for you, and not for the King's house directly.'

Mistress Meggs simpered at that apology like a girl, but her eyes were steely as she tried to judge whether Sir Thomas was speaking with sincerity. 'In that case, of course, it is perfectly all right for Molly to be here...' – her voice hardened slightly – 'even if no one informed me.'

Sir Thomas merely smiled further at that grumbling remark with blank amiability until Mistress Meggs was forced to withdraw slowly, grinding her teeth with poorly concealed anger.

Molly felt almost sorry for her humiliation and knew that the woman would be an even more implacable enemy from now on, looking for any opportunity to sack her for some minor infringement of the rules.

After Mistress Meggs had gone from their hearing, Molly curtsied to Killigrew, while wondering what price she might have to pay for Sir Thomas's apparently kindly intervention. 'Thank you, sir. That was kind of you to take my side.'

Killigrew was in expansive mood. 'Oh, 'tis of no matter. Mistress Meggs can be an officious busybody and deserves to be put in her place occasionally. And why should you not be here, after all? I understand well that you have a genuine interest in playacting, Molly. You are always here watching our rehearsals on your own time, I notice. Even the sad death of Sarah Lusted has not changed that.'

'Indeed I am interested in the actor's art, sir.' Molly was about to say something more but her courage faltered for a second.

'Speak up, Molly,' Sir Thomas said. 'You have something more to say?'

Molly looked at her feet. 'I wonder...'

'Yes?'

Molly cleared her suddenly dry throat. 'I wonder if there might be any chance that I could...could...*read* for a part in one of the plays, Sir Thomas? I believe I could do some of the parts well enough.'

Killigrew came closer until Molly could clearly discern the large pores in his bulbous old man's nose. 'Ah, you have acting pretensions?'

'I do, sir.'

Killigrew smiled reassuringly as Molly backed away slightly from him. 'Do I make you nervous, Molly? You seem to be shivering a little.'

''Tis nothing but the raw cold in here, sir.'

'Ay, I see well the gooseflesh on your arms. You need warming up, my girl.' With that Sir Thomas put his hand on Molly's trim waist, then ran the palm slowly northwards to encompass her left breast.

Molly did not flinch at his touch, although she would have dearly liked to take out the knife from beneath her skirts and slit this old man's turkey throat.

Killigrew finally withdrew his hand as he breathed unpleasing odours into her face. 'Perhaps I can find something for you to do, Molly.' He took her cold hand. 'But I first need to see what you can do in the acting line.' His voice dropped to a whisper. 'Art thou prepared to give me a special audition of thy talents first...?'

*

A few hours later, with dusk falling rapidly, Molly headed home through darkened streets. Tonight was no night for man or beast to be abroad, she thought with a shiver. Candlelight and firelight glimmered faintly behind leaded windows as the snow began to fall again ever more thickly. In the narrow alleyways, the upper storeys of the wooden buildings leaned out so far from each side that often only a thin line of black wintry sky could be glimpsed above. Yet that hardly seemed to provide any protection from the cold, for the wind whistled down these narrow lanes like a knife, and the snow felt like needles of ice against her face. At least with the ground frozen hard underfoot like iron, there was no risk of sinking knee-deep into the street mire like so much of the year, yet this was poor consolation to Molly on the whole. Her feet were so cold and numb in her poor wooden shoes that they felt like mere blocks of ice strapped to her legs.

She had at least not been forced to "audition" for Killigrew today, which was something she was grateful for, since it gave her time to come to a rational decision about how far she was prepared to go to indulge Sir Thomas in return for his patronage. In fact, apart from that feeble grope of her titties offstage, Sir Thomas had been most considerate and cordial today, and had let her stay and watch the rest of the rehearsal without any further hindrance. He had even arranged for her to share some of the grilled capon, boiled parsnip and cabbage leaves that had been brought for the actors' company to eat. But perhaps this was not pure philanthropy on Killigrew's part – Molly wondered suspiciously whether he was fattening her up for his own future delectation. Sir Thomas was known to like a woman of voluptuous shape and perhaps Molly's figure did not quite measure up to his expectation yet after that initial feel he'd had of her breast.

Despite being spared this difficult decision today, Molly knew that Killigrew would ask again in time, of course, and perhaps very soon. He had after all bedded all the other actresses in the company (and several of the actors too, including the handsome Miles Brammer, if Molly's orange seller friend Nell could be believed) so must be in need of fresh conquests for his ageing horn.

Even Sarah had yielded to Killigrew's physical demands, Molly was sure. Sarah had never admitted as much to her but Molly had no real doubts that she too must have given herself to Sir Thomas at least once as the price for being elevated from mere orange seller to actress.

So Molly knew that she would have to come to a decision soon about whether to pay Sir Thomas's asking price, or else be passed over in her acting ambitions for someone even younger. Molly was sure that her fourteen-year-old friend Nelly would happily climb into Sir Thomas's bed the first time she was asked. Nell was so precocious and ambitious that she might not even wait to be propositioned, but do the asking herself.

Molly had crossed Drury Lane by now and had entered a series of alleyways that were even narrower and meaner than those that had gone before. Stopping to catch her breath for a moment at one dark corner, she caught sight briefly out of the corner of her eye of someone behind her. The man was perhaps thirty paces behind her but, on being observed, he quickly stepped out of sight behind a wall, which struck Molly as being sinister behaviour, and warned her that he might be up to no good. She walked on a little more rapidly, before stopping again and turning sharply to see if the man was still there. Yet she saw and heard nothing behind her now but the howl of the wintry wind, the creak of hanging shop and tavern signs, and the groaning of straining house timbers. She shrugged at her own foolish imaginings, then hurried on, trudging through the deepening snow drifts, which now lapped up in places nearly to the sills of the ground floor windows.

She had nearly reached the entrance to her own alleyway off Coal Hole Lane, when, again out of the corner of her eye, she caught a fresh glimpse of a dark shape moving behind her and realized with a thrill of apprehension that she had been right in her earlier suspicions after all. There was indeed a man following her deliberately – a thickset rogue in a patched cloak and feathered hat, who had just turned the last corner behind her, and now stood there brazenly in full view in the alleyway, breathing heavily in anticipation of some action perhaps pleasing to himself, if exceedingly unpleasant for her.

Molly turned to face the man, and appraised him as coolly as she could, while her hand felt feverishly through the pocket of her skirts for the knife that she always carried, in a sheath tied with twine to her thigh.

The man made no move towards her at first, but this was regrettably no proof of any innocent intentions, because a second man – a toothless wiry-haired man, even uglier and more villainous looking than the first, if anything – soon stepped forward from behind the shelter of a house to join him.

Molly felt a shiver of primal fear at the sight of these two devils, but comforted herself with the thought that she was only a few paces from the alleyway leading to her own front door. And that refuge of her own doorway was no more than thirty paces down the alley at the very end. Somehow she had to get to that doorway and across that threshold, and bar the door promptly behind her, before these two villains could follow her.

'What is your business with me, ye poxed devils?' she challenged them defiantly. 'I am just a poor serving maid; I have nothing worth stealing, ye pair of slubberdegullions.'

The first man in the feathered hat lifted his hand into view and Molly gasped as she saw the size of the knife he was holding. ''Tis nothing personal that I must gut thee, Mistress,' he said almost apologetically.

Molly instantly turned and fled, her fear giving her an unexpected surge of speed, even with the thick layer of snow on the ground to impede her. She was able to gain ten yards on the men almost immediately, and to turn into her own alleyway before they could react. Molly almost shouted aloud with relief when she saw that the ground floor door to her lodging house was already open, a faint stream of candlelight issuing from inside. Not only that - it seemed that her roommate Amy was just stepping out of the faintly lit doorway, perhaps on her way to an evening assignation with a paying client.

Amy looked up in alarm as a screaming Molly bore down on her, now pursued closely by the two armed men.

'Return inside, Amy! Now!...*now*....!' Molly yelled but Amy simply stood there in bewilderment.

With Amy blocking the way through the narrow door, Molly had no alternative now but to turn and try and fight off the two men at least temporarily, until Amy could withdraw back into the lodging house.

The first man – Feathered Hat - came at Molly with his stupendous iron blade, but was clumsy in his movements, and clearly not expecting retaliation of any kind. Molly easily avoided his slow and ponderous first thrust and then, pulling her own knife from the secret pocket beneath her skirts, slashed viciously with her blade at the man's ribs. Feathered Hat howled with pain and collapsed into a thick drift of snow like a felled tree.

Before Molly could stop her, Amy threw herself fearlessly into the path of the other man, Toothless, as he came to his fallen accomplice's aid. Toothless, taken by surprise by Amy's aggression, struck at her viciously with some hidden weapon that Molly could not make out in the gloomy light.

Yet that something was clearly a deadly blade of some sort because Amy let out a terrible wail of pain, then staggered and fell in a bloodied heap at Molly's feet...

*

Henry Raven was returning home from an early evening visit to collect some physic for his troublesome colic from a renowned apothecary in Shoe Lane in the city, and his walk home took him by chance across Lincoln's Inn Fields. He was crossing Drury Lane when he heard the sounds of great commotion in the distance – then saw a noisy crowd gathering higher up Drury Lane, led by two elderly officers of the Watch, dressed in greatcoats, and armed with lanterns and wooden staffs.

Raven's curiosity made him follow the two old watchmen and their attendant crowd, whose journey took them all northwards into an area of poor hovels near Holborn. These two decrepit watchmen were typical of the men who were enacted to somehow try and keep the peace in this city, Raven thought, being mostly retired tradesmen of one sort or another, with no more idea of how to uphold the law than of being able to fly. Last year the King had brought in the Act of the Court of Common Council that had been designed to regulate the Watch by improving its efficiency and overcoming its more corrupt practices. This act had led to the watchmen now being known popularly as "Charleys", but otherwise the system seemed as hopelessly corrupt and inefficient as ever, and London's streets just as dangerous and unsafe as before.

In a narrow alleyway just off Coal Hole Lane, an even larger crowd had already gathered at the scene of some tragedy, it seemed. The "Charleys" forced their way through this assembled crowd, while a still curious Raven followed them without hindrance from the other spectators, aided perhaps by his natural authority and the dress of a gentleman.

At the end of the alley, where it opened up slightly into a T-shaped dead end, was a mean lodging house. Lying in front of the entrance to this lodging house, Raven was shocked to see the bodies of two young women lying entwined together in the snow. Even with only the dim light of the watchmen's lanterns to dispel the darkness, it was possible to see that the snow around the bodies was splashed thick with blood and gore.

A slatternly woman spoke up from another doorway and soon attracted the watchmen's attention. ''Ear me, good sirs! I saw it all from my second floor window. These two poor young creatures were attacked by two vicious footpads. They stabbed the maids wivout mercy, then ran off when they heard people approachin' down the alley.'

The older of the two watchmen – a man who must rival Methuselah for age, Raven thought, judging from his snowy white beard and deep wrinkles - prised the two bodies apart. Raven saw with relief that at least one of the maids was still alive since she complained mightily at the watchman's touch. The girl – for she seemed no more than sixteen or so - got slowly to her feet while Methuselah bent down and examined the other woman still lying on the snow.

'This one is dead enough,' he declared almost with satisfaction. 'Sliced clean through the 'eart.'

The live maid stared at him with hatred. 'Leave her be.'

Despite her dishevelled state, Raven suddenly recognized this young woman as the pretty orange girl from the theatre two nights before. She was shivering so violently with the cold and with the emotion of what had happened that Raven instantly took off his own cloak and put it around her.

She stared at him uncomprehendingly for a moment, but gratefully accepted the extra thick woollen cloak. From her behaviour she seemed unhurt to Raven, but it was difficult to say for certain when she was shivering so uncontrollably, and covered with so much blood too.

'Are you hurt, Molly?' he asked her gently.

Her head jerked up in surprise at the use of her name, and Raven detected a flash of recognition despite her dazed state. 'I am not, sir. But poor Amy is murdered by those evil ruffians.'

'Was she a friend of yours?'

'My room mate, sir. We lived in a room just above here...'

Raven glanced up at the miserable cold hovel in which Molly apparently lived. He turned and spoke up to the younger Charley who seemed inclined to show slightly more urgency in dealing with this matter than Methuselah. 'Ye can see these two maids were attacked by someone, so why stand around waiting like this, sir? This other girl will die too unless we get her into somewhere warm soon.' He pointed to the doorway of her lodging, which had thick ice encrusted even on the inside of the doorjamb. 'But she should not be left alone in this place on such a night, or she will certainly freeze in her condition.'

The watchman seemed perturbed by Raven's commanding voice and manner. 'I can remove the body, of course. But I have nowhere suitable to take this other young girl, sir. I cannot offer her free bed and board. Are you offering to look after her tonight, sir?' he asked hopefully.

Raven scowled angrily. 'Of course I will, if she does not object.'

A man in a leather apron sniggered at the back. 'I would take her 'ome too, given 'alf a chance.'

Raven ignored the vulgar man and pressed the two watchmen again. 'My name is Henry Raven, gentlemen. I live in St Martin's Lane, the large house with the green-painted door near to the pond. I am sure that Molly will be happy to talk to you tomorrow about what happened here tonight if you want to call.' He turned to Molly. 'Can you walk, Molly, or should I fetch a sedan chair or carriage for you?'

Molly looked at him with bewilderment. 'I can walk perfectly well, sir. Which is more than what one of those ruffians can do now. His other toothless friend had to drag the scoundrel away after I dealt with him,' she declared with satisfaction.

Raven put his arm around her and led her away through the assembled silent crowd, who now parted for them to pass like the Red Sea dividing for the Israelites.

CHAPTER 5

Monday, 12th December 1664

Molly stirred in her warm featherbed and stretched luxuriously as she finally woke from a deep and satisfying sleep. That was until she remembered where she was, and with a nervous start recalled the terrible thing that had happened the night before.

Wan grey daylight filtered through the shuttered window, but the light was still sufficient in intensity to indicate that it must be well past sunrise. Molly lifted her head from the soft clean-smelling pillow and glanced around the chamber where she had spent the night. She supposed that this was merely an ordinary bedchamber in this house, but it seemed nevertheless a veritable palace to her.

Molly had not been so warm and snug in months as she felt at this moment, with a hearty fire burning through the night in the hearth, three silver candlesticks and a chamber pot at her personal disposal, and a fine dry Turkey carpet underfoot. The walls of this room were of fine white plaster with nary crack nor cobweb in sight, and there were rich Tyrian tapestries hanging on one of the walls. On the table by the leaded window was a polished mirror of silver and a decorated stoneware basin, and in the corner of the room a carved cypress chest full of linen and Turkey cushions. Even the bed was a work of art, with a soft feather mattress and fine silk hangings from the canopy.

This gloomy young gentleman must indeed be a wealthy merchant, Molly decided complacently, or the son of one at least, to be living in such a fine modern house. She knew his name well enough by now, of course – Mr Henry Raven – but nothing much else since they had barely talked yesterday. Last evening he had simply walked with her, or rather half-carried her, to St Martin's Lane as fast as her tired legs could go, and then got his chief servant, a Mistress Bagwell, to put her straight to bed. And Molly, still in shock over the death of her friend Amy, had been in no more of a mood than Mr Raven for making polite conversation...

Molly heard a brief knock at the door, and a young girl of about her own age looked in. The girl seemed a little wary of her, as had Mistress Bagwell last night, but Molly could hardly blame them for that. She doubted that Mr Raven was the type of gentleman who often brought home young women from the streets.

'You are awake, Mistress,' the girl said politely enough, as she opened the shutters. 'My name is Kate; I am the scullery maid in this household. The master asked me to wash and iron your clothes, but they are not quite dry yet. By the by, the nightgown you are wearing is mine. It will take another hour before you can wear your own clothes comfortably again.'

'Then I thank you kindly for the lending of the nightgown. But you need not be so polite to me, young Kate. Call me Molly. What hour is it now?' Molly asked, raising her head from the pillow again. In truth she could scarce recall even what day it might be, after such a long and dream-filled sleep.

Kate wrinkled her high white brow in perplexity. 'I have not heard the church clock striking...err...Molly. So it must still be a little before noon, I am sure.'

Molly gasped and sat up in alarm. 'Nearly noon! I must go to the theatre soon. I start work at two o'clock.'

'Are you an *actress*, then, Molly?' Kate asked breathlessly, wide-eyed with wonder.

Molly would have dearly loved to reply in the affirmative to that question, but honesty prevailed. 'Not yet, but I hope to be in time. I am presently one of the orange sellers at the King's house.'

'Oh, I see.' Kate's eyes fell, disillusion showing. 'Then you are not much higher up in life than me. I thought you were a lady, despite your poor clothes.'

Molly could not help laughing at this solemn, thin little creature with her enormous dark eyes and placid manner. 'No, indeed. Probably I am much lower in social rank than an honest scullery maid, if truth be known,' she admitted uncomfortably.

Before Kate could respond to that frank admission, there came another knock at the open door, and Mr Raven poked his head around it. 'Ah, you are awake, Molly, and look much improved from last night. May I come in and speak with you, even though you are still abed.'

'Surely, sir,' Molly said eagerly. Nevertheless she decided to feign a little more modesty than she truly felt, and pulled the covers up to her neck as she sat up fully in bed.

Mr Raven came and sat in a chair by the bed. Kate was about to go, stepping backwards quietly to the open door, But Mr Raven, clearly uncomfortable to be left alone with Molly, asked the scullery girl to stay for a moment.

Molly could see that this gentleman was still a little shy with her, which endeared him to her somewhat, when she was unused to such modest manners from her male acquaintances.

Mr Raven cleared his throat, before looking Molly directly in the eye. 'I am sorry indeed over the death of your friend. Were you and she very close?'

'Inseparable, sir.' Molly decided it would do her no harm to exaggerate her loss, although, in death, Amy did now actually appear a much sweeter figure than Molly had ever considered her to be when alive.

'Then I grieve for your loss, Molly. An officer of the Watch called an hour ago, together with the constable for the ward of Holborn, to speak with you about what happened last night. They wanted a description of these two ugsome villains who killed your friend...'

Molly felt a fresh wave of melancholy engulf her as she remembered the circumstances of last night's tragedy. Amy could easily have run away, or saved herself by locking herself behind that strong front door. But instead she had selflessly come to Molly's aid and had paid the ultimate price for her bravery. Molly had not truly liked Amy's character before, and had thought her a shallow and selfish creature on the whole. Yet with her death she had left Molly with an uncomfortable debt that could never be repaid now.

'One of the villains might already be dead, the one with the feathered hat,' Molly declared, to a gasp of astonishment from the scullery maid. 'I had a knife of my own to protect myself from such varlets. And I used it to good effect to slash that coward's ribs. The toothless one had to help Feathered Hat away.'

Mr Raven coughed in slight embarrassment. 'Yes, Mistress Bagwell discovered your blooded knife when she helped you undress last night. But it may not be wise to mention this part of your story to the constable, Molly.'

'I have nothing to hide, or be ashamed of, sir,' Molly stated resentfully. 'I was merely trying to save myself from an unprovoked attack.'

Mr Raven almost smiled. 'I agree with you entirely. But the law is full of officious and self-important people who make silly and irrational decisions all the time. So, 'tis better to be silent on this point, Molly, and not give them any scope to exercise their authority with wilful misjudgements.'

Molly smiled primly. 'Whatever you say, sir. I am sure your advice is well-meant.' She examined her benefactor in more detail as he smiled at her in return. He was certainly no more handsome than she remembered from the theatre on Friday evening, with a large bony nose and a dark, roughened complexion, yet he did have a wonderful thick head of hair of a most striking dark hue, and he seemed to possess a younger and sweeter personality here in the comfortable surroundings of his own home.

'You are sure that what happened last night was merely a chance attack, Molly, and has no connection with an earlier event?' Mr Raven asked her warily.

Molly pretended ignorance. 'What is your meaning, sir?'

Mr Raven stroked his beard thoughtfully with his fingers before answering with care. 'My meaning concerns the death of your friend, Mistress Lusted, in the tiring room at the King's theatre on Friday evening. You seemed suspicious of the circumstances then. You even pointed out to me the pinprick of blood on her neck where she might have been poisoned. And you mentioned a mysterious dark lady leaving the scene only moments before.'

In truth Molly had wondered herself if those two villains might have been put up to last night's attack by somebody who wished her harm. Given her suspicions, she was half-tempted now to tell Mr Raven of the earlier attack on her outside the Duke's theatre when she had seen the woman from the tiring room a second time.

Confused thoughts rushed through Molly's mind. *Could that dark lady really have poisoned Sarah in some subtle way, and now be after her too, fearful that she might be able to identify her, or her male companion from outside the Duke's theatre?*

Could the dark lady even perhaps be an actress from the King's company in disguise? This perhaps made more sense than her belonging to the Duke's company since a member of that other company would have no direct motive of jealousy against Sarah, while the other actresses of the King's company certainly would. And actresses were, after all, paid for their ability to become other people – witness Sarah's own transformation that night from her beautiful natural self to the fat and rude maid in Mr Etherege's play.

Yet in the cold light of day this whole notion now seemed to Molly a fanciful and ridiculous theory. Why would this unknown dark lady – even if she were really an actress of the King's company in disguise – wish to murder a penniless young actress like Sarah? Jealousy of a rising young actress scarce seemed sufficient reason to murder anyone.

And now Molly had an even more pressing reason for keeping her suspicions to herself – namely that if she wanted to ingratiate herself with Sir Thomas Killigrew, then the last thing she could afford to do was to go around suggesting openly that Sarah might have been poisoned by a rival actress in the company. *What ructions an accusation like that would cause...*

Molly fluttered her eyelashes innocently as she decided she must conceal her suspicions from the rest of the world for the present, and particularly from this clearly sharp-witted gentleman. 'But you said yourself, sir, that there is no known poison that could kill like that,' she declared, cleverly using his own words against him.

Mr Raven seemed thoughtful. 'Ay, that's true. There is no *known* poison like that. But who can say what number and manner of *unknown* poisons may exist in the world?'

'But how would anyone in the theatre obtain such a substance?' Molly asked reasonably. 'Nay, sir, I now adhere to your opinion, that Sarah died of entirely natural causes. I am sorry to have suggested otherwise. As for last night, it must have been a chance attempt at robbery - that is all. The alleyways around Coal Hole Lane are always dangerous places after all. I have been accosted there before; that is why I carry a knife of my own.'

Mr Raven almost smiled. 'Ye do seem to be a young lady well able to take care of your own safety. But cannot you find a safer and more salubrious place to live?'

'Not with my present limited income, sir. We orange sellers can only earn so much; Mistress Meggs profits by the trade far more than us. But I hope that my situation will improve tolerably in time.'

Mr Raven nodded thoughtfully. 'I trust so too.'

Molly sat up even straighter in bed, and let the cover down sufficiently to give Mr Raven a glimpse of the blue nightgown that Kate had lent her. And a little of her bare arm and shoulder too: it seemed the least she could do for his kindness. 'In the meantime, sir, I must get up. It behoves me still to go to work today.'

Mr Raven almost leapt to his feet, seeing that she was threatening to arise from her bed in a state of undress. 'Must you? Are you quite well enough? You are most welcome to stay in my house until you are properly recovered.'

Molly was sorely tempted to accept this generous offer. She could see well enough that this man was physically attracted to her, although he was scarce aware of it himself yet. She could not help but recall Celia's advice about trying to find a comfortable billet with a kind gentleman of means. Perhaps this was an ideal opportunity for her to worm her way into a wealthy gentleman's affections - or perhaps even into his bed, if she played her cards right.

But something in Molly's honest character rebelled at such a low and deceitful plan. In any case, she was not ready yet to make such a commitment to a gentleman she hardly knew, nor was she content to simply become a rich man's toy. Despite her impoverished circumstances, Molly still needed to feel a degree of independence from the whims of wealthy men. If she had to surrender to the will of a man, then there had to be some compelling reason to justify it, and some compelling reward for her in return. Molly was perhaps prepared to indulge the lustful desires of a man like Sir Thomas Killigrew if need be, because that sacrifice did at least offer in return the enticing possibility of a stage career. At present, the opportunity to perform on stage was still a much greater attraction for Molly Titchen than all the fine possessions of this young gentleman, even with his kindness and well-favoured manners, therefore Mr Raven could not presently compete with Sir Thomas in what he had to offer.

Nevertheless, Molly smiled sweetly at her benefactor. 'That would be most kind of you, sir. But no, I must go soon. I will lose my work at the theatre if I do not appear there today. Mistress Meggs does not tolerate absences for any reason. Any reason except death perhaps...' she added only half-jokingly.

Mr Raven gave her a reproving look for her unseemly levity. 'Then if the constable returns for a description of these two foul villains, I will send him to the theatre to talk with you.'

'Thank you kindly again, sir. I do not know how I can ever properly repay you.' Molly wondered if she should take his hand now and perhaps squeeze it gratefully, or perhaps even give him a glimpse of her bubbies. But in the end she decided wisely against such forward behaviour and limited her thanks to another disarming smile. Although she was not presently disposed to seduce this gentleman, Molly was wise enough to know that her circumstances could change to a point where she might eventually need this man's support, and even loyalty.

Mr Raven and Kate withdrew discreetly from the bedchamber while Molly finally got up from bed. She went over to the window and opened up the shutters fully to look out on the street scene below. Despite the intense cold, the street bustled with activity and noise – the rattle of carts laden with produce going to market, the calls of street hawkers and passers-by, the clanging sounds of trade from a dozen workshops and coaching inns along St Martin's Lane. To the north, the meadows where the May fair was held lay thickly blanketed under white drifts of snow, while to the west and south Molly could make out the wooded glades of Hyde Park and the distant villages of Kensington and Little Chelsea, with their frosted rooftops poking out of a thick mist that seemed to have been smothered across the land by a giant hand, like Devon cream on a scone.

As she surveyed the scene outside, Molly's thoughts returned reluctantly to the death of her friends Sarah and Amy. Although she had told Mr Raven that she no longer countenanced any possibility that her friend Sarah had been murdered, Molly found that she could still not rid herself entirely of these suspicions. Despite her doubts that professional jealousy could be a strong enough motive for murder, Molly found that she still could not abandon the notion altogether that Sarah might have been murdered by a rival actress in the company.

If she could overcome her scruples however, and indulge Sir Thomas Killigrew's perverted pleasures a little, then it seemed possible to Molly that she might gain much closer access to the King's company as an actress in her own right. That would certainly also give her the opportunity to study the other actresses in the company with closer scrutiny and decide whether any of them might have had evil intentions towards Sarah.

And also perhaps discover whether any of them could possibly have gone to the tiring room last Friday night disguised as that dark lady…

In fact, could the bewigged gentleman she had seen with the dark lady outside the Duke's house also be an actor, as well as her accomplice? Despite all her earlier doubts, this notion could not be dispelled easily from Molly's active mind…

*

James Blight had not seen the Thames in such a desolate and frozen state before, and he had lived in London for most of the last five years.

The turgid waters of the river upstream of London Bridge - where the flow was constrained to less than half its potential rate by the many narrow arches of the bridge - were now iced over from bank to bank. And this was no thin insipid skin of ice but a mountainous landscape of bergs and valleys, frozen then part thawed, then refrozen again into a strange eerie landscape reminiscent of the legendary Arctic.

From the stairs on both sides of the Thames – from the Old Swan and Dowgate on the city side, and from Bankside and Falcon Stairs on the south - citizens of every shape and hue were descending onto the ice in vast numbers to enjoy this unfamiliar sensation of walking on water, even as dusk fell on this Monday afternoon. Ragamuffin children with makeshift shoes were skating Dutch-style on the flatter and smoother parts of the ice, while drunken adults made merry in other more vulgar ways with their noisy strumpets. Blight saw the flash of a distant musket as a hunter on the ice took aim at a skein of geese flying low over the river.

London Bridge itself was as dense-packed with humanity as ever, despite being embedded in ice up to the crown of its arches. Some of the older buildings atop the bridge had collapsed over the years and been cleared from the bridge deck, but there were still enough of these medieval shops to limit passage for carts and coaches to a single narrow track in places.

Blight pulled his cloak more tightly around him and forced his broad-brimmed hat lower over his head to try and ward off the severe cold. He wondered as he did how much colder it could possibly get this winter: already there had been reports of sea ice forming in the Thames estuary and on the Blackwater in Essex, something he had never heard of happening before during his lifetime.

He pressed on to the south side of the bridge at Southwark, where the snow-covered rooftops were dominated by the tower of St Mary-over-the-water, and the bulk of St Thomas's Hospital. Yet despite these fine old buildings, Southwark was still a disreputable place, as it had been since Queen Bess's time. The playhouses of Bankside might now all be gone, but the stews and bawdy houses remained, and were as busy as ever.

Blight followed a mean back lane that led him through the area of depressing hovels behind the Bear Garden where shows of cock-fighting, dog-fighting, and bear and bull-baiting were still put on nightly. These were cruel and dirty pastimes in Blight's opinion, and ones that should have long ago been banned as vulgar and uncivilized, demeaning to both man and beast.

Yet Blight had more pressing things presently on his mind than the future of these sordid blood sports, as he came finally to a narrow alleyway that led off the main lane through Southwark. This narrow alleyway was called Rose Petal Lane, yet it must have been named by some wag, or else a blind man with no sense of smell at all, because it seemed that neither dog roses nor burnet roses could ever have possibly grown in such a filthy place. Even the deadly cold could not smother the stink of this pestilential street, or add any allure to the pinched white faces of the whores and doxies who peered out from miserable muddied doorways.

Blight found the house with the black door and the Dutch gables that he was seeking. It was larger than the two-storey hovels on either side, but equally dismal in appearance with peeling shuttered windows, crumbling brick and a general air of imminent collapse. Blight could not believe that his friend Ingledew could be living in such squalor and was half-tempted to turn around, sure that he had found the wrong street and the wrong house entirely. Yet how many Rose Petal Lanes could there be in a place as Southwark?

He knocked with his gloved hand at the door and heard a muffled cry from inside that he took to be an invitation to enter. The door was indeed not locked, and Blight pushed it open with difficulty on its rusted iron hinges to find a plain wooden staircase leading upwards to the first floor.

Blight called out and heard the voice again – clearer now that he was inside – calling out to him in return to come up. The voice was sufficiently like the voice of his old friend and comrade-in-arms to encourage Blight to start ascending the stairs.

There was scarce any light on the staircase, but the glimmer of a candle on the first floor beckoned him on. On the landing he found two doors, one of which was open. He stepped hesitantly into the room with the open door.

The room he entered was a bare and sordid chamber, from what little of it Blight could discern from the single flickering candle on the centre table. A smoky fire burned in the hearth but provided barely any heat to ward off the icy chill. The window on the north wall was not shuttered but there was so little light left in the sky on this wintry late afternoon that it did nothing to dispel the rapidly descending gloom inside this miserable room.

A giant of a man was standing by the window and looking out at the river, but turned sharply on Blight's entry. Blight gasped when he saw that the man was wearing a moulded black paper mask that concealed most of his face, something like those extravagant face masks worn at a royal masque of old.

Blight gripped his sword handle in its sheath, fearful of this apparition, who stood even taller than his own impressive six feet and two inches. The immense height of the masked man did however give Blight some further hope that this might truly be his old comrade-in-arms, because Ingledew had been a true giant as a young man – a full six and a half feet tall. 'Is that you behind that mask, Simon?' Blight asked with a tremor in his voice.

The man turned fully to face his visitor. 'It is, James. Thank you for your attendance on such a miserable cold day – I was not sure that you would think my note to be genuine. Forgive the precautions of the mask, but I need to give you some warning that my looks have changed somewhat in the years since we last met.'

Blight came further into the room, his snow-covered heels clattering on the bare uneven boards. 'I am sure that your face cannot be so much altered that I could not look at it with equanimity, Simon.'

'I am not sure that is true, but as you wish.' With that Ingledew slowly untied the back of the mask and then laid it with due ceremony on the table.

Blight could not prevent a gasp of horror when he saw what lay beneath the mask. Simon had been a comely youth of great physical beauty when they had been boyhood friends in Bedford five and twenty years ago. Even as a fighting man during the Civil War, Ingledew had come through that bloody conflict without a scratch on his handsome face. Yet all that beauty was vanished now, his face a mass of ugly red scars and raddled skin.

Blight was still aghast. 'Wha...what happened to you, Simon? What caused this destruction of your face?'

Ingledew pulled the two chairs in the room closer to the feeble fire and then sat down at one of them. 'Join me by the fire and drink some wine with me, and I will tell you all, my friend.'

Blight accepted the glass of Rhenish wine that Ingledew poured for him, then reluctantly moved towards the fire and took the empty chair, though trying not to look directly at the scarred visage of his old friend. His voice at least was reassuringly the same so Blight did his best to avert his eyes from the putrefaction and corruption of that once beautiful face and take in only his friend's words.

Ingledew sighed. 'As for my vanished beauty, 'tis easy to answer. My scarred face is the result of me catching the smallpox two years ago in Constantinople. I should have died, of course, but it seemed God spared me for some reason.' He laughed humourlessly. 'Or perhaps it was the Devil who found a compelling reason to keep me alive...'

Blight continued to stare into the fire as he sipped his Rhenish wine. 'Of what reason do you speak?' he asked doubtfully.

Ingledew sighed. 'I shall explain that later. 'Tis better that I start my story at the beginning. Or from the moment when I last took leave of you, near twenty years ago after Naseby...'

Blight remembered that dismal June day on that Leicestershire battlefield with vivid recall – a disaster for the Royalist side in the Civil War with the Parliamentarians. It had seemed the end of all their hopes, and the final death knell of England's monarchy, as he and Ingledew had fled the corpse-strewn battlefield together in the hope of perhaps fighting another day. Yet, against all expectations, history had restored the monarchy in a bare fifteen years, and with it Blight's fortunes had prospered inestimably too, despite the disadvantage to him of marrying a stern young Puritan bride.

During his years of exile with Prince Charles abroad, Blight – a single man then - had relaxed the puritan principles of his youth and embraced a surprising talent for diplomacy and politics. And it was this subtle diplomatic ability, coupled with his ready proficiency in five European languages and his tireless efforts on his monarch's behalf, that had made him an invaluable servant to the future King. On the King's return to England, Blight had been quickly rewarded for his loyalty with high office.

Now he was no longer a simple gentleman soldier in the service of the King, but an exalted member of the palace establishment - a Groom of the Bedchamber, no less – and an intimate part of the King's private household. Although Blight had remained enough of a Puritan to decline the offer of a title from the King, he had been rewarded with extensive lands and property, and with other peripheral honours that he craved, such as recently being elected a fellow of the Royal Society. (Yet Blight had to admit to himself that his interest in natural philosophy was perhaps a superficial one at best - at least compared to those more impassioned seekers after knowledge who comprised the main membership of that august society – so it was more the status of being a member that he appreciated rather than the chance to learn the intimate secrets of nature.)

All might have been well with Blight at court if he had not chosen to marry a lusty young bride three years ago. Bernadette, though young and bewitching in the bedchamber, was also a stern Puritan out of it, and had gently persuaded Blight back to the devout religious principles of his youth. Their marriage had not been a long one – Bernadette had died a few months ago of a fever – yet her influence had forced a religious re-conversion on him as profound as that of Saul on the road to Damascus...

Ingledew inspected Blight with more frankness than Blight could easily muster in return, yet the task for Ingledew was a much easier one to bear, of course, given the circumstances. Unlike his old friend, Blight knew that he looked well for his years, with his long dark face still moderately handsome, despite the scar on his cheek from Marston Moor. He was well past his fortieth year now, but because of his unusual height, he remained an imposing figure as he stalked the corridors of Whitehall in his habitual black puritan outfit, even with all the extra weight he had accumulated in recent years from so many lavish palace banquets.

Yet he was also aware that his puritan manners and lack of humour had made him the butt of open mockery by his enemies at court. This mockery had not even stilled when he had been widowed a few months ago: the King's arrogant cronies had despised his plain-speaking young Northern wife Bernadette even more than they had him. The King however had taken no visible notice of these crude attempts to undermine him, so Blight was reassured that his position at court was secure for the present.

Even now, after all these years, Blight could not but compliment himself occasionally on the journey he had made from his lowly origins as the son of a yeoman farmer in Bedfordshire to a high official in the Royal household. Yet, once under Bernadette's influence, he had never been truly comfortable in that high position, and had begun to question almost everything he had once taken for granted, even the moral authority of the King, and his right to rule. Much of this doubt stemmed from the behaviour of the King's courtiers, whose antics seemed to grow ever more degraded and dissolute. Nor was the King entirely blameless in this matter, being all too happy to indulge this decadent behaviour from his unruly friends, particularly Buckhurst and Sedley.

Yet even worse for Blight than the antics of Sedley and Buckhurst was the growing suspicion that the King was secretly a Catholic, and that he intended, by a process of subterfuge and deceit, to make England a papist state again...

'Hast thou been abroad all these years?' Blight asked Ingledew, wondering at the great disparity in their present fortunes, when they had once had so much in common. On that sad day when they had seen their fellow soldiers slaughtered at Naseby almost to a man, Blight had parted from Ingledew with all the affection and sentiment of a true comrade and brother.

Ingledew nodded vigorously. 'Ay, indeed, I was a true wanderer for many years, a man unable to put down fresh roots. I know you were also in exile during the years of the Republic, but I travelled much further afield than you even, into the depths of Asia, to the East Indies, and to wild and uncharted places at the very edge of the world. For the last few years, though, I have been living in Constantinople, and have become half-settled there. You would not believe the things I have seen and done in these last twenty years, James, or what powerful secrets I have learned from the shamans and mystics of these strange lands.'

'You did not find a cure for the smallpox, though,' Blight pointed out tactlessly, the strong wine loosening his tongue a little too much.

'Ah, but I did.' Ingledew showed his teeth in the semblance of a smile, before taking a long draught of his own wine. His face seemed even more grotesque when contorted by this approximation to a smile, Blight thought, his mind half-filled with pity, and half with loathing at his friend's awful fate. 'The Ottoman physicians have long used a method of deliberately infecting patients with a weakened variant of the disease, which then somehow grants them immunity from the more pernicious forms of the disease itself. I used their methods to do my own tests on people without the disease, which worked well enough and proved the general efficacy of the method. None of them developed the full infection when in contact with smallpox sufferers, which astonished me, to be honest. Then I decided I must in all fairness try this method on myself.'

Blight was startled by this story. 'What went wrong with this plan? Something evidently did.'

Ingledew shrugged. 'Indeed so. A servant of mine with a grudge over money – a eunuch from Smyrna – changed the weakened physic I was to use to one more powerful. I caught the disease in its full raging power, yet, as I said, I was spared by some divine – or perhaps devilish - providence.'

Blight gasped again. 'And your treacherous servant? What of him?'

'I could not chop his balls off, of course, so, when I had recovered, I followed him to his lair and sawed his head off instead. But I took my time in doing it, and almost enjoyed the experience...' Ingledew laughed humourlessly, almost the cackle of a Bedlam lunatic.

Blight blanched at that inhuman noise and wondered at the sanity of his old friend. Perhaps his travels and his terrible experiences had soured him permanently and left him half-mad.

Or even worse...*perhaps his sanity had been completely destroyed along with his face...*

Ingledew seemed unsettlingly to understand precisely what he was thinking, so Blight looked quickly away again and diverted the subject away from this dreadful tale of the treacherous servant. 'You have not been back in England at all in near twenty years?'

Ingledew recovered his poise and his appearance of sanity again. 'Only once, four years ago, after the restoration of the King.'

'Ah...' Blight remembered the unfortunate circumstances now. 'Of course...your father...'

Like many families, the Ingledews of the county of Bedfordshire had been brutally divided by the Civil War, with brother taking arms against brother, and father against son. Unlike Simon, his father Silas had been a dedicated supporter of Parliament, and had been both a vehemently anti-Royalist member of the House of Commons and eventually a distinguished Colonel in the New Model Army. Worse still for him, he had been one of the signatories of the King's death warrant, and had therefore been excluded from the King's general amnesty to his old enemies on his return to power.

Blight was disturbed by a guilty thought. 'You do not blame me for what happened to your father, do you, Simon? I was not in such a powerful position at court then as I am now, but I did my best to persuade the King to show leniency towards the regicides.'

Ingledew took his time to respond, the emotions behind that scarred face difficult for Blight to read. 'I blame you not, James,' he said finally and perhaps unconvincingly. 'You were - and are - an honourable man, and I make no quarrel with you. I did write to Lord Clarendon after the trial to use his good offices with the King to intercede and try and overturn this terrible sentence. But Clarendon did not even deign to reply, despite my own record of loyal service to the old King.'

'Were you there that day at Charing Cross, Simon? Did you watch the executions of your father, and Colonel Harrison, and the rest? Blight asked uneasily.

Ingledew grunted. 'How could I not go? I was never close to my father, which perhaps explains why I took the opposite side in that conflict to him. Yet I could not stay away from my father's cruel execution, nor could my sister Carolyn…'

Blight remembered Ingledew's sister, Carolyn. He had known her as a child, a tall and dark girl of determined intellect, ten years younger than her brother. And he had met her again by chance a few years ago in Den Haag in Holland when she had been travelling through that country on business of some sort. Since then he had heard some bizarre rumours from a mutual acquaintance in Bedfordshire that she had later taken up a career as a rich man's whore in Italy, and then, later still, as a government spy for the Hapsburg Empire in Vienna, though neither rumour seemed very likely. Having once been quietly attracted to the woman, Blight would have liked to know whether these salacious rumours had any basis in fact, but deemed that this was not something he could sensibly bring up with her brother at a time like this.

Ingledew was talking still. '…And the manner of his dying changed me irrevocably, and destroyed my good opinion of the King forever. I have seen much human suffering in my life, James – during the war, and in my travels – yet I never saw any men suffer such a barbarous fate as my father and his comrades did that day. Nor did I ever see men bear such evil treatment with such magnificent fortitude and resolve. It taught me to hate the man who had ultimately ordered this barbarity, even though I had spent my youth serving his father.'

Blight closed his eyes slowly, weighing up his old comrade's words with worried suspicion. 'But you left England again?'

Ingledew nodded. 'I did, in disgust. I had given years of service to the old King and in return his son spat in my face. I was angry and bitter, and perhaps inclined to revenge, as was Carolyn. But then was not the time…'

'Then your opinions have mellowed in the intervening four years, I trust,' Blight interrupted hopefully, '…given the healing balm of time.'

Ingledew grimaced savagely. 'Nay, there has been no healing balm of time in my case, James. If anything, my lust for revenge has hardened since I was struck down by the smallpox.'

Blight turned his head and looked worriedly into that terrible scarred face. 'Why have you come here now, Simon? What do you hope to achieve?'

'*Why have I come*? Why, I have come to kill the King, of course,' Ingledew stated simply. 'And I need your help to accomplish this worthwhile task, James …'

*

Blight's blood had turned cold at these words so he took another long draught of wine to steady his nerves. He had been right after all: his old friend *was* completely mad ...

Blight got rapidly to his feet. 'I cannot stay and listen longer to this treasonous talk, Simon. For the sake of our old friendship, and for your service to the King's family, I will not report this conversation, but I suggest you leave the country again as soon as you practically can.'

'It is too late for that. I have already announced my intentions in a letter to the King. In fact I handed it in person to the King's whore.'

'Which one?' Blight asked sarcastically. 'There are so many.'

Ingledew almost laughed at that. 'To his chief whore, Castlemaine. I accosted her two days ago in St James's Park.' He saw Blight's look and understood the meaning of it instantly. 'Worry not! To protect the lady's sensibilities, I wore my mask throughout. Although, being such a notorious whore, I am sure she has seen much worse sights in her time than my scarred face.'

Blight slumped back into his chair again in surprise. No one at the palace had mentioned such an incident to him involving Lady Castlemaine, but perhaps the King and Clarendon had decided to keep the knowledge secret for the moment. 'Did you sign this letter?' he asked wearily.

Ingledew mumbled something to himself under his breath before speaking clearly again. 'As good as. I enclosed the letter with my father's old seal. If there are any intelligent gentlemen providing the King with counsel, they will eventually recognize that seal as belonging to the Ingledew family. Even without it, the contents of the letter should soon reveal the truth of my identity. I want the King to know the name of his nemesis before he dies, or at least to suspect it.'

'Then why did you not simply sign the letter after all?' Blight asked dismissively.

'Because I wish to play the game by *my* rules, not by those of the King and his henchmen...'

Blight held up his hand angrily. 'Desist from this foolish plan, Simon. It can only end in further tragedy for you. Have you not suffered enough pain in your life already?'

Ingledew had not stirred from his chair but now spoke up with equal anger. 'You dare speak to me of foolish notions! I know well that you also have turned against the King of late, just as I did four years ago, even though the motivations for your disaffection may be different. I am sure that you understand now that the King is secretly a papist, and that he is plotting to impose that cursed religion on his people against their will.' Ingledew showed his teeth in a near growl. 'I know also that you are now a convert to the Fifth Monarchy sect, James, and that you openly discussed the possibility of rebellion against the King with a group of plotters only a few months ago. Perhaps fortunately for you, these accomplices of yours were all gross incompetents, and their seditious plotting came to naught. Yet the mere knowledge of your involvement with them would destroy you, if it ever came out...'

Blight tried to stop the sudden shaking of his hands and the tremor in his voice. 'That is nonsense, Simon! Who states such a disgraceful untruth?'

Ingledew leaned forward in his chair. 'I have written evidence of your complicity in the plot from one of your fellow Fifth Monarchists, James. And regrettably I shall be forced to send a copy of this evidence to Lord Clarendon himself, should you not agree to help me.'

Blight was lost for words at this calamity. How could Ingledew have possibly acquired such evidence? All his fellow conspirators were lying low, and nothing of their vague plans for rebellion had been committed to paper as far as he knew.

'I am not a member of the Fifth Monarchy,' Blight claimed desperately.

'You are not only a member; you are one of the high elders of this sect. Your late wife, Bernadette – so I understand – introduced you into the sect two years ago, and you are now one of the secret leaders of this movement.'

Despite his infatuation for his late wife, Blight now cursed his own stupidity at being drawn into this dangerous talk of sedition, even if it had been merely half-hearted musings rather than any deeply conceived plot. 'You cannot succeed in such a plan, Simon! To kill the King is madness!'

Ingledew sniffed coldly. 'With your help, I will do it. And, whatever you might claim to the contrary, you too would prefer the King dead, James. I see it plainly in your eyes. He is as much a hateful figure to you now, as he is to me.'

'That is a gross falsehood. And I have to go, so I will leave you to your sad delusions, Simon. I have a more wholesome meeting to attend now with some gentlemen of distinguished wit and learning...'

Ingledew seemed unimpressed. 'Ah! I suppose that you speak of a meeting with some of your friends from the Royal Society? Yet why would you prize the company of those dilettante gentlemen so highly?'

'And why should I not?' Blight protested. 'They are all nobly inclined men, dedicated to the study of natural philosophy and science.'

'Those poor deluded fools know nothing of the true laws of the universe,' Ingledew snarled, throwing his glass of wine carelessly aside, where it broke into shards against the timbered wall. 'In my travels I have acquired knowledge and powers that would make those dreary natural philosophers of the King's society blink in amazement and wonder.'

Blight stood up again and made a move towards the door to get away from this madman, but somehow Ingledew uncoiled his body from his chair in one swift fluid movement and blocked his way. Ingledew then wrapped a hand like a vice around Blight's throat and lifted him bodily from the ground with one arm.

Blight felt the incredible strength in the man's arm, whose power he had no more hope of resisting than a child fighting an elephant. His vision began to dim to black as the breath was choked slowly out of him, before Ingledew suddenly released him and threw him contemptuously across the floor like a discarded toy.

Ingledew stood over his old comrade-in-arms and grunted triumphantly. 'The smallpox may have destroyed my beauty, James, yet it has also given me such a feeling of strength and rage that I truly believe no power on earth can stop me now.'

Blight tried to get to his feet but the room was still swaying alarmingly, and there was a great roaring in his head as if the sea was washing and crashing inside his skull. Perhaps this was no idle boast that Ingledew had made earlier, he thought fearfully: perhaps Ingledew really had sold his soul to the Devil, in return for his life...

CHAPTER 6

Molly waited nervously for Sir Thomas Killigrew to appear, her sense of trepidation increased by the fact that this was the same private chamber in the King's theatre where she had helped lay out Sarah's body only four days ago. Molly regarded the bed in the oak-panelled room with some sadness, but also with deep misgivings, as she wondered whether she had been wise in accepting Sir Thomas's less-than-cryptic invitation a few minutes ago, when he had met her by chance at the stage door.

'Ay, Molly,' he had declared extravagantly. 'I have a little free time now, so perhaps this would be a good time for you to favour me with that short audition that you promised me. Then I can determine whether you truly have any suitability to go on stage.'

And Molly, despite her depressed state of mind after the deaths of Sarah Lusted and Amy Leatherbarrow in such swift succession, had curtsied politely and said, 'Of course, sir. That would be most generous of you. Where would you like to do the audition?'

Killigrew had paused artfully for a second, as if he had to consider the question. 'Oh, could it be up in my private chamber near the tiring room? 'Tis private there, and will save us from too many distractions.'

Now, a few minutes later, Molly went over to the fire to warm herself while she waited for Killigrew to join her. It was eleven o'clock in the morning, and the King's company were due to assemble on stage in half-an-hour for a further costume rehearsal of *Twelfth Night*. Sir Thomas was presently still downstairs making preparations for the rehearsal, but had promised to appear soon. Molly had changed by now into her fine orange seller's gown, which was far more stylish than any of her own clothes, yet decidedly chilly because of the low cut neckline of the satin bodice. The costume did certainly show off her bubbies to fine advantage, she knew well, yet this was perhaps too much of an advantage considering the old reprobate she was waiting for.

Molly was about to leave, having decided - half-gratefully, half-peevishly - that Sir Thomas was not coming after all, when the gentleman in question breezed suddenly into the room. His voice was tinged with melancholy, though, even if his manner seemed quite as exuberant as ever. 'Molly, you really should have mentioned your situation to me earlier. Are you presently quite up to giving me an...*audition*...?'

Molly blinked uneasily. 'My *situation*, sir? What mean you by that?'

Sir Thomas took tight hold of her right hand. 'I have just learned from some of the company that you have suffered another grievous personal tragedy since Sunday. You were cruelly accosted in the street and your dearest friend in the world brutally slain by villains.'

Molly was completely unable to free her hand from this man's limpet grip - not without using a knife to prise it open anyway. And she had decided, for politic reasons, to leave her knife downstairs in her bag in the orange sellers' tiring room today. 'That is true, sir,' she said with a slight gulp, and a delicate heave of her bosom.

''Tis a scandal how dangerous London's streets have become of late,' Killigrew commented portentously as his eyes dwelt at length on Molly's heaving cleavage. 'These scallywags deserve to be hanged, drawn and quartered at Tyburn.'

'Perhaps they will be, sir. I have given their descriptions to the ward constable, and he has sent word to all the officers of the Watch in the neighbourhood to look out for these men.'

Killigrew patted the back of her hand. 'Ah, such naivety! I would not place too much trust in the feeble officers of the law to right your wrong, Molly.' He released her hand abruptly. 'But enough of such sordid matters. Shall we begin with your recital? I trust you have come armed with some suitable speeches to show off your...' - he hesitated fractionally – '...*talents.*'

Molly wondered if she should make a run for it now while she still had her clothes on. 'What would you like to hear, sir?'

Sir Thomas smiled. 'Anything that takes your fancy. I shall sit here on the bed and merely listen.'

This did not seem quite as bad a prospect as Molly had suspected it might be, although it was daunting enough speaking lines in front of an actor and playwright as famous as Sir Thomas Killigrew.

Molly adopted a suitable theatrical pose, and then began hesitantly with a speech she had long known by heart. '*The quality of mercy is not strain'd. It droppeth as the gentle rain from heaven upon the place beneath: it is twice blest...*'

'Ah, Portia's timeless speech from *The Merchant of Venice*,' Sir Thomas interrupted loudly. Yet from the disappointed look on his face, he seemed unimpressed by Molly's diction and choice of speech even though she had been moderately pleased with the result herself.

Molly cleared her throat nervously, not sure what to do next. 'Should I go on, sir?'

'Yes, but please approach a little closer, Molly. Your voice has a pleasing timbre yet 'tis light in volume and lacks projection. Can you try another speech perhaps, one more suited to your slight voice? Do you know any of *Twelfth Night*?'

Molly moved to within two paces of him. 'I believe I know it all, sir. I have a good memory for lines and usually only need to hear them once to remember them.'

'A proud boast, Molly, but one that I shall treat with due cynicism for the present.' Killigrew gestured impatiently. 'Come closer, Molly...no, a little closer still. Be not shy.'

Molly already felt uneasy at being within two paces of him, and was certainly not prepared to come any closer until she had got a reasonable amount of her recitation out first. She began again with a fresh speech – this one from *Twelfth Night*, as requested. '*If music be the food of love, play on,*' she declaimed, '*give me the excess of it, that, surfeiting, the appetite may sicken, and so die. That strain again! It had a dying fall: O, it came o'er my ear like the sweet sound that breathes upon a bank of violets, stealing and giving odour. Enough! No more: 'Tis not so sweet now as it was before. O spirit of love...!*'

Molly was suddenly aware that Sir Thomas had slid off the bed onto his knees. He slowly lifted up the hem of her skirt, and began studying her legs with rapt concentration. 'Sir!' she complained icily.

'Now, now, we can countenance no false modesty in our profession, Molly. You are speaking the fine words of Duke Orsino there, so I need to know how your legs might look in a breeches role. You know, no doubt, that I did a production of my own play *The Parson's Wedding* earlier this year which was cast entirely with women,' he boasted with a suggestive wink, '...even in the men's roles.'

Molly had indeed seen this version of *The Parson's Wedding,* and already knew it to be a play renowned for its coarse humour. In mitigation of its general vulgarity, it did at least contain some prose readings of John Donne's fine poetry to elevate its content a little for the more literate members of the audience. The "women only" production had however attracted the rowdiest audience to the King's theatre that Molly had ever seen, so that the surviving portions of Mr Donne in the script had been overwhelmed by the general bawdiness, and by the immodesty of the low cut and tight-fitting costumes that the cast had worn. But Molly decided it was best not to make any critical comments at such a delicate juncture in her audition. Instead she asked boldly, 'Then how do my legs look, sir?'

'Very fair – very fair indeed in such pretty silk stockings.' Sir Thomas looked up at her face but did not let her skirts fall to the ground again. 'Go on, go on!'

Molly began again, gritting her teeth. '*O spirit of love! How quick and fresh art thou, that, notwithstanding thy capacity receiveth as the sea, nought enters there, of what validity and pitch soe'er, but falls into abatement and low price, even in a minute: so full of shapes is fancy, that it alone is high fantastical...*'

'That was surprisingly accomplished, Molly,' Killigrew declared, raising a tufted eyebrow. 'Do another speech. Prove your boast and give me something from *A Midsummer Night's Dream.*'

Molly could feel Sir Thomas's hands under her skirts straying higher still to her thighs and beyond. But she breathed out hard and continued with a new piece. '*I know a bank where the wild thyme blows, where oxlips and the nodding violet grows; quite over-canopied with luscious woodbine, with sweet musk-roses, and with eglantine. There sleeps Titania, sometime of the night, lull'd in these flowers with dances and delight...*'

'Delight indeed, young Molly!' Sir Thomas had lost whatever slight reserve he still possessed and now ran his hands up feverishly inside her petticoats to grip her bare buttocks tightly with his fingers.

Molly wondered desperately what a virgin would do in this situation. She gasped a little, as it seemed the appropriate thing to do, then began in a sterner voice: '*Sigh no more, ladies, sigh no more, men were* deceivers *ever...*' - she put particular emphasis on the word "deceiver" - '*...One foot in sea, and one on shore, to one thing constant never. Then sigh not so, but let them go, and be you blithe and bonny! Converting all your sounds of woe into hey nonny, nonny...*'

Sir Thomas seemed not to notice this reproach to male fidelity in her speech and had now run his nimble fingers into an even more intimate area. 'I trust you do not mind me touching your cunny, Molly...'

Molly was sincerely glad at this point that she had not brought her knife with her, otherwise she would have skewered Sir Thomas to his bed with it by now. ''Tis very pleasing and arousing, sir. But can you desist now, Sir Thomas – your hands are icy in the extreme.' She panted a little – genuinely this time - but continued gamely, '*Sing no more ditties, sing no more, of dumps so dull and heavy. The fraud of men was ever so, since summer first was leavy. Then sigh not so, but let them go, and be you blithe and bonny! Converting all your sounds of woe into hey nonny, nonny...*'

Sir Thomas finally did desist and Molly stepped back gratefully from his wandering cold hands. 'Well?' she asked, smoothing down her skirts primly.

Killigrew, still on his knees, frowned up at her. 'Well what?'

'Have I passed the audition, Sir Thomas? Am I fit to join your company of players?'

Sir Thomas climbed to his feet with difficulty. Then he took her hand and gallantly kissed the back of it. 'Undoubtedly, Molly. I believe you may even have a great future ahead of you...'

*

An hour later, Molly sat fuming on the green baize-covered benches in the pit, as the dress rehearsal of *Twelfth Night* went ahead on stage.

Sir Thomas had reneged on his promise almost immediately, merely letting her watch the rehearsals again, rather than letting her play any active part with his precious company, even if only in a walk-on role. Molly could see that she was getting some knowing looks – some maliciously inclined, some more sympathetic - from the actresses on stage, who had obviously been through similar "auditions" in the past in Sir Thomas's private chamber upstairs. Sir Thomas, who was on stage himself to take the part of Sir Toby Belch, seemed entirely oblivious of Molly's sour looks at him from the pit, though - in fact entirely oblivious of her existence at all.

This was hardly progress at all, Molly decided peevishly, since she had long been able to watch the company at rehearsals, even if without the official sanction of anyone in authority. Obviously it was going to take more than one "audition" to satisfy Sir Thomas so Molly calculated dismally how much further humiliation she might have to endure in order to claim her dream of getting onto that stage. Molly had heard that Killigrew had been present at the infamous exorcism of the possessed nuns of Loudun thirty years before, and she had to wonder icily whether he and his debauched companions had perhaps treated some of those nuns with as much freedom as he had just demonstrated during her embarrassing "audition" upstairs. That might explain the so-called "possession" of those French nuns in a simpler and more human way – perhaps the demons that possessed them were merely men like Killigrew, men with lustful thoughts and ways...

Unfortunately for Molly there seemed little alternative to dealing with Killigrew at present because of his absolute power over the King's house. Yet that might change in the future, Molly hoped. Killigrew was a skilled actor and playwright, yet he had gained a reputation as an incompetent theatre manager, and was constantly in disputes with both his actors and the playwrights who wrote for him. Molly had heard some gossip that Killigrew had even had to secretly bribe many of his leading actresses to keep working for him - Elizabeth Weaver, Anne and Becky Marshal, Charlotte Butler and Elizabeth Davenport among them – yet some of them had nevertheless decamped for the rival Duke's company. And many of the best known actors in London - Michael Mohun, William Wintershall, Robert Shatterell, Charles Hart and

Nicholas Burt – disliked working for Killigrew so much that they too had defected recently to Sir William Devanant's company.

Molly put her grievances against Sir Thomas to one side for the moment as she began to immerse herself in the performance of the play, and to enjoy the actors' skills, in particular Mistress Pettican's.

Mary Pettican was undoubtedly the leading actress in the company after the departure of so many of the more established actresses, and was clearly a personal favourite of Sir Thomas. She was a beautiful girl, Molly had to admit to herself, only one-and-twenty, with raven hair and pale unblemished skin, yet capable of playing much more than simple girlish heroines. She had recently played the evil Lady Macbeth with particularly malevolent authority, for example, yet Molly had been equally impressed by the bawdy and abandoned way in which she had portrayed the lusty young widow in Etherege's play *Love in a Tub*. Her skill was such that it was sometimes difficult to believe it was the same person in those disparate roles. Today, on stage, she presented an entirely different persona from those other parts, excelling in her role as the flighty Countess Olivia.

Yet, as she continued to watch this sterling performance of *Twelfth Night*, Molly's admiration was drawn again increasingly to the new girl Jane Golightly, who was portraying Viola/Cesario with charm and verve. Mistress Golightly was wearing breeches in her male guise as Cesario and, dressed that way, and with her fair hair disguised with a curling black wig, she did look and sound unnervingly like a real boy. How easy it was for these actors and actresses to adopt a different character and a different look to their own...!

Molly was reminded again uneasily of her own theory that Sarah Lusted might have been murdered last Friday by a rival actress in her own company, perhaps disguised for the occasion as that tall dark lady she had seen leaving the tiring room. Molly was musing worriedly over this possibility when her attention was drawn to the present scene in the play between Olivia and the gentlewoman in her employ, Maria. Maria was being played by the red-haired Anne Carey...

Anne Carey was Molly's least favourite of the company's actresses - though not because of her acting ability, which was prodigious enough, but because she was a vicious gossip and a shrew who treated the orange girls with contempt. Molly was struck by the green silk gown that Anne was wearing in the part of Maria, and the dark wig she had on, which reminded her slightly of the look of that now infamous dark lady...

Miles Brammer now came on stage in the part of Orsino, and a suddenly suspicious Molly even considered the possibility that he might have been the bewigged gentleman she had seen with the dark lady outside the Duke's theatre last Friday. This sudden suspicion was less to do with any direct resemblance that she perceived between Brammer and that bewigged gentleman, and more to do with the fact that Brammer and Anne Carey were reputed to be sweet on each other, therefore could be part of a conspiracy. Yet despite his male beauty and long muscular legs, Molly had always harboured some slight doubts about Miles Brammer's true manliness. He was so beautiful in fact that he had played only woman's roles in the theatre until that door was finally closed to him a year or so ago. And there were also those scurrilous rumours that he had been bedded in his youth by Sir Thomas Killigrew, whose passions were believed to stray on occasion beyond the female sex to pretty boys.

In fact, now that Molly considered the beardless Brammer in detail, he truly seemed a better physical fit for the mysterious dark lady than any of the actresses presently on stage. That dark lady had been very tall, Molly reminded herself. Both Mary Pettican and Anne Carey were tall too, of course, but not exceptionally so. Yet Brammer certainly fitted the height perfectly, and was also adept at impersonating women. Brammer had appeared in Etherege's play *Love in a Tub* on Friday, but only in the early scenes. Molly struggled to recall whether he had appeared to take his bow at the end of the performance, or whether he had been offstage with the other actors afterwards when she had passed them on her way to the tiring room to help Sarah undress. But it was hard to say because of all the usual noise and confusion at the time. If he had not been there, then he would have had more than enough time after his last appearance during the play to disguise himself as the dark lady and wait in the tiring room for Sarah to appear.

But why would Brammer murder Sarah? He had no reason to hate her as perhaps the other actresses might who felt threatened by her rise. And even if he did murder Sarah using some unknown poison, why would he disguise himself as a woman to do it?

Except that it would, of course, allow him to escape from the theatre unrecognized so perhaps that was enough inducement for him to change sex for the evening...

But if Brammer was the dark lady, then who could have been the bewigged gentleman? Could that have been a *woman in* disguise? It was impossible to say because Molly had only glimpsed his face briefly. But she began quickly to grow dizzy at all this confusion of male and female identities, and returned her attention to the confusion of male and female identities in the play, and to two of the actors in particular.

Christopher Malthouse, who was playing Malvolio in the play, was far less handsome than Brammer - a tall gangly mouse-haired individual but with a fine resonant voice that could electrify an audience. Molly believed him to be from the North - York or Durham or some such extreme Northern place - although she could no longer hear any trace of his origins in his voice. His speciality was heroic drama – he had played Henry V with stirring power in a recent production of the Earl of Orrery's play *The History of Henry the Fifth* – yet here he was making a tolerable show as the pompous Malvolio. In all honesty Molly could never see Malthouse being able to pass himself off as a woman, despite his shaven face, and he was certainly the wrong body shape to have been the bewigged gentleman outside the Duke's theatre on Friday.

The young Irishman Patrick Whelan, on the other hand, was almost as beautiful as Brammer, although more muscular of body and squarer of face, therefore not physically equipped to play a convincing woman either. Molly's little orange seller friend Nell believed Whelan to be a thief and highwayman who had taken to acting to lie low from the law, and Nell always seemed to have impeccable sources for her gossip, so there could be some truth in it. Whelan was playing the clown Feste today and seemed to be enjoying his participation in the rehearsal, although he had given Molly several penetrating looks during his periods offstage, she had noticed, as if wondering what a mere orange seller was doing here at this time, and being allowed to watch the rehearsal from a seat in the pit...

*

After the rehearsal was over, Sir Thomas approached Molly in the pit

She stood up quickly to curtsey, but he indicated to her with his hand to sit down again. Still dressed as Sir Toby Belch, he took the next place to her on the bench, then glanced up at the now empty stage. 'So, Molly, what think ye of our little production?'

'Very fair, sir,' she replied icily. 'But I dare say that I would have enjoyed it much more if I could have joined in. Even if only playing one of the servants in the background.'

Killigrew laughed heartily. 'God's body but you are a difficult girl! You must be a little patient, Molly. I cannot introduce you into the company too swiftly as it would arouse the ire and jealousy of some of my actresses of longer standing. Those established ladies may look sweet but pretty faces do sometimes conceal the blackest hearts.'

Molly agreed silently with that. 'Then how long must I wait, sir?' she inquired coolly.

'I cannot say for certain. But not long, I promise. I do have a special dispensation for you in the meantime, though...'

Molly felt her heart skip a beat. 'Yes, sir? What would that be?

Sir Thomas leaned forward conspiratorially. 'You know well that the theatre is closed on the morrow?'

'Indeed, sir. The company is giving this special performance of

Twelfth Night for His Majesty in the Great Hall at the palace.'

Killigrew nodded enthusiastically. 'Ay, indeed. Well, how would you like to join the company in going to the palace?'

Molly was overjoyed but tried to hide it. 'I would be pleased to go, sir.'

Sir Thomas held up a cautionary finger. 'I cannot promise thee an acting role of any description, Molly. But you can come and help get the actresses dressed for their roles. And, ye never know, I may have *other* duties for you too.'

Molly wondered uneasily whether those latter duties mentioned by Sir Thomas might involve having to allow his hands to roam freely beneath her petticoats again...

CHAPTER 7

Tuesday, 13th December 1664

The meetings of the Royal Society were normally held on Wednesday afternoons at three o'clock, but being close to Christmas, this last session of December had been moved to a Tuesday, and was due to start earlier than usual. It was however promised to be a special afternoon: Mr Hooke, the Curator of Experiments, had made it known that he had something particularly exciting to show the fellows of the society at this final meeting before Christmas.

Henry Raven glanced around the august assembly in the main lecture hall at Gresham College in Bishopsgate. The promise of a special demonstration by Mr Hooke had persuaded almost all of the founding members of the society to find time to attend, and many of the newer ones too. The society was an odd mixture of devout Parliamentarians and staunch Royalists, yet the Fellows' thirst for knowledge and interest in the laws of nature had always transcended their political differences. This coming together of disparate minds and personalities in the interests of mankind seemed in Henry Raven's opinion to offer a genuine way forward for humanity, a hope for a peaceful and prosperous future where man would have won the power to control and utilize the forces of nature for the betterment of all.

The assembled gentlemen in the lecture hall did represent some of the greatest thinkers in the land: Henry Oldenburg, the erudite German secretary to the society, and a man with many important connections across Europe; Dr John Wilkins, the true founder of the society, if a devout Parliamentarian whose beliefs had lost him his academic positions since the return of the monarchy; Lord Brouncker, a gifted man but also a roué, as well as a close confidante of the King; Dr Jonathan Goddard, the eminent physician. Dr William Petty, the famous anatomist who had worked closely with Thomas Willis, the author of *Cerebri Anatome*, was also present today, Raven saw with pleasure; Petty had once studied in Caen in Normandy under the great Descartes himself, and was now the Chair of Music at Gresham College.

The young astronomer and artist Christopher Wren, a protégé of Wilkins during his time at Oxford, and now Professor of Astronomy at Gresham College, was in attendance too, talking amiably with the staunch Royalist Sir Paul Neile, who was one of the main investors in the new Hudson's Bay Company.

The elderly Sir Robert Moray, who had been in the service of the old King many years ago, was seated next to Sir Paul, and gave Raven a small nod of recognition in return for his own more formal bow. Moray, despite his advanced age, was known to be interested in new and ingenious inventions. Raven had heard whispers that in his youth Moray had spied in France for Cardinal Richelieu against the Scottish Covenanters in exile there, yet he had also undertaken extensive correspondence with scientifically minded men across Europe and was the true connection between the court and the new society, enabling it to claim Royal patronage even though the King hardly ever attended meetings personally.

Apart from Hooke, Raven's closest friends in the society were men of similar age and background to himself - the young Mr Abraham Hill, for example, the son of a wealthy merchant. And Mr Alexander Bruce, a gentleman with a particular interest in technical matters related to coal making and the production of coke from coal, which was also a subject that intrigued Henry Raven. If a cheap process could be discovered for turning coal into the more efficient coke, it would reap handsome dividends for him personally.

Another close acquaintance of Raven's was Dr William Croone, a man five years older than him but of similar background. Croone, like Hill, was the son of a merchant, and had been educated at Cambridge – in his case Emmanuel College. He had been named Professor of Rhetoric at Gresham College at the age of only six-and-twenty, but his scientific interests were more wide ranging than mere rhetoric. He was now the Censor of the College of Physicians and the Registrar of the Royal Society. He and Raven had carried out many experiments together at Croone's house, including determining the freezing point of salt water at different pressures, measuring the compressibility of air, making observations of the circulation of the blood in animals, and testing the efficacy of alcohol in preserving animal tissue. Two years ago Raven had been present when Croone had cut out the heart of a carp yet made the remarkable observation that it continued beating for a full fifteen minutes afterwards. The good doctor had also tried bleeding blood from one dog into another on several occasions, an operation that sometimes killed the second animal within a few minutes, and in other cases caused no distress at all. Croone suspected from this that blood was not always as identical as it seemed, and had suggested to Raven that there must be subtle differences in its constituents.

Dr Croone was seated next to a new member of the society, one Mr James Blight, who had been put forward recently for membership by Lord Brouncker. Despite his Puritan dress, Raven had learned that Mr Blight, an extremely tall man of middle age, had been a close confidante of the King during his exile, and was now one of the twelve Grooms of the Bedchamber at the Palace of Whitehall. He had obviously been a man of action at one time because he carried the scar of an old battle wound on his cheek.

The babble of conversation from the audience grew ever louder as the time for the start of the meeting grew closer. Every chandelier in the chamber had been lit to maximum to provide the best possible light to view proceedings. This lecture hall was a distinguished venue for the society to hold its regular meetings. Sir Thomas Gresham, founder of the Royal Exchange, had left his estate jointly to the City of London Corporation and to the Mercers' Company, and his will had provided for the setting up of the college in Gresham's former mansion in Bishopsgate, as well as further endowing it with the rental income from the shops sited around the Royal Exchange which Gresham had established.

The benches in the lecture hall were arranged in semi-circular tiers, one above the other, so that viewing of the dais and the blackboard was facilitated, as well as of whatever delightful experiment Mr Hooke might have to demonstrate. Today, though, there was no interesting arrangement of pumps and tubes and glass vessels on display, but only a number of artist's easels arranged in front of the dais, with the pictures, whatever they were, covered up with hessian sacking. Raven felt obscurely disappointed when he had been hoping for something more interesting today, something that exceeded in ingenuity even Mr Hooke's usually diverting experiments.

For this man was the undoubted true genius of this society, despite still being under thirty years of age. Raven had first met him on a trip to Oxford three years ago when Hooke had been working as assistant to Mr Robert Boyle. Robert Hooke came originally from the Isle of Wight, Raven believed, and had been a sickly child with a pronounced stoop and curvature of the spine, perhaps because of his impoverished background and poor diet. As a boy, he had first trained as an artist but the paint fumes had exacerbated his frequent headaches, so he had given up on that dream and gone to Westminster School to study instead. By the age of eighteen he had taken up a poor chorister's place at Christ

Church, Oxford, where he had come across Mr Wilkins, then a professor at Wadham College, and soon impressed him with his many abilities. At twenty, needing paying work, he had become an assistant to the eminent Robert Boyle, the youngest son of the wealthy and self-made Earl of Cork. The younger Boyle, with time on his hands and no pressing needs to make a living, had developed an interest of his own in natural philosophy after reading books by the astronomer Regiomontanus, as well as those classic works *De Revolutionibus* by Copernicus, and *De Magnete* by William Gilbert. Ten years ago Boyle had moved to Oxford to set up a laboratory where he could perform experiments in pneumatics and electricity, and there he had published his own books, *New Experiments Physico-Mechanicall, Touching the Spring of the Air*, and *The Sceptical Chymist* in which he had renewed his notion that matter was composed of minute particles, as the ancient Greeks Democritus and Leucippus had thought.

Yet Raven knew that much of Boyle's success in his researches had been due to his young genius of an assistant. It was Hooke who had devised an improved air pump – far superior to those devised by the Italian Torricelli – and the clever J-shaped glass vessel with its trapped portion of air that was used to prove Boyle's thesis that the pressure and volume of gases were so intimately related.

After the establishment of the Royal Society to promote natural knowledge four years ago, there had been much debate about who would present the meetings, and in particular who would carry out experiments. It soon became obvious that most of the gentlemen fellows – many of whom were dilettantes when it came to practical things – were also too busy to devise their own regular experiments and demonstrations. Therefore it had eventually been decided to appoint a permanent Curator of Experiments, and Mr Hooke had been the perfect choice for the job…

*

Even though it was still an hour or more to sunset, the light seeping through the tall leaded windows of the chamber had been reduced to a thin sepia brown glow. Without the dozens of candles lighting up this room with such extravagant excess, Raven knew that they would be sitting in virtual darkness - as most people in London were on this winter's afternoon. Wax candles were only for the wealthiest after all, so that most houses were truly dark places where people moved through the gloom from one patch of candlelight to the other. Raven wondered why the collective intelligence of all these gifted men in this room had not come up yet with a more efficient method of lighting than candles. To think what a boon to humanity that would be – to take human society out of the darkness and into the light!

Yet the chemical nature of light, and how it was produced by matter, remained a complete mystery, of course...

Raven sat up in his seat as he saw Robert Hooke finally entering the chamber with his usual bent and shuffling walk. Hooke did not resemble a man of genius in any way, and certainly not a man of fashion either, being dressed in plain dun-coloured breeches and stockings, and a black coat of Puritan cut. Raven got up from his chair and walked down the tiered steps to greet his friend warmly.

Henry Raven was immodest enough to understand that he had many significant talents of his own, including a prodigious talent for business, and a useful taste for the study of natural philosophy. Yet his friend Mr Hooke inspired in him true feelings of awe because this man was so far ahead of him and all of his fellows, in both imagination and intellect, as to be on a different plane of human achievement. His work on timepieces was only one part of this man's unmatched imagination and cleverness.

Raven could only marvel at both the range and subtlety of his friend's achievements. Since last year, Hooke had been keeping daily records of the weather - wind speed and direction, humidity, temperature, the appearance of the sky - and recording air pressure using a portable mercury barometer. He had observed the baroscopical index and found it to predict rainy and cloudy weather when it fell very low, and dry and clear weather when it rose very high. Hooke hoped that his daily observations would eventually enable him to foresee the mutations of the weather at some distance before they approached, something which would be of inestimable value to everyone, but to farmers in particular. Imagine, Raven thought, if farmers could predict the arrival of a storm up to a day before and make suitable preparations to protect their growing crops...

Raven had also seen experiments that Hooke had been carrying out privately in his rooms here at Gresham College where he had dropped lead bullets into a sticky mixture of pipe clay and water to produce craters. Hooke had wondered whether such impacts might perhaps explain the craters on the face of the Moon, yet he had no knowledge of any rain of heavy objects hitting the Moon therefore was extremely puzzled by it. Hooke's general knowledge of astronomy was immense – he had concluded that the spherical shape of planets and stars was the natural result of the same unknown force that held the planets' motion in check. Just last spring, Hooke had observed a dark spot on the surface of Jupiter that proved the planet rotated on its axis, something even the great Galileo had not been able to show.

And only last month in this very chamber Hooke had demonstrated how a dog, strapped down to a table and with its chest cavity surgically exposed to view, could nevertheless be kept alive by pumping air directly into its lungs from a bellows. It had proved to him his thesis that there was something in the air necessary to sustain life, and also to sustain combustion...

Raven nodded at the line of easels in front of the dais. 'Your demonstration appears on the dull and civilized side today compared to some of your recent experiments, Robert. Yet I am glad that your demonstration today will not involve the torture of a dog again, at least.'

Hooke nodded, a little wryly. 'It will not, Henry. I shall hardly be induced to make any further trials of that kind, useful demonstration that it was, because of the distress of the poor creature.' Hooke gave him a secretive smile. 'Yet what I have to show this day may surprise you still. This may even surpass in wonder anything you have seen from me before.'

'And what of the comet, Robert?' Raven asked tentatively. 'Have you come to any conclusions about its motion yet, based on your nightly observations of its position in the heavens?'

Hooke returned a shrewd look of his own. 'Ah! I suspect from that remark that you have come to some determination of your own in this matter, Henry.'

Raven was a little circumspect about revealing his idea, but finally announced it. 'I have been considering the notion that the path of the comet may be a...p...'

'A parabola? I mentioned that possibility in a lecture already, Henry,' Hooke reminded him.

Raven flushed. 'No, Robert, I mean a perfect *ellipse*, as with the path of the planets, only drawn out to an incredible degree of eccentricity.'

Raven was pleasantly surprised that Hooke did not instantly scoff at this bizarre idea. Instead Hooke stroked his patchy beard thoughtfully. 'It is an interesting thought that the comet may be constrained to a *closed* curve; that notion had also occurred to me in my recent private deliberations on the matter. I had not thought of a highly eccentric ellipse, though, I must confess. And it would be very difficult to differentiate between the path of a parabola around the sun, and that of a greatly extended ellipse. In which case, comets may indeed be permanent members of the solar system, but ones whose orbits extend out to immense distances...'

'And which may even return after many years,' Raven suggested eagerly. 'Historical records of comets do suggest that some of them may possibly have been the return of an earlier visitation.'

Hooke nodded. 'I have been thinking the same thing, Henry, even though I could not find a closed curve that would explain it. In particular the comet of 1618 interested me greatly in that respect...'

*

The meeting was called to order as Mr Hooke went to the row of easels in front of the dais. Without ceremony he removed the coverings from the ten drawings on the easels, and was rewarded by gasps of astonishment from the audience at what was revealed.

'You know, gentlemen, that I have been working on a new book which I intend to call *Micrographia* and which will be published by the Royal Society next year. This book will be a summary of my scientific researches to date in many fields. Among them in particular will be my microscopic observations of both the natural and the man-made world. These drawings you see here are some of those that will be reproduced as engraved plates in the new book and show a selection of the astounding things I have seen with my microscope. This first one for example shows the point of a needle; this second one the edge of a razor, this one rock crystals, that one cork cells...'

Hooke went on to describe each of the drawings in detail. No one seeing these drawings could sensibly doubt that Hooke had really seen these things with his microscopes, Raven thought. Raven had in fact seen the microscopes that Hooke used, even if he had never seen these exquisite drawings before. The microscopes Hooke used were of two types: tiny spherical lens with huge magnifying power but annoyingly difficult beasts to hold still, as Raven had discovered from personal experience; and a combination of lenses in a tube six inches long, which gave far less magnifying power than the single lenses, but were infinitely easier to use.

The audience of distinguished men was astounded by the brilliance and unexpected revelations of Mr Hooke's images – bird feathers in scintillating detail, the intricate construction of plant leaves, stunning drawings of insects and woodlice, a fly's compound eye...

*

Afterwards, the meeting took a long time to break up, given the excitement of the audience at seeing these revelatory drawings.

But by seven o'clock, there were only a hard core of devout believers left, still unable to tear themselves away from the brilliance of Mr Hooke's exquisite images.

'Truly remarkable,' a voice observed at Raven's side.

He turned to find the new fellow of the society, Mr James Blight, at his side. Raven noted again the man's extreme height, which was at least two inches more than his own generous height of six feet.

'Yes, indeed. Remarkable,' Raven observed. 'Yet we have come to expect the remarkable from Mr Hooke.'

Hooke, in conversation with Lord Brouncker, overheard that remark and came over to join Raven and Blight, with a wry expression on his face. With his small stooped stature, he seemed even smaller when having to look up at these two tall gentlemen. 'I heard your flattering comment, Henry. But did I truly surpass myself this time?' he asked with a smile.

'That you did, Robert,' Raven agreed ruefully, his awe tempered with a little undeniable jealousy at this man's true genius.

Blight congratulated Hooke warmly on his lecture too. 'What wonders you have revealed to us this day, Mr Hooke! It seems there is nothing in nature that will be closed to our scrutiny in the future. And who knows in what ways mankind will be able to exploit the laws of nature to improve our lot and enable us to do things presently beyond human imagination and comprehension.'

Hooke nodded complacently. 'I would agree, sir. Although some things are perhaps more foreseeable than others.'

Raven intervened. 'And what examples are those? What glittering future do you foresee for us, Robert?"

Hooke smiled. 'Oh, as an example, some system of transporting messages over large distances at high velocity – perhaps even sufficient to outpace a man on horseback...' Blight gasped at that outrageous notion but Hooke barely paused in his discourse. '...I can also see mankind developing mechanical means of motion, through the use of steam for example. Have you not noticed, Henry, how easily a fire can raise the heavy lid of a pot over the fire? We simply need to find a means of turning this power of fire into usable motion so that we can take away so much of human drudgery.'

'And what else?' asked Blight eagerly. 'Do you see any possibility of mankind emulating the birds one day and being able to raise themselves from the earth?'

'I can see no physical reason why not,' Hooke said complacently. 'I am sure that a man will indeed lift himself off the ground by his own mechanical efforts one day. In fact Mr Wilkins and I did some experiments with flying machines in the grounds of Wadham College several years ago...'

Raven thought that notion an absurd one, even coming from Mr Hooke, but he noticed that Mr Blight seemed to take the remark very seriously.

Hooke seemed to take note of Raven's scepticism in his turn. 'You think to doubt me, Henry...'

Raven felt himself redden. 'Indeed I could never doubt anything you say, Robert. But I had never heard of these experiments before.'

Hooke smiled. 'My reticence on the subject is due to the fact that the machines were never entirely successful, and caused me much grief and frustration. Yet I still doubt not that a man will one day ascend into the heavens and compete with the fowls of the air for their space.'

'By sorcery, mean you?' Mr Blight interrupted in a shocked voice.

'Nay, not by sorcery, sir,' Hooke said firmly, 'but merely by using the laws of nature, and turning them to our advantage.'

'So you do believe that the laws of nature are truly fixed and immutable?' Blight asked.

'In what way do you mean, Mr Blight?' Raven replied.

Blight seemed less than composed in return. 'I mean, is it possible for a man to *overturn* the laws of nature? By prayer, or divine providence, for example?'

Raven and Hooke shared a secret look at this point before Raven said, 'You mean, do we believe in the power of miracles? The power of God?'

Blight nodded. 'Yes...there seems no place in your experimental philosophy for God, Mr Hooke. Yet our Lord overcame the laws of nature and rose from the dead, did he not?'

Hooke was careful with his words. 'I do not pretend to try and read all the mysteries of heaven and hell with my little experiments, Mr Blight. There is still much room for faith, even in my imperfect soul.'

'And do you believe in the Devil and his power to overturn the laws of nature too?' Blight demanded.

Raven intervened and decided to be diplomatic. 'With all the misery and evil there is in the world, Mr Blight, no one can doubt the existence of the Devil.'

Blight sighed visibly. 'That is true, Mr Raven. In a softer voice he added, 'In fact, I may even have seen him in the flesh this very week...'

Raven and Hooke shared another long look, as Raven wondered what awful experience had prompted that sudden bewildered and haunted look on Blight's face...

CHAPTER 8

Wednesday, 14th December 1664

As he made final preparations for the play in the Great Hall at Whitehall Palace, James Blight felt that he was in danger of losing his sanity, after the last two days of intense worry. Despite his rational discussion with the learned Mr Hooke at the Royal Society yester evening, Blight was still half convinced that his former comrade-in-arms Simon Ingledew must truly be possessed by the Devil to know so much about his private affairs, and that he therefore had no hope of resisting his manic will.

Blight clung to the hope that perhaps he was simply deluding himself, and that Ingledew had no unnatural powers at all. Perhaps his feat of strength in that hovel in Southwark had been a simple coney man's trick. Blight had seen performers in fairs and street carnivals demonstrate similarly amazing feats of strength, and perhaps that was all there was to it – a simple trick. Yet how had he discovered about his membership of the Fifth Monarchy? That was a secret known only to a handful of people…

Blight cursed again his own naivety and stupidity in openly discussing sedition with other members of the sect. Yet even now, faced with these new dangers, Blight's conversion to the Fifth Monarchy remained absolute, and he knew that he could never return to his former complacent beliefs. It might have been the persuasive tongue of his late wife that had first drawn Blight into the sect yet, even after Bernadette's sad early death, he found he could not simply withdraw. The real mystery was how Ingledew had got to hear of his secret discussions with other members, which had never been more than vague aspirations for a return to proper Parliamentary rule and a Republican form of government. And none of these discussions of the Fifth Monarchy had ever been recorded in writing as far as Blight was aware, so where had Ingledew possibly learned these incriminating things…?

*

On leaving Ingledew last Monday, Blight had made no actual commitment to him over this lunatic plot to assassinate the King, yet neither had he refused definitely to cooperate. For the moment Blight could do nothing but wait and see what would transpire, while trying to give Ingledew the ambivalent impression that he might help if called.

As he continued with his supervision of the preparations for the play in the Great Hall, Blight tried to hide his disquiet as he wondered uneasily if Ingledew could be planning to make use of this occasion to carry out some unexpected action this very day without informing him. The planned performance seemed ready made for unpredictable and dangerous events to occur since the palace was full of strangers - the players and their company of attendants, of course, but also a hundred invited guests and their servants from outside the palace.

Much against his will, Blight had been named by the King as the person charged with making the preparations for this play in the Great Hall. Blight was sure that his enemies at court had put this unlikely choice into the King's head, deliberately to embarrass him. Nevertheless Blight had taken his duties seriously and had tried to organize the event as well as his limited experience in such matters allowed. A raised timber stage, four feet high, had been hurriedly erected over the last three days at one end of the hall, and a vast painted backdrop constructed behind it to give the illusion of the mythical land of Illyria. In front of the makeshift stage, a line of benches had been laid out for the King and his guests to enjoy the play. Great log fires burned in the immense fireplaces at each end of the chamber, and extra chandeliers had been hung from the high hammerhead roof beams to illuminate the makeshift stage with clarity.

All the great officials of the court were here, as well as the intimate friends of the King. Blight saw that the odious Sedley and Buckhurst were here in pride of place in the front row near the King's seat, as was the Duke of Buckingham, who was also presently back in favour.

Lady Castlemaine was also here of course, but forced on these grander social occasions to give precedence to the Queen, Catherine of Braganza. The Queen might be dowdy and plain yet, despite her being a Catholic, Blight had always felt great sympathy for this Portuguese-born lady of refined manners who had been forced to suffer so many humiliations and embarrassments inflicted by her philandering husband – not merely the presence of his *Maitresse en titre* but also the existence of the King's many bastard children around the palace, whom he acknowledged openly and with great affection. Chief among these was the son Charles had fathered by a woman called Lucy Walter while in exile abroad fifteen years ago. This bastard son of the King had been brought to England from France following the restoration by the Queen Mother Henrietta Maria, and the doting King had soon conferred on him the title of James, Duke of Monmouth, as well as a sizeable income. He was now fifteen years old, the same age coincidentally as the King's new paramour...

Blight was interested to see that Castlemaine's new fifteen-year-old rival, Lady Frances Stuart, had been given a seat even closer to the King than Castlemaine herself. Despite her youth, the King was clearly besotted with her, to the point of dereliction of his kingly duties. Perhaps this was a sign that Castlemaine's power over the King was finally on the wane. Blight was not sure that this was an altogether beneficial development, though, since Castlemaine was a political enemy of Lord Clarendon, and therefore a useful counterweight to that gentleman's overweening ambition as Lord Chancellor.

The King's handsome brother was here too, of course – the openly Catholic James, Duke of York - sitting with his wife, Anne Hyde, the daughter of Clarendon. That was a marriage that no one had understood since Anne was such a plain and fat little thing. It seemed almost as if the marriage must have been a secret manoeuvring of the Lord Chancellor, since it certainly had cemented his authority at the court even more tightly than before. Yet Blight was of the opinion that this was in fact a true, if perhaps bizarre, love match, even though James was hardly faithful to her.

The King's other loyal courtiers were also in attendance this Wednesday afternoon: the Duke of Albemarle, who as General Monck had effectively forced Parliament into reinstating the monarchy four years ago; Charles Berkeley, the Keeper of the Privy Purse, who was a rising young man at court; the Duke of Ormond, that stylish and effete Irish gentleman with his long fair hair curling over his lace collar; and Henry Bennet, Earl of Arlington, recently promoted by the King to Secretary of State to the Privy Council, and another of Clarendon's particular enemies at court.

Blight saw that young Mawdsley, Clarendon's chief secretary and agent, was here also, yet looking as apprehensive as he himself felt, despite the conviviality of the occasion. Blight recognized the man sitting next to him as the wealthy merchant Henry Raven, his fellow member of the Royal Society. Mawdsley and Raven seemed on surprisingly good terms: Blight made a mental note of that fact, which was not something he had been aware of previously. A third man, a handsome fair-haired young fellow whom Blight did not recognize, was also obviously part of Mawdsley's own intimate group of guests...

*

In an antechamber of the Great Hall, which had been divided up by painted wooden screens into separate tiring rooms, the actors and actresses of the King's company were making ready for their grand entrance. In a departure from convention, the King had requested that he meet the cast before the commencement of the play, so that everyone, gentlemen included, were making sure that their costumes, wigs and faces were perfect for this unusual Royal acknowledgement.

Miles Brammer was looking wonderfully handsome in his costume as Duke Orsino, Molly thought, even if his face was perhaps decorated in rather too ladylike a fashion with ruby-red lips and thick kohl on his eyelashes. Mary Pettican was suitably regal as Countess Olivia, while Anne Carey (Molly was glad to see) had been forced to change from that lavish green silk gown she'd worn in rehearsal to a rather more dowdy grey costume as Olivia's maidservant Maria, to suit the distinction in social status between their two characters.

Molly noticed that Patrick Whelan, the Irish actor portraying the clown Feste, was still giving her secretive looks, as he had all during the rehearsals. Either this man was enamoured of her – something she sincerely doubted – or else he was suspicious of her (something far more likely.)

In truth Molly was now suspicious of almost the entire company in return and was becoming more and more convinced that one or more of this company had conspired in the death of her friend Sarah Lusted. And if so, then they could also be complicit in the death of Amy Leatherbarrow too, if those two events were connected. Certainly Molly had been more circumspect when returning home from the theatre to her lodgings in Coal Hole Lane in recent days, keeping to the busiest thoroughfares possible and making sure that there were no rogues following her. And when home, she had made sure to block the door with her rough oak table and chair so that no one could get the door open without at least warning her of their arrival, even though such simple precautions would not stop a determined assassin for long. Unfortunately Molly's plans over what to do next if someone broke through her door were less well formed, but she did always sleep with her knife at her side, and was determined not to go easily should she be attacked at home…

Yet, as the start of the play drew nearer and her excitement mounted, Molly's thoughts reverted more to the pleasure of today's performance than to any possible threat to her life. The dressers and backstage helpers had unfortunately not been included in the invitation to be presented to the monarch so that Molly was cursing her ill fortune at not being able to see the King up close. She had seen him many times from a distance in his box at the theatre, of course, but that did not compare with the pleasure of a close inspection of the monarch - and perhaps the even greater pleasure of being examined closely in return. Molly was quietly convinced that the King had taken many a particular note of her as she sold oranges at the start of a performance, even though her friend Nell Gwyn was equally convinced that *she* was the true object of the King's interest. Nell was not here today, of course – none of the orange sellers were here apart from the recently elevated Molly – so this would have been the perfect opportunity to see if the King truly recognized *her* and not her young friend.

Yet it seemed Molly would not get this sterling chance to prove Nell wrong but must stay in this miserable antechamber to help with costume changes while the play went on. Molly had been assigned in particular to assist Jane Golightly in her costume changes, since Jane had to begin the play in her female costume of Viola, but then spend most of the later scenes in her guise of the male eunuch Cesario.

Sir Thomas, in his own costume as Sir Toby Belch, came up suddenly behind Molly and gave her bottom a private hard slap. She scowled at him in return, for which he admonished her lightly. 'Now, be not surly, Molly. You will get your chance to appear on stage in time, I promise.'

Molly wondered how many bruises her bum would have to bear before such a thing would happen, but she forced the appearance of a sweet smile. 'Of course, I thank you for your consideration in promoting me, Sir Thomas, and would never doubt the word of such a noble gentleman as yourself...'

*

As he sat waiting for the play to commence, Henry Raven had made note of Mr James Blight's presence in the chamber. In fact this tall Puritan-looking gentleman seemed to be in charge of preparations for the performance and he was even now arranging for the lowering of the giant chandeliers over the makeshift stage to the optimum level for illumination.

A bell was rung to indicate that the performance would start in a quarter hour. But before that, the cast of twenty or so filed out from the adjacent antechamber and ascended the stage, with a puffed-up Sir Thomas Killigrew marching proudly at their head, dressed in the role of Sir Toby Belch.

Mawdsley, sitting at Raven's side, seemed unusually nervous over something, and made none of his usual bantering remarks in Raven's ear as they watched the cast assemble on stage to be presented to the King.

Raven's other friend, Adam Strange, was his usual roguish self, though, and whispered his appreciation of the beautiful actresses among the company, in particular of Mistress Pettican. 'What a wondrous white bosom that lady has! How I would like to journey through those fine hills and soft vales…'

Raven smiled his assent of that sentiment, but only with half his attention as he was presently rather more interested in measuring the slow oscillations of the great wooden chandelier above the stage than he was in admiring the beauty of the cast assembled on it. Ever the interested observer of natural phenomena, he was following in the footsteps of the great Galileo, who as a youth had noticed in church that the oscillations of a chandelier were only dependent on the length of the rope from which the chandelier was suspended, and not at all on the length of the arc displaced. The chandelier directly above the stage in the Great Hall, which was ablaze with candles, had been disturbed slightly by a draught of air from its neutral vertical position, and Raven had noted that its period of swing matched exactly three of his own heartbeats when measured against his pulse.

To swelling applause from the audience, the King finally stood up from the front row and made his way alone up the steps to the stage, where Sir Thomas met him. Killigrew then escorted the King along the line of actors and actresses, introducing each in turn, who responded with a bow or curtsey as appropriate.

Raven's attention was still concentrated on the chandelier, however, because he noticed it give a slight lurch that noticeably altered its period of swing. Raven's eyes immediately followed the line of the rope, which went around the roof beam above and was then tied to a post on the gallery that ran around the Great Hall at a mid-height level. Raven blinked when he saw that the rope seemed to be tied to the post in only the most rudimentary fashion and that the knot was unravelling rapidly even as he looked...

Raven stood up and shouted a warning, but no one understood the meaning of his anxious message, so that the King and the cast on stage merely stood open-jawed with perplexity, or perhaps anger, at this interruption. Fortunately Raven was near the end of a row in the audience so was able to run towards the stage at once, pointing furiously at the chandelier, which he could now see was going to fall to earth within a few seconds. The King had been about to move along the line to meet the next of the actresses – the one playing the maidservant Maria by her dowdy grey costume – and Raven could see that the chandelier was going to fall directly onto the pair of them unless he could prevent it...

Yet he was still a yard or more from the edge of the stage when the chandelier finally began to fall, so Raven was forced to simply launch himself despairingly into space at the King and the actress in danger, and hope that his intervention would throw them safely out of the path of the descending chandelier. Raven's flight through the air did hit the

King at knee height, but from then on everything became confused. Raven was only aware of a heart stopping impact, a flurry of falling bodies, and then a vast explosion of sound and screams as the heavy wooden chandelier hit the stage and broke into a hundred pieces, scattering burning candles in every direction...

*

Through the part open door, Molly saw that the Great Hall was still in an uproar a half hour later as palace officials and servants of the Royal Household cleared up the debris from the fallen chandelier.

The King – thank the Lord! – was unhurt, due entirely to the brave intervention of a certain gentleman in the audience. Anne Carey had been less lucky, though, receiving a severe blow on the head that had rendered her quite insensible. Molly's dislike of her had been immediately suspended after this horrific accident, and she was now equally as upset about what had happened as Anne's truer friends in the company. Miles Brammer had been affected most of all by the injury to Anne, Molly observed, his face quite white even under all the actor's paint, so perhaps the gossip about their friendship was well founded after all.

Anne had been carried away to a bed in a private bedchamber in the palace where the same gentlemen who had come to the King's rescue was even now attending to her care.

Molly had recognized this gentleman, of course, as her own benefactor on Sunday evening, Mr Henry Raven. She had witnessed the whole incident today in detail, having had her eye avidly pressed to the crack in the door that led to the Great Hall from the antechamber where the cast had dressed for the play.

She had gasped in amazement at Mr Raven's athleticism and courage as he threw himself across the stage in devil-may-care fashion to try and save the life of his monarch. The King had been badly winded by the impact with Mr Raven, but had fortunately been thrown well clear of the path of the falling chandelier, as had Raven himself. It had been by the merest stroke of ill luck that the third person involved in this collision - Mistress Carey - had been flung so far clear by the collision of bodies that she had then fallen off the back of the stage and hit her head with harsh and sickening force against the hard oak floor.

Yet, despite the unpleasantness of the incident, it seemed that the King still wanted the performance of the play to go ahead, if only to demonstrate to everyone assembled that he was perfectly well.

'Yet, if we go ahead, who will play Maria?' Mary Pettican asked fretfully, after Sir Thomas had explained the situation. The cast had returned to the antechamber after the accident to compose themselves, but none of them was in much of a mood to perform, and there was much grumbling and discontent at the thought of having to continue. 'Anne is certainly in no position to recover in time,' Mary pointed out unnecessarily, 'though mercifully she seems not to be in any real danger, according to the gentleman tending to her...'

This comforting advice about Anne Carey's state of health had come a few minutes before from Mr Raven after he had examined Anne and come to the antechamber to tell Sir Thomas and his cast of players of his welcome findings. It would of course have been unthinkable to go ahead with the play if Anne had been killed or seriously injured, but everyone was relieved to know that this was not the case.

Molly had stood discreetly at the back of the group of players while Mr Raven was making this announcement in the antechamber. He had noticed Molly's presence at the rear of the group, she was sure, but he had made no signs of obvious recognition towards her. If anything he had, to Molly's chagrin, taken far more notice of Jane Golightly than he had of her. In fact Molly could have sworn that she detected some signs of mutual recognition between Mr Raven and Jane, and wondered where that acquaintanceship might have originated. Mr Raven had never intimated to her, when she talked with him at length in his own house two days ago, that he was on familiar terms with any of the performers at the King's theatre...

After Mr Raven had departed from the antechamber, Sir Thomas stamped his authority quickly on his recalcitrant players. Despite their many grumblings, Sir Thomas was simply in no mood to disappoint the King. 'I insist that we do the King's bidding and go ahead with the performance.' He turned to Mary Pettican. 'And as for who will play Maria, we have someone here who can play that part well enough, I am sure,' he announced confidently.

Suddenly Molly became aware that everyone was looking in *her* direction. Sir Thomas came over to her side presently and pulled her away into a quiet corner of the chamber where he whispered to her. 'It seems you will get your opportunity even earlier than you expected, Molly. You did boast to me that you knew all the lines of this play. Now is the time to prove your extravagant boast...'

'But, Sir Thomas, I have had no r...rehearsal,' Molly stammered, still aware of all the curious eyes trained on her from the rest of the company.

Sir Thomas looked her sternly in the eye. 'No matter, Molly. Tell me now – can you play this part or no?'

Molly realized that this was likely to be her only opportunity to gain access to this company. If she rejected this chance and let Sir Thomas down, there would be little chance of any renewal of this offer, given Killigrew's unyielding character. 'Then yes, sir,' she stated boldly, hiding her unease, 'indeed I can do it.'

Mary Pettican had overheard this conversation, despite it being whispered in a corner of the room, and she now stepped forward to confront Sir Thomas. 'This will not do, Sir Thomas,' she complained shrilly. 'Maria in the play is supposed to be "small of stature" while Molly here is the size of an ox. Apart from which, we know nothing at all of her acting ability...'

Molly gave Mary a cold hard look in return. 'Madam, you did not complain when Anne Carey played the part, and she is much the same size as me. In fact I believe the costume Anne was wearing would fit me very well, and without modifications, since Mistress Carey and I are so much alike in form.' With that, Molly puffed out her breasts ostentatiously to ensure that Mary Pettican had comprehended her full meaning. 'In fact I would be happy to go to the bedchamber where she presently lies and take the dress off her. I am sure Anne herself will not mind giving up the dress, if it allows the play to go ahead for the King's pleasure...'

*

Given the fraught circumstances earlier, the performance of the play went off with remarkable assurance in the end, if starting an hour later than planned.

Raven and his two companions Mawdsley and Adam Strange had been favoured to sit close to the King in the front row after his brave intervention earlier, and he had spent the last two hours basking in the glow of the congratulations from all the fawning courtiers around him. Suddenly the name of Henry Raven had taken on a new pre-eminence at the Palace of Whitehall, where it had previously been entirely unknown to almost everyone except his friend Mawdsley.

Mawdsley himself seemed even more grateful than the King for Raven's unexpected intervention, and was still congratulating him in whispers two hours or more later over his bravery. 'God's blessing on your beard, Henry! How on earth did you happen to see that falling chandelier, and react so swiftly? I am used to you as a great thinker, but not as a man of action too. Yet no other man alive could have reacted so quick as ye did then, Henry. I am now in awe of you, friend, and you have my undying gratitude for what you just did.'

Raven, too, was modestly congratulating himself for what he had done. In truth he had hardly had time to consider the identity of the man he was trying to save, and his action had instead been entirely instinctive, merely the act of a man trying to prevent the death of a fellow human being. Yet the fact that he had saved the King of all people did put an entirely different perspective on his actions, of course, and did force him to consider the fuller implications of what he'd done.

Raven was no great admirer of the King, but what he had said to Strange several days ago was certainly true - he never wanted to see the country ripped asunder by another civil war. And he was sure that the death of the King in such circumstances as had nearly happened this day might well have unleashed one eventually, since not many of the citizens of this country wanted the King's openly Catholic brother James to succeed him to the throne...

Raven had earlier examined the condition of the injured actress Anne Carey in detail, and was sure from her steady breathing and healthy colour that there was nothing greatly amiss with her. In fact after only ten minutes, she seemed to be showing signs of regaining consciousness, so Raven had simply made sure that she was warm and that someone responsible was watching her. The King himself had nominated one of his pages of the bedchamber for this task – a flaxen-haired young gentleman called Thomas Creed, who despite his youth seemed to have a sensible head on his shoulders, and who promised to call Raven should he see anything amiss with the injured woman. Because of the potential problems of victims with head injuries – for example, due to bleeding within the cerebrum - Raven would nevertheless have preferred to miss the play and stay by Mistress Carey's bedside to be assured of her recovery. But the King would not hear of it and had been determined that Mr Raven should receive the full reward for his service by being allowed to sit at his illustrious side in the front row during the performance.

And after a few minutes, Raven had been so caught up in the enjoyment of the play that he had soon put any thought of Anne Carey to the back of his mind for the present. One point he could not fail to notice with interest about the play was that the young orange girl Molly Titchen had somehow been elevated in the last two days to the status of actress, and had taken over the role of the maidservant Maria from the injured Mistress Carey. Molly had however proved to be an accomplished actress (even if she had clearly improvised one or two of her lines) and one fully capable of convincing the audience that she was a gentlewoman of Illyria. Mawdsley and Strange also noted her presence, of course, and made many whispered bantering remarks in Raven's ear whenever Molly was on stage.

Raven had also taken particular note of the actress playing Viola, Jane Golightly. In fact he had noticed Mistress Golightly in the antechamber earlier when he had gone there to report on the condition of Anne Carey, and, standing near the front of the assembled company, she had seemed strangely familiar to him. Yet when she appeared on stage in her guise as the boy Cesario, Raven recognized instantly where this familiarity stemmed from – because this was none other than

Master John Goodricke, the "boy" he had encountered at the Royal Exchange who had put some serious questions to him about the death of Sarah Lusted. The wig she was wearing as Cesario even looked like the very same wig she must have been wearing at the Royal Exchange. Raven had no idea what Mistress Golightly thought she was doing parading around London dressed as a boy, or what peculiar mocking game she might have been playing with him personally, but he intended to have a serious word with her afterwards...

The play reached its satisfactory conclusion, and the cast were rewarded with a tumultuous ovation, which seemed to Raven as much a thanksgiving for the King's safe deliverance as for the performance of the players, good though they had been.

*

Molly was in a delirium of delight in the antechamber afterwards as the rest of the cast crowded around her to commend her enthusiastically on her unrehearsed performance.

Even Sir Thomas was minded to say, 'Well done, my girl,' and then to give her titties a covert squeeze.

Jane Golightly was more circumspect in her appreciation, but she did come forward and kiss Molly tenderly on the cheek. 'That was a wonderful lively performance you gave.'

Molly appreciated this compliment, given that she knew she had mangled some lines, and made up others, and also given that this girl had been a marvel in her role as Viola/Cesario. Jane was now back in her Viola costume that she had changed to for the last scene, yet Molly was still struck by how well she could portray a boy on stage, almost as if she had been born to the role...

*

Raven wanted to get back to his patient, Mistress Carey, but the King was a difficult man to escape from easily. Even though his friends Mawdsley and Strange had disappeared already from the Great Hall, both having urgent business to attend to elsewhere this evening, the King insisted that Raven stay behind and be introduced personally to his close circle, including the infamous Lady Castlemaine herself.

Raven was soon captivated by Lady Castlemaine's glowing and bountiful beauty, and by her openly flirtatious ways. This truly was a wondrous-looking lady, Raven decided, as she bowed and rewarded him with a warm smile, and her heartfelt thanks, for having saved the King from serious injury, or perhaps even saving his life. 'That was a most athletic leap that you performed onto the stage,' she commented, eyeing Raven from head to foot with seeming approval. 'You must be extremely well made to execute such a difficult manoeuvre. I could never do such a thing...'

'Certainly not in those tight corsets of yours,' the King said with a wicked smile. 'Though I am sure you would give it a creditable try, Barbara,' he added even more salaciously.

Lady Castlemaine smiled faintly at the compliment, and fluttered her fan to hide the pink glow of pleasure in her cheek.

The Queen, when she was introduced to Raven by the King, was more modest in her gratitude, but brightened up when Raven spoke a few words of halting Portuguese to her. 'Ah, you speak my language, Mr Raven!' she said in surprise.

''Hardly at all, your majesty,' Raven admitted quickly. 'Yet I have visited your beautiful sunny land several times.' Despite the fact that she was no match in the beauty stakes for the well-endowed Lady Castlemaine, being rather sallow of complexion and with plain features, Raven was quickly drawn to Queen Catherine's decorum and gentle grace.

Eventually Raven did manage to make his apologies to his Royal hosts in order to go and see to Anne Carey. However his progress was halted when he passed the antechamber where the theatre company had dressed, as a lady opened the door and obstructed his way.

Raven saw that it was the beautiful Mistress Golightly...

She did not seem at all embarrassed to be caught out in this way, more amused by his reaction, if anything. 'Mr Raven, may I have a word,' she asked, glancing into the room behind her.

'Ay, gladly,' Raven said.

'You probably have some questions to put to me, but could I first ask for your discretion in this matter?'

Raven was confused. 'Discretion?' He examined her again closely: in this feminine guise she was a pretty creature with her golden shoulder-length hair and her vivid blue eyes. Raven wondered how he could ever have mistaken her for a boy, even in breeches and a dark wig.

She hesitated. 'I can understand why you are surprised to see me here masquerading as a woman...'

Raven was entirely disconcerted now. *Surely she was not still claiming to be male?* In this dress, she looked most womanly, and distinctly alluring.

Raven was lost for a reply for a moment, but did eventually say, 'You do still claim to be *Master* Goodricke then?'

She blinked slowly. 'Of course. Who else would I be?'

Raven regarded her with suspicion. 'Then why are you here, dressed like this?'

Mistress Golightly sighed in a most feminine way. 'I love playacting, Mr Raven. And, for reasons that I shall not attempt to explain or justify, I find my best expression in female roles. Four years ago it would not have been an issue; I could have worked openly as a man taking female roles. But now times have changed and I have to pretend to be female all the time, not merely on stage, in order to work.'

Raven was still disbelieving of her story. 'You do seem more natural in the role of Viola than of Cesario.'

She smiled faintly. 'That proves only the depth of my acting ability, sir, and confirms what I said myself. Or perhaps it proves your own inclinations. You would rather that I was a Viola than a Cesario, it seems, but alas nature has decreed otherwise.'

Raven frowned, still unconvinced. 'You mentioned my "discretion"?'

'Yes, sir. I ask that you make no mention to anyone of the existence of John Goodricke. To the company I am only Jane Golightly.'

Raven coughed disbelievingly. 'And to Sir Thomas?'

'Ah, Sir Thomas! He does know the truth. He has the habit of undertaking "intimate" auditions with his players that make it difficult to conceal such things from him.'

Raven was beginning to accept that she might be telling the truth after all, although it was a difficult tale to swallow. 'Does your family know what you do?'

'I am an orphan, sir. I never knew my father, and my mother died five years ago. It was she who gave me the name Goodricke. She would have been disappointed to learn what I do for my living, and I would not want the knowledge of my profession to get abroad to her friends and acquaintances.'

Raven nodded uneasily. 'Then your secret is safe with me. But if you do wish to keep this confidential, why were you abroad that day at the Royal Exchange in the guise of John?'

'I wanted to know some details about the sad death of Sarah Lusted. One of the other actors in the company, Miles Brammer, told me that you had inspected Sarah's body for signs of foul play, and found none. Yet I wanted to hear the truth from you directly. It was easier for me to borrow the costume of Cesario to go in search of you since a male costume confers freedom of movement and action that is denied to most ladies. And Miles told me that you frequent the Royal Exchange most mornings.'

Raven thought that this Miles Brammer seemed to know a lot about him, for someone he had never spoken to. But his attention for the moment was occupied more with the person standing in front of him. He was still not entirely sure of the motives of "Mistress Golightly" and whether she might be playing mischievous games with him. 'If we should meet again, how should I address you?' he asked uncomfortably.

Jane smiled. 'I am glad that you think we might meet again, and I thank you for your kind consideration. Since you will only ever see me in this female guise from now on, sir, by all means address me as Jane

Golightly. It will make my life easier. And I think you do seem to prefer me dressed this way,' she added with deliberate emphasis...

Raven, breathing surprisingly hard, was aware that they had been joined by a third person. Jane excused herself and departed rapidly when she saw that it was a palace official.

Raven realized that the newcomer was Thomas Creed, the page of the bedchamber who had been assigned to the care of Anne Carey.

'Yes, sir, what is your will?' Creed asked, standing to attention.

Raven's mind was still diverted after his conversation with the enigmatic Mistress Golightly. 'My will? What do you mean by that?'

'Why, sir, someone came to the bedchamber and said you needed to speak with me urgently.'

Raven raised his eyebrows. 'What fellow was this? '

'I hardly saw his face, sir. He sounded like a gentleman so I assumed he was one of your party.'

''Twas not one of my friends, Mr Creed,' Raven declared. 'I think perhaps we should return at once to the bedchamber where Mistress Carey is lying. How was she when you left?'

'She looked finally to be nearly awake, sir. She was moving a little, and making low sounds of pain.'

'Then I had better see her at once,' Raven said, moving rapidly towards the door of the Great Hall

Creed led the way from there up to the bedchamber in question, which was reached from the Great Hall by a maze of corridors and staircases. According to Creed, this distinguished-looking chamber had in fact been the King's own bedchamber at one time and was a wondrous large room, decorated to resemble the Louvre. The bed on which Anne Carey lay had crimson damask covers, while the special alcove in which it stood was separated from the rest of the chamber by gilded railings hung with two great Flemish draperies. The floor was of French marquetry, with hangings and tapestries on the walls, and the ceiling was a grand allegorical scene showing Astraea, daughter of Zeus and the embodiment of justice, returning to Earth to bring a new Golden Age.

Yet Mistress Carey could not enjoy any of the splendours of this former Royal bedchamber because she was no longer breathing...

CHAPTER 9

Thursday, 15th December 1664

James Blight tried to adopt an air of calm, as he stood on the raised perimeter gallery in the Great Hall, near to the fixing post to which the fallen chandelier had been tied. Yet his stomach was churning with so much distress and anxiety that he feared its consequent bubbling and stirring must be audible at quite twenty paces away. Blight did not take kindly to being interrogated by Lord Clarendon and his pretty young secretary Mawdsley but he knew that these two were almost the closest of the King's advisors now, and he would therefore have to satisfy them as to his proper conduct if he wanted to remain with the King's household.

It was the morning after that near-disastrous performance of *Twelfth Night,* and Blight realized that he was not only under some suspicion of neglect from the King's chief counsellors, but perhaps even under the greater shadow of some suspected complicity in a deliberate plot to do hurt to the King. The irony of course was that he was entirely innocent of any part in the falling of the chandelier, and had presently no conception at all of how this near-calamity could have occurred. Yet it seemed too much of a coincidence that such a thing should happen now so soon after his meeting with Simon Ingledew, so Blight believed intuitively that Ingledew must have had some malevolent hand in this ill-timed incident. Which meant that the madman must have other agents in the palace household who were doing his bidding, besides himself, or else Ingledew was truly gifted now with sufficient occult powers as to be able to untie a rope by a mere effort of will from some remote location…

Blight gave up these distracting thoughts concerning Ingledew's possible occult powers as he tried to maintain a believable aspect of innocence under the pressure of the difficult questions he was facing. 'I can only say, my Lord, that I walked around the gallery immediately before the play began, to check that the chandeliers were all set to the desired level, and that all the ropes were securely tied in place. This particular knot was most firmly secured, and could not possibly have unravelled of its own volition.' Blight had decided that it was a better strategy to concur with the notion that this had been a deliberate act, rather than admitting it might be due to his personal neglect. He would lose his position in the household instantly if this incident should be ascribed to a dereliction of duty on his part. And he was perhaps protected by his long association with the monarch from genuine suspicions of more treacherous conduct.

Clarendon regarded Blight coldly. 'If you say so, then I must believe you, Mr Blight. You are a man of undoubted integrity after all, an example to us all.' Despite a frosty smile, the intent of Clarendon's words seemed entirely contrary to their literal meaning, and Blight was forced to bite back a sharp riposte. He could not afford to make an enemy of this man openly, when he was already the butt of so much contempt at court from the King's close circle of rakes and wits.

In all the years they had known each other, Blight had never formed a close relationship with Lord Clarendon. In fact he had always disliked the man and been intensely jealous of his hold over the King; yet at the same time he could not help but admire Clarendon's protean abilities.

Clarendon had certainly made the most of his opportunities in life, and seemed to have had an uncanny knack of always making the right choice when two distinct paths beckoned. This unerring political talent for following the right course had enabled him to achieve the highest political office in the land, despite his modest background as only the third son of a gentleman, and a mere lawyer. According to what Blight had heard of his early life, Clarendon had not even been a good law student during his time at the Middle Temple forty years ago. His abilities then had been more conspicuous than his industry, and his time had been devoted more to general reading and to the society of eminent scholars and writers than to the study of law treatises.

Blight was fifteen years Clarendon's junior, so had not known him as a young lawyer, of course; he had first encountered Clarendon in person during the Civil War when he had been plain Mr Edward Hyde, although Hyde was even then a man much senior to him in status, so their acquaintance had hardly been that of equals. Hyde had gone on to serve in the King's council as Chancellor of the Exchequer, and had been one of the more moderate figures in the royalist camp. But by the end of the war, his moderation had alienated him from the old King, and he was made guardian to the Prince of Wales, with whom he fled to Jersey in '46. By such a chance happening was the founding of

Clarendon's present power established.

These days, the King seemed to rely on Clarendon's counsel even more than formerly – even though he was also known to resent Clarendon's increasing interference in his personal life and his stern moralizing about his many mistresses. Clarendon had benefited greatly last year after his main political rival, George Digby, Earl of Bristol, had been banished from Whitehall for trying to have Clarendon falsely accused of treason. This coup had left Clarendon with unassailable power for the present, even though he still had many enemies at court, notably the King's rising favourites Henry Bennet and Charles Berkeley. The King had given Clarendon full charge of conducting the growing conflict against the Dutch, and, provided that war went well and ended in a favourable outcome, Clarendon's power seemed destined to become permanently enshrined. With this power had come vast rewards, far greater than any Blight could ever aspire to. Just last year, the King had named Clarendon as one of the eight Lords Proprietors who had been given title to a huge tract of land in North America for a new colony. This new English colony was to be called Carolina after the Latinized form of the King's name, and would add considerably to the existing ones in Virginia and New England.

Blight was honest enough to admit to himself that his jealousy of Clarendon was perhaps one more reason for him having turned secretly against the King.

Clarendon's young secretary Mawdsley was in a sombre mood as he inspected Blight with worried eyes. 'I am sure that you did indeed perform your duty diligently, Mr Blight, therefore this was clearly no accident. Someone must have gained access to this gallery immediately after you had finished your rounds, and loosed the knot deliberately.'

Blight reminded himself that he had still not been informed officially of any letter threatening the King's life so had to be wary in his response to this. 'Your expression suggests that you have some particular reason to fear for the King's safety, Mr Mawdsley...'

'Indeed we do have such reason, sir, but we must keep this knowledge confined to the most senior members of the King's Privy Council for the moment.' Mawdsley did not choose to elaborate further, and Blight felt some considerable anger at this young man's quiet insolence.

Clarendon now directed a question of his own at Mawdsley, which Blight took with relief to be a sign that he was no longer suspected of anything malicious. 'Surely someone would have seen any person skulking on this gallery before the play started, Mr Mawdsley, would they not?'

Mawdsley shook his head. 'I fear not, my Lord. There was much noise and confusion in the hall below, and everyone's attention was on the stage. So it would have been a comparatively simple matter for someone to slip away for a minute to this gallery. The gallery is also up in the shadows of the roof so that even if someone below happened to look up, they would see very little to recognize.'

Blight listened to this discussion with interest as he considered the circumstances of yesterday's incident in more detail. If that falling chandelier was truly Ingledew's doing, was it a serious attempt on the King's life, or just a further warning of what was to come? Blight was forced to wonder too, by the manner of the incident, whether Ingledew might not be intent on implicating *him* deliberately in the plot. The incident yesterday did almost seem designed to incriminate him since he had been the person responsible for the good order of the chandeliers. Yet Blight could not imagine for the moment how incriminating him would favour Ingledew's overall plan, nor why Ingledew should do such a thing when he needed his help.

Blight now turned his troubled mind to the dead actress. Had her death truly been accidental, or had Ingledew also murdered her for some unknown reason? *Had she perhaps seen something – perhaps the person who had gone to the gallery and untied the chandelier knot - and therefore had to be silenced...?*

*

Raven had received a message from Mawdsley at his home early this morning asking him to come to the Great Gate of the palace at ten o'clock.

Mawdsley was waiting at ten for his arrival, but instead of leading him into the main complex of buildings between the river and the Banqueting House, crossed King Street into the jumble of buildings known as the "Parkside". Most of the King's courtiers had self-contained apartments of one sort or another inside the palace, Raven knew. Lady Castlemaine for example had sumptuous apartments near the Holbein Gate that were superior even to the Queen's own private apartments. Yet the palace was so overcrowded with the King's vast household of nine hundred souls that many of the King's less influential friends now had to make do with lodgings on the park side of King Street. The Duke of Albemarle, for instance, had been given the rundown buildings around the Cockpit, built a century ago as a tennis court by King Henry, while Ormond - who in fairness spent most of his time in Ireland - had been limited to possession of the Tiltyard Gallery.

Mawdsley did not enter any doorway in the Parkside buildings, though, but followed instead a brick-arched passageway that led through the jumble of Tudor buildings to the parade ground beyond. Yet he did not pause on the parade ground either, but proceeded at pace into St

James's Park, which was glazed white in icy splendour on this harsh winter morning. Despite the cold, groups of finely attired ladies and gentlemen were promenading in the park, while on the parade ground a line of red-coated soldiers marched and drilled, and cleared the ice off their frozen cannon. In the frigid white mist above the snow-covered meadows, a herd of roe deer seemed to have been turned by the intense cold to a pattern of statues.

Mawdsley did not speak much until they were fully into the park and out of earshot of any other people taking the air. 'So, that was an interesting evening, was it not?' he finally proclaimed dryly.

'It was indeed.' Raven decided to come to the point quickly. 'Have you had the chance to investigate what happened in detail yet, Anthony?'

'I have, Henry.'

'So, do you believe that the chandelier fell by accident?' Raven queried.

Mawdsley cast him a wry look. 'I do not. I do not believe in such convenient accidents of nature, particularly when someone has made a threat against the King's life...' Mawdsley went on to tell Raven of the letter from the "Harbinger of Death", and of the dramatic manner of its delivery to Lady Castlemaine, and in particular of the direction given by this masked madman for the King to look out for the comet presently in the constellation of Taurus.

'Then perhaps you should have taken more precautions yesterday,' Raven commented dryly, on hearing the full story. 'Perhaps the play should not even have gone ahead, given this clear threat.'

Mawdsley rubbed his gauntleted hands together in a violent manner that suggested extreme frustration. 'The King would not hear of it, Henry. He will not give in to such threats. His personal courage is very great, you know. Nor will Lady Castlemaine, who I see is taking the air today on the other side of the lake as usual, despite the threat to her safety.' He sighed in frustration. ''Tis just as well that I have instructed an armed man to watch her without her knowledge. I would pay for it with my head if anything happened to that King's strumpet...'

'She does seem a cool and self-possessed lady,' Raven observed, as he glanced at her across the frozen expanse of water.

Mawdsley grunted. 'I trust you have no ambitions in that line, Henry, despite the warm smiles she favoured you with yesterday. Lady Castlemaine is very free with her favours...but not to anyone under the title of Marquis, I believe,' he added dryly.

Raven smiled. 'Why tell me this? You cannot seriously think that I aspire to the King's chief mistress.'

Mawdsley made a wry face. 'Of course I do not – you would not be so foolish. But I do need your help to identify the author of this letter that was handed to Lady Castlemaine. I thought I might be able to identify the origin of the seal at least, but I have not even been able to do that much. In fact I have made no real headway at all in hunting this masked individual to earth, and already it has been five days since I was given the task by my Lord Clarendon.'

Raven was still looking across the lake to where Lady Castlemaine and her maid were walking. Castlemaine had a very elegant and sensual walk, he decided; it seemed as if she was always performing for the pleasure of men, even when undertaking as routine a task as promenading in the park. 'I would need to see this threatening epistle,' Raven pointed out distractedly, 'in order to be of any help.'

Mawdsley, having first looked around anxiously to check that no one else was close, reached inside his coat and withdrew a letter from deep inside an interior pocket. 'I have the evil thing with me, as it happens.'

Raven took the letter from Mawdsley's gloved hand. In doing so, he could not help but notice how well his friend was dressed today. Mawdsley was always accoutred well these days of course, but this particular morning he was every inch the grand court gentlemen, with his long velvet silver-buttoned coat, his Rhinegrave breeches decorated with ribbons and bows, his silk stockings, his walking stick, muff, snuff box, and lace handkerchief. His manner of walking had changed recently too, Raven had noticed – no longer the undistinguished plebeian walk of his student days, but now the swaggering, elegant movement that was expected of a Restoration gentleman in order to carry off the full weight of his layers of fabric and ribbons. Mawdsley now took great delight in his extravagant costumes, from the tips of his square-toed high-heeled shoes to the great plumes of his broad-brimmed hat. Raven, with his lesser interest in fashion, could only hope that Mawdsley would not take this delight in his appearance too far and end up as one of the King's mincing fops like Sedley or Buckhurst.

Raven read the interesting letter through, and then said thoughtfully, 'I know not this seal. Yet the content of the letter does reveal much detail about the man's character.'

Mawdsley blinked, his eyes becoming moist and red with the cold. 'Then I would be obliged if you would enlighten me, Henry.'

Raven scanned the letter again. 'Obviously this is a man well versed in religion since much of his language is culled from the King James's Bible. Yet he has clearly lapsed from religion and is perhaps in the depths of a great moral despair. He also has a particular grudge over the death of Colonel Thomas Harrison and the other regicides, which suggests a close personal connection with one or more of them.'

Mawdsley nodded in agreement. 'I recognized that latter point myself. I have consequently been investigating various gentlemen of Republican sympathies, and in particular those who were friends or family of the regicides. Yet most of the friends and relatives of those executed men who are still living have long since fled the country.'

Raven grunted ironically. 'Then one of them has possibly returned.' He asked Mawdsley what extra precautions had been put in place to protect the King's life in the face of this threat.

Mawdsley seemed ill at ease. 'The King's personal guard has been informed of the threat but no one else.'

'Why not? Why has the whole palace household not been informed and told to be on their guard?'

Mawdsley became even more defensive. 'My master Lord Clarendon deems it better not to raise the spectre of panic and suspicion within the palace. He says he has full confidence in me finding this man quickly.' He bit his lip anxiously. 'That is why I need your help, Henry. You have certain talents which may assist me greatly. Is there anything else you see in this letter that might enable us to narrow down our search?'

Raven handed the letter back to Mawdsley. 'I would say this man has a scientific background.'

Mawdsley was puzzled. 'How dost thou determine that? Is that simply because he mentioned the comet? Most educated people in London have heard of the comet. Even Lady Castlemaine knows of it,' he added abrasively.

'When the man spoke to Lady Castlemaine here in the park, he made reference to the comet presently being located in the constellation Taurus. I do not believe that one common man in a thousand would know in which constellation the comet presently lies. But a man with knowledge of astronomy would...'

Mawdsley stopped walking and dug aggressively at the snow with the point of his walking stick. 'So we must look for a madman who has some connection with the regicides, and who also has some knowledge of science. I have been to meetings of the Royal Society with you, Henry, and, to be honest, most of its illustrious fellows seem more than a little mad to me,' he said dryly, 'especially your strange friend Mr Hooke.'

Raven laughed. 'Your sensibilities must be a little more finely tuned than mine to detect madness then, Anthony. Although I would admit that Mr Hooke does demonstrate a little eccentricity on occasion.'

'*Eccentricity*? The last time I ventured to join you at Gresham College, your Mr Hooke tortured a dog by opening its chest and pumping air directly into its lungs with a bellows. That poor animal was in mortal agony.'

Raven frowned. 'I hope you do not seriously consider Mr Hooke as a candidate for this would-be assassin, Anthony.'

Mawdsley relented. 'Of course I do not. But do you have any alternative choices?'

Raven stamped his frozen feet on the hard white ground. 'Have you considered Mr James Blight?'

Mawdsley turned his head warily. 'Why would you mention that gentleman's name? You have some particular reason for suspicion there?'

Raven sighed, watching his breath turn to floating ice crystals almost immediately as it dispersed through the air. 'He is a new fellow of the Royal Society. At our meeting this week, he asked Mr Hooke some very strange questions, and did seem slightly deranged. Also I saw him yesterday up on the gallery in the Great Hall where that chandelier was tied. So it would have been easy for him to have loosened the rope deliberately.'

Mawdsley had of course considered this possibility but had quickly discounted it, as he explained to Raven. 'The man has served the King loyally for many years.'

'Opinions change. Men's minds turn. Loyalties erode. I only raise his name as a possibility,' Raven said apologetically, 'someone perhaps worth the watching.'

Mawdsley remained sceptical. 'And did he also murder this actress Anne Carey? What is your view of that mystery? You examined her body. Did she truly die of the injuries sustained in falling off the stage? Or did someone assist her across the Styx with some extra malevolent effort?'

Raven became sombre. 'The identity of the man who called the page Thomas Creed away from Anne Carey's bedside is certainly a mystery. I know it was not you or Adam, but it could have been almost any other gentleman in that Great Hall. Where did you go at the end of the play anyway? I did not see you afterwards.'

Mawdsley frowned. 'I went to consult urgently with Lord Clarendon. And to show Adam out of the Great Hall – he needed to get home as he is much engaged with the preparations for a forthcoming legal case…'

Raven was still deliberating intently with himself over the death of Anne Carey, which he could not but blame himself for. If he had sat with her as he had wanted, if he had been more forceful in refusing the King's invitation to watch the play, then she might still be alive. 'Master Creed could give me no helpful guidance as to this man's appearance, apart from believing him to be a young man.'

'Did no one else go to the chamber where Anne Carey was lying?' Mawdsley asked.

'No one who would have harmed her.' Raven had made enquiries of Thomas Creed, and the only other person the page could remember visiting the room, apart from Raven himself, had been young Molly Titchen, who had come before the play went ahead to remove the gown that Anne had been wearing on stage and to replace it with something warmer. According to Creed, she had been alone with Anne Carey for some time. *But surely Molly would not have harmed her?* And the fact was that Anne had been alive and breathing for long after Molly's visit anyway.

Yet Raven was still reluctant to mention Molly's name to Mawdsley at all given the relentless ribbing from him that seemed to result at the mere mention of her name. Raven returned his thoughts instead to the mysterious male visitor whose behaviour was much more suspect than Molly's since he had called Creed away quite deliberately. 'If this man's behaviour was entirely innocent, why did he not come forward afterwards and make himself known to me? Ergo - he had some devious reason for drawing Thomas Creed away from the chamber. I cannot be certain but I believe Anne Carey was smothered with a pillow. In her weakened condition, with her head injury, she could not have struggled long – a minute at most. I believe now that this same person must have also killed Sarah Lusted at the King's house last week. Someone is deliberately murdering actresses from the King's company.'

Mawdsley gasped. 'Then we truly have a devil at work...'

Raven agreed. 'Ay, but is it the same devil who wishes the King dead? Or do we have two devils at work here...?'

CHAPTER 10

Thursday, 15th December 1664

That same afternoon, Henry Raven came again to watch the daily performance at the King's house.

This was unusual behaviour for him – a second voluntary visit to see a play inside a week. Or perhaps it could even be counted a third, if the special performance yesterday at Whitehall Palace were taken into account, although his presence in the Great Hall had perhaps been more in the nature of an obligation than a pleasure. Truly it seemed that he possessed a growing addiction for the world of the playhouse, and one which was possibly quite as severe a case now as his friends Mawdsley and Strange.

Yet the real attraction for Henry Raven at the King's theatre was perhaps something simpler than merely a newfound love of comedy and drama. Perhaps it was merely the fact that he had heard that Molly Titchen was due to perform here today...

The play was Mr Dryden's new comedic masterpiece, *The Rival Ladies*, in which two society women, disguised as pages, enthusiastically pursued the same man in a hectic game of sexual cut and thrust.

As ever, the King's theatre in Bridges Street was filled to capacity with a boisterous audience whose ribaldry, high spirits and low humour could scarce be contained by the theatre walls. Sometimes the enthusiasm of the crowd grew so feverish at the convoluted and farcical nature of the plot that some of them seemed ready to erupt onto the stage and join in the bawdy action, given half a chance.

Raven, alone in Mawdsley's private box, was free to enjoy the performance for once without the distractions of having to make conversation with his friends, or to defend his motives in being here. On stage, under the forest of blazing chandeliers, the performance of the play did truly entrance him, enlivened as it was by Mr Dryden's witty dialogue, but also by the brazen costumes and general bawdiness of the plot.

Molly was not playing a major role in the play, but merely a bit part as a glamorous Royal courtesan. In her high wig, and with her face painted porcelain white, and her lips carmine red, and with a black half-moon patch on her cheek, she was almost unrecognisable as the young orange girl Raven had first met a few days ago. In that particular gown she was wearing, with all its rigid boning and corseting, her waist was compressed to such a tiny circle, and her bosom inflated in turn to such an equally impossible level, that the attention of the audience was fixed avidly on her charms whenever she was on stage.

Yet it was not only the fact that she looked the part that claimed the audience's (and Raven's) attention, but also that she moved, talked and behaved exactly like the real thing. For a girl with her common background – or was it perhaps *because* of it? - she managed to convey the behaviour of a high-class courtesan with unerring accuracy. With her lively movements on stage, she suggested the graceful, sensuous vitality expected of such creatures. Raven had seen the way that even normal ladies of society in London aped French manners these days at masques and balls, preening and prancing like pigeons, fluttering their eyelashes, and manipulating their skirts and their charms with a complete knowledge and assurance about the effects they were creating. And Molly mimicked that behaviour with perfect timing and ineffable mockery, particularly in her use of her fan. The fan was of course a society lady's most important accessory, and was as important a weapon to a woman in the game of love as was a musket to a soldier on the battlefield.

Watching Molly's bewitching if brief performance, Raven became gradually convinced that she was basing her portrayal of this lady on Lady Castlemaine herself, which was a bold thing to do if it were true. When Molly received some earthy and leering remark from a small bald man in the pit – 'Can I come up on stage and see your precious white bubbies up close, my lady?' - she improvised a reply in character that soon silenced him and brought the house down. 'You had better not come on stage and stand close by me, sir, else, with your hairless head and your short stature, it might look like I have three tits in place of the usual two…'

Even the indolent fops, complacently combing their wigs in the box opposite to Raven, seemed vastly amused by that riposte.

Molly did however still have some stiff competition for the attention of the audience, since the main parts in the play – the two rival ladies of the title - spent most of their time striding around the stage in men's breeches and showing off their fine legs. Even though Raven found his attention concentrated most on Molly when she was on stage, he had to admit that the sight of Mary Pettican and Jane Golightly dressed in tight breeches was an arresting one too.

If Mistress Golightly truly was a young man, then this was an extremely subtle performance by "him", Raven thought, because he played the male page with just the right hint of underlying femininity to suggest that this really was a girl pretending to be a boy, and not a boy pretending to be a girl pretending to be a boy…

*

At seven in the evening Raven was waiting in the intense cold at the stage door to the theatre, when Molly finally appeared.

With her face scrubbed clean, and wearing her own plain woollen clothes, she looked like a simple maidservant again, so much so that no one else in the small crowd of onlookers recognized her at all as the high class courtesan from the play.

They recognized the actor who was with her, however, as one Patrick Whelan. The crowd pressed around him in their enthusiasm to shake his hand so that Molly was able to slip away from his side quickly. She seemed relieved to have escaped from the company of this Mr Whelan despite him being a handsome and personable-looking young man. She saw Raven waiting in the alleyway, but perhaps unsure that he was here waiting for her, seemed reluctant to come over and speak to him until he smiled and beckoned her over with his lantern.

'May I walk with you to your home, Molly?' Raven asked, doffing his broad hat in gentlemanly fashion.

'Of course you may, sir,' she said with equal politeness. 'But to what do I owe this privilege?'

Raven replaced his hat and tightened his cravat against the fierce wind that was scouring the alleyway and driving the snow into deep drifts against the timber and brick walls of the darkened playhouse. 'There are things I need to discuss with you, Molly. Important matters.'

'Then shall we talk as we go, sir,' she suggested diffidently. 'Brrr…'tis too cold tonight to stand still and converse.'

'Ay, indeed. I have brought a lantern because the way to Coal Hole Lane is very dark and incommodious.'

Molly seemed uncomfortable. 'That is of no matter because I have quitted my lodging there for the present.'

'That seems sensible, in view of what happened to your friend. It seems a dangerous neighbourhood.'

Molly sighed in melancholy fashion. 'It is, sir. Yet I still blame my own actions as much for Amy's death as the dangerous circumstances of our neighbourhood.'

Raven decided to let that remark pass, doubtful that she really blamed herself in any serious way. 'Where is your new lodging, Molly?'

Molly brightened up. 'If you follow me, sir, you shall see in due course. 'Tis not much further than Coal Hole Lane.'

They set off, taking a shortcut through the end of the alleyway that led to Drury Lane. Being a fashionable street, Drury Lane was still busy with passers-by on foot, and heavily congested with sedan chairs and closed carriages, in spite of the dense covering of snow and the biting wind. The sedan chair men seemed about to come to blows with some of the coachmen, as their annoyance at being unable to find a path through the clutter of vehicles in the street began to reach breaking point.

Raven was concerned at Molly's poor apparel, a world away from that glamorous costume she had been wearing today on stage, yet equally unsuitable for warding off this dreadful winter cold. 'Are you warm enough dressed like that, Molly? Your cloak seems very thin.'

'I am made of stern stuff, sir. And you too apparently. Despite this weather, I see that you do not use your own carriage much, sir,' Molly observed. 'I imagine that you do keep one, sir?'

'I do. In fact I have just taken delivery of a new carriage of very light construction, built especially by a coach maker, and sprung to my own design. But I use it only seldom within the city,' Raven answered. 'I have to stable my horses, including my favourite mare Bessie, a good quarter mile from my house, and 'tis irksome to make the carriage ready unless I have a journey of at least five miles in mind. Within the city I prefer to walk or ride, and it is presently too dangerous to ride a horse with the streets so icy and slippery.' Nor did he have a dedicated coachman, Raven could have added, since this was another one of Martin's many special duties. Raven could well have afforded a dedicated coachman, of course, yet there was a parsimonious side to his nature that balked at paying some elderly driver to sit around on his large backside for long periods at a time.

Molly accepted Raven's explanation without comment, though she did seem irked that he could not have swallowed his principles for once, and brought out his closed carriage on such a vicious cold night as this. From Drury Lane Molly led the way north and east through streets and alleyways that grew progressively more dismal and darker with each passing step. The snow had begun falling again almost as soon as they had set off from the theatre, and with the wind so northerly in direction, blew painfully into their faces.

As they went on their shivering way, Molly congratulated Raven on his bravery and quick thinking yesterday, and particularly on saving the King from serious injury or even death. 'The King may give you a knighthood for such bravery, sir. If not, he is most ungrateful.'

Raven flinched a little in embarrassment at the effusive compliment, which seemed excessive for what he had done. 'It was not so heroic as you think since it was over in the blink of an eye. I scarce had time to think over what I was doing.'

'How could such an accident have happened?' Molly asked, puzzled. 'Even in the playhouse, I doubt that such a thing could be allowed to happen. The chandeliers in the theatre are checked most carefully.'

Raven was careful in his reply. 'Perhaps it was simply carelessness in tying the chandelier. Or perhaps there were darker forces at work.'

Molly's eyes widened. '*Darker* forces? Was it a deliberate act, then, think you?'

Raven avoided replying, since he was not free to mention the threat against the King.

Molly wrapped her arms around herself and shivered violently as she reached a corner between two narrow lanes, and was hit by a sudden blast of cold air. 'I was sorry that you did not speak to me yesterday after the play,' she said lightly. 'Are you perhaps ashamed of any public association with me, sir?'

Raven looked sharply at her, not sure how seriously her remark was intended. 'Not at all, Molly. I would never suffer any shame at being in the company of such a pretty girl as you. I was much distracted yesterday, that is all.'

Molly nodded thoughtfully. 'That is true. You were much distracted, as were we all by what happened. Yet you still found time to speak to Jane Golightly,' she complained with slight peevishness.

Raven smiled. 'I am making amends now for my inattention to you yesterday, am I not? You performed most excellently in *Twelfth Night* by the way, although even that was quite eclipsed by your accomplished performance today. And your riposte to that man in the audience was most memorable.'

Molly almost blushed. 'Ah! You heard that! I am mortified to have said such a vulgar thing, even though I was severely provoked.'

Raven doubted that she truly meant that, and thought that she was still acting a part of some sort. He shivered again under the blast of this awful northerly wind. 'But whence comes this sudden elevation in your fortunes, Molly? On Monday you were a mere orange girl. Yet by Wednesday you are on stage in front of the King and you steal the show from your fellow players. To what do you ascribe this sudden rise in your fortunes?'

Molly smiled. 'I believe that Sir Thomas admires my ready spirit and wit, and was prepared to give me a chance because of it…although, if I am frank, then perhaps the fine shape of my legs when displayed in breeches' roles might also have had some influence on his decision,' she added in a whisper. Molly then sighed at the look on Raven's face. 'I am sorry, sir. I see I have shocked you again with my saucy opinions.'

'Nay, Molly, you have not shocked me,' Raven denied unconvincingly. Yet he was as much amused by her forthright opinions and frank tongue as he was shocked.

Molly weighed up his response carefully, then clearly decided to adopt a more demure tone. 'Circumstances have also favoured me in my ambition to be an actress, sir. Anne Carey's injury was a particular stroke of good fortune for me, sir, if very ill for Anne herself. It pains me to profit from another person's misery, but I still could not sacrifice my one chance, could I?'

'No, indeed.' Raven finally got to the main reason why he had offered to walk home with her tonight. 'I have no wish to make you fearful, Molly,' he warned her. 'But there are aspects of the sad death of Anne Carey that make it look not like an accident, but instead like callous and deliberate murder...'

Raven noted that Molly did not seem at all surprised by this revelation.

He went on. 'I believe she was smothered to death. The blow she received to her head in falling from the stage was severe, but not enough to kill her in my opinion...'

Molly interrupted eagerly. 'That was my thought too, sir. When I went to the bedchamber where she was lying, in order to recover her stage costume, she seemed almost on the point of waking up. Her breathing was regular and her skin was warm and had a good colour. I did not see any reason to fear for her life. I was most shocked and disconcerted when I discovered that she had apparently succumbed later to her injuries.'

Raven held up the lantern so that he could see her face in the driving snow. 'That was my belief too, Molly, else I would never have left her. Yet someone deliberately called away the page watching her – someone who knew my name and my part in tending to this injured woman. When the page and I returned to the bedchamber, we found Mistress Carey suffocated by some unknown hand.'

Molly said nothing to that, so Raven continued. 'Anne is now the second actress from the King's company to die within a week in suspicious circumstances, and the coincidental nature of these occurrences must excite some curiosity and concern. Of course, the death of Anne Carey could be entirely unrelated to the death of your friend Sarah Lusted, yet it would be foolish to deny any possibility of a connection. What say you on this matter, Molly? At my house this week, you said that your suspicions over Sarah's death had now abated and that you were satisfied that she died of natural causes.' Raven frowned.

'But were you entirely honest, or merely telling me the things you thought I wanted to hear?'

Molly looked sheepish. 'I did not tell you the truth,' she admitted ruefully. 'I thought from the first that Sarah's life was taken by some wicked person, and I have never really changed my mind in that respect. I believe truly that Sarah was murdered by the dark lady I saw leaving the tiring room. I also believe that this lady may be one of the actresses in the King's company who had adopted a clever disguise for the occasion. I am also sure that she used some strange poisonous substance to penetrate Sarah's body through that small wound in her neck, and that she could have a gentleman accomplice...'

Raven was annoyed. 'Why did you not tell me this before when you were at my house, Molly? Why did you dissemble so?'

Molly flushed, despite the cold. 'I beg your pardon, sir, but I had my reasons. It would make my life exceeding difficult at the theatre if I were to make such accusations known, especially since these actors and actresses are now my fellow players.'

Raven now understood her reasons, and mollified his angry tone, even if not being entirely satisfied by her excuses. 'And what of the men who attacked you in the street? "Feathered Hat" and "Toothless", you called them. Do you believe they too could be part of this insidious plot?'

''Tis possible,' Molly conceded uncomfortably.

Raven had completely lost track of where they were by now, blindly following Molly into the maze of alleyways north of Lincoln's Inn Fields. 'Yet what reason do you truly have to think that this dark lady in the tiring room might be one of the actresses of the company in disguise? You said that you did not recognize her – yet you know all the actresses of the company well enough by sight, and would not be easily fooled by a different costume or wig.'

'That is true enough,' Molly admitted. 'Yet who else would want Sarah dead – and now Anne too - except one of her rival actresses? Who also would have the opportunity, and would also know that Sarah would be alone in that tiring room at that time, in order to discard her cumbersome costume first before the other actresses returned? This woman could have been waiting in the tiring room for Sarah to appear...'

'An actress from the company could not have planned yesterday's events ahead,' Raven pointed out thoughtfully. 'She could not have foreseen that Anne Carey would be hurt in that way, and would be left to lie in a bedchamber in the palace.'

Molly stopped in her tracks, the snow covering her thin shoes and the trailing hem of her skirt. 'No, but an actress, or an actor accomplice perhaps, might easily have taken advantage of this chance occurrence to do the deed.'

Raven was unconvinced. ''Tis hard to believe that mere jealousy of a fellow actress could drive a woman to such an intricate plot. Could there not be some better reason why someone would take against Sarah Lusted and Anne Carey? Did they have anything else in common, besides being young actresses of ability and wit?'

Molly began walking again, pulling the hood of her cloak tight about her head. 'I cannot think of any particular thing they had in common, apart from their age. They were both twenty years old, but did not look alike in any way. Sarah was from Islington, while Anne was from East Anglia, I believe, the town of Ipswich. Anne was also an orphan, like Sarah, which I suppose is something of a coincidence.'

Raven was bemused. 'So do you suggest that some evil and deranged soul in the company is murdering orphaned actresses for the sake of it?'

Molly sniffed coolly, not liking his dismissive tone. 'I would scarce make such a ridiculous claim as that, sir.'

Raven would have liked to believe that it was an entirely ridiculous notion, but was constrained by a niggling doubt. 'Are there any other actresses presently in the company who are orphans?'

Molly wrinkled her brow as she went through the list of actresses in her mind. 'Only Jane Golightly, I believe. She is an orphan from the town of Warwick, or so she told me anyway. But she is a strange girl of very shy and secretive habits, so I am not sure I believe everything she says,' she added complacently.

Raven wondered from that remark whether Molly suspected something of "Jane's" true nature. Could she perhaps perceive a Master Goodricke under the feminine costumes and the long golden hair?

Molly was still reflecting quietly. 'I too am an orphan, of course, and now an actress of sorts with the company.'

This was an interesting point that Raven had not considered before. 'I doubt that *you* are in any danger from any other actress in the company, Molly. I am glad, though, that you have moved out of Coal Hole Lane -' he glanced around uneasily as he finally began to realize Molly's likely destination – 'yet this area we approach now seems hardly more salubrious or safer. This is Whetstone Park, is it not?'

Molly seemed reluctant to admit it. 'It is, sir. I lodge now with my mother.'

Raven was taken aback. 'By your "mother", I take it you mean Madam Celia Hornett?'

'I do, sir. Did someone tell you of my connection with her, sir, or have you perhaps favoured her premises previously with your own custom?' Molly asked innocently.

They had finally reached the alleyway in which Celia Hornett's infamous bawdy house was located. This little street was officially named Rope Lane, but known familiarly to all and sundry as Gropecunt Lane, which summed up the chief preoccupations of its visitors perfectly. Although Raven had never been inside Madam Hornett's establishment, he had been to the door before, half-tempted on occasion to savour its infamous delights. It was a rambling three-storey house built before the Civil War, and gave no indication from the outside of its inner sinful workings, having merely the appearance of a sober merchant's house. 'No, I have not been to her premises before,' Raven answered uncomfortably, 'but Sir Thomas did mention your connection to Madam Hornett to me in passing. Do you really intend to lodge in this bawdy house, Molly?'

'I fear that I do, sir. But I lived there from a little girl and I have my own room on the last landing. So I shall be safe enough under my mother's watchful gaze.'

Raven frowned. 'Safe? Really? In a bawdy house? In any case, Madam Hornett cannot be your real mother if you are truly an orphan as you claim.'

'Of course she is not. My real father, Mr Titchen, was a draper in Fetter Lane in the city, and he and my poor mother were killed in a fire more than fifteen years ago. Madam Hornett took me in as a baby, and she will continue to take good care of me, sir, despite the lack of any of her own blood flowing in my veins.'

Raven was still concerned for her welfare. 'Yet will ye. be safe from Madam Hornett's pestering customers?'

'Do not concern yourself, sir, over my welfare. I shall board up the door very firmly to them all.' She turned and looked up at him, her voice reduced to a whisper. 'Unless you call of course, sir, in which case I might be persuaded to lower my defences briefly.'

Raven felt himself stiffen instantly at that provocative remark, but was not sure how to respond with equal seduction, without appearing ridiculous. His own talents for flirtation were still on the rudimentary side when faced with such a quick-witted and saucy girl as this. 'Then I trust you will be safe here, Molly. But please make sure from now on that you never walk home alone late at night from the theatre... '

*

At eight o'clock, Raven knocked at Adam Strange's door in Bow Street and was confronted by the dour Mistress Bilby again.

He was conscious that because she was standing two high steps above him, her eye level was several inches above his, and that her dark eyes were appraising him from that lofty position with even chillier candour than usual.

'Is Mr Strange at home,' Raven asked her.

Mistress Bilby nodded briefly. 'He is, sir, but he has just returned late from working at his chambers in the Middle Temple and is very fatigued.'

Raven tried to maintain his good temper, despite the woman's insolent look and manners. 'Nevertheless, may I come in and see him for a short time?'

Mistress Bilby sometimes seemed less a servant than a self-appointed guardian of Adam's free time. But she finally acceded with a small bob of her head. 'Of course, sir, Please go through to the ground floor parlour. I will bring you some refreshment presently.'

Raven found Adam reclining in his high-backed settle by the usual crackling log fire.

'Ah, the hero of the hour,' Strange said mockingly. 'Welcome, Henry. Come and sit and tell me everything. I heard that after I left the palace yesterday, there was a sad conclusion to your heroic action, and that the poor lady who fell from the stage eventually succumbed to her injuries.'

Raven took a seat by the fire and explained at some length his true suspicions over the death of Anne Carey, having been given leave by Mawdsley to tell Strange everything he knew about yesterday's incident, and even of the threat to the King. Mawdsley trusted his friend Strange's integrity and discretion completely, despite his sometime jocular manner. Raven left out, however, any reference to Molly Titchen when mentioning the coincidence of the deaths of two young actresses from the King's company, and his fresh suspicions in the matter. Raven had no wish to have his growing feelings for that girl exposed to more of his friend's gentle ridicule.

After hearing Raven's thoughts concerning these mysterious events, Strange ran a hand across his strong jaw, his blue eyes almost twinkling. 'What an exciting and eventful life you lead for a coal merchant, Henry! Plots against the King...plots against actresses...'

'Tis no laughing matter, Adam,' Raven said, disconcerted by his friend's lack of sensitivity.

Strange became more subdued in his manner. 'Ay, perhaps you are right to query my levity, Henry. Yet I deal with the miserable consequences of human behaviour so much in the course of my daily work that humour is oft the only escape for me from forbidding melancholy and gloom.' He cocked a wry eye in Raven's direction. 'Yet with regard to the threat made to the King, are you truly that concerned over his fate, Henry? Despite what you said to me a few days ago, would you truly not prefer a republic in this country?'

Raven would not be drawn too far in answering such a charged question, although there was something valid in what Strange said. 'I made my position clear enough to you the last time you asked me this question, Adam. A unified England is what I seek. And if it takes a King to keep us unified, then the monarchy must be preserved in perpetuity, as far as I am concerned.'

Strange seemed unimpressed by that answer. 'Yet I sense that this business of the deaths of these actresses intrigues you more than the King's fate.'

Raven blinked slowly. 'Why would you say that?'

Strange laughed. 'Because you are more personally involved, Henry.' Strange slapped his friend affectionately on the shoulder. 'I saw the way you looked at that strumpet Molly on stage yesterday. You definitely have some ambitions there now, I am sure. 'Tis the one advantage of these baggy breeches that gentlemen wear now that they disguise many a manly erection. I am sure, though, that I detected a great stirring in your Rhinegraves every time young Molly bestrode the stage yesterday.' Strange looked at Raven knowingly. 'In fact from the look of you, I would guess that you have been with her this very evening.'

Raven grunted defensively. 'Only to escort her home from the theatre. She was attacked most savagely last Sunday night, as I told you yesterday.'

Strange breathed out slowly. 'Then I am surprised she is not in hiding, Henry, if you truly believe her to be in danger too.'

Raven nodded. 'She is not exactly in hiding, Adam, but I have advised her to take precautions. For one thing, she has left her former lodgings in Coal Hole Lane for somewhere safer.'

Strange rubbed his hands by the fire. 'Knowing her history, I think I can hazard a firm guess as to where she might have gone.'

Raven smiled. 'Surmise all you like, Adam, but I do not intend to tell even you where Molly has gone...'

*

In her tiny garret room at the top of the bawdy house, Molly lay in bed and reflected over her long talk this evening with Mr Raven. She regretted now making that forward remark about letting her defences down should he come to call. He had looked quite shocked again at such forwardness on her part.

Yet she was sure that she was right about him: he was most certainly interested in her. The signs were there for all to see. During the performance this afternoon, she had noticed his eyes following her every time that she strode onto stage, and felt his earnest gaze far more than anyone else's in that audience. Yet she realized that he was not used to common and direct girls like her, and that if she truly wanted to attract him, she would have to moderate her flirtatious instincts a little and behave in a more ladylike manner with him.

Yet, knowing how men truly were, she doubted that he would want her to be *too* ladylike...

Molly shivered violently under her coarse blankets. This room might be safer than the one in Coal Hole Lane, but it was certainly no warmer or more comfortable. Yet with the door firmly barred with thick planks against any illicit entry, and with the large chamber pot under the bed to prevent any need for her to wander further abroad tonight, she did feel entirely secure here, if still frozen to the marrow.

As Molly began to drift off into sleep, she made a list in her head of all the people at the theatre she intended to keep a close eye on from now on.

Miles Brammer for one, of course...

He was the one actor in the company – being beautiful enough, and slender enough of form - who might have been able to realistically disguise himself as that tall dark lady without her seeing straight through his guise. She tried again to recall whether he had been offstage with the other actors after the performance of Etherege's play *Love in a Tub* on Friday when she had passed them on her way to the tiring room to help Sarah undress. But she still could not say for certain because her mind had been elsewhere.

Until yesterday, Molly had thought Brammer to be possibly enamoured of Anne Carey. Yet in the end, after everyone's initial shock had worn off yesterday, he had seemed no more affected by her death than the rest of the company, so the depth of his commitment to her had to be questioned. Perhaps his preference for Anne had been mere affectation, designed to conceal his true nature and feelings...?

As for Christopher Malthouse and Patrick Whelan, Molly had no particular suspicions of either of them, except that Patrick Whelan had made a point of meeting her this evening in the theatre after the performance and walking with her to the stage door. He seemed uneasy in his manner towards her too, which Molly found a continued cause for curiosity...

Molly had definite suspicions now concerning Mary Pettican, whose dislike and jealousy of her since her elevation to the company was plain for all to see. But was this simply a woman's natural jealousy of a rival, or did this dislike originate from something darker and more sinister lurking beneath the surface?

Molly also gave some thought to Mistress Meggs, who now hated her with even more venom than Mary Pettican for her unexpected promotion from orange seller to the privileged status of actress. In her youth Mistress Meggs had perhaps dreamed of such a thing happening to her, and she clearly detested anyone who had the temerity to achieve what she could not. When Molly had run into her this afternoon before the performance of *The Rival Ladies*, Mistress Meggs had smiled obligingly at her and whispered her congratulations on her new role in life, yet Molly could see that beneath the skin she was spitting blood. Truly that dreadful false smile she had displayed on her raddled old face had been a most disturbing and ugly sight...

And Jane Golightly...

What of that strange, fey girl...?

Molly's idle musings about Jane Golightly were however ended abruptly when she heard a discreet knock at her door. Getting out of bed with a shiver, she tiptoed across the cold wooden planking. 'Yes, who is it?'

' 'Tis me, Molly,' a voice whispered on the other side of the thick oaken door.

Molly recognized Celia's distinctively husky voice.

'May I come in?' Celia went on, after Molly made no reply at once.

Molly reluctantly slid the door planks aside and let her in. 'What do you want, Mother?'

Celia smiled tentatively at her. 'Shall I stay with you tonight, Molly? It is terrible cold outside – the icicles hanging from the roof eaves must be two feet long! We can keep each other warm tonight, just like when you were a child.'

Molly ran back to her bed. 'As you wish, Mother. But please barr the door securely behind you with the boards.'

In a second, Celia was in bed with Molly, almost buried under the layers of blankets. 'Molly, I want to say something to you before we sleep. I am most proud of you appearing on the stage at the King's company. And yesterday, performing at the palace itself! 'Tis a truly wonderful achievement! I did not think you so talented, but it seems I underestimated my own sweet daughter.'

Molly shivered to hide her pleasure at the compliment. 'It seems you did, Mother,' she said complacently.

Celia touched her arm under the blankets. 'Yet two actresses of the company are dead, and in strange circumstances. I worry about your safety, sweetheart.'

Molly finally snuggled up to her for mutual warmth. 'Do not fret so. I have sufficient friends to look out for me.' Yet many likely enemies too, she could have added.

Celia smiled and took her hand under the blankets. 'Like that gentleman who escorted you to my front door this evening. A most obliging young man he looked. Who is he?'

'His name is Henry Raven. I yet know little of him, Mother, but he has a fine house in St Martin's Lane, and his maidservant told me that he has considerable estates in the county of Dorset.'

Celia snuggled up to Molly even more tightly. 'It would be a feather in your cap to land such a prize as that, Molly. But ye must play him with care, and not let him slip your line...'

'I will make sure my hook bites deep and firm, Mother...' Molly said with a sleepy smile.

Celia ran her hands down Molly's body. 'My, such wonderful firm duckies you have now, Molly, and what long beautiful legs. I can see why this Mr Raven is so attracted. And even if he gets away from you by some ill luck, just think what a fortune those physical treasures of yours could make you here in my house.'

Molly yawned tiredly. 'Yes, Mother. But I would rather that they be my fortune on stage, than the subject of constant abuse in your house...'

Celia seemed disappointed with that remark. 'Then I suppose your wishes must take precedence over mine, as ever. Perhaps you are right, though. Good night, dear,' she said, kissing Molly's cheek softly.

CHAPTER 11

Friday, 16th December 1664

On Friday morning, Raven went to the King's theatre again, assured in his own mind at least that the wish to see Molly Titchen again played no part in that decision whatsoever, and that he was here merely to pursue some further enquiries into the matter of the dead actresses.

The theatre was empty apart from the actor's company who were in the middle of their usual morning's rehearsal. Raven sat on one of the green baize-covered benches that sloped gently back from the stage, where Sir Thomas Killigrew had graciously consented to talk to him about the deaths of Anne Carey and Sarah Lusted.

Killigrew still had half his eye on the rehearsal continuing on stage, though, and seemed remarkably uninterested in the fact that two of his actresses were now dead within a week, apart from the obvious problem of replacing them somehow with equally gifted young women. 'Surely the death of Anne Carey was merely a distressing accident, sir,' he said. 'While you told me yourself, as I recall, that Mistress Lusted died of some innate heart defect.'

Raven sighed. 'That is what I thought at the time, sir. It seemed the most likely explanation. Yet the death of this second actress obliges us to dig deeper and perhaps suspect darker forces at work.'

Sir Thomas shook his head in violent disagreement as the players on stage finished their scene. 'Who would possibly have cause to murder these sweet young actresses, sir? No, Mr Raven, I cannot accept such bleak suspicions. I saw with my own eyes that Anne Carey struck her head when falling off the stage under your impact. I perceive your reasons for saying what you do. You perhaps feel the finger of guilt at your part in her death – however unintentional it was. She must have been more severely injured by the fall than you suspected, that is all – perhaps an important blood vessel ruptured inside her head and consigned poor Anne to an early grave. You must not blame yourself, sir, but should take pride in the fact that you saved the King by your act of bravery. It was the lesser of two evils that Anne died in place of the King, and I take pride – as I am sure she would too, if she were still here - that her death may have enabled the King to live…'

Raven could hardly blame Killigrew for taking this stance, of course. Perhaps Sir Thomas even believed this complacent view of events, which also coincidentally made his life much simpler than the possibility of his actresses being murdered. If it had not been for that mysterious man who had called the page Thomas Creed away from Anne Carey's bedside, then Raven's own suspicions would have been much lessened. And it was only Anne Carey's death that had truly renewed his suspicions over the circumstances of Sarah Lusted's death, rather than Molly's continued doubts on the same score.

Raven became aware that a young lady was approaching them from the side of the pits. Killigrew stood up to welcome the lady, then introduced her to Raven as Mistress Mary Pettican.

Mistress Pettican gave Raven a pretty curtsey. 'I am pleased to make your acquaintance, sir.'

Seen up close, Mary Pettican was not quite as beautiful as Raven remembered her from the stage, despite her raven hair and her clear skin. There was a coldness in her eyes, and a sharpness to her chin that spoiled the perfection of her image. Raven remembered her as the lusty young widow in Etherege's play *Love in a Tub,* and as the silly Countess Olivia in *Twelfth Night*, but in her present mood she reminded him more of when she had played the evil Lady Macbeth in a recent production here with such malevolent authority.

'May I speak with you privately, Sir Thomas?' she requested, with an apologetic glance in Raven's direction.

They went away into a quiet corner together for five minutes. Raven could not hear any of the details of their whispered conversation, but clearly it was an ill-tempered one - on Mistress Pettican's side at least.

Killigrew eventually returned to Raven's bench and sat down beside him. 'My apologies for that interruption, good sir. Mistress Pettican is a little out of sorts because I have given Molly her part in the play this afternoon.'

Raven suddenly realized that the play being rehearsed was the same one as he had watched yesterday: Mr Dryden's play, *The Rival Ladies*. This was confirmed when Molly appeared on stage dressed in the page's costume that Mary Pettican had worn yesterday, followed by Jane Golightly in similar garb.

'Molly did very well yesterday in a small part,' Killigrew explained, 'so I wanted to see how she would look in breeches as one of the main rival ladies. These are two women disguised as pages pursuing the same man...'

'Yes, I saw the performance yesterday,' Raven interjected.

Killigrew smiled. 'Ah, then you know well what a success Molly was.'

Molly took no visible note of Raven's presence in the pits and went straight into her scene with Jane Golightly.

Raven watched her performance with pleasure, and could not help but compare it mentally with Mary Pettican's from last evening. On the whole he thought Molly's better - more charm, more vivacity – even slightly better diction, surprisingly.

Sir Thomas too was enthusiastic as he whispered asides in Raven's direction. 'That girl is a prodigious talent, Mr Raven. Quite unexpected too in one so young, and of such lowly birth. She truly does possess an exceptional memory for lines, and seems to be able to slip in and out of character at will. I am sure that if I asked her to play a doddery old man with a limp, she would take a passable stab at it, such is her talent for mimicry and her understanding of human behaviour. I hardly wish to say this but the deaths of Sarah and Anne have provided one unexpected beneficial effect for the company, in bringing Molly to the fore. To think...I might never have given Molly her chance but for those sad occurrences...'

Raven was left to reflect on that uncomfortable truth for a moment. Finally he said, 'Mistress Golightly also plays convincingly in a male guise.'

Killigrew nodded with a knowing look. 'Ay, *very* convincingly.' He gave a leery smile. 'Yet Molly looks much better in breeches than Jane, does she not? I knew she would, of course,' he stated with satisfaction. 'Those legs of hers will certainly make me a fresh fortune in time...

*

Molly finished her scene with Jane with relief. She had not expected Mr Raven to be here again this morning, and she found his presence at rehearsals acutely disconcerting for some reason.

What were Mr Raven and Sir Thomas discussing so intently? she wondered.

Offstage, Molly felt someone touch her back softly, and turned to find her orange seller friend Nell standing there, her eyes sparkling with pleasure.

'Molly, I have not had the opportunity to congratulate you yet for gaining admittance to the company,' Nell said, taking her hand and clasping it warmly. ''Tis a wonderful thing!' Nell was apparently delighted to find Molly there by accident and have the chance to pass on her congratulations, even though she was clearly envious of Molly's recent elevation to actress in the company. That envy had led to a certain degree of coolness and ill temper on Nell's side yesterday whenever Molly had happened to run into her in the King's house. But now, for whatever reason, Nell's good opinion of Molly seemed to have been restored, and she was all amiability.

Molly kissed her cheek in return. 'Thank you kindly, Nell.'

Nell blinked innocently as she asked a leading question. 'And was the audition with Sir Thomas a very severe and penetrating one? They say he has a most fearsome horn for such an old gentleman.'

Molly laughed. 'Nay, not too fearsome. I am sure he would be most willing to audition you too, Nell, if you ask him.'

'Then I certainly shall –' Nell grinned cheekily - 'but perhaps I must wait a week or so for a more propitious time of the month.'

Nell did certainly have the personality and ambition to become an actress herself, Molly knew, as well as the looks – a pretty oval face, entrancingly clear skin, hazel eyes, thick brown eyebrows and tawny hair. She had a petite turned-up nose too, and a curvaceous figure, and most especially, a pair of long shapely legs that would look extremely fine in tight breeches. Her main disadvantage was that she was near illiterate at present, which would make it difficult for her to read and to learn lines. Molly was sure however that the ever generous Sir Thomas would find it in his heart to overlook those shortcomings, given her many other advantages.

Nell's mother Helena was a bawdyhouse-keeper too, so she and Molly had more in common than merely their wish to become famous actresses. Yet Celia was a very ladylike woman by comparison with Helena Gwyn, who was frankly a drunken pipe-smoking, quarrelsome harpy. So Molly had to admit that her childhood had been much easier than Nell's because of this essential difference in the characters of the two women who had brought them up. Nell had told Molly several wildly different stories about who her father might be, varying from a common blacksmith to the Earl of Berkshire (although Molly tended to believe the former as being far more likely.)

'Perhaps you would help me sometime with my reading, Molly,' Nell suggested hopefully. 'I can hear the words well enough, but I have some trouble lifting them off the page with my eyes alone.'

Molly smiled. 'Of course I shall help you, Nelly…'

*

A little later, it was Jane Golightly who came and sat beside Molly offstage as they waited to start the next scene. 'That last scene was very good, Molly. I marvel at your ability to memorize lines so quickly. I have done this play three times already, yet still need prompts from time to time, such is the speed of the dialogue, and the many naughty puns.'

Molly was hardly listening to her, her mind still dwelling on Mr Raven's unexpected presence here. While she was happy enough to see him, she hoped that he was not passing on to Sir Thomas any of her suspicions of her fellow members of the cast. That would finish her acting career before it had even started…

Thoughts of Mr Raven and her long discussion with him last night did however prompt a question in Molly's mind. 'You told me once that you were an orphan, Jane.'

Jane blinked slowly. ''Tis true enough. I never knew my father. And my mother died when I was fifteen.'

Molly nodded. 'Then you were not truly an orphan since you were already full-grown before your mother passed away. I on the other hand lost my real parents in a house fire when I was but a babe.'

Jane seemed putout by Molly's statement. 'Then 'tis true that your case was perhaps sadder than mine, although my situation was melancholy enough, believe me. My mother was a strange creature who gave me little in the way of true affection…'

Molly decided that it might be better to leave this delicate subject of Jane's childhood, which clearly still caused her much pain. Instead she indicated the direction of the pits with a subtle turn of her head. 'Do you happen to know that gentleman who is sitting in front of the stage talking to Sir Thomas today, by any chance?'

Jane followed the direction she had indicated and frowned slightly. 'Nay, I think not.'

Molly thought her reply a little too quick. 'Then 'tis strange, because I thought I saw you talk with him at length on Wednesday at the palace.'

Jane was flustered. 'Ah, is that the same gentleman I spoke to then?'

Molly narrowed her eyes disbelievingly. 'I believe it is.'

'Then you could be right. But he merely complimented me on my performance as Viola, nothing more. I cannot recall his name.'

Molly was sceptical of that statement, sure that Jane had her eyes firmly set on Mr Raven for herself. 'Then I can enlighten you, Jane. I believe his name is Henry Raven…'

*

Raven was leaving the theatre by the stage door when Jane Golightly appeared suddenly at his side from a darkened corner. She was still dressed in her costume as a page, yet contrived nevertheless to look more female than male. Whatever reproductive organs nature had conferred on her, Raven could not think of her as a man no matter how vainly he tried.

Raven bowed uncomfortably. 'Good day, Mistress.' He dropped his voice to a whisper. 'Yet it seems you are in the guise of Master Goodricke again.'

'That is no guise, sir, as I told you. I trust it does not confuse your feelings about me too much, sir.'

In truth, Raven's feelings about this enigmatic creature were intensely confused.

'May I ask what you and Sir Thomas were talking of earlier, Mr Raven?' she asked.

'It was naught to do with you, believe me,' Raven said quickly.

'I am glad of that, sir. You did promise to keep my secret, and I trust you are a man of your word.'

'I am indeed,' Raven promised. 'Now if you will forgive me, I must take my leave.' With that Raven made quickly for the door, suddenly anxious to be away from this puzzling person.

Jane Golightly or John Goodricke? Whoever this person was, whether male or female, she aroused in him strange and unfathomable emotions...

*

Still mulling over the contradictions of the mysterious Jane Golightly, Raven walked from Bridges Street to the Strand. The snow had stopped falling for a few hours in the morning, and the sky had cleared to an unsullied cerulean canopy, yet the cold was as fearsome as ever. The entire population of London now seemed to consist of a vast thronging army of people with pickled red noses and pinched white cheeks, nursing violent sneezes, hacking coughs and chilblains the size of bunions. The bright sun, reflecting off the dazzling snow and ice underfoot, contrived to light faces in an unfamiliar way, so that the craftsmen and journeymen and ragged children on the street, the fops and rakes in their sedan chairs, and the silk-gowned ladies rushing by in their carriages, all seemed to wear the same strange unearthly glow.

Raven had an appointment at noon with one of his shipping agents at the Royal Exchange so, on reaching the Strand, set off briskly eastwards, as he had been much longer at the King's theatre than he intended. He wondered whether he should have spoken to Molly while he was at the theatre – she had complained of his inattention to her at the palace on Wednesday, after all, and he had no wish to appear deliberately aloof and unfriendly with her. Yet Raven thought that his growing liking for Molly was a thing perhaps better kept to himself for the moment, and perhaps even from Molly herself. He knew not where this relationship with Molly might be headed, but in the meantime he was finding her to be a most entertaining and sprightly girl to be with, as well as one who stirred in him unusually erotic and lustful thoughts for such a normally sober man...

In twenty minutes of hard walking Raven had reached Ludgate Hill, and was about to turn northwards at St Paul's for Paternoster Row and Cheapside, when he espied a tall figure ahead of him that he vaguely recognized. In fact it was the man's extreme height that first attracted

Raven's attention and then forced his eventual recognition of the gentleman in question. It seemed that Mr James Blight was alone and on foot like himself, which Raven thought was unusual behaviour for such a distinguished member of the King's household, who might be expected to travel any distance only by carriage or sedan chair.

Raven recalled that he had mentioned Blight's name to Mawdsley yesterday in passing as a possible suspect for the business of the falling chandelier at Whitehall Palace. But he had made this comment this only because of the particular circumstances of Mr Blight being in charge of the preparations for the play in the Great Hall, and certainly not because he knew anything disreputable against the man. Based on their conversation on Tuesday at Gresham College, Mr Blight was certainly an odd gentleman but he was in all probability also a true and loyal servant of the King, even if his Puritan demeanour made him stand out noticeably in that colourful court of ambitious scheming politicians and decadent rakes.

Raven could see from the clock on the tower of St Paul's that he was already a full half hour late for his appointment at the Royal Exchange, so decided on reflection - knowing that his shipping agent, Mr Vine, was a busy and impatient man who was unlikely to have waited at the Exchange for him - that it might be a more fruitful use of his afternoon to follow Mr James Blight instead and see where this gentlemen was walking so purposefully...

*

Mr Blight followed Watling Street through the city, then Canning Street, and then finally turned right at Fish Street where he headed down the steep hill to London Bridge.

Since Blight was distinguished by both his black Puritan garb and his great height, Raven found him as easy to follow as an injured crow in the snow. Blight seemed to have no suspicions that he might be under observation, and never turned his head even once to look behind him. In fact he seemed so heavily preoccupied with his own thoughts that Raven thought that a musket could have been discharged right next to him and yet the man would still not have deigned to twist his neck to inquire as to the cause of the metal ball whistling by his lowered head.

Blight crossed London Bridge without pausing even to look into any of the shops and taverns on the way. It seemed Blight was intending to visit Southwark so Raven wondered whether he was perhaps a frequenter of the Bear Garden with its shows of cock-fighting, dog-fighting and bear and bull baiting. Or perhaps, since he was a widower according to Mawdsley, it was the stews that attracted him...

Yet Raven doubted that – there were bawdy houses much closer to Whitehall than the dirty back lanes of Southwark, after all, and of a much more pleasing quality too than the miserable pox-filled stews of Bankside. And if Blight merely wanted a woman, there was no doubt an army of buxom ladies willing to come to Whitehall Palace to satisfy his male desires, should he command them. Mawdsley had told Raven that the apartments of Whitehall were awash with low women at night, who seemed to come and go at will to satisfy the whims of the mostly male household.

As Blight headed into the maze of alleyways behind the Bear Garden, Raven was sure that he must have some definite destination in mind, and that his purpose here must be a dubious one to have brought him to such an unsavoury place. Blight reached a stinking side street called Rose Petal Lane from the sign, and Raven began to think that he might have been wrong in his surmise about him, because this was clearly a sinful neighbourhood and one even worse in appearance than Rope Lane in Whetstone Park. Raven had never seen so many miserable pinched faces as the whores and painted doxies who peered out into the alleyway from their miserable hovels, hoping to find custom on this dismal afternoon.

Blight stopped at a house with a black door and tall Dutch gables, which was a more substantial property than the leaning and patched hovels on either side, but no more welcoming in appearance, with iced-up windows, worn brickwork and a marked air of squalor. The building was such a poor and stinking hole that Raven could scarcely believe that this was really Blight's intended destination.

Yet Blight entered the house immediately, not even knocking at the door, but merely pushing the black door open on noisy rusted hinges, which familiarity suggested that he might be a regular visitor here. Raven caught a glimpse of a plain wooden staircase leading upwards before Blight closed the door behind him...

*

Blight called out to warn Ingledew of his arrival and then ascended the staircase with heavy and unwilling feet.

He had his sword with him, and was seriously considering using it on Ingledew as the only way to escape from this nightmare.

He had thought over what he had seen in this room four days ago, and had convinced himself by now that Ingledew had no special occult powers, merely possessing the strength of a raging madman, and probably also having a very good network of spies and informers to support him. This renewed conviction that Ingledew was an ordinary mortal after all had emboldened Blight to consider running him through with hardened steel in order to shut his mouth permanently. Ingledew's strength would be of no use to him with twelve inches of cold steel sliced through his heart. In truth it would be a blessing to dispatch the man from his now dreadful life, Blight told himself, given that the pitiful scarred wretch was half-mad, and but a foul shadow of the noble soldier and handsome Englishman he had once been.

As on his first visit, Blight found that there was scarce any light on the staircase, but the light of a candle on the first floor beckoned him on again. On the landing he found the same open door and stepped hesitantly over the threshold.

A fire burned in the same hearth as before, yet still this miserable room seemed frozen like an ice cavern.

Ingledew stood by the fire, wearing his frightening mask. But he took it off at once when Blight entered the chamber.

Ingledew motioned him to take a seat by the fire, but Blight wanted to get this over with quickly, and decided it would be much easier to run the man through from a standing position.

'Why are you here today, James?' Ingledew asked peremptorily. 'I did not request a meeting with you. I told you to await my next instruction by messenger at the palace.'

Blight's voice sounded hoarse and strange even to himself, and his heart was beating wildly beneath his cloak. 'Simon, tell me. Did you arrange for that incident in the Great Hall at Whitehall two days ago?'

'Incident?'

Blight was not fooled by the pretence of surprise in Ingledew's voice. 'I mean causing that chandelier to crash down on the assembly, and nearly killing the King…'

Ingledew finally nodded impassively. 'Ah, that incident! Yes, I may have had something to do with it…'

Blight took the reply as a full confirmation of his suspicions. 'How did you contrive to make that chandelier fall? I checked the ropes myself just before, and the knots were all secure.'

Ingledew grunted. 'I have no need to tell you all my secrets, James. 'Tis enough for you to know that I have many people to do my bidding. I have also told you that no power on earth can stop me in my righteous quest against this papist King, yet it seems you choose not to believe me.'

Suddenly, before Blight could even move to resist, Ingledew had shot across the room at bewildering speed and engaged Blight's head in a painful arm hold. Blight was again powerless to resist; this time it felt as if his head had been gripped in an immense vice, and that the bones of his skull might splinter at any moment. Without relaxing his hold with his right arm, Ingledew used his left hand to press the blade of a vicious-looking knife against Blight's throat, drawing a line of blood with the point of the blade. 'Do you really believe me so stupid as to fail to comprehend your intentions in coming here like this, James?' he hissed. 'Yet I fear that you are no longer the well-formed soldier of your youth, so please abandon this foolish notion of inflicting violence against me. With that capon-lined belly of yours, you are so slow and cumbersome that you would not get within a yard of me before I slit your throat.'

Ingledew was so confident in his abilities to physically outwit Blight that he did not even attempt to disarm his former friend but simply stepped away from him contemptuously, and even turned his back on him deliberately.

Blight felt humiliated by this disdainful dismissal but had no choice but to accede, given the truth of what Ingledew had said.

Ingledew kicked a nearby stool with his foot and slid it closer to the fire. 'Now, sit by the fire, James, and we shall drink a draught of Italian wine together like civilized men.'

Blight reluctantly sat on the offered stool by the fire and tamely accepted a pewter tankard of red wine from Ingledew.

In the stark glare from the fire, Ingledew's face looked even more dreadful today than Blight remembered from his last visit, and he was filled with loathing and disgust for this vile monster that his friend had turned into. Yet even though he was sore afraid of the man, Blight still tried to put up a token show of resistance to his will. He took a long drink of the red wine, which steadied his nerves a little. 'Despite all these powers of which you boast, Simon, you still failed miserably in your first attempt to kill the King.'

Ingledew sneered at him in return. 'If that is your judgement, then you misunderstand me abysmally, James. I did not want to kill the King in such a pathetic manner as that. This trivial matter of the falling chandelier is merely a warning salvo in the game, a demonstration to our decadent monarch that I can kill him wherever and whenever I like. It would truly have been an embarrassment to kill the King in such a facile and demeaning manner as that. When the King does die, I want the whole of Europe to witness his inglorious demise and to be appalled by the manner of his dying. Men will write about this moment for a thousand years to come, and my name will ring through the annals of English history as the man who freed this country from a tyrant.'

He is a madman, Blight thought dismally. *The pox did destroy his mind as well as his face. There can be no doubt of it now...*

'Did you kill that actress from the King's company too?' Blight asked, for want of something to say.

Ingledew sipped his own wine. 'I did not. I have no interest in actresses – vain, stupid creatures.'

Blight did not believe this mild protestation of innocence. 'Then who did kill her, if not you or one of your agents?'

Ingledew reflected. 'Tell me who was in the audience in the Great Hall that night, and perhaps that might inform me.'

Blight believed this request to be a deceiving one on Ingledew's part, but nevertheless went through all the names he could remember, as he tried to recover his equanimity. Many of the guests he did not know by name, though. He had got to the names of Mawdsley and his companions when Ingledew interrupted. 'Ah, yes. This man Raven was the man who actually saved the King's life.'

'Yes.'

Ingledew nursed his goblet complacently. 'Then I should thank him. It would have been most unfortunate if the chandelier had actually killed the King and destroyed all my coming pleasure at the deed. It was certainly not what was intended.'

'And yet you still deny killing the woman, Mistress Carey?'

'I do. And thou shouldst learn to have more faith in my word, James. But I believe I can surmise who might have murdered that actress, if not their reasons.'

Blight was sceptical. 'What reasons could anyone have to murder an actress? Who would do such a thing?'

Ingledew smiled. 'That must remain my secret for the present, James. The knowledge might be a useful tool to me in extracting cooperation for my own plot. I would not want you to spread this knowledge abroad without my permission.'

As on his last visit, Blight began to feel overpowered again by the malevolent atmosphere of this room. His head was spinning in a most unpleasant way from the effects of the strong wine, and his stomach threatened to heave involuntarily. There seemed almost to be a subtle miasma of evil rising from the floorboards of this dark chamber, and the suspicion of even worse things lurking in the corner shadows - nameless and inhuman things...

Ingledew's scarred face had taken on an even more terrible and inhuman aspect as he said, 'Pay heed to this, James if you want to live. I will tolerate no further disloyalty from you. You will do my will without question in the future, else you will pay a terrible price for your perfidy. Is that fully understood...?'

CHAPTER 12

Friday, 16th December 1664

Raven had waited for a long time in the cold and stink of the alleyway for Blight to reappear. It seemed to have been the best part of an hour since Blight had gone inside that sinister black door, he thought, and this was soon confirmed to him by the sounds of the tower clock of St Mary-over-the-water striking two o'clock.

He certainly had not expected Blight's visit to this dismal place to last so long otherwise he would not have countenanced this simple plan to wait for Blight to reappear, and might instead have forced his way immediately into that miserable house to investigate what went on there. Yet the longer Raven waited, the less he felt like doing anything impetuous that would warn Blight that he was under suspicion...

Raven's vigil in the alleyway had prompted much curiosity from the whores in the house three doors down from the black door, who did their best to tempt him across their own uninviting threshold with flashes of white arse and pink tit. Yet Raven had stuck manfully to his unrewarding task so far. Even the jeers of the local ragged children, who begged incessantly from him but were equally quick to show him their own bare backsides in mockery when he failed to deliver sufficient coins, did not distract him from his purpose.

It seemed likely now that Mr Blight intended to stay in that miserable hovel all afternoon, so Raven, frozen to the bone and with almost no feeling left in his feet, finally contemplated abandoning his self-appointed quest. In fact he was just about to do exactly that, and to escape from the continued pestering attention of the women and the local feral children, when he heard the sounds of someone leaving the house by the black door, as evinced by the clatter of noisy footsteps coming hurriedly down the staircase inside. Raven hastily retreated further down the lane and stepped back out of sight into the narrow gap between two hovels.

Peering around the corner from his hiding place, Raven saw Blight leaving that miserable house almost at a gallop. In fact he seemed in such a veritable panic to get away from that grim building that he heeded not how he slipped and stumbled on the icy cobbles, but went even faster and more recklessly if anything. His erratic skidding progress would have been a comical thing to observe but for the expression on his face, which precluded any possibility of amusement at the sight. The same filthy boys and girls who had mobbed Raven now followed Blight and repeated their unseemly begging on him, but got naught for their efforts. Instead, all half-dozen of them leaped back in fright when they glimpsed Blight's face.

Raven could not blame these street urchins for their sudden scattering in alarm because the look on Blight's face as he snarled and spat at them was such as to cause nightmares to even a grown man. Raven did not believe that he had ever seen such a haunted look on a man's face before, with such staring eyes, and with the skin marked by such a dreadful bloodless colour, as if all the life had been simply drained out of his body in that evil house. It seemed almost as if Blight had looked into the fires of Hell itself in that house and seen the evidence of his own eternal damnation lying in wait for him...

Raven was minded to follow Blight to his next destination, but had a feeling that in his clearly shocked and distraught state, the man would merely scurry home to the shelter of his own apartments in Whitehall as fast as his feet could carry him. Something had happened inside that house with the black door to cause Blight this great terror - certainly he had not worn such a terrible expression when he had entered that house an hour ago - and therefore the house and its occupants seemed perhaps worthier of further investigation than Mr Blight himself.

Yet Raven decided to be circumspect and not to approach the black door directly just yet. Instead he went in search of a nearby tavern or inn where he hoped that he might pick up some useful gossip about the house and its occupants.

The nearest such public place was a considerable distance away, though - The Pope's Head in Bankside – so Raven was unsure that the regular patrons of this busy coaching inn would have much information about the occupants of Rose Petal Lane.

Yet he need not have worried. He had not been in the taproom long, after ordering a quart of ale from the buxom young maidservant Peg, than he got into conversation with three locals. These men were loquacious enough as it was, but became even more so when Raven offered to share his ale with them. These three men had resplendently biblical names - Isaac, Hezekiah and Daniel – and resplendently biblical beards to match, yet their habits and conversation were hardly biblical, being peppered with profanities and bawdy humour.

After much talk of the bitter weather, of the coming war with the Dutch, and even surprisingly of the comet, which all these three gentlemen had seen with their own keen eyes, Raven finally brought the subject around to the one that interested him most at present. 'I have just visited one of the bawdy houses in Rose Petal Lane...'

Daniel, who was an old bearded seaman with a scrap of tarred pigtail and a swollen red nose that suggested regular losing bouts with the Dutch gin bottle, sniggered. 'Then, sir, I shall not sit so close, for fear of what I might catch from you...'

Raven smiled frostily but did not take offence. '...And coming out, I heard such a commotion as would rouse the dead, from a house three doors down. A large house with a black door that has seen better times...'

'I've seen better times too, come to think of it,' Isaac interrupted, warming his palms at the blazing log fire. This was a younger man than Daniel but with the gnarled hands of a carpenter.

Raven ignored this distracting comment. 'Who lives in that house to make such an ungodly commotion, do you think?'

Hezekiah, an old coachman with wild grey hair that seemed to support much crawling life of its own, spat a stream of dirty brown spume into a spittoon. 'I know the house you mean. And as for who lives there, why it be the Devil himself.'

The old seaman Daniel agreed, although such a hardened man did not look the type to be afraid of anything on God's earth. ''Tis true. The children around there are all afeared of him...'

Raven remembered the wild children in Rose Petal Lane. 'I did not notice much fear in them.'

'Oh, that is mere bravado,' Isaac muttered. 'They run quick enough when the Devil shows his face.'

Hezekiah, who seemed the natural leader of this group of intoxicated philosophers, butted in. 'But he does not show his face, does he, Isaac? At least I have never seen it in the few months he has been here. He wears a mask, sir - a black mask over the whole of his face,' he explained to Raven.

Raven nodded in understanding. 'Perhaps he is merely a man returning from distant lands who has been disfigured by the Pox, and not the Devil at all?'

Isaac weighed that notion up. 'Well, he could be poxed, of course. There's plenty around here who are. But I think this man has some even worse affliction than that...'

The maidservant Peg had returned to collect some empty tankards, and had overheard most of the latter part of this conversation. She was a pretty if knowing creature, Raven thought, who seemed, like Molly Titchen, well capable of taking care of herself, even in a rough Bankside coaching inn. 'That man *is* the Devil, truly,' she declared to Raven. 'I heard from my friend Agnes that one of our local thieving rascals broke into that house recently to see what he could get. Only he got a lot more than he bargained for...'

'What would attract a thief to such a filthy place? Raven asked her curiously.

Peg gave him a knowing smile in return. 'Ah, sir, it seems that there were many deliveries to the back of that house – barrels of wine and other goods – so it seemed likely this Devil's basement cellar was stocked with good things, despite the decrepit state of the house from the outside. Yet when this young thieving rogue came out of that house, he was empty-handed and running for his life. My friend Agnes said that his hair was turned snow white and that he had aged forty years in as many minutes. Of course I never seed this myself, but Agnes knows this man well enough. No, this devil man is truly evil. They say he can cast spells and do things that would turn a virgin to stone.'

'I doubt that should worry you, then, Peg,' Isaac said sarcastically, for which he received a sharp slap on the face from Peg in return, although in a good-humoured fashion rather than administered with any true venom.

Raven pretended to be impressed by these wild stories. 'Do any of you know this evil man's name?'

Hezekiah shifted his old bones on his stool. 'He is known by the name of Beelzebub, or so the local children call him anyway...'

*

Raven was not a man susceptible to gossip and rumour, yet the story of the young thief with his hair turned instantly to white did give him some pause for thought. And the way Mr James Blight had looked when leaving that same house in a near panic did add some extra credence to Peg the barmaid's unsettling story.

Yet dusk was falling rapidly on this bleak mid-winter afternoon, and Raven did not want to traipse all the way back to St Martin's Lane without something to show for his efforts today.

With the fall of dusk, Rose Petal Lane was quiet at least, with all the wild children finally departed to their rough sleeping places. No feather beds and roaring fires to tide those untamed children through the night, he guessed, but scraps of food, and miserable spaces on cold kitchen floors, if they were lucky. Even the whores had retreated inside to get away from the cold, or perhaps they had finally lured some passing trade into their warm if diseased clutches.

Raven looked up at the forbidding façade of the house with the black door. He could see what looked like a candle shining through the window on the first floor of the house, but otherwise there was no sign of life – not a sound from within, not even the murmur of a voice or the creak of a loose floorboard.

Logic told him that he should approach this problem indirectly and try and break in from the back to discover what went on in this mysterious house. Yet, even if he overlooked the story of the young thief with his hair turned instantly to white, the penalty for burglary was hanging. And while Raven doubted that he would suffer such a harsh penalty if he was caught in this house and accused of such a crime, he decided that directness was perhaps the best solution in this case after all.

Therefore he knocked loudly and confidently on the black door, but to no avail at all. The heavy silence from within persisted, as stubborn and penetrating as the silence of a graveyard.

Three subsequent knocks, each louder than the one before, did not elicit a response from within either, so Raven then tried simply pushing the door open. The hinges showed some initial resistance to his fists yet the door was not barred or bolted on the inside and did open easily enough in the end when he put his shoulder forcefully to it. Obviously the man inside believed that his devilish reputation was quite sufficient by itself to discourage unwanted visitors.

Raven saw a flight of bare wooden steps leading upwards, which encouraged him to continue, despite the murky gloom inside the house. He put a careful foot on the first step, waited for a second to listen for any response, then took a further step. By such wary and tentative steps did he find his way unchallenged to the first floor landing, where an open doorway provided further encouragement to continue his slow and measured progress.

Raven entered a room that was as cold as a grave, despite the embers of a fire in the hearth. A solitary candle burned fitfully on the window ledge. A man stood by the dying fire and turned slowly towards Raven on hearing him enter the room, to reveal a sinister masked face. Raven could not restrain a gasp of surprise at this forbidding sight, even though he had been warned what to expect. Perhaps he should not have been so quick to disbelieve and mock the stories of Daniel, Isaac and Hezekiah – or even of the maid Peg…

Raven would have liked to turn and make a hasty exit at this point, but something made him hold his nerve in the face of this giant sinister figure. The man seemed of immense height in the flickering shadows, perhaps approaching six and a half feet tall.

The man did not attempt to explain his sinister masked appearance, but said merely, 'What do you want here, sir? What is your business?' It was an educated voice, Raven could tell, if breathless in tone. But whether the breathless quality in his voice was natural, or induced by exertion or excitement, was impossible to say.

'Excuse me, sir, I look for the home of a man called Hooke.' Raven used the name of his friend from the Royal Society as a convenient falsehood. 'Forgive me, I must have erred in my directions and come to entirely the wrong house.'

'There is certainly no man called Hooke here,' the masked man said coldly.

'Then I beg your pardon for my unwarranted intrusion...' Raven took the opportunity in the long pause that followed this apology to glance quickly around the room. Yet there was nothing here to give any clue as to the identity of this man: bare floor boards, a few pieces of rough-hewn furniture, ice crystals encrusted on the outside of the window like salt, that single sputtering candle. Even with his expression hidden from sight behind that immovable mask – or perhaps because of it - the giant's unsettling presence did excite some fearful thoughts in Henry Raven.

Raven was quietly convinced by now that this man must indeed be the same individual who had confronted Lady Castlemaine in St James's Park, and then threatened the King's life. He began to think of ways in which he could possibly restrain this giant, and perhaps bring him bound to Whitehall to face the justice of the King, but it would not be easy with such a large and powerful man. Raven began to feel for the handle of his sword – perhaps the threat of force would be enough to pacify this man and make him pliable to his will...

Yet in truth he doubted his ability to arrest this giant of a man without help. Better to beat a safe retreat, and to return with reinforcements to take this man safely into the King's custody.

Raven began to back away with a bow, when the man made a comment that brought him to a sudden halt again.

'Would that be Mr *Robert* Hooke you wished to see, Mr Raven...?'

Raven was so astonished that this man should already know his name that he could say nothing rational in response.

The man continued speaking with scarcely a pause, moving closer as he did. 'Yet ye must truly be lost if you mistook this place for Gresham College...'

Raven was not able to utter a sensible reply before the man suddenly flew at him in a great and violent rage. The man unleashed a great scything blow at him with an iron poker that had been concealed at his side. The head of the poker whistled through the air with such malevolent speed that all Raven saw was a blinding flash of movement before darkness engulfed him…

*

Raven groaned as he woke up, and found he was still in the same cold room. He had no comprehension of how long he had lain here insensible, yet he did not think it could be for more than a few minutes.

The masked man was gone, together with the lone candle, and Raven could only curse his ineptitude at letting this devil slip through his fingers. The man would not come here again of course; otherwise why should he leave him here alive to report this meeting?

Yet perhaps this was a sign that the man must still retain some semblance of humanity behind that sinister masked visage? After all, he had not slit his victim's throat before he left, something which he could easily have done.

Or it was simply that the man did not want the aggravation of the hue and cry that would inevitably follow a brutal murder? So far, the man had only made threats, after all. Even if he had been responsible for the falling chandelier in Whitehall Palace, no one had died directly from it…

Raven climbed painfully to his feet, and waited for the darkened room to stop spinning. His head did eventually clear a little, although the price for this clarity was that it felt as if it had been cleaved in two.

Yet he was anxious to be gone from this place, which still retained its sinister atmosphere even with that man gone from it…

Raven stopped in mid-step as he had an ominous thought. *Had the man really left the house at all?* Raven listened intently and thought he heard a sound from below – a strange sputtering sound that he could not identify, yet seemed unsettlingly familiar.

Perhaps the devil was merely downstairs in the cellar making preparations to leave, and it was simply that Raven – with his thick skull – had woken from his stupor more quickly than expected.

Raven decided to waste no further time in leaving, but nevertheless was forced to move carefully because of the penetrating darkness, and because of his suspicions that he was not alone in this house after all.

Feeling his way out of the doorway and then down the staircase, one step at a time, Raven realized that the sound he had thought he heard must be real, for it was growing ever louder here.

He moved on downwards, anxiety making his head ache even worse, with the increased blood flowing through it.

Then his foot snagged on something on the stairs and he bent down to examine it. His wandering hands eventually found a line of thread or wire.

Then, with panic rising in his throat, Raven realized where he had heard that distinctive sound before.

It was the sound of a fuse burning – *the type of fuse used to fire a cannon...*

Then the staircase suddenly erupted beneath his feet with massive force, and he felt himself lifted from the ground like an autumn leaf in a black storm...

CHAPTER 13

Saturday, 17th December 1664

Molly was washing her face in a bowl of icy water when she heard a rush of feet on the narrow staircase up to her garret, and Celia burst breathlessly into her room.

'Your prospects must indeed be looking up, Molly. There are two fine gentlemen in the parlour downstairs waiting to see you.' Celia was clearly impressed with the improving social level of Molly's acquaintances since being elevated to the role of actress, but seemed less impressed with her tardiness, and with her general unladylike appearance first thing in the morning, inspecting her frankly with a critical stare.

Molly glared at her in return. 'What do these gentlemen want with me?' she demanded ungraciously.

Celia continued her critical examination of Molly's pinched white face and goose-pimpled arms, which even Molly was prepared to concede did not look too enticing at this time of the day. 'Truly I know not,' Celia said absently. 'They did not see fit to confide in me.'

'Have you secretly arranged this visit with some ulterior motive in mind, Mother? I tell you that I am not for sale,' Molly added suspiciously, as she shivered half-naked over her washing bowl.

'I am entirely innocent in this matter,' Celia declared huffily. 'I have no comprehension what these gentlemen want with you, but I suggest it will do you no harm to find out. Come, Molly, 'tis nearly light already, and you are not even decent yet,' she complained.

'Oh, I am not decent enough even for a bawdy house, am I not? I do not have to be at the theatre until ten o'clock for rehearsals, therefore I shall dress as I please at this time of day, Mother.' Molly yawned heavily as she regarded her own image in the sliver of polished metal fixed to the wall that served as her mirror. 'And especially when most others in this house of yours do not stir their bodies at all before noon.'

'But then they do keep unsociably late hours, and work very hard,' Celia rejoined tartly.

Molly eyed her balefully. 'I work diligently at my trade too, Mother. What are the names of these two gentlemen below?' she demanded. 'Did you learn that much from them, at least?'

Celia simmered resentfully. 'I did. They are a Mr Mawdsley and a Mr Strange.'

Molly frowned on hearing those two unexpected names, one of which certainly meant something to her. 'Then tell them I shall be down in five minutes. I think perhaps I had better put on a dress first, though.'

Celia was relieved that she was finally taking the visit of these two handsome gentlemen more seriously. 'Yes, you certainly should, Molly. Wear the blue satin one I gave you yesterday as a gift. It has a neckline that shows off your sweet bubbies to admirable effect...'

*

Mr Mawdsley was extremely apologetic at disturbing Molly so early, which was gentlemanly behaviour that she appreciated. Yet she appreciated even more the fact that this young man was so handsome – nay, beautiful was the truer word! - as he stood crisply to attention in Celia's parlour, with his fine features lit to advantage by the chill grey snow light seeping through the parlour window from the cobbled lane outside. Molly was glad that she had forced Celia to leave the room, otherwise she knew that her mother would have been ogling this distinguished gentleman and his friend by now in a most shameless huswife fashion. 'Excuse us calling on you at this Godforsaken hour, Mistress,' Mr Mawdsley said again, repeating his apology for disturbing her for about the fourth time. 'You remember me, I trust?'

Molly nodded as she also took in with pleasure his substantial height, and the way his shoulder-length brown hair curled so strikingly over his rich lace collar. Those handsome curls and that chiselled jaw were indeed hard things for a girl to forget, even if the sad circumstances of their first face-to-face meeting had been a considerable distraction to her mind. 'I do remember you, sir. You are a friend of Mr Raven. I saw you at the theatre with him on the evening that my poor friend Sarah died. And I believe you were also in the audience at the palace on Wednesday to watch our performance of *Twelfth Night*. May I ask, sir, what you want with me? And how did you happen to know where to find me? 'Tis not common knowledge that I am living here.'

Mawdsley seemed hesitant to explain, and this long pause gave Molly further time to note his long velvet silver-buttoned coat, his Rhinegrave breeches decorated with ribbons and bows, his black silk stockings, and his silver-topped walking stick. Yet for all his sartorial style and French manners, he did not give the impression of being a fop and a wastrel.

'As for finding you, my friend here, Mr Strange, guessed where you might be staying. Mr Raven had made mention to him that you had changed your address of late - Mr Raven had some concerns for your safety in your previous abode, I believe, because of the unexplained deaths of two of your fellow actresses - and Mr Strange thought it most likely that you would come here to stay with Madam Hornett.'

Molly had no idea that Mr Raven had been discussing her situation with his gentlemen friends, and did not quite know whether to be happy or upset at being the subject of these gentlemen's gossip. On reflection, though, she resented the thought rather more than she appreciated it, particularly the fact that these gentlemen knew all too well that her adoptive mother ran an infamous bawdy house, and that she was here living with her. 'I am sure there is naught to Mr Raven's suspicions, sir,' she said hurriedly, still anxious that no word of her suspicions should get back to Sir Thomas Killigrew. 'But your friend did show some kind concern for my welfare, which I could not but be grateful for, even though I think the dangers exaggerated.'

Mr Strange now interrupted. Molly remembered him too, both from the theatre, and from the performance of *Twelfth Night* at the palace, although she had never spoken to him. If anything she thought him an even more decorative addition to this room than Mawdsley - tall, fair-haired and youthful, with a soft pink complexion that would be the envy of any woman. He dressed in a more sober and less expensive fashion than his friend Mawdsley, so Molly suspected that he might not perhaps be as wealthy as him, and certainly not as well-to-do as Mr Raven. 'Perhaps you can repay Mr Raven's kind concern for you with a similarly generous act in return,' Mr Strange said solemnly. 'We are very concerned for the safety of our friend...'

Molly felt the blood drain from her face at these ominous words. 'Has something happened to Mr Raven, sir? Is that what you have come to tell me?'

Mawdsley took up the lead again. 'We do not know what has become of Mr Raven,' he admitted. 'But we know that he never returned to his home last night, even though he was expected. His manservant came to Mr Strange's house in Bow Street to check on his whereabouts this morning – Mr Raven often stays there overnight, but not this time...'

Molly bit her lip. 'He is not here with me, if that is what you suggest, sir.'

Mawdsley shook his head wryly. 'I make no judgement of my friend, Molly, or of you. I only seek to find him because I am concerned for him...'

Strange interrupted again. 'Have you no intimation at all where he might have gone?'

Molly sank down slowly on the wooden bench seat by the fire, as her mind raced. 'None, sir. I have not seen Mr Raven since yesterday, sir. He was at the theatre before noon, but then left without speaking to me. I have no notion where he went after that...'

*

After Mr Mawdsley and his friend had left – both clearly genuinely worried for their friend Mr Raven – Celia came into the parlour and sat down opposite Molly, with a knowing look written plainly on her face. 'So what did those gentlemen want, Molly?'

Molly glanced up at her archly. 'You listened at the door, did you not? Was that not sufficient for you to hear everything you wished?'

Celia bridled at that. 'No, it was not. I attempted to listen, but those gentlemen, for all their immense size, both speak very soft.'

Molly was tempted to dissemble further but, worried too for Mr Raven's safety, did not have the heart at this moment for such a game. 'It seems Mr Raven has not been seen since noon yesterday. Those gentlemen are his friends, and are anxious over his safety.'

Celia tut-tutted. 'Oh dear, oh dear. That would be a great pity if Mr Raven has fallen victim to some mean footpad or villain, and is lying dead or injured in a gutter somewhere. What a waste of a young man's life that would be, and you clearly so close to landing him!' Celia sat back in her seat and became more philosophic in tone. 'Yet such a black cloud has a silver lining at least. His gentlemen friends are even more handsome than Mr Raven, and seem uncommonly interested in you themselves.'

Molly looked at her with annoyance. 'You advised me but two days ago to get my hooks deep into Mr Raven, as if he were the greatest prize in the world that I could ever expect to land.'

'That is true. But I had not seen his friends then,' Celia argued complacently.

Molly shook her head sadly. 'Mother, you are a fickle creature as ever, I see.'

'Ay, that is also true, But 'tis simply the way of the world,' Celia answered sharply. 'All we humans are fickle in our affections...'

*

Mawdsley and Strange walked back from Whetstone Park across Lincoln's Inn Fields, and from there took a four-horse carriage borrowed from the palace household to the Royal Exchange to see if there were any reports of Raven there.

There they soon learned from Raven's own shipping agent, Mr George Vine, that Raven had arranged an appointment with him at the Royal Exchange yesterday at noon, but had failed to appear. Normally Mr Raven was extremely punctilious about keeping appointments so Mr

Vine did wonder whether Mr Raven might be ill or otherwise indisposed.

Mawdsley and Strange were about to escape from the clamorous crowd of merchants and dealers in the main courtyard and return to the West End, not knowing where else to look for Raven for the present, when Mawdsley happened to overhear two merchants talking. His ears instantly registered that an unusual incident must have taken place close to the city.

'Excuse me, sir,' Mawdsley interrupted one of the merchants. 'Could I trouble you to repeat what you just said?'

The merchant, a well-fed individual in the wine trade, was content to share his knowledge. 'Did you not hear the explosion yourself, sir? It was truly a deafening noise, fit to burst the gates of hell itself...'

Strange pushed himself forward through the milling crowd to join Mawdsley. 'What has happened, sir?'

The merchant stroked his luxurious beard. 'Why, there has been a great explosion in Southwark last evening, in a street called Rose Petal Lane. Three houses are completely destroyed, and many people are supposedly dead, although they must mainly be whores in such a place of ill-repute. I wonder you did not know – I thought everyone in the city must have heard the uproar.'

Mawdsley shared a concerned look with Strange, who seemed equally worried that this explosion might have something to do with Henry's unexplained disappearance.

Mawdsley was not aware that his friend frequented the stews of Southwark, but he and Strange agreed that they must investigate at once.

In twenty minutes their carriage had carried them through the city and across London Bridge, the Thames now a solid vista of low white mist filled with jagged floes of ice that groaned and shifted against the stone piers of the bridge. Once on the south side of the Thames, the progress of the carriage became slower and slower due to the state of the roads. The lanes of Southwark leading to Rose Petal Lane eventually became so narrow and so obstructed with deep drifts of snow that the coachman was finally forced to stop in the street to the south of the Bear Garden and let his passengers walk from there.

The site of the explosion was however easy enough to locate from the crowds of the inquisitive and the poor who had come to gawp at someone else's distress. Mawdsley had never seen such a scene of devastation and carnage before, with three houses reduced to a large hole in the ground filled with brick rubble and broken timbers, and the buildings on either side of this cavern leaning at a most alarming angle that suggested imminent collapse too. Only the power of gunpowder could explain this level of destruction, Mawdsley thought, as he saw that the dwellings had been ripped apart as if they were made of paper, even down to their basement cellar walls.

There was so much confusion among the crowd of spectators - so much wailing and misery and anguished noise - that Mawdsley and Strange could at first find no one to give them any sensible account of what had happened here.

Eventually one passer-by – a toothless old crone of a woman, who must have been over fifty – did give some sensible answers to Mawdsley's urgent questions. 'Ten dead, so they say. Mainly women from the bawdy house next door.' The woman showed her gums in a leery smile. ''Tis my good luck that I am too old for the game of Venus now.'

'So, Mother, were there any survivors to say what truly happened?' asked Strange, with a rueful look at Mawdsley.

The woman reflected on that, her toothless old jaw adding extra emphasis to her pointed chin and protruding brow. 'Someone informed me that they did pull someone alive from the wreckage. A young gentleman, by all accounts, although terribly injured, they say. They took him to The Pope's Head coaching inn in Bankside. Perhaps he died later...'

Mawdsley and Strange thanked the old woman quickly, gave her thruppence for her pains, and took themselves quickly to that well-known coaching inn in Bankside, prepared for the worst.

The Pope's Head was a large coaching inn with several public rooms – taproom, parlour, coffee room - arranged around a cobbled coach yard. A double tier of bedroom galleries, with clumsy old wooden balustrades bordered three sides of the yard. Two coaches, covered in icicles, were standing under a sloping lean-to roof – the drivers, no doubt, awaiting fresh horses being brought from the stables to continue their journey to Dover and Rochester. Yet the yard was presently devoid of any human presence in this terrible cold, all of the drivers and their passengers having clearly withdrawn to the comfort of firesides inside. After a search through the public rooms, Mawdsley and Strange soon encountered the landlord, a middle-aged man of vast girth, and a complexion so ruddy that it seemed as if he had been staring into a red-hot fire these many hours.

When they explained their purpose to him, the landlord pointed with a melancholy finger up the stairs to a bedchamber on the first floor. 'Your Mr Raven is lying in state up there.'

Mawdsley and Strange ascended the stairs with a heavy heart, sure that all they would find in that chamber would be the mutilated body of their friend, laid out ready for burial. But instead, when they slowly pushed open the heavy oaken door, they found their friend dressed in a nightshirt and sitting up in a feathered bed, and being happily administered to by a buxom young maidservant, who was ladling soup generously into a bowl for him.

Raven's face was decorated with a few minor bruises, but for a man who had been found yesterday in a collapsed building, he looked remarkably healthy and content with life.

Mawdsley gave him a wry look before exclaiming, 'By God's blest mother, thou art all right, Henry...!'

*

'Ye must be the luckiest man in all creation, Henry!' Mawdsley observed yet again, after seeing how little his friend seemed to be hurt. In truth Raven had suffered much more hurt than he let on to his friends, despite the lack of evidence of it in his face. His body was considerably bruised and battered, yet somehow he had survived that gigantic explosion with no permanent injuries. The Lord God must indeed have been looking out for his welfare yesterday...

Peg the maidservant had left them alone by now, though she had clearly been reluctant to leave, and had smiled seductively at the two handsome young gentlemen in an attempt to be allowed to stay. Eventually, though, she had accepted with disappointment that her services were no longer needed for the present, and she had departed with the empty bowl of soup and her other ministering aids. Raven could see that her interest in him had instantly dimmed when his two handsome friends had arrived. It was a story that had often been repeated throughout his years of friendship with Mawdsley and Strange at Cambridge, and more latterly here in London. Quite unintentionally, those two were forever stealing away the attentions of his occasional female admirers. Yet Raven could still not hold the beauty of his friends against them when those same handsome faces also registered so much clear concern for his own welfare.

'Why did you send no word to us of what had happened, Henry?' Mawdsley complained, after his initial pleasure in finding his friend still alive had worn off a little.

Raven was forced to smile. 'I was truly in no condition to think clearly until this morning. And Peg the maidservant was most kind in her attentions to me...at least until you two arrived...' he added dryly.

After many more exclamations of joy from his friends at his miraculous escape from death, Raven began to tell his story. With the after effects of shock still inhibiting the clear workings of his mind, Raven rambled a little in his discourse, jumping back and forward in time, and not giving his friends the most understandable of narratives.

After this jumble of facts, Mawdsley asked Raven to start again, and to take his time.

Raven took a long breath. 'I believe that I met your "Harbinger of Death" face to face yesterday, Anthony,' he said simply. 'I even spoke briefly with him before he got away from me. He has been living in that house in Rose Petal Lane for several months, I believe.'

This was something Mawdsley had clearly not expected – that Raven should have tracked this man down with such remarkable ease and celerity. Raven saw that Mawdsley was elated at the news, if trying his best to hide it. 'You truly think that this man is the same one who has threatened the King's life?' Mawdsley asked sharply. 'The man who confronted Lady Castlemaine in the park?'

Raven sat up higher in bed and pulled his nightshirt tighter around him. For all that a fire burned brightly in the grate of this cheerful bedchamber, the room was still far from warm. 'I can scarce doubt it. And my admiration for Castlemaine goes up in leaps and bounds when I see the measure of the villain that she stood up against.'

Mawdsley smiled. 'I am sure that the admiration is returned in equal amounts, Henry. She has mentioned your name to me several times since your heroic exploits on Wednesday. I believe she wants to reward you in some personal way for your heroism: I can only trust that this personal reward will not require the removal of your breeches first, although - knowing the lady - I am scarcely confident of it.' He became more serious. 'So what did this devil have to say for himself?'

Raven tried to remember, although his memory of that encounter was hazy at best after its dramatic conclusion. 'Not much, as I recall. Although I believe I was right in my suggestion that he must have some connection with the world of science and invention, even if only a remote one. He knew the name of my friend Robert Hooke, and not one man in a thousand would know *his* name. And, not only that, he recognized *me* too.'

Mawdsley was surprised at that. 'Did he, by Jesu? Then perhaps that gives us a further clue to his identity.'

Raven nodded. 'Ay, perhaps it does. I have certainly never met that man before. He has a very distinctive voice which I am sure I would have recognized if I had heard it before. But it may be worth speaking to my friends and colleagues at the Royal Society to see whether any of them can identify this man from his description and his habits…'

Strange had not taken part in this discussion so far, but now, warming himself by the fire, he turned his head and intervened for the first time. 'But no one has seen this man's face, Henry,' he pointed out.

Raven pondered that. 'Yet he is also an immense height - close to six and a half feet tall, I would say – which should narrow down the list of potential names. And there are all these other indications about his background and history to guide us in our search too.'

Strange continued with his questions, his interest clearly piqued by the reports of this evil man. 'Is his mask a disguise, do ye think? Or an affectation? Or is it that the man has been hideously disfigured by injury or the pox perhaps?'

Raven glanced at the leaded window at the sounds of a coach being readied in the yard below, with much jingling of harnesses and colourful expletives from the coachmen and yard hands. 'The locals do seem to think he may be scarred from the Pox, although no one has seen him without his mask as far as I could establish, therefore that could be mere gossip. He had certainly become an infamous figure in the neighbourhood in the few months that he had been dwelling here.'

Mawdsley was deep in thought. 'It seems that I must be right too, then, and this man has probably been abroad for several years.' He glanced at Raven almost accusingly. ''Tis a pity ye could not apprehend this dangerous man yesterday. He could be anywhere by now. How did he get the better of you anyway, Henry? You are a useful man with a sword.'

Raven shook his head ruefully. 'He is a formidable looking individual and I was not sure of my ability to restrain this man single-handed. So my plan was to return quickly with help and take him into the King's custody. Yet he gave me no time for that, and attacked me with a poker, and knocked me insensible, almost as soon as I entered his lair. I doubt that I have ever seen a human move with such speed before; in faith his physical abilities did seem almost supernatural. When I came to my senses, the man was gone.'

Strange came over to the bedside. 'And what of the explosion? Was that an accident?'

Raven laughed humourlessly. 'No, it was certainly no accident. The man must have had a stock of gunpowder in his cellar – he did receive deliveries of barrels of something there, according to what I was told – and he must have set the house to explode deliberately. Almost as if he was expecting someone like me to appear there, and had set the trap accordingly. '

Mawdsley frowned. 'Yet how would he know that you would appear that very day?'

Raven remembered the evil atmosphere of that strange house. 'I know not. Perhaps he is in league with the Devil. Or perhaps he *is* the Devil. The local people do call him by the name Beelzebub.'

Mawdsley flinched. 'Are you serious, Henry?'

Raven chose not to answer that, unsure of what to say. Despite his logical and rational mind, Raven did believe that there were forces of evil at large in the world that could not be fully explained by rational philosophy and experiment.

'How came you there in the first place, Henry?' Strange was minded to ask. 'How did you find this house in Rose Petal Lane? Did someone bring you reports of this Beelzebub?'

Raven realized that he had omitted one major fact from his story. 'Nay, it was also quite by accident. I followed someone here to Southwark. A gentleman who excited my curiosity.'

Mawdsley leaned forward in his chair in anticipation. 'Who was this gentleman?'

'It was Mr James Blight that I followed,' Raven finally admitted, after a long pause. 'I spotted him walking alone in the city, and was struck by his odd demeanour, so I followed him. He led me straight to that black door...'

Mawdsley swore. 'A foutre for that man! Blight! I cannot believe it! A traitor! The man was a loyal servant of the King during his exile, and has been given great rewards in return. Why would a high official like Blight – a Groom of the Bedchamber, no less - turn against his own monarch?'

'We cannot be so certain that he has,' Raven cautioned him. 'All we can be sure of is that Blight certainly does know this man.'

Mawdsley stood up angrily. 'Yet Blight's complicity in this plot would easily explain the matter of the falling chandelier. I shall have Blight arrested at once on my return to the palace! He will soon give us the real name of this Beelzebub, and where to find him now.'

Raven hesitated. '...Assuming he knows that much. It may be that Blight only knows the house in Rose Petal Lane, and would not know where else the man might hide.'

'He must know his real name at least,' Mawdsley said balefully. 'And that name would furnish us with a much better chance of finding this man.'

Raven nodded. 'Perhaps, but torture does not always provide the quickest way inside a man's head. Would it not be better to merely observe Blight closely for the next few days and to give him some rope to hang himself with? I do not understand what his relationship with this masked Beelzebub is, but 'tis not a simple one, I am sure. Blight may not know the man's present whereabouts, but at some point Beelzebub will approach him again for some reason. Blight might then lead us directly to him...'

Strange had a thought. 'Might not this Beelzebub already be dead in the wreckage of that house in Rose Petal Lane?'

Raven scoffed at that notion. 'Not one chance in a million, Adam. Beelzebub was covering his tracks deliberately yesterday by blowing up that house, leaving not a scrap of evidence behind. Yet I believe he could have done so with a much less destructive plan than that.'

Mawdsley grimaced. 'Then why did he blow up that house and kill so many innocent people in such an evil fashion where there was no need of it?'

Raven moved aside the bedclothes in preparation to get up. 'Because I think he has passed from the realms of normal human conscience to a world of shadows and evil where nothing much matters to him any more: not human life, not human companionship, not compassion or consideration for his fellow men. Not even the laws of God make any appeal to what is left of his conscience. That is my view of the man I glimpsed yesterday. He lives now in a netherworld between Hell and Earth, and knows he is damned for all eternity, and simply wants to take the rest of mankind with him on this hellish journey.'

'No human could have descended so far into the pit of inhumanity, no matter how tormented his soul,' Strange suggested hopefully.

Raven shook his head. 'This man has. I had thought that the fact that he did not simply slit my throat yesterday when he had the chance was perhaps some sign of a residual humanity in him. But I think the truth is that he did not want me to die so easily. He wanted me to perish violently in that explosion. Or perhaps to be permanently maimed by it – left legless or blind, or disfigured, as he appears to be.'

'Surely no man can be so evil as to think like that,' Mawdsley said sombrely. 'Yet if that truly was his aim, then God has subverted his intention by bringing you out of that inferno alive and whole.'

'If very bruised,' Raven said, getting gingerly to his feet. He winced at the pain in his legs and side.

Yet his deliverance yesterday had truly been close to a miracle, he had to admit. He could remember now being lifted through the air like the ball from a cannon, and feeling the house literally coming apart around him in dust and noise and confusion.

When he opened his eyes a few minutes later, he had thought himself dead, until he felt the stinging cold on his cheek. And then someone's hand had been laid on his brow – a woman's, he thought - and had gently cleared the dirt and dust from his eyes with fresh snow.

It had felt like being reborn...

*

An hour later, Raven had recovered his strength sufficiently to return from Southwark to his home in St Martin's Lane with Mawdsley and Strange. He could not have walked so far in his still sore condition, yet the well-sprung carriage that Mawdsley had borrowed from the Whitehall palace stables made the journey comparatively painless for him, despite the freezing weather and the rutted and potholed roads on the way.

Dora Bagwell fussed over him even more than usual on his return, then rushed him straight to his bedchamber when she heard the story of what had happened to him. There, without any ceremony she stripped him of his clothes, and washed his body gently from head to foot in hot soapy water. Then she applied various unguents, lineaments and ointments to the many cuts, scrapes and bruises on his body. Back in her native Dorset, Dora had been known for her healing arts – her father had a deep knowledge of country herbs and their uses in curing maladies, and he had passed much of this learning to Dora as a girl: how the orange coloured sap from the greater celandine could burn away warts and corns, the use of the white fumitory for banning melancholy, the efficacy of treacle mustard for treating insect bites, how the stems and leaves of burnet saxifrage could be used to staunch bleeding and heal wounds. Certainly Raven found the ointments that Dora applied to his naked body infinitely soothing and cooling to his skin, and felt much recovered after this intensive treatment.

When she was done, Dora inspected her handiwork with an unsentimental eye. 'I see no sign of permanent damage to your body, Master, so you have been extremely fortunate.'

Raven was already confident that he had suffered no lasting injuries, but was glad to hear Dora's confirmation. Certainly he had no broken limbs, and his pain, although considerable, was all due to superficial cuts and bruises, and gave him no cause to believe that his major organs had been damaged in any way. Perhaps being on the staircase at the side of the house had protected him from the worst of the blast, which had been two floors below in the cellar.

Dora helped him under the sheets as she advised him to stay in bed for a few days. 'Kate was in a most tearful mood last night when you did not return,' she told him with a smile. 'She thinks of you almost as her father now.'

'I am scarce old enough for such a role as that yet, Dora,' Raven responded with a wry look.

Martin appeared now at the door of Raven's bedchamber and had his own slightly aggrieved say. 'You should not have gone to such a place alone, Master,' he complained.

Raven grimaced ruefully. 'I shall not do it again. You can be assured of that, Martin.'

They left him alone to rest after heaping up the fire with more coal. Adam Strange had already taken his leave by this time and returned to his own home, after Raven had thanked him most heartily for his concern, and for his help.

Yet Mawdsley was still in the house, and he now came and sat by Raven's bedside for five minutes, much to Dora's obvious annoyance as she left the chamber. 'I shall take my leave of you now, Henry,'

Mawdsley said, 'while you get some sleep. In the meantime I will deliberate over your advice concerning Blight. I will have to tell Lord Clarendon of our suspicions, though. If he orders Blight's immediate arrest, then I will have to go along with that plan. I dare not defy Clarendon on such matters. But he is usually mindful of my opinion, and I do err to your judgement that it would perhaps be better not to warn our madman enemy that we know of Blight's involvement yet.'

'Madman?' Raven queried Mawdsley's use of the singular. 'I would doubt sincerely that this Beelzebub acts alone. I am sure he has other willing helpers besides Blight – as you know, the King has made himself many enemies in this country over the last four years.'

Mawdsley was thoughtful. 'I am glad that *you* are not one of them, at least, Henry. You proved your ultimate loyalty to the King when you saved him on Wednesday. Even though you are no great admirer of the King, you would never lift a hand against his rule.'

Raven said nothing to deny that, yet was not quite sure that this was absolutely true. He was a political pragmatist, after all, not a believer in the divine right of kings. Yet he certainly preferred the rule of this king to the possibility of another civil war. Civil rebellion could only be justified in Henry Raven's opinion in order to remove a despotic and tyrannical king who defied the general wishes and needs of his people. And Charles, for all his shortcomings and failings, and his ill-advised repressive laws and taxes, was no tyrant. Not yet anyway…

Mawdsley stood up and regarded his friend with an affectionate eye. 'There is yet another favour I need to ask of you, Henry.'

Raven raised his head painfully off the pillow. 'Gladly. Just name it. I owe you for your concern today.'

Mawdsley smiled faintly. 'You may not be so glad when you hear what that favour is. You will recall that I told you that Lady Castlemaine has mentioned your name to me several times, and is desirous to show you some "special favour" for your bravery and quick thinking. She has invited you in particular to her apartments in Whitehall this evening for an "exotic entertainment". Can you be there at the Holbein Gate at seven o'clock this evening? I had already promised her that you will be there, and I will never hear the end of it if you fail to appear. I will send a carriage for you, of course…' he added hopefully.

Raven was reluctant to agree. '*This* evening? I am still in much pain, Anthony, despite Dora's soothing ointments.'

'The party is still six or more hours away. And the King will be there too, of course,' Mawdsley assured him swiftly, 'and he is most anxious too for you to attend.'

Raven shrugged with resignation. 'Then I can hardly refuse such an invitation, can I, despite my bruised condition. Provided no one expects me to dance a reel or a jig, then I believe I will have the strength to attend...'

*

At six o'clock that same day, Molly made her way home from the theatre. She had changed quickly after the performance this afternoon and decided to go straight home, rather than take wine with the rest of the cast afterwards, as was becoming her habit.

The third performance of Mr Dryden's play *The Rival Ladies* had gone extremely well, Molly decided complacently - perhaps even better than last night. Molly had enjoyed again the sensation of striding around the stage in tight breeches, brazenly showing off her legs as she gave life to Mr Dryden's witty dialogue. The performance had quite driven the audience to raptures, she thought - though whether it was Mr Dryden's words or her own long shapely legs that drew the greater applause from the masses was not easy to say. Tonight she was in a mood of intoxication even without the benefits of a glass of wine: the rush of excitement and exhilaration that came after performing on stage truly drove all other thoughts and concerns entirely from her mind.

Yet as she walked home through the snowy streets, her cares and suspicions about her fellow players gradually came flooding back. Particularly of Jane Golightly now...

Working so close with Jane over the last few days had made observance of her character easier, yet the result was not clarity in Molly's mind, but rather confusion. Molly had previously dismissed her as merely a sweet and fey creature – a little dreamlike and unworldly in character perhaps, but perfectly pleasant.

Yet closer inspection of her character revealed different things – including a much steelier nature than Molly had initially supposed. She was also intensely private; she did not like to undress completely in front of the other actresses, Molly had noticed. Perhaps this was simply maidenly modesty, yet Molly wondered if there might be more to her secretive behaviour than that...

Jane had also been in rather sombre mood today, and that dark mood had inhibited her usual lively performance so that Molly was sure that she had outperformed her in the play this afternoon, being much brighter and more vivacious in her own competing role. Molly had even given the final cheeky epilogue out of character and openly teased the audience with her lines in the play about the staircase of love, which she had embellished with her own naughty improvisations. Sir Thomas had been mightily pleased both with Molly's general performance, and with that improvised epilogue, which he was convinced would bring in full houses next week too for further performances of *The Rival Ladies*. He had been disappointed, though, at Molly's rapid departure from the theatre tonight, although he had consoled himself by giving her bum a tight squeeze with his hand as she slipped past him in the gallery outside the tiring room.

That was yet one more secret bruise to add to all the others that she had from Sir Thomas by now. Yet a few bruises and indignities still seemed a price worth paying for achieving her dream…

The snow had started to descend heavily again on this Saturday evening, and the sky was heavily overcast, yet by some mysterious process there still seemed enough light on the streets to see by. The winter had barely started, yet it felt to Molly as if the world had been frozen forever. As she trudged through the snow on her way home to Whetstone Park, Molly found it hard to remember a time when she had last felt warm; and the delights of last summer in the fields north of the city – apple blossom and fresh mown hay, and long drowsy sunlit evenings full of moths and blackbird song – seemed a lifetime ago.

Although, with regard to keeping warm, Molly had discovered that those breeches she wore in *The Rival Ladies* did hold the warmth of her body with admirable effect, so she had taken the bold decision to keep them on tonight under her own skirts and petticoats. And the effect was most gratifying – her nether regions did feel distinctly less chilled than usual – so perhaps this was a useful lesson for the future.

Molly suddenly remembered walking this same route home two nights ago with Mr Raven, and began to wonder guiltily what might have befallen him. She hoped indeed that he was all right, despite the concerns of his friends, and that nothing dreadful had happened to him. She had heard no word later that he had been found, although everyone in the theatre had been talking about the reports of a terrible explosion in Southwark in which many people had been killed…

Although his two friends were certainly more beautiful than him, Molly was not as fickle a creature as her mother, and still had a high regard for Mr Raven. He was a man with a good and loyal heart, she believed, and a sweet nature, which was a feature rarely to be seen in people so wealthy. Molly had determined this partly from her own observations of the gentleman, of course, but also from the opinions of his own house servants. It was most unusual for servants not to have an ill word to say in private about their master, and even more unusual for a master not to be taking liberties with his young female servants. Yet Molly was sure from her talk with the young maidservant Katie Soule that Mr Raven had always treated that girl with perfect propriety and almost daughterly affection.

So although Misters Mawdsley and Strange had certainly excited Molly's female interest, they had not displaced Mr Raven yet from her growing affections…

Despite her promise to him never to walk home alone, though, Molly realized guiltily that she was doing exactly that tonight. Perhaps for the simple reason that she did not know whom from the theatre to trust to be her companion.

By the time she had crossed Drury Lane and was in the maze of near-deserted alleyways to the west of Lincoln's Inn Fields, she was regretting not taking Mr Raven's advice, though...

Someone was following her again....

She was almost certain of the fact yet the person this time was clearly more adept at disguising his intentions than had "Feathered Hat" been six days ago. In glancing back from time to time, Molly was never able to get more than a glimpse of this shadowy figure. Yet she was sure that this elusive fellow was following her with some evil purpose in mind, and not merely sharing her route home.

Molly had got to the last turning before Celia's bawdy house when resentment boiled up inside her and she decided rashly that she must do something about this before the man had her trapped in the dead end of Rope Lane. Turning the final corner, there was no one in sight in the darkened alley ahead, but Molly could hear the reassuring sounds of life coming from the other houses on each side so was confident someone would come to her aid if she shouted loud enough. She reached under her skirts for her knife, then remembered with an unmentionable word that she was still wearing the breeches from tonight's performance and that her knife was back in the tiring room at the theatre. She was about to move quickly on when the man turned the corner too and caught her there in the alleyway with her skirts hitched halfway up her legs.

She had no time to try and identify her pursuer – the light in the narrow confines of the alley being too little for such a task anyway - but in her panic at being caught in this compromising position, simply lashed out at him with her right fist.

The man took her fist square on the end of his nose, and collapsed in an untidy heap in the snow. But he did not react violently, merely resentfully, as he lay on the snow and felt his bloodied nose. 'What's the matter with you, Molly? Why did you strike my noddle like that, you ungrateful creature?'

She recognized Patrick Whelan's voice in the near darkness. 'What are you doing here, Patrick?' she demanded suspiciously. 'You live in Red Cross Street, do you not? That's a good mile from here.'

Whelan got slowly to his feet, still trying to stem the steady drip of blood from his nose. 'I am just looking out for your interest, Molly,' he said evasively.

'What has my interest to do with you?' Molly asked warily.

Whelan hesitated. 'You were attacked in the street last week. Sir

174

Thomas thinks you are a valuable property now, so he asked the company for someone to volunteer to keep an eye on you when you walk home, and make sure no harm comes to you.'

Molly was still suspicious. 'Yet why would you volunteer for such a duty? It takes you a long way from your own journey home.'

Whelan stepped closer, his face a blur in the dimness, before admitting reluctantly, 'Because I love thee, Molly. That's why...'

CHAPTER 14

Saturday, 17th December 1664

Lady Castlemaine's apartments in the palace complex were located in a rambling Tudor building near the Holbein Gate, yet, despite being relatively far from the King's own private apartments, were as sumptuous in interior decoration and furnishings as Raven had been led to believe, with elegant oak roof beams, new panelling to the walls, and hangings of crimson Genoa damask. On the walls of her main salon were masterpieces by Holbein, Jan van Eyck and Rubens, which Raven guessed the King had merely lent her, not given her. The pictures by Rubens were distinguished by their erotic content, having much rampant female flesh on display. Raven thought that the women subjects in these pictures displayed strikingly similar proportions to Lady Castlemaine herself yet she could not possibly have been the model for any of them since Rubens had been dead a full quarter century.

On entering the main salon in company with Mawdsley, Raven was relieved to find that this evening's soiree was to be a modest affair by palace standards, merely a small gathering of thirty or so of Castlemaine's closest friends and allies at court.

The King was here, of course, and his disreputable friends Buckhurst, Sedley and Buckingham too, but there was no sign of those more severe gentlemen, Clarendon, Ormond or Arlington. The Queen was most certainly not here – she might have been obliged by the King to recognize Lady Castlemaine officially as one of her Ladies of the Bedchamber, but it was well known that she would never voluntarily come to her rival's own lair in the palace.

From the choice of assembled guests, Raven judged that this was to be a night that Lady Castlemaine had devised purely for the King's pleasure, something to take his mind off his many troubles. Raven did wonder why Lady Castlemaine had been so insistent on *him* attending, though – he was undoubtedly a fish out of water in this decadent and complacent company…

James Blight was an absentee too, Raven noted, though it would have been a considerable surprise to have found that man here in this frivolous company. Raven doubted whether that puritan gentleman, even if he was not presently languishing under the dark shadow of suspicion, would ever be invited to one of the *maitresse en titre's* soirees. Mawdsley had already let Raven know that Clarendon had accepted his advice for the moment not to arrest Blight outright, but merely to keep him under close observation. Clarendon had appointed three of his own agents to this delicate task which had relieved a thankful Mawdsley of any direct responsibility.

Mawdsley whispered an aside to Raven as they were introduced to the assembly and led to a table where a lavish repast was about to be served. 'How is the pain in your limbs, Henry?'

'Tolerable,' Raven lied. 'But I still will not take to the dance floor this evening.'

Mawdsley smiled. 'I believe you use your injuries as a convenient excuse for not partaking of an activity which you find so dull and inconsequential. Yet there should be no need to test your sore muscles and sinews on the dance floor tonight. There will be dancing later, of course -' Mawdsley pointed to the musicians in the gallery at one end of this long narrow room, quietly attending to their lutes, viols and spinet - 'but there will also be many other less strenuous activities to enjoy - card games, and other naughty teasing games brought over from the French court – which you might be able to enjoy even in your delicate condition. And Lady Castlemaine usually finishes the evening with something special – tonight she has promised an "exotic entertainment", which is something I am looking forward to with pleasure, based on past experience. Last time she had the acrobat Jacob Hall perform, and he was something wondrous to behold, being able to undertake stupendous vaults and summersets on the floor, and even to throw himself head first through a ring of real fire. 'Tis a wonder the palace did not burn down afterwards, though…'

*

Raven found that contrary to his expectations he was indeed enjoying this evening, despite the many residual aches and pains in his body. The banquet at the start had been a feast of most unusual dishes from distant lands, and he had then indulged in several enjoyable card games, if excusing himself from the dancing and the more raucous games that followed.

Lady Castlemaine had been most gracious and solicitous to her guests throughout the evening. Away from the eyes of the Queen, the

King was openly flirtatious with her, although he did not limit his seductive behaviour to her alone, Raven noticed. Raven himself was once again favoured by some personal notice from the King, and, during the dancing, sat and talked with him in a quiet corner for some minutes, covering every subject on God's earth, from the new American colony of Carolina to Mr Boyle's discovery of the "spring of the air".

When the King had left him to rejoin the dancing, Lady Castlemaine came over immediately and sat by Raven's side in his place. After thanking him yet again for his heroic action in the Great Hall on Wednesday, she asked him politely, 'Are you not dancing, Mr Raven? Are none of these beautiful ladies on the floor to your taste?'

'They are very much to my taste, madam. But alas I hurt myself in a fall from a horse yesterday and bruised myself considerably –' this was the excuse that he and Mawdsley had agreed on to avoid answering any awkward questions about the explosion in Southwark – 'so I must beg to be excused this evening from such exertions.'

'Then of course I understand.' Lady Castlemaine was wearing a distinctive black patch on her cheek, and now turned her head so that Raven could admire it at leisure, and the interesting contrast it made with her ivory skin. 'You are not exerting yourself much at present yet I observe that you still seem a little uncomfortable in the surroundings of my humble apartments,' she went on, after turning her head to face him again. 'Are they not to your liking?'

'No, indeed they are much to my liking,' Raven assured her hurriedly. 'They give me great pleasure, as does the society of these noble and interesting people. '

Lady Castlemaine fluttered her fan to signal mild disbelief. The plate of her fan was painted beautifully, Raven noticed, showing wood nymphs in a forest glade, while the stick was made from ivory and tortoise shell, and intricately carved.

'Perhaps it is the manners of the men in this room that are not to your liking,' she declared finally. 'They are certainly popinjays, to be true, with their ribbons and their bows, and their elegantly controlled flourishes.'

Raven regarded the gentlemen presently on the floor. 'Yet these gentlemen need to adopt a certain degree of swaggering movement in order to make the most of those layers of fabric and ribbons with which they are adorned.'

Lady Castlemaine laughed gently, before whispering, 'Yes, you are probably right to despise these peacocks – all except the King, of course.'

'Of course,' Raven agreed quickly, as he tried to recall what Mawdsley had told him earlier of Lady Castlemaine's interesting past.

Her personal history had many similarities with that of Adam Strange, it seemed. Her grandfather, he knew, came from the powerful Villiers clan, and was a half-brother to the first Duke of Buckingham, old King James's favourite. Her father, Viscount Grandison, had died of wounds received at the siege of Bristol in the year '43, when Barbara Villiers, as she was then, was but three years old. Her uncle Ned Villiers had been a founder of the resistance group the Sealed Knot, and had been one of Clarendon's most valued agents and political allies during the Commonwealth. Like the Stranges, the Grandisons had lost everything in the service of the crown, while Barbara's mother's merchant family, the Baynings, had apparently squandered their wealth in grand and pointless drainage schemes in the Fens. And although Barbara's widowed mother had later married the Earl of Anglesey, his estates too were sequestered in time, leaving Barbara Villiers penniless as a young girl, and forcing her to survive as best she could among the dangerous royalist circles of Interregnum London...

Raven felt her eyes closely examining him, and, uncomfortable at such frank attention from such a grand and sophisticated lady, he turned his gaze again to the dancers on the floor. Many of these gentlemen did overdo their flourishes and hand gestures to a ridiculous extent, and minced, rather than strode, across the dance floor. Raven almost laughed when he saw one particularly foppish gentleman give such an abrupt twist of his head that he almost unseated his vast curling wig.

'It does seem that the court of King Louis has much to answer for,' Raven said dryly, which made Lady Castlemaine smile in agreement as she followed the line of his eyes.

'Yet you yourself are not entirely immune to the dictates of fashion, I can see,' Castlemaine went on after a moment, studying his costume with a critical eye. She fingered his lace cuffs, and looked down at his feet. 'Expensive laces at the cuffs of your shirt sleeves, and on your cravat. Very elegant stockings of French silk. And your shoes are extremely elegant as well: that square toe and high heel suit your shapely leg well.'

Raven smiled ruefully. He felt like a little boy being chided by a grown woman, though in reality Lady Castlemaine was two years his junior. 'Ay, I accept the charge of gross hypocrisy, ma'am. But nevertheless I draw the line at wearing petticoat breeches - or cannons, those silly decorative frills below the knee.'

Castlemaine accepted that without further argument. 'And how do the women on the floor compare with the men in the matter of style?'

'High fashion suits the needs of a lady better,' Raven said tactfully, 'and adds much to their natural charms of grace and vitality.'

''Tis true. A lady must indeed have a graceful, sensuous vitality, and must be dressed well to show off this vitality to proper effect.' Lady Castlemaine blinked innocently as she glanced down at her own impeccable costume. 'Gowns have changed considerably in shaping and silhouette since the return of the King, you may have noticed. For example, see how my bodice is now much lengthened and narrowed compared to those of ten years ago. And the neckline is, as you see, low and oval in shape, and no longer edged by a wide lace whisk as previously. And if I were to stand up, you would observe no doubt that my upper skirts extend in the back to a considerable train, and that the waist has become extremely small. You have no idea of the pain I had to endure to be laced into my corset this evening, Mr Raven...'

Raven glanced guiltily at this point in the direction of the King, yet he seemed to be in too much of a flirtatious discussion of his own with a beautiful young girl to worry over what his mistress might be getting up to. Lady Castlemaine followed the line of Raven's eyes, and her smile faded to a scowl for a moment as she noticed the pretty young girl with the King, before recovering quickly.

Raven could not help but compare these fine ladies on the floor with young Molly Titchen, and would have infinitely preferred to see that young actress up there on the dance floor, dressed in those same rich brocades, satins or embroidered silks, and wearing high-heeled shoes decorated with rosettes of ribbon and lace, rather than her own poor wooden soles.

After a lull in the conversation, Lady Castlemaine changed the subject, seemingly aware of Raven's discomfort with her flirtatious talk, and taking pity on him for it. 'I believe you have recently become a member of the King's society of gentlemen philosophers, Mr Raven,' she continued. 'I would love to come to one of your meetings, to see what mysterious things you gentlemen discuss.'

'You might find it very dull, madam,' Raven warned her.

'Surely that great comet in the sky cannot be considered dull.' She frowned. 'Do you believe that comets are truly portents of disaster, Mr Raven?'

'No, ma'am, I do not,' Raven declared emphatically.

Lady Castlemaine narrowed her eyes in perplexity. 'Then what are they, sir? These mysterious ghostly things? His majesty showed me the comet through his own telescope last evening, and I was startled by its appearance, with a long tail like an angel...'

'I believe they are simply members of our solar system – like the planets, only much smaller – which circle the Sun at a great distance, ma'am. But for some reason, they are perturbed from time to time from this distant path, and then approach much closer to the Sun, and to the Earth.'

'Then why do they have a tail? Planets have no tails…'

Raven was surprised by her persistence. 'Perhaps they are composed of lighter materials than rock – perhaps comets are simply large balls of ice, and the tail is caused by the heat of the Sun causing the ice to melt.'

Lady Castlemaine seemed astounded by that idea. Raven had realized by now that she was not only a flirtatious lady, but also a much cleverer one than she was given credit for.

But then perhaps he should not be too surprised at this because she had led an extraordinarily eventful life for one still young – Mawdsley had told him that she had become the mistress of the Earl of Chesterfield from the age of sixteen, for example, then married the worthy but wealthy Mr Roger Palmer at nineteen, even though brazenly continuing her affair with Chesterfield. But, according to Mawdsley, it had been in Brussels just before his restoration, that the King had met the beautiful Madam Palmer, and been overwhelmed by her. On the King's return to England, she and her husband had been quickly moved into a house in King Street opposite the palace. Since then she had had four children by him, all ostensibly Palmer's, but all equally acknowledged by the King as his own.

Raven wondered what the wealthy cuckold, Mr Palmer, thought of all this. He had been bought off with the title of Earl of Castlemaine, and large estates in Ireland, yet it seemed he loved his wife too and was not quite as accommodating a cuckold as he might have been, even for his King. He was certainly nowhere to be seen tonight, Raven had noticed…

Lady Castlemaine finally excused herself from Raven's company. 'If you will allow me, I have to go and make preparations for the climax of the evening. I hope you will appreciate the entertainment I will be presenting to my guests shortly. It should be most stimulating and exciting.' She rose gracefully to her feet, showing the beautiful curls dangling on each side of her pretty head, and then sauntered across the room, turning every man's head as she did so.

Watching her leave, Raven admired her complete devotion to her art, and was as entranced by her as every other man in this room – she was undoubtedly the *maitresse* supreme...

*

Mawdsley, who had been taking his full enthusiastic share in the dancing, came over on the completion of a gavotte, a dance recently introduced from the French court, and took the seat recently vacated by Lady Castlemaine. Perhaps because he could still feel the warmth of that lady's presence retained on his chair, he was moved to talk in even more intimate fashion about her.

'A Royal mistress must indeed be a resilient creature, Henry. And

Lady Castlemaine has shown herself to be most resilient - even tenacious - in her duties. To give the lady her dues, she has adopted the libertine manners of the male courtiers here with gusto, and even matched her lover's infidelities...'

Raven wondered what had loosened Mawdsley's tongue so drastically, and in such a dangerous place, where his inopportune comments might be easily overheard. With a warning touch of his hand on Mawdsley's shoulder, Raven tried to get his friend to change the subject.

But Mawdsley continued to ramble, and Raven realized that he had drunk too much wine for his own good. '...She has also had to endure constant stories about her sexual appetites and practices. For example, I have been told by one person here tonight that Lady Castlemaine knows all the variations shown in Aretino's *Postures*...'

Raven was shocked. 'You mean that infamous book from Renaissance Venice.'

Mawdsley nodded. 'Indeed...and, not satisfied with that infamy, that she has also tried out Mr Jacob Hall, the famous acrobat and rope-dancer, to see if his tumbling limbs were as satisfying in private as in public performance.'

Raven put his fingers to his lips in a desperate attempt to make Mawdsley come to his senses. This was utter foolishness – to indulge in salacious gossip about the King's mistress in her own apartments, and at her own party...

Mawdsley waved an admonitory finger of his own. 'Yet I suppose she must try something to keep her hold on the King. Despite all her charms, they say her power over His Majesty is waning rapidly.'

Raven followed the direction of Mawdsley's eyes. 'You see that pretty girl talking to the King presently,' Mawdsley said. 'That young lady is Mistress Frances Stuart, recently arrived at court. The King is reputedly mad for her, but so far she has resisted all his advances. She was born in exile in Paris, I am told, but was sent to England last year by the dowager queen Henrietta Maria to act as lady-in-waiting to Queen Catherine.'

Raven inspected the young lady covertly. 'She looks but sixteen.'

Mawdsley smiled. 'No matter. Lady Castlemaine was barely older when she took the Earl of Chesterfield as her lover. Mark my words, in a year or two, Castlemaine will be pensioned off somewhere with a better title, and a house a safe distance away from the palace.'

Raven sighed. 'Tis a sad thing if it is true.'

Mawdsley shrugged drunkenly in response. 'Tis the way of the world, Henry.'

Raven nodded coldly. 'The way of this court perhaps. Yet still a sad thing...'

*

The final entertainment of the evening was about to commence, and everyone in the assembly had returned to sitting in ordered rows of chairs to watch proceedings.

There was an expectant hush because it seemed that Lady Castlemaine could always be relied on to come up with some diverting entertainment as the climax of her parties. A brocade curtain had been hung at one end of the room, behind which the preparations for this entertainment were still apparently underway, and the mysterious sounds coming from behind the curtain were intriguing enough to raise the expectations of Lady Castlemaine's select guests even further.

Lady Castlemaine herself had disappeared from view so it seemed she might be taking some part in the entertainment in person. In her absence, Raven saw that her rival Frances Stuart had quickly stationed herself next to the King in the front row of seats. The King's cronies, Sedley, Buckhurst and the Duke of Buckingham, were in the front row too, if unusually subdued for once.

Raven and Mawdsley, a little neglected now in Lady Castlemaine's absence, had only been able to find seats near the back of the assembly, together with the other less favoured guests.

Then a uniformed page stepped forward and drew the curtain aside to reveal a stage framed by a painted wooden portal, with a back curtain of black velvet behind. The interior of the stage was filled with strange, exotically painted cabinets, boxes and mechanical contraptions, including what looked like a medieval crossbow.

Mawdsley was disappointed. "Tis but a magic show...'

Yet his interest was aroused again when a masked woman strode on from stage left. The lady might have been wearing a white Venetian mask that covered most of her face, but Raven saw that this was clearly Lady Castlemaine herself because she was still wearing the same costume as earlier in the evening.

Then a second figure appeared from stage right onto the makeshift stage, a figure whose daring costume drew even more gasps from the audience than had the masked Lady Castlemaine – these gasps, ones of delight and astonishment from the gentlemen, and ones of outrage (if perhaps feigned outrage) from the ladies.

This second visitor to the stage was indeed an arresting sight - a statuesque masked lady half a foot taller than Castlemaine, and attired in the diaphanous costume of an odalisque: golden silk turban, loose purple breeches, and with her swelling breasts practically bared under a thin blouse of muslin.

Like all the other gentlemen in the room, Raven was instantly diverted by the sight of this woman, particularly when Mawdsley told him in a whisper that he believed her to be an Austrian woman from Vienna called Marie-Theresa von Kladowitz, a renowned magician and illusionist who toured the courts of Europe giving performances of her strange arts. 'Madam von Kladowitz is known to dress for her shows in the exotic costume of a female concubine,' Mawdsley added, but not explaining the source of this unexpected knowledge.

Then followed a half hour of amazing illusions and tricks, mostly performed by the odalisque alone, but with occasional help from the masked Lady Castlemaine, as for example when Castlemaine entered into one tall open cabinet, and then mysteriously vanished from sight after one puff of red smoke, only to reappear from the side of the stage immediately afterwards.

Raven had seen magic tricks before at street fairs and carnivals, but nothing to remotely match the wonder and surprise of these illusions. In fact they scarce seemed to be illusions at all, but more like demonstrations of occult knowledge.

The audience of the King's favourite courtiers had gasped at all the tricks, but were driven to frank amazement when the odalisque took Lady Castlemaine's left hand, and then, without any apparent effort, rose vertically a foot into the air as if on wires. Yet Castlemaine then withdrew her hand, leaving the odalisque standing only on fresh air, and used a wooden hoop to traverse the levitated woman from head to foot to prove that there could be no wires holding her in place.

Such was the extravagance of these illusions that even most of the gentlemen in the audience hardly noticed the woman's provocative costume and naked breasts any longer, but only the magnificence of her performance.

Neither Castlemaine nor the odalisque had spoken throughout these splendid tricks, and this silence only served to emphasize the highly erotic nature of the performance. The King had certainly lost interest in Mistress Frances Stuart for the present, his attention concentrated instead firmly on the stage. Although whether it was the sumptuous figure of Lady Castlemaine that attracted his attention more, or the statuesque Madam von Kladowitz, was a possible subject for debate.

Raven wondered what the climax of such a scintillating display of tricks could be, and was mildly disappointed when the odalisque finally picked up the crossbow on the stage, and loaded a bolt into the breech. Was this to be merely a display of her accuracy with the crossbow? It seemed a small thing after what had gone on before. Yet his interest quickened rapidly when it appeared that Lady Castlemaine was to be the willing target.

Lady Castlemaine walked to one end of the stage and then turned, with her profile to the audience. The odalisque came forward, inspected her with intimate detail, and then placed a large green cooking apple on Lady Castlemaine's head. Her high coiffure of curls and waves was more than adequate to keep the apple in place, without the need for any further restraint.

The odalisque then stepped back ten paces to the far side of the stage. The page who had attended to the curtains, now came forward when prompted by the woman and tied a blindfold around her masked face.

Even the King gasped aloud at this, but did not stop proceedings.

The odalisque took up her position, guided by the page, who sighted her approximately in the right line. Lady Castlemaine coughed to indicate her position to the masked woman with the crossbow. The woman raised the heavy French crossbow to a horizontal position and took blind aim.

Raven held his breath as did everyone else in the salon. This was dangerous enough, even if she could see properly, never mind blind. *Surely she would not really fire a bolt at that apple...?*

The King looked intensely worried and tried to get to his feet. But Mistress Stuart restrained him from rising and said loudly, 'Nay, Charles, Barbara will come to no harm. 'Tis naught but a trick. The bare lady will not really fire a bolt. I have seen this trick performed before at the French court.'

A hush descended on the audience. Raven could hear his heart beating furiously as he waited for the climax. Yet when it came, the climax was even more frightening than he had imagined. Instead of firing the crossbow at Lady Castlemaine, the odalisque turned slowly instead and aimed the crossbow directly at the *audience...*

Or in particular at the King...

Raven knew that there was something terribly wrong now. Who knew who might be dressed in that odalisque costume? Perhaps it was not this Madam von Kladowitz at all, but some deranged ally of Beelzebub?

Yet this time, even if his body had not been a mass of aches and pains, Raven had no chance to react as he had with the falling chandelier. The woman simply fired the crossbow without hesitation, and the bolt shot through the air and impaled the King's head against the back of his chair.

Panic and confusion erupted; the guests screamed in unison - even Lady Castlemaine had become quite hysterical, Raven had time to notice.

Then a pall of dense green smoke filled the room, adding to this bedlam...

When the smoke cleared a little, Raven saw that the odalisque was gone, and that Lady Castlemaine was left on stage, sobbing in disbelief at the impaled figure of her lover...

CHAPTER 15

The Lord's Day, 18th December 1664

At eight o'clock on the morrow, Mawdsley and Raven shared a breakfast of bread and cheese and cold roast beef with Adam Strange in the kitchen of his house in Bow Street, while they discussed the bewildering events of the evening before. The kitchen was a long stone-flagged room at the back of his comfortable house, with a long oaken table in the centre, and roofed over with high timber beams from which presently hung a line of game birds, and even gamier rabbits, on hooks. On the freshly lit fire, a hanging pot of stew was beginning to bubble.

On request, Mistress Bilby had left her master alone with his visitors for the present, although, from the sour look on her face, she had not much liked being asked to relinquish her kitchen, even for a few minutes. Raven guessed that she ran the other house servants, Will and Hannah, with a rod of iron and an exceedingly sharp tongue, and was normally the unchallenged queen of this little domain.

Strange was envious when he heard of the startling events that he had missed last evening in Lady Castlemaine's apartments. 'I wish I had been there to see the King assassinated in such a bold and reckless fashion.'

Mawdsley gave him a sour look in response to such unseemly levity, and chewed morosely at a thick rind of mouldy cheese. ''Tis no laughing matter, Adam. Despite his bravado afterwards, I saw that the King was a severely frightened man.'

Raven grunted. 'He has good reason to be frightened, after what happened. The King was but a quarter inch away from bloody death last night; such a narrow escape from the grave tends to concentrate the minds of even the mightiest of men, and give them pause for thought.' He reflected for a moment. 'And the incident perhaps reminded him of the unpleasant fact that his own father died on the block only a short distance away from where he was sitting…'

'Or - more pertinently perhaps - that his grandfather, the French King Henri le quatre, actually died at the hands of a devious assassin,' Strange suggested.

Mawdsley agreed with a wry nod of his head. 'Indeed so. The King does arise from a troubled pedigree. He must be well aware that not many of his Stuart ancestors have lived long enough to die peacefully in bed of old age. It was exceedingly fortunate in this case that the bolt from that crossbow merely impaled itself through the King's wig and not through his skull. Otherwise…'

Raven looked up in surprise from selecting a slice of roast beef. 'You truly think that this close miss was by accident and not design?'

Mawdsley was bemused. 'Do you not?'

Raven grunted dismissively. 'I doubt it very much that this Madam von Kladowitz - if that was indeed her last night - would miss her target, when she accomplished everything else so perfectly, including spiriting herself out of the palace afterwards by magic. I believe therefore that events transpired exactly as they were supposed to.'

Mawdsley frowned. 'Then what was the purpose of this action, if not assassination? It seems an excessive amount of trouble to have taken merely to frighten the King and his entourage.'

Raven deliberated for a second. 'I cannot agree. The devil behind this wants the King to suffer agonies of fear before he finally meets his maker, otherwise why would he warn the King of his intentions…?'

Mawdsley leaned across the table in Raven's direction. 'I take it then, Henry, that you believe this man Beelzebub to be behind this outrage?'

Raven nodded grimly. 'Oh, yes. It would be a great coincidence if two separate groups of assassins were presently at work to instil terror in the King.'

Mawdsley reflected for a moment. 'Then this woman – be she really Madam von Kladowitz or a clever impostor - must be in league with him.' When Raven said nothing in reply, Mawdsley continued, 'This devil seems to be able to have his agents come and go at will, even within the King's own palace.'

'It seems so,' Raven agreed. 'Last night's events were all part of his slow insidious plan, as I see it: he certainly does not wish to grant his victim a quick and convenient dispatch with a crossbow bolt. And apart from terrorizing the King, the manner of that performance last evening also humiliated the monarch greatly in front of that assembled company of his closest friends, as it was clearly intended to. I imagine that no one has seen the King's real hair for several years, apart from his intimate friends and family, so that must have been a mortifying experience for him to have his real short-cropped hair exposed to the scrutiny of that whole assembly.'

Mawdsley pursed his lips. 'Ay, indeed. Even I was surprised to see his close cropped skull. And his hair so grey and thin too, for a man not yet five-and-thirty. Yet they say that his young cousin King Louis was losing his hair similarly, which prompted his decision to adopt a youthful-looking wig of rich brown curls.'

'Yet it did not require every gentlemen in England and France to follow this vain French example,' Raven suggested dryly.

Even Mawdsley had to smile at that. 'It would be most tactless of an ambitious courtier to display a head of his own luxuriant natural-coloured hair to a King with thinning grey locks of his own.'

Strange laughed. 'Yet it has not stopped you doing exactly that, Anthony. Or are you considering wearing a wig yourself, despite still possessing a head of your own thick and shining hair, merely to fall in line with the King's fashion?'

Mawdsley was reticent to give a clear answer to this question, which surprised Henry Raven, who had expected a swift rebuttal. Perhaps Mawdsley was indeed contemplating such a tactful course in order to stay in favour at court...?

Raven smiled grimly at the thought of what a man must do now to curry favour at Whitehall. Even that old tyrant King Henry had never forced his courtiers to wear silly wigs. 'Ay, but I would vow that the King has more pressing matters to worry him at the moment than merely his disappearing hair.' He looked at Mawdsley. 'Have you been able to discover yet how this woman managed to effect her escape from the palace?'

'I have not,' Mawdsley admitted, 'but I believe that she must have had inside help. Even though it is much easier to escape to King Street from Lady Castlemaine's less secure apartments than from the King's privy quarters, it still requires intimate knowledge of the layout of the palace buildings, which no casual visitor would normally possess. The woman must somehow have changed her costume on her way out of the palace, as well, and it is difficult to see how she could have done such a thing without help...'

'Why do you think she must have changed her dress?' Strange asked.

Mawdsley grunted. 'While it is all too common to see half-naked women fleeing from the palace at night –' he coughed apologetically at this frank admission – 'I think even the most complacent Whitehall guard would have noticed a woman in King Street wearing a golden silk turban and purple breeches. Not to mention sporting naked breasts in the freezing snow...'

Raven reflected on that. 'Even if she had help, though, her escape seems to have been quite as incredible as most of the tricks she performed yesterday. I imagine the King's guard has been scouring the streets of Westminster this morning for this woman, Madam von Kladowitz.'

Mawdsley answered reluctantly. 'They have, of course – and further afield too - yet none can say if this truly was the real Madam von Kladowitz, or a clever impostor.'

Raven had a thought. 'How was it that this woman was invited to perform her tricks last evening? How did she inveigle herself into the palace?'

Mawdsley cleared his throat delicately. 'The truth is a little difficult to ascertain. But 'tis my belief that she made a personal approach to Lady Castlemaine, who was taken in completely by her clever tricks and charm.'

Strange intervened. 'So Lady Castlemaine must have seen the lady's face? This woman performer could not have presented herself to her in a Venetian mask.'

Mawdsley pondered that. 'I imagine so. But then no one knows what the real Madam von Kladowitz looks like, so Lady Castlemaine can hardly be blamed for not recognizing her as an impostor...'

'If impostor she was,' Strange said thoughtfully. 'From your accounts, it is hard to credit that the real Kladowitz could be any more accomplished at trickery and illusions than this supposed fake.'

Raven agreed silently with that. 'Yet Lady Castlemaine did not really perform with this woman, as we all thought, did she?' Like everyone else, he had been entirely taken in during the performance by "Lady Castlemaine" - but not by her screaming antics afterwards, which were most unlike any reaction that could have been expected from the real lady in question.

'No,' Mawdsley admitted. 'That was Castlemaine's little joke for the King. It was in reality her maidservant Henrietta Pask who performed on stage with the odalisque. Henrietta had rehearsed the act in secret with "Madam von Kladowitz" for two days beforehand. Lady Castlemaine herself viewed the whole performance last evening from a secret viewing gallery in the roof of her apartments...'

'For the success of which, she must have been congratulating herself heartily until that last dreadful minute. Did the real Castlemaine perhaps not see how the odalisque managed her escape from that room?' Raven asked.

Mawdsley gave Raven a shrewd appraising look. 'I did ask Lady Castlemaine that very question afterwards, But she did not see anything herself of how the woman escaped; in the confusion afterwards, and with the main salon filled with coloured smoke, she was too distraught to think clearly, and simply rushed down from the viewing gallery to the

King's aid. She was surprised, though, that this "Madam von Kladowitz" managed to escape with such apparent ease from her apartments, with their rabbit warren of corridors and stairs, even though the woman did have the run of the place for two days beforehand while she was practising her act with Henrietta, so could perhaps have worked out a suitable escape route during that time…'

'Then perhaps there is no need to suspect an accomplice inside the palace after all?' Strange interrupted.

Mawdsley paused to think about that. 'Perhaps that is true, although I still tend to the notion of an inside accomplice. Whatever the truth, Lady Castlemaine is most profoundly shocked by what happened, although it is said that her rival Mistress Stuart is positively thrilled by the evening's events.'

Strange laughed. 'Why does that not surprise me?'

Raven had a question for Mawdsley. 'What of Mr Blight? Could he have had a hand in expediting the woman's escape? Could he be the missing accomplice?'

Mawdsley shook his head reluctantly. 'Unfortunately not. Lord Clarendon is still having Blight watched constantly in the hope that he leads us to Beelzebub again. According to Clarendon's men, Blight did not stir from his own apartments yesterday evening, nor did he receive any visitors, or even a messenger of any sort. Clarendon will continue having Blight watched for the present, but his patience is not unlimited, so he may order his arrest eventually. I dislike the thought but I might have to be involved in Blight's questioning, if it comes to that…'

'And with his torture?' Raven added sharply.

Mawdsley grimaced. 'I fear so.'

There was an uncomfortable silence before Raven broke it finally. 'Yet there are some encouraging signs in all this,' he said.

Mawdsley was surprised. '*Encouraging?* The King was almost murdered last night in his own palace! What is there in all this dangerous business that could possibly encourage me?'

'Just this,' Raven explained. 'For a man with supposedly supernatural powers, this Beelzebub seems to rely a great deal on flesh-and-blood accomplices to do his handiwork. And given that his accomplice from last night was well versed in the arts of trickery and subterfuge, it suggests that Beelzebub's powers may owe more to the world of smoke and mirrors than to a genuine pact with the Devil…'

Raven was a little startled at this point by the return of Mistress Bilby. He suspected from the lack of footsteps preceding her entry that she had been listening at the kitchen door to at least some of their discussion, and he was struck for the first time by the thoughtful and intelligent expression on her face, so different from her usual hard scowl. She seemed suddenly younger and more attractive with this gentler expression on her face, and for the first time, Raven had an inkling of what qualities Adam might see in her as a servant.

In fact, Raven noticed that Strange now shared a quick secretive glance with her that spoke volumes and suggested that there might even be an unlikely intimacy of sorts developing between master and servant in this house.

Yet even if Adam were becoming embroiled in an inappropriate relationship with his own servant, Raven could hardly find the will to fault his friend's lack of judgement when he himself was becoming equally involved with a sixteen-year-old actress...

With all the challenging situations he had faced in the last two days, Raven realized guiltily that he had given little thought at all in that time to Molly Titchen's welfare. Mawdsley had told him of his visit to Madam Celia Hornett's premises in search of him, and Raven realized that he should have let Molly know that he was all right. Granted that he was still sore and bruised from enduring that explosion in Southwark, and that last night he had almost witnessed the death of a King, yet he still bemoaned his inattention to the fate of that vivacious girl. He did believe now that she was in some kind of danger – perhaps even mortal danger - although for reasons that he could not remotely comprehend. A sixth sense also suggested to him the possibility that Molly's uncertain situation at the theatre, and the deaths of those two actresses, were linked in some mysterious way to the death threat to the King, although he had no evidence on which to base this supposition.

Yet Raven decided that it was now time to stop neglecting Molly's situation, and so he resolved to see her today, or at least send her a message assuring her that he was well...

*

At almost this same moment, Molly Titchen's thoughts were equally concentrated on a person of the opposite sex, although not on Mr Henry Raven as it happened, despite her continuing concern over what fate might have befallen that gentleman since Friday. Her thoughts were concentrated instead on her fellow thespian Patrick Whelan. As she walked from Whetstone Park to Drury Lane on this overcast and freezing winter's morning, under a sky that seemed to have been hammered together from solid sheets of pewter, she was wondering how much credence she could give to Patrick's protestations of love the evening before. On the whole he had managed to sound remarkably convincing, although sincerity in men was such a rare commodity, and one that Molly came across so seldom, that she was ill equipped to judge the manifestations of this fine quality. On the other hand, she was well used to seeing the darker side of men's natures, and was an expert at discerning male duplicity. Therefore, given her prejudices about the male sex, she erred naturally towards that darker interpretation of Patrick's behaviour, and had by now convinced herself that there must be some deceitful motive concealed behind his claims of affection.

She also remembered her orange seller friend Nell's opinion that Whelan was a ne'er-do-well, a former highwayman who was on the run from the law, which was a considerable additional black mark against him, given that Nell was usually most astute in her judgements of men. Nell had not however said where she had obtained this secret knowledge, yet, for a fourteen-year-old orange seller, she seemed always to have impeccable sources of information. In fact Molly could not recall any piece of gossip or scandal that Nell had passed on to her privately that had not turned out subsequently to be proved true.

As Molly reached Drury Lane, however, thoughts of Patrick Whelan were instantly dispelled from her mind by the sight of another of her fellow thespians. Miles Brammer was walking a little ahead of Molly down Drury Lane, and seemed to be behaving even more oddly than usual, carrying a large bulging canvas sack, and displaying clear signs of furtiveness. Rehearsals at the theatre were not due to start for another two hours at least – Molly had come early in order to learn her lines for the new play they were planning to rehearse today, *Sir Politic-Would-be* – so she suspected the theatre was not Brammer's immediate destination.

Although his furtive manner suggested that he had no wish to be followed, Molly's curiosity got the better of her, so she decided to disoblige him and follow him anyway. Her guess that Brammer was not going directly to the King's house was soon proved correct because he did not cross Drury Lane to Bridges Street, but cut instead through a back alley leading to the north end of Bow Street.

Even though it was just after nine o'clock on the Lord's day, Brammer made no further diversions, but went directly to a stable yard at the back of the Cock Inn. The yard appeared to be closed for normal business, but Brammer gave a quick intricate knock at the high timber gate and was soon admitted into the large cobbled yard inside by an unseen gateman.

After the gate had slammed crisply shut behind Brammer, Molly followed in his steps and stood at the closed gate for a moment. This alley behind the Cock Inn was a dismal place at the best of times, but today the gloomy nature of the place was made even worse by the heavy grey lowering sky. The gloominess of the scene was such that it seemed to Molly as if some giant hand had nailed a solid sheet of metal over the entire city of London during the night, trapping its occupants inside this cold grey world. Yet the depressing weather seemed to have no dampening effect on whatever was going on inside that stable yard.

From the various noises issuing from the other side of that tall gate –
mostly boisterous exclamations of delight and excitement, it seemed -
Molly judged that there had to be a considerable crowd assembled in
that stable yard, even at this time of day. Molly had a strong inkling by
now of what the crowd might be doing there so early on a Sunday: she
guessed that there must be cock fighting or something similar going on
inside, with heavy wagers being made no doubt on the outcome of the
contests. This was certainly against the law on the Lord's day - which
probably explained Brammer's furtiveness on his way here, Molly
decided.

Molly was curious to see inside, and spied a sizeable knothole in the
wood of the gate that might do the job. It was set very high in the wood,
at rather more than a comfortable eye height for her, but by standing on
tiptoes she could just get her eye to it and see into the yard, if only over
a restricted angle.

She soon saw that she had been right in her general supposition. A
group of men of all classes, from ragged ruffians to bewigged
gentlemen, were assembled in a ring around the middle of the yard, and
were in a fever of excitement over something. From within the ring,
came the sounds of growling and yelping, and vicious snapping of teeth,
so this looked to be a meeting for fighting dogs, not cockerels.

Since Molly could only see a narrow slice of the spectators through
her knothole, there seemed little likelihood of catching a glimpse of
Miles Brammer in her restricted line of sight. But she was proved wrong
almost immediately in her pessimistic supposition: by chance Brammer
was standing directly in her view, on the far side of the circle of
spectators, still with his unopened sack in his hand (which perhaps
contained his own fighting dog, Molly now guessed.)

Molly had not expected this pretty actor to have a taste for gambling
and dog fighting, but that seemed to be all there was to this clandestine
morning visit to this stable yard, so Molly's interest began to wane
rapidly.

*That was until Molly caught sight of the two ruffians who were standing next to
Brammer, one on either side of him...*

Molly felt her heart thud wildly as she recognized "Feathered Hat"
and "Toothless", the two rogues who had murdered poor Amy
Leatherbarrow, and who had almost done the same for her.

Not only that: these two were clearly close confidantes of Brammer,
judging from the frequent amiable exchanges between the three of
them...

Molly, still straining to her maximum height on tiptoes, saw that
Feathered Hat seemed unfortunately to have recovered from the knife
wound she had given him a week ago, which was a great pity. Molly

decided that she really must invest in a knife with a much longer and sharper blade, then, next time perhaps, she might be able to deal with these two villains properly...

And with Miles Brammer too, the deceitful and treacherous rogue...

*

Molly had a stroke of luck then because the next person that she saw arrive at the back gate of the stable yard was none other than her friend Nell Gwyn, laden heavily with a tray of pies obviously intended for the spectators at the dogfight.

Nell spotted her friend at once, despite having that heavy wooden tray balanced on her head. 'Watch yer, Molly. What are you doing here, skulking and shivering in the cold? I did not think you would be one for dog fighting. Would you like one of these pies before I take them in?' Nell offered generously, after she had finished greeting her friend. 'My sister cooked them only last evening. They are real beef pies – no dog or horsemeat – honest!'

Molly politely refused the offer of a meat pie – if they had been made by Nell's sister, Rose, then they were certainly full of dog meat, and maybe even worse sorts of offal than that... 'They look delicious but no, thank you kindly, Nell,' Molly said lamely. 'But if you are about to go inside the stable yard, can you do me a favour?'

Molly went on to ask for Nell's help in trying to discover the names of the two ruffians who were presently in company inside with her fellow actor Miles Brammer, and perhaps to listen in on their conversation, if she could.

Molly had never discussed the deaths of Sarah Lusted and Anne Carey with Nell, but Nell was a smart girl, and seemed to suspect herself that something at the theatre was not right. 'What has provoked your interest in Brammer and his two rough companions?' she asked suspiciously.

Molly attempted a coy look. 'I am only interested to discover what Mr Brammer is up to with those two disreputable-looking men. Perhaps he should be warned about mixing with such people. They do not seem his type of companion at all.'

Nell nodded in understanding. 'Ah, I think ye still have the hot flushes for Miles, don't you, Molly? That is why you plague his steps so, and want to know his every business.'

Molly pretended that this was indeed the case, as it seemed the simplest way to elicit Nell's help.

Nell shook her pretty tawny curls and gave a resigned smile. 'I cannot blame you for wanting to bed Brammer because he is such a pretty boy. But I warn you again, Molly, not to expect too much of Miles. For one thing, I am sure that he likes the taste of a cock up his own bum, more than the other way round. And for another, he leads women on when he has no real interest in them. Like poor Anne Carey...'

But in the end, after Molly had pestered her some more, Nell agreed to spy on Brammer and his companions when she went into the stable yard to sell her pies.

In fifteen minutes she returned, having sold all her pies very quickly, and laughing heartily as she counted out her coins.

'Why do you laugh so, Nell? What was so funny in there?' Molly asked suspiciously.

Nell was still counting her profits with satisfaction. 'Oh, there might be a few belly aches and over brimming chamber pots among those gents tonight, that's all -' she saw Molly's critical eye and added quickly – 'but only because of the speed they gobbled those pies down, I swear, not because of what's in them...'

Nell had been less successful, though, in overhearing anything of what Brammer had been saying to his companions, as Molly had asked her to. Brammer had recognized her of course from the theatre and – whether that was the reason or no - had shut up tight as a drum whenever she had come in close proximity to him. He had not even bought one of her pies, which was even more annoying to Nell.

Yet Nell had managed nevertheless to discover one very useful pieces of information. From one of her regular customers inside, she had learned the names of Brammer's two ruffian companions, who were both apparently regular visitors to the dog fighting matches behind the Cock Inn.

Thanks to Nell, Molly now knew her attackers' names: it seemed that "Feathered Hat" was called Job Parish and "Toothless's" real name was Caleb Wedderburn...

*

Molly left the alley behind the Cock Inn soon afterwards, being already much later for the theatre than she had intended. Once in the King's house, she found a quiet corner behind the stage and tried to put everything else out of her mind as she read through her scenes in the Duke of Buckingham's play *Sir Politic-Would-be*. The play was a disappointing one compared to *Twelfth Night* or *The Rival Ladies*, being an unsubtle and bawdy satire on the politics of the Commonwealth. Molly liked bawdy humour well enough in its place, but delighted in sparkling dialogue even more, something that was distinctly lacking in this effort at playwriting by the King's favourite. Christopher Malthouse was to play the lead for a change, rather than merely a supporting role, although Molly doubted that any of the other leading actors would begrudge him this particular part.

At eleven o'clock, a messenger boy brought her a letter addressed to her personally at the theatre. Molly had never received such a letter before – not one on such high quality paper, and written in such a beautiful hand anyway – and opened it eagerly. She was relieved to find that it was a brief letter from Mr Raven, informing her that he was returned from his business, and was in good health, despite the concerns expressed yesterday by his friends Mawdsley and Strange. Molly was relieved to hear this news, although she had already doubted that anything too ill could have befallen Henry Raven. Mr Raven seemed to her one of those solid, blessed and sober citizens to whom nothing truly bad could ever happen.

A little before noon, the whole cast was assembled on stage for a read through of the script, which went well enough, considering that no one in the company knew the play well. Even Sir Thomas seemed thoroughly out of sorts today, Molly thought, and could hardly raise sufficient enthusiasm to squeeze any pert female bottoms that came within his reach, even her own.

Mary Pettican played a preposterous lady of manners in the play with her usual skill and aplomb, while Jane Golightly was the downtrodden and fragile heroine of the piece, a part that seemed ready made for her.

Molly's own part was as a common and vulgar strumpet, which was perhaps a part equally ready made for her, she could not help but think.

Patrick Whelan read his own part of an officer of the New Model Army with quiet dignity, disguising his normal Irish brogue with a passable impersonation of a plain speaking Puritan Englishman. At one point, Molly, forgetting her belief that he was being duplicitous towards her, had favoured him with a pretty smile, for which she received a shy and encouraging smile in return, despite him still sporting the cut on his nose that she had given him. Perhaps she was wrong about him, she thought; perhaps he really had developed some true affection for her over the last few days...?

Yet Molly was sure that she was entirely right to distrust Miles Brammer, that snake in the grass. Molly had barely been able to disguise her contempt every time that Brammer had read one of his lines in the play as a bawdy parson. Molly was certain now in her own mind that Brammer was the dark lady's accomplice, the man she had seen outside the Duke's house dressed in that outlandish French wig. It must have been *him* who had hired those two rogues, Parish and Wedderburn, to shut her mouth permanently. But, if that were so, then who was the tall dark lady? Molly had formed no better idea yet as to her true identity. She had no particular liking for Mary Pettican or Jane Golightly, yet surely it could not be either of them who had murdered Sarah in such a heinous fashion? Apart from the fact that Molly could not believe either of them to be evil enough to do such a thing, there was also the practical point that neither was tall enough to be the dark lady, except if they were wearing six-inch heels anyway...

Yet, even if it was one of these two women who had killed Sarah, neither of them could possibly have killed Anne Carey because they had been on stage in *Twelfth Night* as Olivia and Viola. Nor could Brammer have done it, Molly remembered: he had been playing Duke Orsino in the same production, and had never been out of sight of the rest of the company that whole evening. But this objection applied equally to all members of the company, which implied that Anne Carey's murderer could not be an actor or actress at all.

Nor could any of the company have been responsible for the falling chandelier either, which thought left Molly entirely at a loss.

Yet the incontrovertible fact remained that Miles Brammer *did* know the two men who had murdered Amy Leatherbarrow, so he had to be involved in this conspiracy somehow...

*

Upon finishing rehearsals for the day, Molly walked to Raven's house in St Martin's Lane in late afternoon to tell him of her suspicions about Miles Brammer, and to give him the names of Parish and Wedderburn, in particular. With Mr Raven's standing in the community as a wealthy man of business, she thought that he would be far more likely than her to get a respectful hearing if he took these accusations to the Ward Constable or Beadle.

But on knocking at Mr Raven's door, Molly was disappointed to discover that he was not at home. The servant who answered the door was Kate Soule, the pretty if thin girl who had looked after Molly last week in this very house.

Kate recognized Molly in return of course, and seemed from her respectful manner to have heard from somewhere – perhaps from Mr Raven himself – that she had now been promoted at the King's house from orange girl to actress. 'Please come in and wait, Mistress Titchen. I believe Mr Raven has gone with Mr Mawdsley to the palace to discuss something. I am sure the master will be returning soon, though. He said that he would be home before dark.'

But Molly felt uncomfortable at the idea of waiting in Mr Raven's house for an indeterminate period of time, so declined to wait. She asked Kate to give him a message that she would be most obliged if he would call at the theatre when he had the opportunity, as there was something important she wished to discuss with him.

As Molly walked away down St Martin's Lane, though, she could not help glancing back at the façade of that fine substantial house, and reflecting on what it might be like to be the mistress of such a secure and prosperous home. She remembered the intense way that Mr Raven had looked at her on stage three nights ago, and was quietly confident that with suitable encouragement and the use of the erotic arts that Celia had taught her she could indeed find her way into his bed if she so wished.

It would certainly make Celia happy if she became Mr Raven's *maitresse*. Yet would it truly make her happy? That was a more difficult question to answer…

*

With the biting wind and the deep snow underfoot, it took Molly a good half hour to walk back from St Martin's Lane to Whetstone Park. When Molly entered the downstairs parlour of the bawdy house, she found Celia sitting by the crackling fire, looking a little downcast.

Molly asked her what was wrong.

Celia sighed gently. 'I am afraid that "Sir William" is here yet again, and has chosen Marion to vent his manly frustrations on.' Celia saw the look on Molly's face and became defensive. 'I tried to persuade him to take another girl this time – one of the better built girls who can cope with his brand of chastisement…'

Molly turned instantly on her heel and stormed up the stairs to Marion's room on the second floor, where she heard the sounds of considerable violence and abject moans from within.

Molly did not bother to knock, but simply burst in through the unlocked door.

Marion lay face down on the bed with her hands and feet bound to the bedposts, her legs spread-eagled and her bare buttocks marked with the ugly red welts and scars inflicted by "Sir William's" cat o-nine tails.

Sir William turned his head languidly and appraised Molly with a contemptuous stare. 'Ah, reinforcements! 'Tis about time. Come here, my sweet. Lift your skirts and climb onto the bed alongside your friend here.'

Molly smiled at him, then raised her skirt slowly with a mock show of desire. But when she reached the knife strapped to her thigh, she quickly dropped her skirts again and held the knife to Sir William's fat white throat. 'I see you like a little blood to flow, Sir William. How about we let a little of yours gurgle from your throat to join Marion's sweeter blood there?'

Sir William was too astonished for a moment to reply, but then started to bluster. 'I like a bold strumpet. Now take off those skirts and let me have a good look at you. I think you might enjoy the taste of the cat on your soft white backside too.'

'I doubt if it is as soft and white as your backside, sir,' Molly snarled. 'And if you do not move that soft white arse promptly and leave this room, I promise you I will decorate it with much deeper cuts than you have chosen to visit on poor Marion here.'

Suddenly Sir William realized that this mad, wild-eyed girl was in deadly earnest, and started to back away from the bed. 'I shall complain about this deplorable behaviour of yours downstairs, girl, and your days working here will be numbered. In fact I promise that I will bring the constable at once to arrest you for this infamous conduct...'

Molly waved the knife in his face, and Sir William turned instantly and fled, though wearing only his shirt, which flapped over his fat white legs like a loose sail. As he slid and bumped down the stairs in his panic, Molly shouted down after him. 'And I promise you that I will chop your manhood off and feed it to the alley cats if I ever see you in here again, sir.'

As Molly was untying a weeping Marion from her undignified position, Celia appeared at the door of the bedchamber and shook her head wryly. 'What a girl you are, Molly! I shall have no business left in this house if I do not allow a little spanking of my girls.'

But Molly only held a tearful Marion in her arms and glared at her balefully. 'Then 'tis shame on you, Mother...'
*

Still seething with anger at the pain and misery that this obnoxious man had inflicted on sweet young Marion, Molly went outside into the alleyway to shout her frustrations at the empty night sky. She was so consumed by her anger at first that she was quite oblivious of anything going on around her.

Only at the last second did she sense that someone was standing behind her in the alleyway.

She turned quickly and saw a silhouetted figure standing there in the gloom. The figure of a woman - *a tall dark lady*...

Too late Molly realized her danger and turned again and fumbled for the door to the bawdy house behind her.

But instantly she felt a hand reach over her face from behind, a hand that felt like a vice holding her jaw. This was no woman's hand, though – no woman ever had strength in her hands like this.

Yet somehow, in her feverish desperation to try and escape from this choking hand over her face, Molly did manage to bite a finger and loosen that inhuman grip for a brief moment. And in that second, she was able to see that the man who held her in this awful grip was wearing a black facemask. Gasping and writhing, Molly ripped off that mask with her free hand and saw in the dimness a face out of a nightmare...

Then something struck her hard on the back of the head, and she dived into a black lake as deep and impenetrable as the far reaches of Hades...

CHAPTER 16

Monday, 19th December 1664

Henry Raven had returned home very late on Sunday evening, and received the message from a yawning and apologetic Kate Soule that Mistress Titchen had called earlier in the day and would like to see him on an important matter. Raven had been annoyed at returning so late because he had spent a long fruitless day at the palace at Mawdsley's request, yet nothing had been achieved that might remotely help them find the mysterious "Madam von Kladowitz". The woman had achieved such a remarkable disappearing trick from Lady Castlemaine's apartments that Raven had suggested only half-facetiously to Mawdsley that she might truly have occult powers at her disposal after all, rather than merely the cunning tricks of a magician.

By the time Raven did arrive home, it was too late an hour to set off for the King's theatre – he imagined anyway that Molly must be long gone to her own home by then - so he resolved to see her tomorrow when she next returned to the King's house for rehearsals. He reasoned that the matter could not be that pressing, otherwise she would surely have accepted Kate's invitation to stay until he got home.

Yet Raven's first appointment on Monday was not at the King's house, but at Gresham College in Bishopsgate where he went to consult Robert Hooke on what was also an important matter to him. This time, though, he had Martin drive him to the city in his grand new closed riding-carriage, rather than walking there as was his custom. He was still bruised and sore from his exploits in Southwark two days before, even after a second administration of Dora Bagwell's magic potions to some intimate parts of his body last evening. Last night, as he had finally retired with his night candle to his bed, he had been struck again by the miracle of his deliverance from that collapsing house, and had said a heartfelt prayer of gratitude to God before finally yielding to sleep.

His sore condition did also give him the perfect excuse to use his new carriage this morning, which, being built to his own design on scientific principles, was a much lighter and better-sprung vehicle than his previous cart-like carriage, and one that could in consequence be pulled by a single strong horse. The interior could accommodate four passengers at a pinch, yet in truth was really only comfortable for one or two because of its small size. The quality of the suspension was still not perfect either, but much better than the old, and Raven was grateful today for that improvement, as the carriage made its way through London's frozen and rutted streets.

On gaining admittance to see his scientific friend, Raven realized with amusement that Mr Hooke was even more untidy in his appearance and habits when in the confines of his own private rooms at Gresham College than when he was attending meetings in his capacity as Curator of Experiments, though previously Raven had not thought a greater slovenliness possible. On this icy Monday morning Hooke was wearing breeches covered in some noxious chemical, and his coarse woollen stockings were clearly not of a pair, being entirely different colours. His bent and shuffling walk was even more pronounced than usual for such a young man, so that it seemed as if his head had sunk somehow into a depression between his shoulder blades. Yet, despite his slovenly appearance, he had been most welcoming when Raven appeared unexpectedly this morning outside the door to his private rooms. Raven was pleased to know that he was one of the few people in London whose society Mr Hooke could freely tolerate.

For all his general lack of worldliness, Hooke was however as sharply observant of normal human and social behaviour as he was of scientific phenomena. He noticed instantly, for example, that something was amiss with Raven's physical condition, even without much external evidence. 'Ye seem to be in some pain or discomfort this morning, Henry,' he observed. 'Have you suffered an accident?'

'A minor one with a horse, Robert, that's all. Nothing to be concerned about,' Raven assured him hurriedly, not wishing to be drawn into long explanations of the strange events in his life over the last week.

Hooke showed Raven through to his parlour where a fire burned brightly, bringing light and warmth to this comfortable room on an otherwise cheerless day. Raven wondered whether the coal burning in that grate might not be from his own mines in the north; it was entirely possible as one of his colliers – the *Anne Raven*, renamed recently for his late mother - had delivered several tons of best quality Durham coal to Billingsgate Wharf in the city only last week.

Raven was glad to see that Hooke was settling into his commodious new rooms at Gresham College. In the early days of this learned society, when Hooke had still been an assistant to Mr Robert Boyle, and only visiting London occasionally from Oxford to attend meetings, he had usually stayed during those visits at the home of Boyle's sister, Lady Ranelagh, in Chelsea. Raven imagined that staying with such fashionable people must have been an uncomfortable and trying experience for a simple and unsophisticated bachelor like Hooke. Luckily the post of Curator of Experiments with the Royal Society - with its testing requirement to produce three or four considerable experiments a week – had also brought with it a salary of eighty pounds a year, and these pleasant rooms in Gresham College itself. Thanks to the good offices of the fellows of the society (and of Henry Raven in particular), Hooke now had a library, a parlour, and two smaller rooms on the ground floor at his disposal, as well as a garret above for his own servant. In these rooms Hooke could carry out his clever explorations of the laws of nature at his leisure, and with no one to criticise his manners, the cut of his coat or the unfashionable colour of his breeches.

Lord Brouncker had also had the recent notion to promote Mr Hooke even further for his good work, to the title of Gresham Professor of Geometry and Cutlerian lecturer, which posts would bring him even more rewards in due course. Yet no man could say that a person of genius like Mr Hooke was not fully deserving of this consideration.

Although Raven had come to talk this morning about more practical matters than natural philosophy, he inevitably found himself engaged first in a scientific discussion. It was almost impossible for Henry Raven to encounter Mr Hooke, and not be instantly consumed with curiosity at what interesting natural phenomena Hooke might be presently engaged in studying and explaining. An encounter with Mr Hooke was almost like peering through a gateway into the future, and getting a glimpse of the wondrous things that mankind might eventually be capable of.

Raven was particularly interested when he discovered that Hooke was presently experimenting with gunpowder and trying to explain the origins of its awesome explosive power. Hooke took Raven into the small room next door – clearly a former kitchen from its fittings - where his did most of his experiments, and showed him a complex assemblage of glass retorts and beakers and flasks and tubes, filled with various chemicals, bubbling slowly over a fire. 'I have shown with this simple little demonstration that neither charcoal nor sulphur can burn without the presence of air, Henry, but that the other ingredient of gunpowder – saltpetre - will do so readily...'

'And what does that mean?' Raven asked, intrigued.

Hooke smiled mysteriously. 'In my forthcoming book *Micrographia*, I intend to show that combustion in air is made possible only by a substance inherent, and mixed with the air. And my researches here have proved that this substance inherent in the air is very like - if indeed not the very same - as that which is fixed in saltpetre.'

'You mean saltpetre contains a vapour within its solid form that is naught but part of the air?' Raven was startled by this idea.

Hooke nodded emphatically. 'Exactly. And this part of the air is the most important constituent of all because I believe it is necessary not only to sustain combustion but also to sustain life itself...'

Raven blinked slowly, understanding. 'You think this is the same substance that we need to take into our lungs when we inhale?'

Hooke peered into one retort and examined the mysterious purplish vapour arising inside with a penetrating eye. 'Yes, and we use this vapour that we inhale to help consume our food, which then provides us with the vital spirit to live and move and think.'

This was a revelation to Raven. 'So this means that digestion is naught but a form of slow burning?'

Hooke raised his head from inspecting the bubbling retort. 'I did not think to put it quite that way, but it seems as good a description as any.'

'And what about the power of gunpowder?' Raven inquired. 'Where does that arise?'

Hooke straightened his weak back with an effort. 'That seems to be merely burning too, but at such an extreme rate that the vapours produced soon exceed the capacity of the container in which the gunpowder is held. It is this frantic outpouring of vapours in a confined space that I believe gives gunpowder its frightening destructive power.' Hooke frowned. 'Did you not hear of that frightful explosion in Southwark on Friday last...?'

'I did indeed,' Raven interjected dryly, but otherwise elected to stay quiet on this particular subject.

Hooke barely paused for breath before continuing. '...That conflagration must have been the result of gunpowder exploding, though why any sane man would keep barrels of this dangerous stuff in his own cellar is hard to say. The man must have been mad...'

'Yet *you* keep gunpowder in your cellar, Robert, do you not?' Raven pointed out with a smile.

'True,' Hooke agreed amiably. 'Therefore one might suspect my sanity too, perhaps. Yet I keep only tiny quantities, and I am also most careful when experimenting with such violent compounds. I do not wish to turn my home here at Gresham College into mere rubble, like those poor houses in Southwark.' Hooke cast Raven a shrewd look. 'Is it about this explosion that you have come to consult me, Henry?'

'Indirectly, yes,' Raven finally admitted. 'I am interested in finding this madman who might have kept that gunpowder in that cellar in

Southwark.'

Hooke seemed confused. 'What is your role in this business, Henry? You are a merchant and gentleman, not a member of the Southwark Watch.'

'My friend Mawdsley has asked for my assistance in finding this evil man,' Raven explained. 'He thinks my scientific knowledge might help track this villain down.'

'I see.' Hooke had met Mawdsley when Raven had brought him along to a recent meeting of the society, and knew him to be secretary to the Lord Chancellor, and therefore a person of influence at Whitehall.

Raven continued. 'I have evidence that this dangerous man is acquainted with you in some way, Robert, or at least knows you by reputation.'

Hooke looked startled by this revelation but did not query how Raven knew such a thing. 'Are you sure that this man himself did not die in the explosion?'

Raven smiled grimly. 'No, I am not entirely sure. Yet I doubt sincerely that this man is dead, although he perhaps wishes us to believe it. According to what I have heard from Mawdsley, the victims whose bodies have been dug out so far from the wreckage in Southwark are all local women and children.' He went on to describe the nature of the man he was searching for. 'I believe this man to be someone formerly of culture and learning, and with at least an interest in natural philosophy. He may even have a touch of genius about him, but that genius is now subsumed by evil and inhumanity.'

Hooke was subdued in response. 'Is there anything else you can tell me about this individual?'

Raven remembered the chilling look of the man. 'He is extremely tall, perhaps six and a half feet, which should narrow down our search considerably. Not one man in a thousand is such an immense height. He may also have been living abroad for several years, and he may be disfigured now by the pox or some other calamity.' Raven had another thought. 'And he could be connected in some way to one of the regicides who were executed at Charing Cross four years ago.'

Hooke deliberated over that while he went over to the iced-up windows to stare at the forbidding snow-laden sky outside. After a few seconds of reflection, he turned to Raven again with a long sigh. 'There is one man of my acquaintance who fits your description, Henry, although I had thought him dead of the plague. I met him and his sister briefly in London four years ago. He had heard of my ability to make the most powerful and efficient air pumps. He was desirous that I make one for him, which I did. He said that he wished to do research into the nature of Torricellian vacuums.'

'What was this man's name?'

Hooke frowned. 'His name was Simon Ingledew. As a young man, Ingledew had fought on the Royalist side in the Civil War. Yet his father was the infamous Parliamentarian Colonel Silas Ingledew of the New Model Army, who was executed at Charing Cross with Harrison and the others. He died a most barbarous death.'

Raven tried to hide his elation at finding a plausible name for this villain so easily. 'Did you meet Ingledew before or after the execution of his father?'

'A few weeks after, I am sure. Ingledew intended to return to the East where he had been living for many years among the Ottomans. He did strike me as a man of some genius, particularly in his knowledge of the anatomy and workings of the human body, which seemed much superior to mine. He told me that he believed he had discovered a possible cure for smallpox, which would have been a wonderful thing, if true.'

'Was he disfigured in any way?'

Hooke shook his head vigorously. 'Nay, that is why I hesitated to name him at first. He was a most handsome man of five and thirty, and of an immense height, if brusque and superior in his manner. His sister, Carolyn Ingledew, was also very tall and splendid-looking. They were both naturally embittered, though, after the awful death of their father.'

Raven came and stood by the window with Hooke. 'And…?'

Hooke shrugged his narrow sloping shoulders. 'I met them only a few times, over a period of several weeks. I eventually supplied Ingledew with his air pump – the best I ever made, I think - for which he gave me the generous sum of ten pounds. I met him for the last time in Deptford – at the Anchor Inn - from where he was intending to take ship with his sister to Flanders, and thence beyond. I did exchange some desultory correspondence with him later on scientific matters, but then I heard two years later that he had died.'

Raven blinked slowly. 'From whom did you hear this?'

'I received a letter from his sister to that effect. She too was still living abroad. I believe she wrote the letter from Vienna. She did tell me in her letter that she was working as a performer and actress on the Vienna stage. I must admit I was very surprised by this assertion because she seemed a most respectable young gentlewoman to me when I met her. But I imagine she had to do what was necessary for a lady in her position to survive…'

Raven felt his heart racing at this unexpected information. It seemed a notable coincidence that "Madam von Kladowitz", the illusionist and performer who had almost impaled the King of England with a crossbow bolt, was supposedly Austrian, and from Vienna too. Could that perhaps have been Ingledew's sister who had given that magic show at the palace two days ago? If so, it would certainly explain her connection to the plot. 'Do you still have this correspondence with Mr Ingledew and his sister?' Raven asked.

Hooke glanced around the untidiness of this room with an ironic smile. 'Back in my rooms in Oxford somewhere, perhaps. And buried under a thousand other letters...'

Raven said nothing but merely smiled faintly in wry acknowledgement that Hooke was not the most punctilious of men for keeping things in good order.

Hooke became more assertive. 'If you are right about Ingledew being still alive, then he might be the man you seek, Henry. Even four years ago, Ingledew struck me as a volatile and unpredictable man of genius, someone who might be capable of great good in the service of his fellow men, or perhaps – if the pendulum of his mind happened to swing the other way – of great evil towards his fellows. And, if the latter, who knows what additional terrible knowledge this ingenious man might have acquired during his years abroad to use against the rest of mankind...?'

*

With Martin driving the tiny carriage as it bumped over the frozen ruts of the city streets on its way west, Raven was left alone in the narrow back seat to ponder the story that Mr Hooke had told him. The route took the carriage first southwards down Bishopsgate Street, passing all the many coaching inns that filled this street from end to end to accommodate passengers setting out on the North Road: the White Hart to the north of St Botolph's, the Dolphin, the Flower Pot, the Wrestlers, the Green Dragon, the Angel and the Black Bull. This latter inn, Raven knew, had been a venue for the Queen's Men theatrical troupe seventy years ago, and its most famous actor Will Shakespeare, though Raven himself had always preferred drinking in the nearby Catherine Wheel tavern where he had spent many happy hours with his friends Strange and Mawdsley. The late Sir Paul Pindar – the famous merchant who had become King James's ambassador to the Ottoman Empire - had lived nearby to this inn in a fine house, and, before buying his present home in St Martin's Lane, Raven had been minded to make an offer for this excellently situated house in Bishopsgate, only to be firmly rebuffed by Pindar's son, who had no intention of selling.

The carriage rattled on down Threadneedle Street, then into Cheapside, which was thronged with street traders and stalls as usual despite the arctic cold. The winter was showing no signs of releasing its hold on the city yet; if anything the cold seemed to be growing even more intense with every passing day so that the very air crackled with frigidity. The cold did have the useful effect of inhibiting the usual foul London smells, but even such cold as this could not defeat entirely the collective effects of horse and cattle dung, dead rats, refuse from hospitals, slaughterhouse offal, and the evil-smelling premises of glue-makers, candle-makers and tanners.

From the relative comfort of his back seat, Raven listened to the familiar cacophony of street cries as his carriage made its way along crowded Cheapside: *"Twelve pence a peck, oysters!"; "Knives, combs or inkhorns"; "Hot baked wardens!"; "Crab, crab, any crab!"; "Buy my fat chickens!"; "Who will buy my flounders!", "Buy a fine singing bird, sir!"; "Small coal for sale…!"*

And among all these vendors of eels and pea soup and tripe, and stallholders selling sheep's trotters and livers, were the throngs of jugglers, entertainers, beggars, pickpockets and whores who made a living on these cold streets entirely by their wits. The beggars and thieves were of many proliferating kinds these days, Raven knew: priggers of prancers; abram-men, who counterfeited insanity; hookers or anglers; rufflers, uprightmen and palliards. Raven could hear a man with minstrel inclinations singing *The Merry Milkmaid,* a popular new song on the streets, but his voice was ill suited to the melody and the man was soon rounded on by a gang of low class ragged villains who bared their arses at him, and then pelted him with disgusting offal to silence him.

The jostling of the Cheapside crowds forced Martin to stop the carriage for a moment outside a coffeehouse, and Raven, glancing through the main window of the establishment, saw the gentlemen at the long communal table inside engaged in an intense and vulgar debate about the King. He even thought he heard the name "Castlemaine" mocked loudly by one red-faced gentleman, and wondered sadly why that beautiful lady should be the subject of so much venom and malice from the masses.

A fight had meanwhile broken out in the street ahead of the carriage between two particularly ugly rogues who had drawn knives on each other. Somebody in the crowd called out for an officer of the Watch but Raven knew there was never more than one constable and half-a-dozen watchmen to police each ward of this teeming city, so neither of these rogues had too much fear of being caught and dragged up before the bench.

Eventually the fight stopped when one of the men fled, and the crowd ahead began to thin, so that Martin was able to stir his mare Bessie into movement again. The immense black shadow of St Paul's loomed ahead of them, blotting out the snowy sky. After Ludgate Hill, the going was easier still, with most of the crowds behind them now.

From Fleet Street, Raven caught glimpses of the frozen wasteland of the river, as gaps appeared in the sprawl of tiled roofs and thatched roofs to the south. St Bede's church was decorated in a thick glaze of white, while the wooden landing stages of Temple Stairs and Whitefriars Stairs were almost buried under hillocks of ice. In normal weather the heavy green waters of the Thames would lap comfortingly against the walls and watergates of Dorset House and Essex House and the other waterside mansions, providing the main thoroughfare of this city. Yet, given the vicious cold of this endless winter, with boats frozen solid at their moorings, no one would be leaving those grand riverside mansions by water any time soon, Raven decided wryly.

Martin finally turned off Fleet Street at Wich Street, then entered fashionable Drury Lane. The people on the streets here had more elegance than the crowds of Cheapside, but even these promenading ladies and gentlemen looked frozen to the marrow in their fashionable costumes. The collapsible parasols carried by the ladies were little use against this bitter north wind, although the gentleman's wigs were perhaps a useful addition for once in protecting many a balding head. Raven was amused to see that even in this weather, some of the ladies were wearing patches, which did at least form an interesting contrast to their pinched white cheeks.

Martin eventually pulled the carriage to a halt outside the main entrance to the King's house in Bridges Street. Raven stepped out at once, only to see a worried Sir Thomas Killigrew waiting just inside the main door.

Sir Thomas recognized Raven at once and beckoned him inside with a wave. Raven found Killigrew was deeply distracted, though, and far from being in an amiable mood. 'Young Molly has not appeared today,' he confided, after Raven had asked him what was wrong, 'yet she is due on stage this afternoon in *Sir Politic-Would-be*. I sent Mr Whelan to her home to inquire as to her well being, and he found Mistress Hornett to be in a most distraught state. There was some altercation last night inside her home, it seems. Molly went into the street later to recover, and simply disappeared. Mistress Hornett has not seen her since...'

Raven was deeply concerned by this unsettling news particularly when he remembered that Molly had called at his house yesterday, presumably with some important news to impart. He cursed himself now for wasting so much time at the palace yesterday trying to uncover the tracks of this so-called "Madam von Kladowitz" when he should have been helping Molly instead. Sir Thomas led a worried Henry Raven into the main part of the theatre where they found a dejected company waiting on stage. One young Irish actor in particular was almost in tears as he approached Sir Thomas. 'Something terrible must have happened to Molly to keep her from appearing for rehearsals today,' he said. ' 'Tis my fault entirely, Sir Thomas, I should have looked after her better.'

Sir Thomas put a reassuring hand on his shoulder. 'Nay, 'tis not your fault, Patrick. Let us hope that we are wrong, and that Molly has merely been held up by something trivial.'

Raven was not convinced of that optimistic hope, though. Molly must have come to his home yesterday with some particular purpose in mind. Had she perhaps discovered some fresh evidence about the deaths of the two actresses in the company? *Or a worse possibility...*had she gone in search of the murderer herself?

Raven became aware that Jane Golightly was standing near him, and clearly wished to say something to him in private.

He led her into a private corner behind the stage to hear what she might have to say. She was in female garb, of course, and entirely feminine in appearance so that Raven had almost forgotten by now her bizarre claim to be a man. 'Is Molly in trouble, Mr Raven?' she asked with apparently genuine concern.

Raven nodded soberly. 'I believe she is. Perhaps even in great peril.'

Jane looked downcast. 'Then I am distressed to hear it. Could her disappearance be something to do with the deaths of Sarah and Anne?' she asked in a whisper, casting nervous looks around her.

Raven was thinking rapidly. 'Alas, it could be so. Do you know anything of where she might be? Did she say anything to you yesterday before she left the theatre?'

'Only to do with the play we were rehearsing together - *Sir Politic-Would-be*. Nothing of Sarah or Anne.' She had a sudden thought. 'I did however notice her looking at Miles Brammer from time to time during rehearsals yesterday, and I thought I detected some hostility on Molly's part, although I could be entirely wrong.'

Jane had mentioned Miles Brammer to him before, and Raven could not help but look in the direction that Jane indicated with her eyes. Raven recognized him at once as the actor who had played Duke Orsino in *Twelfth Night* at the palace. Brammer was a most handsome young fellow, with an almost feminine prettiness to his beardless face.

Jane turned her eyes back to Raven. 'Molly is a sweet girl at heart, so I hope that no harm has come to her.'

Raven agreed. 'My sentiments too...' His face was impassive but, inside, his mind was churning at the thought that by his negligence he might have let Molly Titchen suffer a similar fate to her fellow actresses Sarah and Anne...

*

*Cold...deadly cold...*such a terrible cold as she had never known before...

This was Molly's overwhelming thought when she woke from a much disturbed sleep on this frigid Monday morning.

She found herself lying on a straw mattress on a wooden floor, her hands and feet tightly bound, and with hardly any feeling left in them at all. The single window was shuttered tight, but a little light penetrated cracks in the wood so she knew it was already morning. Yet she was no longer gagged or blindfolded, so she reasoned she could not be anywhere where it might help to shout to raise an alarm. That feeling was reinforced by the fact that she had been taken such a long way from the city by her abductors. Tied up in the back of a four-wheeled cart, and gagged and blindfolded securely too, she had tried to guess her route as the cart trundled slowly through the night. She was sure that they had gone right through the city, and then across London Bridge. The sound that wooden wheels made when traversing the stone pavement on the bridge was quite different from the normal sound they made on streets of frozen mud. Molly had expected the journey to stop not long after that, anticipating her destination to be somewhere in Southwark. But that crossing of the bridge turned out to be only the start of her journey, which went on for another uncomfortable hour or more...

The discomfort of the journey took the edge off her fear, in some strange way. Yet she was deeply fearful of the tall dark woman and her hideous accomplice, and what they might be intending to do to her.

She had no doubt that this was the woman she had seen leaving the tiring room in the King's house on the night of Sarah's death, even though the woman was much more plainly dressed now. It was a comfort at least to know that the dark lady had not been one of the actresses of the company after all (although it also made her motive for harming Sarah more mysterious, and left Anne's death unexplained entirely, since how could this dark lady have even been in Whitehall Palace that night...?)

Yet, despite her clear identification of the dark lady, Molly doubted sincerely that the scarred man with her could be the bewigged gentleman she had seen outside the Duke's theatre in company with her.

It was true that she had not seen the man's face in any detail – from the front she had only got the briefest impression of the man as he struck out at her with the blade of his sword - but what little she had seen suggested a handsome young man, not this scarred and raddled face from a nightmare.

At least she had only been abducted by the two of them. There had been no sign of their other likely accomplices, Feathered Hat and Toothless – Parish and Wedderburn, as she now knew them.

This led Molly to assume that the bewigged gentleman she had seen outside the Duke's house must have been Miles Brammer after all. That was entirely possible, given his known connection with Parish and

Wedderburn.

But if it were true, it suggested a very large and worrying conspiracy to murder actresses of the King's company for some unknown reason...

Tied up on this straw mattress in this bitterly cold room, Molly wondered where exactly she was, and why her abductors had brought her here at all. Why had they not simply slit her throat back in Rope Lane?

The cart must have travelled many miles beyond Southwark so she could be anywhere in the Kent or Surrey countryside. She was now imprisoned in a tall house or inn - and somewhere high up in the building, like an attic or garret room, judging from the sloping roof beams, and by the number of stairs she had been carried up by the man at the end of her journey by cart, while still blindfolded and gagged. Yet from the sounds of lapping water and raucous gulls outside, she thought she must be somewhere near the river still. And since the river was still apparently flowing here, she must be well downstream of London Bridge, perhaps at Deptford or Greenwich, where the river was tidal.

Whatever their reasons for leaving her alive, though, her abductors had made a bad error of judgement because Molly was far from giving up...

Molly cast her mind back to her altercation last night with that blackguard "Sir William". It seemed she might have some reason to thank that slimy rogue now because after the fight with him, she had been careful to replace her knife in its secret place beneath her skirts just in case he came back to the bawdy house.

And lying on her cold straw mattress, Molly could feel that knife in its sheath still strapped comfortingly to her right thigh...

CHAPTER 17

Monday, 19th December 1664

It took Molly several hours of determined effort to free herself from her bonds.

With her hands tied tight behind her, and her feet and legs bound rigidly together too, it took a considerable degree of bodily contortion, and ingenuity, to get her fingers into a position to reach the knife strapped to her thigh. Even then her hands were so tightly bound, and had so little feeling left in them with the cold, that she had extreme difficulty manipulating them into a position where she could direct the blade at the ropes tying her wrists.

At best she could get only her right forefinger and thumb to hold the handle of the knife, and then to begin sawing through the ropes with a patient back and forward motion of that finger and thumb.

Patience was the key word because many minutes of such sawing seemed to make no visible difference to the thick ropes at all, as far as she could tell from feeling the cords with her fingers. The slight nick she had made in the ropes seemed no more than a paper cut deep. But she summoned up fresh supplies of mental strength from somewhere deep inside her, and continued sawing blindly. At least she could feel some resistance to the movement of her blade, which meant that she had to be sawing through something. She just hoped that it was not one of her own fingers she was sawing through, but given the lack of feeling in them, it seemed to be a possibility. Molly had the disconcerting thought that she could probably saw through her entire hand at present without feeling a thing.

Yet, in the end, with a sudden rush, the ropes simply fell apart as if by magic, and she found her hands were free. It was then a much simpler matter to untie the bonds around her legs and ankles, but a considerably longer matter to try and restore some feeling back into her frozen limbs. She walked up and down in the chill dark attic, beating her arms and legs vigorously into motion, and wondering whether she would ever feel warm and comfortable again.

When the blood did start to flow again in her extremities, she felt great relief, but also agonizing muscular spasms in all parts of her body. The straw mattress looked very inviting now, and she was sorely tempted to subside back onto it again and rest for a while. Yet she reminded herself that she was still a prisoner of these evil people, so this was no time to rest on her laurels.

It suddenly occurred to her that she was probably late by now for rehearsals for *Sir Politic-Would-be*, a thought that left her even angrier with her abductors than all the other indignities and pain they had inflicted on her. Her part as the strumpet in that play would no doubt be given instantly to one of the other young girls in the company and, if they were any good at all, Molly would no doubt find her stage career short-lived indeed. The thought of having her stage career destroyed in this way before it had even started made Molly's blood boil with fresh resentment against this dark lady and her masked accomplice, to add to all the other reasons she had for hating this evil pair of villains.

Forcing her limbs to move with a conscious effort of will, Molly stumbled her way to the shuttered window. She was reluctant to open it for fear that someone outside might be looking up from below and might spot instantly that she was free of her ropes. So instead she found a large knothole in the warped timber and peered through that. She found she had been right in her supposition, and that she was imprisoned at the top of what seemed to be a tall merchant's warehouse or storehouse by the river. The lighter grey of the sky in her view suggested that the sun had risen in that direction this morning, so Molly judged the storehouse faced more easterly than north. There was deep snow lying on the low riverbanks opposite, she saw, and a surface crust of blue-white ice reached out from the banks into the shallows of the river, yet the main channel was flowing normally and was open to shipping. Molly moved her eye back and forward over the knothole in the wood, and glimpsed a forest of masts in the river, their tall black lines and spidery rigging almost at her eye height, and outlined in stark contrast against the bleak white uniformity of the far shore.

Her view through this small hole in the wood was exceedingly limited, yet still sufficient to reveal that the river appeared to curve sharply to the west again upstream of her position, so Molly decided she must indeed be on the outskirts of the village of Deptford on the Dover road, perhaps quite near the Royal Naval dockyard.

By chance Molly knew Deptford a little, since this was Celia's birthplace. Celia had sometimes brought her to this village as a little girl, at a time when Celia had been regularly in the company of a seagoing gentleman of means known as "Captain Tommy", who happened to lodge in Deptford too. This gentleman might even have been a real captain in Cromwell's navy for all Molly knew, although she doubted it somehow. All she could remember of him now was that he had been a handsome and kind-hearted gentleman, with a fine head of fair hair and twinkling blue eyes. He had died in the West Indies of a fever, so Celia had told her, and Celia had never much wanted to return to Deptford again afterwards.

Molly tried to recall what she knew of the village from her visits as a little girl. Once just a fishing village, and the last stopping place before London for coaches coming from Dover and Canterbury, it was better known now as the home of the King's Navy Yard, as it had been since old King Henry's time. The deep ford that had given the village its name - across the River Ravensbourne where it widened into Deptford Creek before joining the Thames - had now been replaced by a stone arch bridge, but no one had thought fit to change the name of the village to suit.

Molly tried to peer downwards through the knothole in the window shutter and saw that there appeared to be a wooden landing stage below at river level, a branch of which led out into the charcoal grey waters of the Thames. All colour seemed to have been leached out of the wintry river scene below, leaving it as a shifting pattern of greys and blacks. No vessels were berthed presently at the landing stage that Molly could see, and there seemed to be nobody working below on such a painfully cold day, as evidenced by the presence of a bold red kite that was standing in plain view at the end of the landing stage, and picking complacently at the carcase of some dead rodent.

Molly began to review her means of getting out of this building unseen. It was a straight sixty feet drop from this shuttered window down to the landing stage and river, and, even if she could climb down a vertical brick wall unaided like a spider, she would be plainly visible both from the ships in the river, but also — more pertinently perhaps - from the lower windows of the warehouse. It could be that she had been left alone in this storehouse therefore perhaps it didn't matter about trying to remain unseen. Yet Molly doubted that her abductors would have left her alone here: she was sure that the man with the terrifying face was still here skulking somewhere in the building, waiting to carry out whatever evil fate he had in mind for her.

Molly wondered about the possibility of using a more direct route to get out of the building, and tentatively tried the door to the attic room, but it was predictably locked, despite the fact that she had been bound hand and foot as well. These villains were clearly taking no chances of her escaping from this room. Molly bent down and peered through the keyhole of the door. There was no key in place on the other side, so she was able to make out a dismal dark landing, and the beginnings of a narrow wooden staircase that spiralled downwards into the gloomy interior of the building below.

Not being able to open the door without a much better tool than her knife, Molly was forced to re-examine her hopes of leaving by the window. Given the apparent lack of any human presence below – through the knothole, the red kite was still chewing confidently at his carcase on the landing stage – Molly decided she would have to take the risk and open the shutters. Yet even so, she did it very tentatively, hoping that the slow opening of the shutter would not attract any unwanted human attention from below, and warn her captors that she was free to roam. With the shutters finally fully open, and no glass to protect her, a great blast of icy wind suddenly blew in from the river, causing Molly to shiver violently from head to foot. Yet she could not afford to turn back now, especially as she could see for certain that there was no one standing below. A quick glance down confirmed the impossibility of climbing down, though. Even a trained monkey could not climb down such a sheer wall, she thought with exasperation. The entire front face of the building was a tall timber frame in-filled with smooth brick, and with no significant projections of any sort – not even the odd nail or projecting beam – to help her find a way down.

Yet above her head was something that gave Molly a little hope - a gnarled wooden lifting-beam that jutted out a good ten feet from the gable wall above. Yet there was still a major problem to overcome before she could exploit that beam: even by standing precariously on the window ledge, with her back towards the river and the icy wind gusting around her skirts, and with her arms and fingertips stretched upwards to their limit, Molly could still not quite reach the underside of it.

She jumped back down from the window ledge and quickly scanned the room for anything that might help. Apart from the straw mattress on which she had lain, there was virtually nothing in the room. Molly was about to give up in despair, until she remembered the ropes she had been bound with. She had cut the ones tying her wrists, though, and what was left was too short to be of much use to her. But she had untied the ropes around her legs and ankles, and she found a serviceable length of ten feet or more remaining among the discarded remnants. If she could loop that length of rope around the lifting beam, then she might be able to lift herself onto the sloping roof above. What she would do then she had no idea, but simply had to hope there was some feasible way off the roof other than the way she had come.

Standing on the window ledge again – with the red kite on the landing stage below still acting as her unofficial unpaid watchman as before – she found it a surprisingly simple matter to throw one end of the rope around the beam, and then to feed it back down to her level. After tying the dangling ends together and making the rope secure, she could now support her weight with it. Yet to climb up that rope she would have to step off the window ledge into space and rely on the strength of her frozen hands and arms to pull herself up. Her courage almost failed her when she looked down at the long drop below her, but her simmering resentment against these evil villains who had abducted her strengthened her resolve, and she quickly launched herself upwards into space. Hands gripped tight to the rope for dear life, she shinned up the rope with all the speed and strength she could muster. In a few moments she was able to pull herself onto the flat top of the beam and take a well-earned rest. She blew some pathetic warmth back into her icy hands while from far below the red kite looked up for a second from its meal and regarded her with usual raptor suspicion. Yet the bird seemed remarkably unimpressed by Molly's climbing feat (despite her own feeling that she deserved some considerable applause from someone for this display of bravery) and soon returned its attention to its unappetizing meal.

It was but a short step up from the top of the beam to the edge of the sloping roof. Once Molly was on the roof, though, she wondered whether it would not be better to return instantly to the garret. The roof stepped up and down in a series of ridges and valleys, with several tall brick chimneys penetrating the ridge lines. The roof was clad in clay tiles, but these were now covered in a thick carpet of snow. Underneath the snow, Molly's probing fingers soon revealed a skin of ice as smooth as glass. At the eaves, the ice spilled over the edges of the roof into spectacular hanging icicles of a prodigious length and diameter.

Molly saw that her storehouse was but one of a series of three similar buildings, whose combined storage capacity must be vast. She guessed from the colour of the landing stages in front that the building to her left was used to store coal, while the one on the right was apparently for grain. Her own building seemed to be a general storehouse for all sorts of materials and goods.

The grain store looked the most promising of the two adjacent buildings to try and reach because it had an external timber staircase that ran down one corner of the building, from roof to river level. Yet there was a six-foot gap separating her roof from that of the grain store, which seemed as wide and forbidding as a ravine…

Could she jump such a fearsome-looking gap, from one steep snow-covered roof to another? It seemed a certain way to die…

Molly moved along the central ridge of her storehouse roof, looking for a saner alternative. As she paused at the back of the main chimney in order to get some respite from the arctic blast of the wind, she heard the sound of distinct voices coming from a room below.

She realized at once that the chimney was acting as a perfect conduit for channelling sounds upwards, and she could hear these people below almost as well as if she was in the same room with them.

The voices were of a man and a woman, and, after hearing a few words, Molly soon had no doubts of their identity. This was undoubtedly the evil couple who had abducted her last night...

*

Their talk was of surprising things at first, though.

The man spoke up first in a cultured voice. 'Tell me, sister. What is the famous young Emperor Leopold like?'

The woman was talking in the more rapid tones of the two, yet her voice sounded equally cultured to a shivering Molly on the roof above. 'His many names and titles are impressive, at least. Leopold Ignaz Joseph Balthazar Felician, Holy Roman Emperor, King of Hungary, King of Bohemia. And his lineage is equally impressive: he is the second son of the emperor Ferdinand the Third and his first wife Maria Ana of Austria. His maternal grandparents were Philip the Third of Spain and Margaret of Austria, and he is also a first cousin of his greatest rival, Louis the Fourteenth of France...'

'Impressive lineage indeed,' sneered the man.

The woman did not react to that belittling remark. '...Leopold was intended for the Church, but his prospects were changed abruptly by the death of his elder brother Ferdinand ten years ago of smallpox, when he became his father's heir...'

The man sounded bitter. 'Then the brother was lucky to die so quickly and not have to face the agonies I suffer every time I look in the mirror. But what of Leopold as a man? Is he handsome? – I have not seen his likeness drawn anywhere.'

The woman sniffed coldly. 'You have not missed much pleasure there: Leopold is not at all handsome. He is in truth physically unprepossessing. It proves that ancient lineage does not count for everything...'

'He is ugly like me, then?'

'Not like you, brother! You were a most wonderfully handsome man, and it pains me greatly to see your beauty destroyed by that cursed disease. Leopold was however born short and sickly, and he has inherited the Hapsburg lip to a degree unusual even in his family. His gait is slow and deliberate; his air pensive, his address awkward, his manners uncouth, and his disposition cold and phlegmatic.'

The man laughed. 'He sounds a delight! Yet, despite his cold and phlegmatic disposition, did you not sleep with him anyway, sister?'

The woman sounded unapologetic. 'Of course I did: I could hardly refuse his advances – how can one refuse a Hapsburg emperor? - and he was a proficient lover, if a little distant.'

'You were of great service to him outside the bedchamber too, I believe,' the man suggested with a grunt.

'I was. As you know, the Ottoman Empire had begun to interfere in the affairs of Transylvania, always an unruly district of Leopold's empire. So Leopold dispatched me personally to that province early last year to discover who was promoting this unrest. I soon discovered that the Sultan had purchased the loyalty of two Transylvanian noblemen who were acting as his *agents provocateurs*. This interference by the Sultan could not be tolerated for long by Leopold, and as a result war broke out again between his empire and the Ottomans last year. In August this year, Leopold gained a notable victory over them at Saint Gotthard, and by the Peace of Vasvár forced the Sultan into a humiliating treaty which amounted to their virtual surrender in Transylvania.'

'And how much of this victory was due to the intelligence that you provided Emperor Leopold with?'

The woman laughed. 'At the risk of sounding immodest, all of it. I informed Leopold of the identities of these two traitorous noblemen in Transylvania, and they were quickly arrested and hanged. The Sultan was then suddenly deprived of all his former secret intelligence within Transylvania...' The woman changed the subject with brutal suddenness, which almost made Molly jump at her freezing listening post on the roof. 'Why have you brought that girl here alive, brother? Why have you not slit her throat immediately as I asked?'

The man's voice was subdued. 'Perhaps I tire of doing your dirty business for you, sister. Why do you want this girl dead?'

'Because she might be able to identify me, brother.'

'I doubt that exceedingly. This girl clearly knows nothing of your true identity. She is naught but a simple orange girl turned actress...'

'Do not slight the profession of actress, brother! It has stood me in good stead over the years. I do even feel some degree of sympathy for this girl when she has probably had to submit to Sir Thomas Killigrew's pathetic little pistol in order to get her chance to appear on stage.'

Molly, shivering on the roof, was outraged at that slander. Sir Thomas was known to have a most serviceable member for such an elderly gentleman...

The man laughed cynically. 'And did you not perform the same service for Sir William Davenant in order to get your opening into the Duke's company earlier this year?'

The woman was clearly disconcerted. 'I certainly did not pleasure Sir

William willingly, 'tis true enough. But I ask again: why have you left the girl alive? You may be right that she cannot identify me, but I simply cannot afford to take the chance.'

'Then, if you are so keen to see her dead, be my guest. She is lying upstairs, trussed up like a capon. I will even provide you with a sharp knife that you may slit her throat with equanimity.'

The woman became hesitant. 'Despite my career as an intelligence agent for the Emperor and others, I have never had much taste for killing in cold blood.'

The man sneered again. 'The deaths of those two other actresses did not appear to cause you a similar fit of conscience, sister.'

'Those were different. The one in the palace was insensible already. And the first one in the theatre took just the prick of a thorn. Give me that same thorn and I will do the same now for Molly Titchen, without any qualms.'

'Alas I have no more of that particular thorn, or of that delicate poison with which it was tipped.'

The woman sounded annoyed. 'Then *you* slit her throat, brother! I did your bidding at the palace on Wednesday last, at great risk to myself, and put the fear of God into our merry monarch by loosening the rope on that chandelier...'

'You forget - that was not exactly at my bidding, sister. I asked only that you create some sort of worrying disturbance. I did not ask you to murder anyone. You did that entirely of your own volition.'

The woman growled almost. 'I was at the palace on your instruction! You will not deny the much riskier action that I took a few days later, though, I presume. That was certainly at your bidding. So you owe me recompense for that, brother. '

'Hah! You enjoyed every minute of that experience, I'll wager, showing your magic skills, and your seductive body, to that attentive courtly audience. I would have said that the balance sheet between us was still in your favour. If anything, you owe *me* further service, sister.'

'You were surprised when I told you that Henry Raven was at Lady Castlemaine's party, were you not?' the woman asked in a goading tone. Molly, listening above by the chimney, became even more attentive at the mention of Mr Raven's name.

'I was *most* surprised,' the man admitted without rancour. 'I had thought him dead and buried under a ton of rubble at my former nest in Southwark. That wealthy young gentleman seems to have an unpredictable talent for survival. But it matters not. Neither Raven nor his friend Mawdsley can stop my plans now.'

The woman did not reply to that for a moment. When she did, her voice was quieter. 'Why did you want the King humiliated in that way? I could have put that bolt straight through his head; in fact I was sorely tempted to, given the vulgar way that he looked at me throughout that show.'

The man simmered with anger. 'That would be too easy a death for him. I want Charles Stuart to understand what true suffering is like. Do you have no urge for revenge against him for what he did to our father?'

The woman was scornful. 'No, I have not. Our father was a foolish idealist at best, who deserved his sorry fate. I look out only for myself.'

The man's anger subsided quickly, and he laughed almost at his sister's cold and calculating cynicism. 'So why did you want these no-account actresses dead, if it has nothing to do with revenge? And now you want this Goodricke person dead too. Why is that? How do their deaths serve you, sister?' Molly was listening so intently now that she had almost forgotten the dreadful cold, as she wondered who on earth this Goodricke person might be.

The woman seemed reluctant to answer. 'I had no particular enmity for either of these actresses, since you ask. They simply stood between me and something I want - it was no more or less than that. Goodricke is now the final obstacle that stands between me and my reward.'

Molly heard the man get to his feet and begin to pace the floor deliberately, the clunk of his boots on the wooden planking echoing up the chimney.

The woman sounded defensive. 'I commend you again on the efficacy of the poison you gave me to use on Mistress Lusted. Are you sure that you have none of that subtle poison left? It made for such a sweet and painless death that it scarce seemed a crime.'

The man laughed sourly. 'Yet it certainly was a crime, sister, and one for which you will hang if you are caught, believe me. The poison I gave you is a chemical confection made from the juice of a rare East African fungus. It stops the heart almost instantly once it penetrates through the skin and into the blood stream. I commend you in return for finding the vein in her neck so accurately with that piece of Jerusalem thorn I gave you. She must have died in a second and never known a thing.'

The woman did not seem minded to accept the compliment. 'At least when I kill, it has some purpose, some reward. With you, it seems entirely without reason. Revenge is for children, brother! There will be no reward, financial or otherwise, for your worthless mission. If you kill the King eventually, what then? His papist brother will simply rule in his place. Where is the benefit for you in that? And after you have done this deed, where would you go from there, brother? With your ravaged face, and with the fortune that you made in the East gone, there is no refuge for you in Europe. You can never rejoin polite English society again, Simon – that way of life is now closed to you forever, looking as you do.'

The man was still pacing angrily. 'I do not intend to stay in Europe, sister. A new world beckons me. I shall make a fresh start in the Americas as soon as my work is done here. Perhaps among the savages of the New Wrld, my scarred appearance will be more acceptable than it would be in Drury Lane.'

'How can you make a new life for yourself when you are virtually penniless?' the woman snapped. 'Do you expect me to give you the money?'

'Rest assured, I shall not need your financial help. I shall not be penniless after the deed is done.'

'You mean after the King is dead?' The woman then gasped aloud as a thought apparently occurred to her. ''Tis not the King's death that you truly seek at all, is it? You could have killed him thrice over already, if you wished. I see it now...'

'What see you, sister?'

'The threat to the King's life is merely a distraction to draw attention away from your real target. You probably intend that James Blight will be blamed for the attacks on the King, while you escape. And this storehouse below us is filled with enough gunpowder to blow half the King's ships in the nearby dockyard to kingdom come...'

The man grunted with satisfaction. 'Perhaps your skills have not entirely deserted you since you gave up working as an agent for Emperor Leopold.'

'Who is paying you, brother?' the woman pressed him.

The man seemed reluctant now to answer.

The woman laughed triumphantly. ''Tis the Dutch of course. Who else would want to mortally wound the King's navy, but their main rivals at sea?'

Molly gasped at this fresh revelation but the man below did not bother to deny it. 'Does it offend your patriotism, sister, that I should take the money of the States General to use against my own country?'

'I told thee, brother. I look only to my own interests and work for anyone that will pay me well, even a papist emperor. Thou wilt hear no arguments in favour of patriotism from me. Now, what of the girl upstairs?'

'I have told thee already: I do not believe that she is a threat to thee or to me. Therefore I will let her live for the present. '

'Why? Has her pretty rump incited your lust?' Molly, listening above, was instantly angry at being dismissed as merely a pretty rump by this evil woman.

'Perhaps it has,' the man went on. 'But she may be useful to me in another more instructive way than merely satisfying my lust. You see, I have one final present for King Charles's kingdom too, and this girl seems ready made for my purpose. Trust me, though, she will die in the end, and in a far worse way than even you could imagine…'

The woman sounded uncomfortable for the first time. 'Evil seems to have infected your soul, brother.'

'And yours, *sister*,' the man responded quickly.

'Perhaps so,' the woman agreed. 'We shall have to let God decide in the end which of us has become the wickeder.'

The man was not finished. 'I have one more favour to ask, sister. Concerning your two henchmen…'

'What of them?'

'Can you lend me the services of one? I have much hard lifting to do in the next few hours, and only a few men to help. One more strong pair of arms would not go amiss.'

'Then, provided you pay him, and provided he is agreeable, you may take Parish, the taller one with the feather in his hat. The other one – Wedderburn – I still have need for, to help me deal with Goodricke, since you have no more of your clever poison…'

'Thank you, sister.' The man hesitated. 'This may be our last meeting in this life, I fear. Will you embrace me one last time, despite the ugliness of my face.'

'Gladly, brother…'

A long pause followed. 'Remember though, brother. Do not let that girl live, unless you are sure she can never come back to haunt us.'

'Trust me, sister. She is already as good as dead…'

*

On the roof Molly was shaking uncontrollably by now, and not merely with the cold any more.

Returning to the edge of the roof a few minutes later, she leaned her head over and was just in time to see a cart pulling away down the frozen track leading away from the river to the main London road. There were two figures riding up front on the cart, both heavily muffled, but no doubt the dark lady and her villainous toothless accomplice Wedderburn.

Molly padded slowly back to the chimney, leaving another row of tracks in the snow on the roof. She was back in time to hear the man below bark an order to some minion. 'You had better go upstairs and check on that girl. I am not sure I trust your friend's knots.'

Molly panicked when she realized she had only a few moments grace before her escape was discovered. And they would soon work out from the disturbed snow on the lifting beam where she had gone. Molly quickly slid up and down the next ridge of the roof until she was on the side of the building away from the river, where it came closest to the roof of the adjacent grain store. Then, with a quick prayer, she simply ran along the last ridge and launched herself into space, trying to reach the equivalent ridge on the adjacent grain store roof. Somehow she managed to make the other side with two feet to spare, yet there was nothing for her to grab on to, and she began instantly to slip off the ridge sideways towards the rear of the building. Sliding on her back down the snow-covered slope, she did her best to brake her motion with her heels. But it was to no avail on the icy surface, and she slid over the overhanging eave like water going down a pipe.

Yet her luck held, because she did not slam into the hard frozen ground sixty feet below, but fell instead into a deep mound of straw and cattle dung at the rear of the grain store, which was giving off so much heat that it was steaming in the frosty air. Molly disappeared into this warm mound of filth, only to soon roll out again.

The smell was disgusting; she was covered head to foot in this hot foul mixture. But she was alive, she was back on solid ground, and she was suddenly warmer now than she had been all day.

The surprising thing was that no one seemed to have noticed her fall from the roof of that storehouse, neither from the many ships anchored on the river, nor from inside the storehouse itself. Perhaps it was because she had fallen off the rear of the building rather than the side facing the river. The lane at the back of the storehouses was presently devoid of any human life or activity, which was extremely fortunate, but perhaps not surprising given the arctic weather. Yet her escape from the attic room must still be discovered soon, Molly reminded herself, and a hue and cry would result.

Nevertheless Molly was not yet prepared to simply run for it. Instead she found her way to the back of the storehouse where she had been imprisoned. Here there were cobbled bays for loading and unloading goods onto carts, but with no one presently working. Apart from the storehouses, there was nothing else here: a bleak wilderness of leafless trees and gaunt black hedgerows, a cart track with deep frozen ruts, and wintry fields over which a scouring wind blew drifting snow.

Molly saw that the back gate to the storehouse was open, though, and before she had time to debate the wisdom of her move, found herself sneaking inside to take a further look.

As the evil sister had said, the lowest floor of the storehouse was packed with crates and barrels, row after row of them, some stacked four high. Molly was shocked at the number of barrels, though, despite what she had heard earlier. If these all contained gunpowder, there seemed enough to blow the entire city of London to eternity.

Then Molly heard a strange scurrying sound, like the sounds of tiny feet against metal. She wormed her way further into the storehouse, hiding behind barrels as she went, although, in truth, anyone with any sense of smell at all could have detected her in her present stinking state at a hundred paces. Yet something inside this storehouse smelled even worse than Molly did at present, and she soon found the origin of that foul smell and that scurrying noise.

Cage after cage of animals, each pacing back and forward, their sharp black eyes devouring her in the semi-darkness.

Black rats…

Hundreds of them…

*

Molly got out of that dreadful place as soon as she could, and made her way back to the river side of the building again. Perhaps she could find a boat to take her back into London as far as the bridge anyway. Although what boatman would take her in her present disgusting foul state, and without any money, she could not think.

She had just reached the front corner of the building when a pair of powerful hands suddenly locked around her neck from behind and dragged her backwards by her hair.

Molly recognized her assailant instantly as Parish, the man who had killed poor Amy in Coal Hole Lane.

Even Parish seemed intimidated by the smell of her, though, Molly was mortified to see. But at least it allowed her to free herself from his grip and to turn and face him.

She backed away from him to the edge of the landing stage.

Parish followed her, his mood ugly. 'How did you get free then?' he asked her, puzzled. He smiled balefully, showing hardly any more teeth than his toothless friend Wedderburn. 'You stink of cow shit, Molly, do ye know that?'

He grabbed her again by the throat with his outstretched right hand and pushed her back to the very edge of the landing stage until she was standing, balanced uncomfortably, on the last plank. 'I believe I owe thee some bloody retribution for knifing me last time when I was not expecting it, young Molly. That cut you gave me caused me some considerable pain and discomfort, so I feel I should return the favour in kind. Now that ye have no knife, I feel much safer with a wildcat like you, Molly Titchen…'

Molly gritted her teeth. 'Why would…ye think…I would have…no knife, Mr…*Parish*,' she said triumphantly.

Parish saw her right hand suddenly move with dizzying speed, then felt a massive pain in his left side, as if he had been hit by a sledgehammer. He barely had time to glance down disbelievingly at the knife buried in his chest up to the handle, before toppling face forwards into the icy waters of the River Thames…

CHAPTER 18

Monday, 19th December 1664

It had just finished striking eleven times on the Whitehall Palace clock when Anthony Mawdsley found the King on the flat roof of the Council Chamber where he kept a small telescope for late night observations.

Mawdsley bowed low. 'Excuse me for disturbing you so late, your majesty, but Lord Clarendon told me that you were still awake, and making observations of the comet tonight.'

The King straightened up from peering through the eyepiece of his ten-feet-long refracting telescope. Mawdsley had not seen this impressive new brass and gold instrument close up before, but it seemed that the King spent much of his free time making observations with it from the roof of Whitehall Palace. 'Indeed I am still awake,' the King admitted without rancour. 'Yet I could not waste such a wondrous clear night as this in mere drowsy sleep. This small telescope is no match for the magnifying power of the one that Sir Paul Neile had made for me for the Privy Garden, but being so much shorter, it is infinitely easier to manoeuvre.' The King glanced up at the sky. 'The heavens are a wondrous sight tonight, are they not, Mr Mawdsley, even with only the naked eye.'

Mawdsley had to agree as his eyes took in the majesty of the heavens above. Today had been a miserable snowy day, yet tonight the air had magically cleared, leaving an extraordinary night sky, ablaze with celestial wonders. He doubted that he had ever seen the stars appear with such compelling clarity before. And the earth below seemed a different place too, silent and still, and bathed in ghostly starlight. Arrayed below this vast starry sphere, the rooftops of London seemed huddled for protection from the cold under their crisp white coating of snow. It occurred to Mawdsley as he watched his own icy breath rise towards the heavens that it must have been on just such a peaceful night as this that the magi had travelled to Bethlehem to witness the birth of our Lord…

'Do you know much about the heavens, Mr Mawdsley?' the King asked him curiously, having noticed his visitor's eyes straying upwards.

'Alas no, sire,' Mawdsley said apologetically.

'Then let me show you some of its wonders.' The King went on to point out the outlines of the main winter constellations: Orion the Hunter, Taurus the Bull, Auriga the Charioteer, Canis Major and Minor, the Great and Little Dogs. Mawdsley was struck by the King's boyish and enthusiastic tone as he described this wondrous natural spectacle, which carried no hint of anything patronizing or didactic in its message, but merely the pleasure of one human being in enlightening another. Mawdsley followed the line of the King's outstretched hand as he pointed out the brilliant open cluster of the Pleiades, the yellow star Capella and her attendant "kids", fiery red Betelgeuse as bright as a ruby, brilliant Rigel, the belt of Orion, the limitless stars of the Milky Way. And the fierce blue-white glitter of the dog star Sirius, which seemed so close to Mawdsley that he felt he could knock it from the sky by merely throwing a pebble.

The famous comet, on the other hand, was a slight disappointment to Mawdsley, being neither particularly bright nor particularly prominent, although it was spread over a prodigious area of sky at least.

'Do you know, Mr Mawdsley, that we have no idea how far away these stars are?' the King said. 'Yet their lack of any measurable parallax means that they must be infinitely further away than the planets. Yet even the scale of our own solar system eludes our best scientific minds at present, even the ingenious Mr Hooke and Mr Wren…' The King fought back a yawn. 'Yet you did not come here merely to listen to a lecture on astronomy, I think. You have something to tell me…'

'I do indeed, sire. I have brought important tidings. Mr Raven has this evening sent me a message, which I have just read. He believes that he may know the identity of the man who has threatened your life…'

The King waited in eager anticipation. 'Yes, go on…'

Mawdsley took a deep breath, as he wished he had thought of this name himself. 'Raven believes the man to be Simon Ingledew…'

The King frowned. '*Ingledew*…? That is a familiar name to me.'

'Yes, it should be, sire. If you will allow me to remind you, Simon Ingledew served on your father's side during the Civil War, which is why I had never thought of him as a candidate for such treachery. He also left England after Cromwell's victory, and has not been heard of in his homeland these many years, although there were reports that he was living among the Ottomans. Yet he is also the son of Colonel Silas Ingledew, who was one of your father's greatest enemies… '

The King swore softly under his breath. 'By God's lid! Of course!

That Ingledew was one of the cursed regicides!' He paced up and down a little before turning to Mawdsley again. 'And what think you of your friend's opinion? Is he right about the younger Ingledew?'

Mawdsley nodded solemnly. 'It seems entirely possible after considering the evidence. I have examined the foul letter that was handed to Lady Castlemaine in the park, and the pattern of three oak leaves on the wax seal does indeed bear some resemblance to the Ingledew family crest.'

The King planted one gloved fist firmly into his other palm with clear satisfaction. 'Then we have him. Now that we know his name, we can soon run him to ground!'

Mawdsley had more to say. 'Mr Raven has a further cogent theory about this insidious plot. Simon Ingledew has a sister, Carolyn, who has lately been living in Austria. Mr Raven believes that *she* might be none other than the woman who fired the crossbow bolt at your head two nights ago.'

The King laughed uneasily at the memory of it. 'I shall not forget that provoking moment in a hurry, Mr Mawdsley. But can that brazen hussy dressed in the guise of a half-naked odalisque truly have been an Englishwoman? And the daughter of a stern Puritan like Silas Ingledew?'

Mawdsley made a wry face. 'It seems that she could. Carolyn Ingledew is known to have worked as a performer and actress on the stage in Vienna so she and "Madam von Kladowitz" could indeed be one and the same person.'

The King was elated so much with this revelatory news that Mawdsley began to realize for the first time how seriously he had taken this sinister threat to his life. 'Mr Raven's case appears plausible on the face of it, then - perhaps even convincing,' the King said spiritedly.

'Yet we must not drop our guard, sire,' Mawdsley warned. 'Not until we apprehend Ingledew and his sister anyway, and discover whether they are truly the guilty parties.' Neither Mawdsley nor Clarendon had yet confided to the King their suspicions of James Blight, and Mawdsley decided to leave matters that way for the moment. Yet it would be interesting to see if he could discover any past link between James Blight and the Ingledews...

The King agreed. 'Of course we should not drop our guard, Mr Mawdsley. It goes without saying. Yet I am tolerably reassured that this threat is simply the work of a lone madman –' he laughed – 'or a lone madman and his deranged hussy of a sister anyway.'

Mawdsley hesitated. 'Do you plan to stay here on the roof the whole night, sire? Is that wise on such a fierce cold night as this?'

The King smiled. 'You sound very like the Queen, Mr Mawdsley, who is always telling me to rest and conserve my strength. Or Lady Castlemaine too, for that matter…although that lady is being a little more circumspect in giving me her opinions for the last day or so, since the embarrassment of her little soiree nearly led to my demise…'

'Perhaps the Queen is right to advise rest, sire. You have a busy day tomorrow.'

The King smiled charmingly. 'Nay, we have been talking an hour or more, Mr Mawdsley, so 'tis already midnight. So I have a busy day *today*.'

'Even more reason to rest, then, sire.' Mawdsley thought ahead to the grand ceremony that was due to be held at the Royal Dockyard at Deptford in the morning.

Three of the King's warships had been through a major refit during the last few months in the vast dry dock at Deptford, in preparation for the inevitable war with the Dutch. And tomorrow would see these three vessels re-floated, and then re-dedicated with great ceremony within the dock, with the King and all his chief officers of state on board. Afterwards the ships would be hauled out through the gates and into the river so that the common people of England could witness the might and grandeur of the King's navy. Foremost among these three vessels was the *Royal Charles*, a first-rate three-decker ship of the line, and the acknowledged pearl of the King's navy. She had been built by Peter Pett at Woolwich dockyard nearly ten years ago for the navy of the Commonwealth of England, and named the *Naseby* in honour of Cromwell's recent decisive victory over the Royalist forces during the Civil War. Yet the King nevertheless had a great affection for this ship because it was the vessel – hastily renamed in his own honour - that had sailed to Holland four years ago to bring him back to England from his long exile abroad...

The King was still reluctant to leave for his bed, despite his clear tiredness. 'I will not retire just yet, Mr Mawdsley, but I promise I shall stay only for a few minutes more. Before you go to your own bed, though, Mr Mawdsley, please come and look at the form of the comet through the telescope. It may seem no more than a streak of pale luminescent cloud when seen with the naked eye, but it looks much more impressive when viewed through a lens.'

Mawdsley allowed himself to be persuaded, and was duly startled by the appearance of the comet. Magnified, it did truly have a malevolent look, plain white in colour yet with a vast elliptical head, a pronounced curving tail, and intricate and unexpected details. ''Tis truly a wondrous object, sire,' Mawdsley agreed with genuine interest.

The King was pleased at Mawdsley's reaction, yet wary too. 'You do not believe that comets are harbingers of some terrible human disaster, do you, Mr Mawdsley?'

'I do not, sire. That is mere superstition.'

The King frowned worriedly. 'Yet, with the comet reaching such a climactic phase this very night, I do wonder if the ceremony at the dockyard tomorrow should go ahead. Perhaps we are tempting providence in ignoring this sign in the heavens.'

"Tis too late to change the plan now, sire,' Mawdsley almost snapped. 'A vast crowd will be there at Deptford, and we cannot disappoint them.'

The King sighed with a deep note of melancholy. 'Worry not, Mr Mawdsley. I was not being overly serious, merely thinking aloud. Of course the ceremony must go ahead. The Archbishop of Canterbury will be there to bless the *Royal Charles* and her sister ships in their future service to the crown, while most of the Privy Council will be in attendance on board too. It should be a magnificent occasion.'

Mawdsley felt compelled to say something positive to raise the King from his fey and melancholic mood. 'Fear not for your safety at the ceremony, sire. You will be surrounded by thousands of your navy men and loyal subjects so one lone madman like Ingledew can do nothing. Naught will go amiss.'

The King slapped him affectionately on the shoulder. 'Of course it will not! Yet I would like you to invite your Mr Raven to the ceremony, if you will. For some reason, I take great comfort from that man's presence. He seems a most gifted and able individual. He saved my life once already in the last week, which perhaps explains this sympathy I feel for him. And now he has certainly identified this sinister enemy of mine, so inspiring even more gratitude on my part.'

Mawdsley was not sure what to say to such an encomium for his friend. 'He will be grateful for your good opinion, sire. I shall try and persuade him to come, but he is a busy man and he may have an engagement elsewhere...' Raven had also informed him in his letter of the disturbing news that Molly Titchen had gone missing from her home last night, information that had given Mawdsley some pause for thought. Mawdsley had mocked Raven many times over the last week about his supposed infatuation for that orange girl, but now he realized for the first time, from the sad tone of Henry's message, that his friend was genuinely taken with that pretty strumpet, and was worried for her life.

Mawdsley became aware that the King was waiting for him to say something further on the subject of Henry Raven. 'I shall go to his house at first light and make sure he comes with me to Deptford, sire.'

The King smiled tiredly. 'Make sure you do so, Mr Mawdsley. If Mr Raven is still reluctant, say it is a Royal command...'

*

Snuggled up in a warm feather bed for the night , Molly Titchen was glad tonight that she had been born a comely and well-endowed girl, otherwise she was sure that she would have frozen to death today out on those wintry marshes near Deptford. It might be a man's world – in fact there was little doubt of it in her mind - yet there were times when it was a great advantage to be a pretty woman...

She thought back to events earlier in the day. After escaping from the vicinity of the storehouse by the river - and still in a highly emotional and abject state after that final violent act of her escape - she had not had any clear idea in her mind of what to do next, beyond knowing that she had to find some warm shelter quickly, otherwise she would perish from the cold.

And then to rid herself of these stinking foul clothes...

She was mortified at the thought of anyone seeing her in this bedraggled and wretched state, and smelling worse than a cesspit. Especially if it were anyone from the theatre. She could only imagine Mary Pettican's superior smirking face if she should turn up at the King's theatre looking and smelling like this.

Yet Molly knew that the journey back to London was too great a distance to contemplate walking in her condition anyway: she would be dead of cold before she got halfway. Somehow she had to find somewhere to rest and recover her senses - somewhere warm and inviting like a barn - although such places were likely to be thin on the ground in the bleak fields and marshes that bordered the village of Deptford. It was already well past noon, Molly observed, and the short winter's day would soon be coming to an end. In fact there was so little light on this dismal snowy afternoon that it seemed as if dusk was already falling. The thought of being trapped out on these marshes overnight made her heart thud with panic, a feeling which forced her to keep moving in her desperate search for shelter, despite her terrible fatigue. She naturally headed west at first, a direction that took her away from the river, which ran near north to south at Deptford.

Yet there seemed no refuge on her way west that could remotely offer shelter: the track leading back to the main London Road from Deptford was no more than a dismal line of bare hedgerows that meandered through a wilderness of snow-covered fields, bare copses and the odd abandoned hovel that looked too cold and desolate as a refuge even in Molly's distressed state. The way ahead seemed entirely devoid of life – no reassuring coach tracks, or even the imprints of human feet; no sounds of voices, just the threatening howl of the icy wind and the scouring drift of the snow. The only good thing was that the snow on this track was so hard-packed already that she was leaving no clear footprints of her own that could be followed by any pursuer.

Molly could not see any sign of a warm barn or an inviting farm outbuilding ahead where she might be able to get some shelter and try to bring back some warmth to her shivering body. The snow had started falling yet again, obscuring the view behind her with thick driving flakes so that she could no longer even see the tall shapes of those distant storehouses where she had been imprisoned.

Then she came to a crossroads where the road joining seemed more promising of human activity since it showed the fresh wheel tracks of a passing cart. Molly doubted this could be the main London road itself – it still seemed too little used for that - yet perhaps it might lead her that way. The left turning seemed the more promising of the two alternative directions; there were certainly more wheel tracks in that direction, although not all fresh ones. Yet she followed that way anyway for a while, hoping that her instincts for finding the right road would prove to be sound in this case. Dragging her icy feet step by step, she finally espied a farmhouse of some sort in the distance, set back a little from the road at the end of a track that wound its way through a gnarled stand of leafless silver birch trees. Although this was the largest building she had seen since fleeing the storehouse by the river, this was certainly no rich farmer's house, but merely a poor smallholding of some sort. Yet when she investigated further, Molly found that there was a barn of sorts at the side of the farmhouse, and a neat yard in between surfaced with compacted stone and cobbles. The cottage itself was sheltered by a straggling line of poplars whose bare branches sighed and moaned in the relentless east wind.

Molly jumped suddenly when a voice challenged her from behind. 'What do you want here, girl?'

Molly turned around sharply to see a well-built man of forty regarding her suspiciously from just inside the barn.

'I have suffered an accident, sir,' Molly explained timidly. 'I need food and shelter, or I shall freeze to death.'

The man seemed kind-hearted for all his plain round face, unkempt hair, and black Puritan garb. 'You had better get inside in the warm, then. I will just fetch more wood for the fire, then I will join you.'

Molly did not need a second invitation, but went inside the cottage at once, and straight over to the fire. It was a poor place but spotlessly clean, she saw, with an earthen floor laid with the remnants of last summer's meadowsweet, white-washed walls and low oak beams that showed the mark of the adze on their flanks. A heavy cauldron of water was bubbling over the fire.

The man entered after her, encumbered with logs of wood, so Molly turned and curtsied politely. 'Where is your wife, sir?'

'In the graveyard down the road,' the man answered gruffly, as he bent down and filled the scuttle by the fire with the fresh supply of firewood. 'My children are both there too to keep her company.'

'I am sorry to hear it, sir,' Molly said, abashed.

''Tis of no matter now. They are in a better place than in this vale of earthly sorrows.' The man prodded the fire back into life with an iron poker, but Molly noticed that he was giving her a close inspection out of the corner of his eye as he did so.

Molly coloured as she became aware of his close scrutiny. 'Have you somewhere where I could wash myself, sir. I am ashamed of the smell I have brought into your fine house. I fell into a ditch.'

'It must have been a ditch filled with cow shit, then, girl,' the farmer said in lighter vein. 'Yet I have smelled much worse than you in my time.' He pointed with a stubby finger. 'There is a tub in the scullery at the back, and you can draw as much water as you need from the well. And I have a cauldron of hot water over the fire here to warm thy ablutions should you need it. Thou art most welcome to use that.'

Molly nodded her gratitude. 'Thank you kindly. But cold water will do me well enough, sir.'

The man stood up and regarded her with a friendly eye. 'Nay, girl, thou art frozen to the bone, so take the hot water. I can always heat some more. What age are you, girl?' he asked curiously.

'Sixteen, sir. And what is your name, sir, that I may address you properly?'

The man held out his hand. 'My name is Crabtree, John Crabtree.'

She accepted his hand, but only after rubbing her palms on the cleanest part of her dress to remove the worst of the filth. 'I am Molly Titchen, sir.'

'Well, Molly, get those filthy clothes off while I fetch the water for you. Then you can tell me where you sprung from on this raw afternoon...'

Now, many hours later, Molly woke in the middle of the night and thanked God she was a comely and well endowed girl. The tall tub of warm water in which she had bathed this afternoon had been a wonderful blessing, and Mr Crabtree most attentive to her needs once she smelled half decent again. He was a nice man at heart, if terrible lonely. Molly had learned a little of her host's personal history while eating a supper of boiled pig trotters with him this evening. Mr Crabtree had been a carpenter in the dockyard at Deptford until last year, but had then taken over this smallholding on the death of his older brother. It had proved an unhealthy and fateful place for his family, though. His wife had died six months ago of a fever, followed quickly by his young son and daughter, leaving him on his own to raise his pigs and chickens on this windswept marshy holding.

And perhaps his loneliness and need for human company explained his manner, which was an odd mixture of brusqueness and shyness. Yet, shy of her or not, he had seemed happy enough to share his bed with her tonight, and presently slept soundly under the same covers with her.

Yet Molly did not truly mind this forced intimacy; the man had clearly not enjoyed the company of a woman in a long time, and a kiss and cuddle with him before sleep seemed a fair trade for a warm bed for the night, and food in her belly. She was even wearing his late wife's nightdress, and tomorrow she might have a choice of the dead woman's day clothes to choose from, even if the only colour to choose from appeared to be black.

Molly turned over uneasily in bed and wondered what to do on the morrow. Mr Crabtree had promised to take her on his cart back into Deptford and even to lend her the fare for the coach from Deptford back to London Bridge, which would save her the long cold walk. She would have to return to London as quickly as she could and tell Mr Raven what she had discovered. She was confident that she would be able to help him catch that evil man and his sister before they could do any more damage, or kill any more innocent people...

But who was this Goodricke who still stood in the way of the dark lady's ambitions? Molly asked herself. There was no one in the King's company of that name that she knew, so at least none of them at the theatre had anything more to fear from the woman, which was a blessing.

Yet, as she tried to get back to sleep, the thought of the evil scarred brother was perhaps a greater worry to Molly than the dark sister. What terrible deed was he planning with so much gunpowder at his disposal...?

Did the man truly intend to attack the King's ships in his own dockyard, and do the work of the damned Hollanders for them? It seemed utter madness for him to contemplate such a thing – surely he could never hope to succeed against the collective might of the King's navy?

Yet, before taking the coach to London tomorrow, Molly thought that perhaps she would have to try and persuade Mr Crabtree to take her first in his cart to the dockyard in Deptford. Perhaps, with Mr Crabtree's help, she could warn the gentlemen of the King's navy that a madman was on the loose and that they should take due notice of any suspicious visitors to the Royal dockyard...

Mr Crabtree turned over in his sleep too and snuggled up close to her. He was a powerfully built man and Molly could feel his hard stomach muscles pressed against her back and buttocks. She moved her own trapped hand out of the way and discovered accidentally that he also had a most formidable erection in his sleep. But she was not disconcerted by this discovery; she was used to the rough habits of men and understood their physical needs very well after her time working in Celia's bawdy house. And in truth this was actually a pleasant way to drift off to sleep, in a warm straw bed, and in the company of a grateful man, especially when she remembered the cruel way she had been treated by that other monstrous man last night...

CHAPTER 19

Tuesday, 20th December 1664

The clear conditions that had provided a starry sky overnight had persisted into morning so that the Royal dockyard at Deptford was bathed on this early Tuesday morning in brilliant low sunlight. The red disc of the sun lay poised above the snow-covered hills of Kent, casting pale rose shadows across the whiteness, and picking out the shapes of woods and copses, and the intricate buried patchwork of fields. The sunlight was scarce strong enough to melt any of the snow and ice that encumbered the fields and marshes along the river in a thick white blanket, yet it added immeasurably to the cheerfulness of the scene. For the first time in many days, the dour clouds and mist had even lifted from the distant rooftops of London to the west, and revealed the city in a more beneficent and glowing light.

Standing in the vast dockyard at Deptford among the most important people in the realm, Henry Raven was inspired to considerable pride - as any patriotic Englishman would be - by the magnificence of this enterprise, which looked a splendid hive of activity in the clear morning sunlight. This dockyard was a veritable city of its own, peopled by a swelling army of shipwrights, carpenters, chandlers and smiths, who swarmed in great profusion all over its wet docks and dry dock, its great storehouse and slipways, its lifting derricks and sawpits and mast houses.

The dry dock alone was nearly two hundred feet long and presently housed three of the greatest ships in the King's navy, including the *Royal Charles*, while every one of the slipways leading down to the water was occupied by a warship that had been hauled up from the icy river for repairs to its barnacle-covered hull. The gate to the dry dock had been opened last evening to slowly flood the dock, and the vessels inside were now floating freely again for the first time in many months. The refitting work had been undertaken at a reckless and inhuman speed because these ships were urgently needed at sea again. Raven was standing in a private sequestered area at the west side of the dry dock, an area presently reserved for the King and his guests as they waited to board the *Royal Charles*. But he felt uncomfortable among these fine people and their insincere talk and exaggerated manners, and had deliberately chosen to wait a little apart from them in the company only of Anthony Mawdsley. He was sore and chafed too after the journey from London, which was a further reason for his slight ill temper. His carriage might be a new design with improved iron springs, yet its lightness of construction, constricted size and narrow hard seats meant that it was still far from comfortable on these frozen country roads, and the jostling and many bumps he had received on the way had added considerably to the pains and bruises he was already enduring as a result of the explosion in Southwark four days ago.

The King's favourite companions, Charles Sedley, Lord Buckhurst and the Duke of Buckingham, were in the King's close company as usual on such grand occasions, Raven observed, which was no surprise to him given these gentlemen's penchant for basking in any reflected glory. All three of these reprobate courtiers seemed in particularly boisterous mood today as if they were already drunk on strong Italian wine.

Nearby, the King's handsome brother, James, Duke of York, was talking in affectionate terms with his plain and dumpy wife Anne Hyde, the daughter of Clarendon. And the King's other loyal courtiers were also here in force on this cold and sunny Tuesday morning: the first Earl of Clarendon himself of course, standing silently with the other senior members of the Privy Council - the Duke of Albemarle, Charles Berkeley, the Duke of Ormond and Henry Bennet, the Earl of Arlington.

The King was conversing presently in a private corner with his Queen, Catherine of Braganza, and with his bastard son James, Duke of Monmouth. Raven was struck by the amiability of the Queen towards her husband's pretty young son, who was turning into an undoubted peacock in his blue velvet coat and white silk stockings. This boy's presence must be a constant nagging reminder to the Queen of her own failure to provide the King with a male heir, Raven thought, which should have made her hate young Monmouth, if anything. Yet he could see from her genuine warm smiles that she clearly doted on the boy, and his soft pink cheeks and curling brown hair.

The real surprise for Raven was that Lady Castlemaine should be here - and looking lovelier than ever. She seemed to have overcome her embarrassment at the unseemly events of Saturday night, smiling an innocent greeting at Raven through a crowd of other guests, as he bowed to her in return. Though whether the Queen had forgiven her for nearly causing her husband's death on Saturday was an interesting and presently irresolvable question. Today, of course, Lady Castlemaine was forced to give precedence to the Queen, and was only here, Raven supposed, in her official role as a Lady of the Queen's bedchamber.

The atmosphere in the yard was convivial today, almost carnival-like, with a large boisterous crowd of the King's subjects, decked out in their best smocks and coats, gathered behind the end wall of the dry dock to witness the blessing of these giant ships after their re-fit. The mood of celebration among this patriotic crowd belied the solemnity and serious purpose of this occasion, as everyone here had to be aware that these fighting ships were soon off to war against a new and formidable enemy.

Mawdsley bowed an acknowledgement of his own to Lady Castlemaine, who favoured him in return with a most becoming smile. He turned to Raven, looking extremely pleased with himself after receiving such a warm smile. 'Art thou not glad that I persuaded thee to join the King's party today, Henry? Is this gathering not truly a wondrous sight?'

'It is indeed,' Raven admitted, '...though there was no "persuasion" involved in what you did,' he added dryly. 'You practically dragged me from my comfortable warm bed.' Mawdsley had indeed arrived at his front door in St Martin's Lane long before dawn this morning, and had forced a recalcitrant Dora Bagwell to rouse her master from his sleep. Mawdsley had then cajoled his yawning friend to come to Deptford immediately at the King's personal invitation, and was simply not prepared to brook any refusal. In the end Raven had acceded, and ordered Martin to make ready his own new carriage and his favourite black mare Bessie for the journey into Kent, but only because he had already been intending to make a journey to the Pool of London later this day anyway to go on board one of his own colliers before she set sail for the continent. The vessel – the *Anne Raven* - had already left Billingsgate Wharf and was presently moored in the river near Deptford waiting for a favourable tide this afternoon. Therefore it had not been too much of an imposition for Raven to go to the Royal Dockyard first, although he certainly had not admitted this much to Mawdsley. 'Yet I hope you have told the King that I must leave the celebrations early to go on board my own ship before she sets sail for Antwerp. 'Tis not so grand a vessel as the *Royal Charles,* yet I am just as proud of her as the King is of his namesake.'

Mawdsley smiled. 'I believe that affection is more because the vessel is named for your late beloved mother than because she has any great beauty of line.'

Raven looked towards the river, and spotted at once the distinctive masts of his Whitby collier, the *Anne Raven,* moored among all the other vessels in the shallows just upstream of the dockyard. 'You are right, of course. Yet the *Anne Raven* is a fine seagoing ship for all her plain looks, and I am most anxious to show her to my manservant Martin.'

Mawdsley made a wry face. 'You still wish to persuade him to move to the God-forsaken Tyne to manage your coalmines there? Is that why you want to show him that collier? It would certainly be a bold choice to give such a young and untried man so much power all at once. But I pity poor Mr Gibney nevertheless! I thought you liked that man...'

Raven was in two minds himself about this matter, so did not particularly enjoy his friend's bantering tone and now wished that he had never discussed this radical possibility with him. 'I do indeed, so it would be a great wrench to lose his regular company. Yet 'tis no banishment for him; this job could be the making of Martin, I wager. And, for all your prejudices about the North, Anthony, Newcastle is no miserable place of exile, but a fine prosperous town, built in a most imposing situation on steep crags above the river.'

Mawdsley smiled as he regarded the bleakness of the river in front of them. 'If the Thames is in such a frozen state as this, I cannot imagine in what state the Tyne must presently be. The ice must be a mile high.'

Raven smiled in return. 'As usual, Anthony, you exaggerate greatly...' Given that his trade depended on this river, Raven was glad to note that even in this harshest of winters the Thames was still fully navigable this far downstream. Yet, despite being passable, the river was still so thick with granulated ice on the surface that the water had the consistency of a dense cold syrup.

The thought of this bitter winter weather distracted Raven for a moment from mere thoughts of trade and commerce, as he remembered guiltily that there had been no word of Molly Titchen now for nearly a day and a half. What if she was out in this terrible cold somewhere...?

Or could she even be dead? he wondered bleakly. It was difficult to imagine any other reason why she would stay away from her mother and her friends without telling them where she'd gone. Or, even more, why she would stay away from the King's theatre, which she clearly loved with a passion.

Mawdsley had noticed the shadow cross his friend's face and understood immediately what he was thinking of. 'Is there any word on your strumpet Molly?' he asked lightly.

Raven still blamed himself for her disappearance, which made it even worse for him. 'None that I have heard.'

''Tis not your fault that she disappeared, Henry,' his friend admonished him gently.

Raven snorted angrily. 'Then whose fault is it? No, I should have paid her far more attention. I knew she was in danger from someone at the theatre, and yet I chose to ignore her plight.'

Mawdsley stamped his feet against the cold. 'You did not ignore her plight, Henry; you did what you could for her. But you have been rightly more preoccupied these last days with the threat to your monarch's life. It may be harsh to acknowledge it openly, yet a certain threat to the life of the King has to take priority over a possible threat to the life of a mere actress...' Mawdsley leaned forward and dropped his voice to a whisper, as he noticed someone standing behind Raven. 'Mr Blight is here today with the King's party, Henry, so please mark your manners to him and treat him with due respect. Lord Clarendon and I have kept his treachery to ourselves for the moment. We still have hopes that he might lead us to this man Simon Ingledew in due course.'

Raven tried not to glance around. 'You are truly satisfied that Ingledew is the man you seek?'

Mawdsley nodded. 'Indeed. I have made some enquiries overnight about Ingledew, and I have little doubt that he is the Beelzebub that we seek. According to an acquaintance of Mr Blight at court, Ingledew and Blight were boyhood friends in Bedfordshire, it seems, and then fought together in the King's service during the Civil War.' He grimaced. 'My only regret is that I was not the first one to think of his name.'

Raven shrugged carelessly. 'You may take full credit for it, then, should it prove correct. I seek no reward for it.'

'Alas, 'tis already too late. I told the King himself who was responsible for this insight. That is one more reason why the King wanted you here today. I believe he now regards you as his particular talisman. It seems almost that he believes that no harm can befall him when you are near.' He saw Raven's uneasy expression. 'Worry not, Henry. I have done my best to counteract this odd impression, and I am sure it will pass from the King's mind eventually, provided we catch Ingledew...'

Raven looked up sharply. 'Have there been no fresh sightings of Ingledew since that explosion in Southwark?'

Mawdsley glanced around uneasily, as if suspecting the man might even be in the vicinity at this very moment. 'No, none at all.'

'I can see that you are worried that Ingledew might wish to perpetrate some act of terror here today, are you not?' Raven nodded in the direction of the swelling crowds at the end of the dock. 'In truth, he could be any one of those people standing over there – most of them are so wrapped up against the cold that no one can see their faces.'

Mawdsley denied it heartily. 'Nay, one man on his own can do nothing against the King today. His majesty will be protected by a dozen men at all times…'

*

Now that the water level in the dock was finally high enough, a gangway had been laid from the quayside to the mid-deck of the *Royal Charles* between its quarterdeck and forecastle. As the King and his guests began to make their way in line to the gangway, Raven took the opportunity to turn his eyes skywards and admire the magnificence of this great fighting ship, whose tall oak masts and furled sails towered above them.

The *Royal Charles* was truly an awe-inspiring sight, and one that would hopefully put the fear of God into any Dutchman foolish enough to attack her. Following the refit, she now had a hundred cannons on her three decks instead of the previous eighty, enough to blow any ship on earth out of the water. At 1,229 tons, she was also far larger even than the *Sovereign of the Seas*, the first three-deck ship of the line, built by Phineas Pett, Peter's father. Since buying his colliers, Henry Raven had acquired some considerable knowledge of ship construction himself and he noticed that the *Royal Charles* had a more rounded hull than warships of old, while the stern was also much lower and sleeker than the vessels of half a century ago. The carving on the stern was less ornate too – although still decorated with the King's standard - and made the ship appear a lot more seaworthy and easier to sail perhaps than her predecessors. The *Royal Charles* also had the new royal sail, Raven noted, and the even newer innovation of staysails, which were attached to the stays that held the masts up and were triangular in shape like those of the strange Arab ships Raven had seen plying the North African shore in the Mediterranean…

As he brought his eyes back to deck level, Raven became suddenly aware that James Blight had fixed his gaze momentarily on him. In that brief instant when their eyes met, Blight's haunted look and haggard face gave away his guilt as clearly as a deathbed confession. Raven was sure from that bleak despairing expression that Blight knew all too well that he was now suspected of treachery towards the King, and that his days were numbered…

The King and Queen were the first to board the *Royal Charles*, followed by the Archbishop of Canterbury, Gilbert Sheldon. Raven knew little of Sheldon other than what Mawdsley had told him, but Mawdsley's view of him as a malevolent influence on the King seemed an undeniable truth: the man was all refinement and mildness on the surface, but inside Raven suspected that he was indeed all malice and deceit. What was beyond question was that Sheldon had taken a far harder line than the King and Lord Chancellor in his designs for the restored church, and that the contentious Act of Uniformity was far more his invention than Clarendon's. Physically Sheldon was perfectly cast for the role of Machiavellian religious plotter, being dark-haired, beetle-browed and intense-looking.

Clarendon and the more sober members of the Privy Council then boarded the *Royal Charles* with slow and deliberate ceremony. The equally dignified members of the Navy Board were just assembling to follow the courtiers on board in their turn when something caught Raven's attention out of the corner of his eye, some flash of light in the assembled crowd at the end of the dry dock. Puzzled, he turned his head in the direction of the crowd for a moment, but saw nothing to excite his interest at first, so assumed he had been simply mistaken.

But then he saw a flash of light again and realized that someone was indeed signalling to him after a fashion, perhaps with a piece of polished metal. Raven scanned the distant figures in that direction, trying to identify who might be signalling surreptitiously to him. One person stood out immediately among the group - a tall young woman dressed in Puritan black who even put her hand in the air as if waving to him...

It was difficult to see in that direction because the sun was still low in that quadrant of the sky and reflecting dazzlingly off the snow-covered hills beyond. Raven squinted his eyes into the bright sun, still doubting that the woman could truly be signalling to him.

But then he recognized her and his heart filled with unlikely joy...

An astonished Raven whispered an urgent message in Mawdsley's ear. 'Excuse me one minute, Anthony, but I believe that a friend is signalling to me from over there. And she seems to have something important she wants to tell me.'

Mawdsley looked around in confusion, but Raven was already gone from his side. Mawdsley swore to himself as he wondered how he would explain the loss of his lucky talisman to the King...

CHAPTER 20

Tuesday, 20th December 1664

Raven tried to conceal his great pleasure and relief at finding Molly alive and well, yet was entirely unsuccessful in that minor deceit. 'By all that's sacred, how came you here, Molly?' he said, beaming at her like a happy child. He regarded her thin black clothes with concern, though. 'Yet you are half-froze. And why are you dressed in sober black like a Quaker?'

Raven realized suddenly from her hesitant look that the stolid middle-aged Puritan fellow standing at her side was someone known to her, and not just an accidental companion.

Molly introduced him politely. 'This is John Crabtree, Mr Raven. Mr Crabtree has been of great service to me in my troubles.'

Crabtree appeared as uncomfortable as Raven as Molly uttered these words, but he shook Raven's proffered hand anyway, then stood a little aside from them in a dignified fashion to allow them to talk freely.

Raven lowered his voice to a whisper. 'Mistress Hornett said that you had disappeared. Where have you been these two days?'

Molly too kept her voice low, with so many curious bystanders watching them. 'I was abducted outside my home, sir, and brought forcibly here to Deptford...'

Raven cast an eye in Crabtree's direction, but Molly instantly corrected that mistaken assumption. 'Not by Mr Crabtree, sir, but by a most evil masked rogue. Yet the poor devil should not be blamed for wearing a mask because he is exceeding ugly under that mask, with a face that would cause great fright to any woman or child that saw it. And to most men too perhaps...'

Raven was shocked by this revelation. 'You mean you were taken by *Ingledew*?'

Molly looked puzzled. 'I know not the monster's name, sir, but he is a most evil man who is planning some great retribution against the

King.'

Raven made no answer as he struggled to understand why Ingledew would have abducted Molly of all people when she was nothing to him. Yet it could not be coincidence that he had taken her, so somehow there had to be a connection between Ingledew and the King's theatre...

'I have encountered just such a man in the last few days, Molly,' he finally said. 'I believe his name to be Simon Ingledew. It was he who was responsible for that great explosion in Southwark on Friday that killed many people...'

Molly gasped. 'Then it must truly be the same wicked individual who abducted me.'

Even though thoroughly confused by events, Raven eventually framed a sensible question. 'Where exactly did Ingledew take you, Molly?' *And why did he not simply kill you, like Sarah and Anne?* he wanted to add, but thought better of it.

Molly looked over to the *Royal Charles* where a line of red-coated soldiers had now arrived on the dockside to the sounds of drum and fife. 'He took me to a great storehouse by the river near here and tied me up in an attic room there,' Molly told him. 'One of three tall storehouses in a line, with a wharf for ships in front. 'Tis but a quarter mile or less upstream from here.'

Raven knew the storehouses and the wharf of which she spoke, because his own colliers had berthed there occasionally. 'Why did he take you there?'

Molly shrugged her shoulders. 'I know not, sir, except that he and his accomplices had some devious purpose in mind. The woman wanted to kill me...'

Raven blinked. 'What woman?'

'The man's sister,' Molly explained in a rush. 'She is the dark lady I saw leaving the tiring room in the King's theatre.'

Raven gave a gasp of understanding. *Ingledew's sister...*Of course! So that was the connection with the King's theatre – *Carolyn Ingledew...*

Raven was gratified that he had apparently been right in his conjecture about her helping her brother in his plot against the King. Yet he had never suspected that she might also have some direct connection with the death of the actresses from the King's theatre...

Molly was taking still. '...This vicious woman killed Sarah with some poison that her evil brother provided. She was also responsible for that chandelier falling at the palace last week, before our performance of *Twelfth Night...*'

Raven frowned. 'How do you know all this, Molly? Surely they did not admit all this to you openly...'

'Of course they did not, sir. But I managed to escape from the attic room in which they held me, and climbed onto the roof of this storehouse. And down the chimney I happened to overhear a lot of their conversation when the man and his sister were conversing covertly in a room below and congratulating each other on their mutual wickedness. That is how I know something of what he plans to do…'

'And what is that?' Raven demanded impatiently.

'He is plotting some severe action against the King. I know not what exactly, but he has been paid for this treachery by the Dutch…'

Raven became even more disturbed. 'The Dutch? So this is not simply an act of personal revenge by Ingledew against the King?'

Molly shook her head vehemently. 'I think not, sir. I found a way down from the roof of the storehouse and was able to get away into the surrounding countryside. That was when Mr Crabtree kindly helped me otherwise I would have froze to death on the marshes. But before I left, I made a point of looking around the ground floor of the storehouse, and I found it was loaded to the rafters with barrels…'

'Barrels?' Raven asked uneasily.

'Yes, barrels of gunpowder, I am sure. And Ingledew – if that truly is his name - had several accomplices there to help him, apart from his sister. One of them was the toothless man who murdered my friend Amy in Coal Hole Lane. By the way, I know his name now, sir: it is Wedderburn. That was the reason I called at your home on Sunday evening – to tell you I had discovered this rogue's name. But after they abducted me, I soon learned much more about this villain and his confederates.'

'Was the other man who attacked you and Amy not there? The rogue with the feathered hat?' Raven asked.

For the first time Raven had a feeling that Molly was not being completely honest with him as she avoided his eye. 'I did not see the other man, sir, though he could have been there.'

Raven looked over to the tall masts and rigging of the *Royal Charles* where a drum roll from the line of musket bearing soldiers on the dockside announced the imminent start of the ceremony of blessing the ships. A solemn hush fell over the crowd in turn as they watched the King and his guests on board fall silent.

Despite the call for silence, Molly whispered into Raven's ear. 'Ingledew intends to blow up the King's ship, I fear, perhaps with the King and his council on board.'

It would certainly be an audacious plan, and one the Dutch would no doubt be happy to pay a King's ransom for, Raven thought. But even if Ingledew had a vast supply of gunpowder at his disposal, it would not be a simple matter getting all that destructive power within reach of these vessels. 'How would he achieve that?'

'I could not discover that yesterday,' Molly said, still whispering intimately in Raven's ear, 'but Mr Crabtree knows that storehouse of which I speak, and he took me back there this morning to have a secret look from a safe distance. Yesterday there was no vessel moored there, but early this morning there was a large Kent sailing barge with red sails berthed at the wharf by the storehouse, and there were men loading it up with barrels. Hundreds of barrels…'

Raven breathed in sharply. 'What happened to this barge?'

'It set sail not long after we arrived.'

'Upstream or downstream?' he asked, almost snapping at her in his concern.

'Upstream, sir. It went around the next bend in the river and Mr Crabtree and I lost sight of it.'

'How many men were on board? And was Ingledew one of them?'

Molly concentrated her memory. 'I believe there were half a dozen men on board, sir. And the scarred man must have been one of the party because the storehouse seemed completely deserted afterwards.'

'What of this man Wedderburn? Was he also on the barge?' Raven asked.

'No, sir. I saw him leave on a cart the day before, heading towards the London road.'

Raven had a sinking feeling in his stomach as he contemplated events. Once this ceremony of blessing the ships was over, the *Royal Charles* and the other two vessels would be hauled out by rope into the river channel. At anchor in the main channel, and with sails furled, they would be helpless to manoeuvre out of the way if a vessel loaded with gunpowder should suddenly descend on them like a fire ship. Raven looked around the dockyard in sudden desperation, wondering what to do for the best.

The obvious course of action would be to go on board the *Royal Charles* and warn Mawdsley that Ingledew might be afloat nearby in a sailing barge with its holds full of gunpowder. But with the Archbishop of Canterbury presently intoning an endless prayer, which would no doubt be followed by an even longer sermon and blessing, it was out of the question for him to simply force his way on board at this juncture.

Raven decided rapidly on an alternative plan of action. 'We need to get on the river in a ship of our own, Molly. Then we can foil Ingledew, should he appear in his Kent barge.'

Molly almost laughed aloud at this ambitious plan. 'Where could you hope to find a ship at your disposal so quickly, sir?'

Raven pointed to the grey line of the river. 'See those tall masts over there, with the top sails just going up. That is my own ship, Molly, the collier *Anne Raven*. I think we should make haste and go on board…'

From the surprised look on her face at that casual pronouncement, Raven thought that he had quite taken the wind out of Molly Titchen's own sails for once …

*

Within twenty minutes or so, Raven and Molly were on board the *Anne Raven*. It had been a simple matter to leave the environs of the dockyard and find Martin and the carriage waiting at a nearby inn by the river, the Anchor Inn, and then to signal by hand to the crew of the collier to send over a boat to pick them up from the nearby landing stairs.

Before leaving the dockyard, Raven had invited Mr Crabtree along, but the man, clearly uncomfortable with the worldliness and bawdy language of the crowd around him, had declined to accept his invitation. Yet Crabtree had taken Molly's hand in a most intimate way before departing, so Raven had wondered at their odd relationship which seemed to border almost on the affectionate. Had she perhaps known this man before, to explain this strange intimacy? Or was she just very accomplished at exploiting older men with her feminine charms? On due consideration, Raven suspected the latter...

Yet this Mr Crabtree was a stern looking Puritan old enough to be her father, so Raven had no thoughts of any jealousy concerning the man. Surely Molly could not have been truly intimate with a stern man of that age? Raven himself was ten years older than Molly, and that decade difference in their ages seemed a large enough gulf by itself to have to bridge between a man and a woman, never mind twenty or thirty years...

Once on board the *Anne Raven*, Henry Raven made his presence known to the captain, a plain-speaking Newcastle man of fifty called Charles Armstrong. Raven was well acquainted with Captain Armstrong, of course, although he had frankly never formed any great rapport with the man, and employed him only because of his exemplary seamanship, nothing more. This blunt-talking Northerner soon made no secret of the fact that he did not like what he was hearing, when Raven explained the potentially dangerous situation.

Armstrong was never exactly deferential towards the owner of his vessel, but today he was even more recalcitrant and moody than usual, treating Raven as if he were some sort of deluded madman. 'And what do you expect me to do, Mr Raven, if this Kent barge with the red sails heaves into view?' he asked abrasively. 'I have no cannon to blow it out of the water. Even if I had, I would refuse to do it, because it would be murder. Where is your evidence that this barge has been taken over by a madman who has filled it with gunpowder?'

Raven glanced at the unlikely figure of Molly – the very image of a Quaker girl in that demure garb and plain black coif - standing amidships talking in subdued tones with Martin; this did not seem the most opportune time to explain to Armstrong her part in this drama, or the fact that he was basing his case for action entirely on her veracity and intuition.

'The King's ships presently have no useable weapons either, since they have no powder on board to fire their cannons,' Raven pointed out. 'Nor will they be able to manoeuvre out of the way if some burning vessel filled with gunpowder should bear down on them. A Kent barge on the other hand is eminently well equipped to manoeuvre in the river, by virtue of its shallow draught and nimble sails. We must try and prevent that barge getting close to the *Royal Charles*. It is our patriotic duty as Englishman...' he added hopefully.

Armstrong eyed him sourly. 'The word "patriotism" is invoked all too often by rogues who have not one ounce of such a commodity in their own bodies,' he said brazenly. 'And I have particular qualms about giving my own life to save the neck of a King such as this, who takes perverse delight in victimizing his own subjects.'

'I understand your feelings, Captain. Yet we cannot simply stand by and watch a disaster happen. Are ye with me or not? If you are not, then I will take over command of this vessel myself.'

Armstrong nodded curtly. 'Then 'tis better that I give my life for a worthless king, I suppose, than hand over the care of this ship to a landlubber, sir. So I am at your disposal...'

Raven went amidships and joined Molly and Martin. 'We have Captain Armstrong's reluctant cooperation, Martin, but I still do not trust his commitment entirely so I would be obliged if you would keep a close look on him, and watch what orders he gives to the hands...'

After Martin had gone aft on this delicate mission, Molly said in an annoyed voice, 'I overheard much of your conversation with the master of this vessel, sir. Yet the captain of this ship is your servant, is he not? He should do your bidding without question, as a wife should.'

Raven smiled. 'I doubt that a ship's captain is always as obliging as that in his actions. Or a wife too, for that matter.'

'Then shame on them. If I were a good man's wife, I would always do his bidding, even if I heartily disagreed with him. 'Tis the bargain a woman must make when she accepts a husband. And a captain who accepts the charge of a vessel from its owner should do the same...'

Raven said nothing to that, merely scanning the river upstream, so Molly continued. 'Is this ship truly yours, sir? I thought you spoke in jest when you pointed it out to me on the river.'

Raven patted the gunwales. 'You saw the name on the hull when we boarded, did you not?'

Molly admitted that ruefully. 'Then you must truly be a man of great wealth and power. I had not thought you quite so high.'

'Why did you think that?'

'Because you seem a modest man of sense to me, sir, unlike most very wealthy and powerful men,' Molly answered honestly.

'Then perhaps I will get less sensible in time, as I get older and richer,' Raven suggested dryly, though in fact he was touched by what she had said.

Armstrong had got the *Anne Raven* under way by now with a fair head of sail, and now he managed to bring her around through a hundred and eighty degrees to face upstream, which was a considerable feat of seamanship in this crowded river channel. Raven saw that the ceremony on board the *Royal Charles* was still continuing in the flooded dry dock, and for once had gratitude for the verbosity of English archbishops which was clearly extending the length of the ceremony. It might be another hour yet before the King and his guests finally disembarked, and the process of slowly hauling out the ships from the dry dock by capstan rope could begin. There was also a thick crust of ice at the dock gate that would have to be removed before the ships could leave, although a few men armed with sea axes would make short work of that small problem, so that could not be relied on to delay the entrance of the ships into the river for long.

Raven was just congratulating himself that they had an hour or more to prepare for Ingledew when he saw a vessel approaching from upstream out of the low white mist on the river. His heart began to beat faster as he saw that it was indeed a sailing barge with red sails. Not only that, it was approaching at reckless speed, its sails making full use of the strong north-easterly wind.

Molly too had gasped when she saw the barge. ''Tis him, 'tis the evil man.'

The vessel was still three hundred yards away, yet Raven could clearly make out the tall masked figure in the stern, directing the helmsman. As if to confirm the identity and purpose of the vessel beyond doubt, Raven saw that even its deck was packed with kegs and barrels. 'Never mind, Molly. Ingledew cannot inflict any damage on the King's ships while he is out here, and they are safe within the dry dock.'

Molly frowned. 'But what if he does not wait, sir, but simply charges his way into the dry dock?'

Raven was shocked into silence for a moment. 'That would be madness...suicidal madness! He would have no means of escape.'

Molly looked worried. 'Perhaps escape is no longer what he seeks, merely final retribution...'

Raven saw instantly from the track of Ingledew's barge that Molly's intuition was right. Ingledew was hugging the far north shore as close as he could, presumably in order to give himself enough space to turn into the open dock gates at a near right angle. In fact the vessel already seemed to be turning even as Raven looked, as the boom of its main sail swung outwards in response to the change of rudder direction.

Raven raced aft and shouted an order at Armstrong. 'The barge is trying to sail directly into the dry dock. We have to get to the gate first and block their entry.'

Armstrong did not look happy with that order, but accepted it nonetheless, and took over the helm of the *Anne Raven* himself. The collier was a slow and ponderous vessel in a river, whereas the red-sailed barge was purpose-made for such an environment, so this seemed like a race between a great lumbering tortoise and a fast and nimble hare. Yet the tortoise had the shorter distance to go and had the simpler task of obstruction, while the hare had the more delicate task of finding the precise line to take it through the narrow dock gates at high speed.

Raven saw the barge converging on the same spot immediately in front of the dry dock gates as his own vessel, and tried to calculate who would get there first, hare or tortoise. The *Anne Raven* was moving so slowly and cumbersomely at first that it seemed like no contest between the two, and that the barge would sail though the opening into the dry dock with half a minute to spare. But in his urgency the helmsman of the barge made a mistake in his course, and then had to subsequently correct his direction, which cost him valuable time. Whereas Armstrong, for all his abrasive manners, understood his tortoise vessel intimately, and judged its speed and direction perfectly.

In the end, the tortoise reached the gate of the dry dock ten seconds ahead of the hare. The barge was going at such a rate of knots by this time, though, that it could not deflect from its chosen course, and plunged into the side of the *Anne Raven* like a knife into a cow pat.

Raven felt the gigantic impact and heard the wooden hull of the collier disintegrating beneath his feet. He cursed himself for not realizing what would inevitably happen, yet even if he had, he would not have changed his plan. The sinking of his own beloved ship had to be a price worth paying to keep that madman out of Deptford Dry Dock.

Armstrong put his hands to his mouth and called on his crew with powerful tones to abandon ship, which was already awash with water at deck level and settling rapidly at the bows. Raven saw that the crew of the fast sinking barge were already abandoning their own vessel, having lowered a boat from the stern for just this purpose. Yet one man on the barge at least was making no move to abandon ship – the tall baleful figure in the stern. He had taken off his mask, and Raven saw his exposed face for the first time, bearing all the destructive scars of that terrible scourge, smallpox. It was then that Raven spotted a burning fuse on the deck of the barge – the madman might not be able to get his vessel through to the dry dock, yet he clearly intended to blow his vessel and the surrounding area up anyway, and hope to inflict some damage on his enemies.

Armstrong's crew were similarly trying to lower a boat from the stern of their vessel by now, but Raven had spotted a better alternative means of escape and shouted to Molly and Martin to come forward with him.

Raven tried to calculate how long they might have before the barge blew itself to kingdom come. When it did, the explosion would undoubtedly take the *Anne Raven* with it too, whose own holds were still half-filled with coal, and with the lethal explosive vapours that Durham coal was known to give off. Yet Raven saw that they had a small chance of escaping before the coming conflagration. The collier was now wedged by the impact with the barge against the outer limestone wall of the dry dock and spanning the open gate. In this position, the bows of the collier, although settling fast into the water, were very close to a vertical wooden ladder fixed to the half-immersed stonewall.

Raven arrived first in the bows of the *Anne Raven*, skidding to an ungainly halt in his urgency. The lower rungs of the nearby ladder were covered in kelp and other marine weed, and looked none too strong, yet they did offer the best chance of escaping the vessel quickly. The bows of the ship were unfortunately a yard or two short of the ladder, though, so it would take a significant jump to reach the rungs.

Martin and Molly joined him and instantly realized his intention when they saw the inviting ladder so close.

'You go first, Martin!' Raven ordered, not wanting Molly to have to try this difficult jump first. Martin instantly stepped up onto the gunwale at the bow, and launched himself into space. Being young and athletic, he made the leap look easy enough, which reassured Raven enough to help Molly up on the gunwale too.

She looked back at him with worry, yet Raven saw that she was remarkably self-possessed for a young girl in this perilous situation. She glanced down at her puritan black skirts and ripped the hem apart so that it did not hinder the movement of her legs too much. Then, gritting her teeth, she jumped towards the ladder with all the power she could muster. One of her feet landed precisely on a rung, but then slipped on the kelp-covered surface. Yet she managed to recover somehow, grabbing a higher and drier rung with her right hand, and getting both of her feet on the ladder again eventually.

A relieved Raven was just about to get up on the gunwale too in preparation to jump when he heard the sound of a musket firing, and saw a lead ball viciously strike the wall of the dock, not a foot away from

Molly's head, leaving a giant chip in the limestone.

'Keep climbing,' Raven urged her, as he looked around for the user of the weapon. Inevitably he saw that the musket was in the hands of Ingledew in the stern of the barge. Even though it was fast settling by the bows, it seemed Ingledew had no intention of leaving his vessel, but was determined to go out in a blaze of imagined glory...

Raven could see that Ingledew had re-loaded the musket and was about to point it at Molly again. It seemed that he was determined that she of all people should definitely not survive, although the odds of any of them surviving seemed presently remote. Yet the fact that Ingledew was concentrating his evil attentions on Molly quite enraged Raven, and, before he knew what he was doing, he had run across to the other side of the deck of the collier and vaulted across the gap onto the deck of the barge.

That was something that Ingledew had not expected, as Raven came at him in the stern of that vessel, snarling and threatening like a madman.

Ingledew pointed the musket at him, but Raven did not mind that as it enabled Martin and Molly to finally make it to the top of the ladder where they turned to look back at him with white strained faces.

Ingledew was half a head taller than Raven and looked down at him with contempt. 'My sister told me I should have killed that girl, yet I foolishly did not heed her advice.' He deliberately pointed the musket at Raven's face, directly between his eyes. 'Move one inch and I shall blow your head off. We shall both wait here for the end. It cannot be long; the fuse must be nearly spent. And be assured: this is one explosion that even a lucky soul like you cannot survive.'

'You want to die?' Raven asked in wonder.

'I do now,' Ingledew said bleakly. 'Life has become a bleak and unrelieved hell for me.'

'Not as bleak and unrelieved as the one you are heading to,' Raven said. 'But I do not care to wait for oblivion...'

With that Raven simply launched himself head first over the side of the barge and into the icy waters of the Thames. The shocking cold of the water made him gasp, yet he forced his arms and legs to keep moving as he swam away from the stricken vessel as fast as he could.

He knew that Ingledew had probably moved to the side of the vessel too, and could be pointing the musket at his head right now. Any reasonable shot would kill him from this distance, and Raven tensed himself as he waited for that violent impact to rip into the back of his exposed head.

Yet for some reason, Ingledew did not fire...

Eventually Raven stopped in exhaustion and treaded water fifty paces from the barge. He saw that everyone else had got off the two vessels by now apart from Ingledew. Armstrong and the crew of the collier were standing off in their boat a hundred paces downstream, while the crew of the barge were rowing upstream in their equally small boat as if their lives depended on it.

Ingledew raised his musket in mocking salute to Raven in the water, as the barge finally exploded in an immense ball of fire that lifted both trapped vessels bodily out of the water and then scattered their remains far and wide...

CHAPTER 21

Tuesday, 20th December 1664

Anthony Mawdsley stood on the dock wall and looked down at the shattered remains of the *Anne Raven* in grim disbelief. The hull had been completely ripped apart by the explosion, and all that remained were broken timbers and pieces of scorched canvas floating in the icy shallows. Of Ingledew's sailing barge, there was even less remaining. 'I am sorry for the fate of your ship, Henry – especially as it carries your mother's name - yet 'twas sacrificed in a noble cause.'

Raven shivered at his side, even though wrapped heavily in blankets that had been donated for his comfort by a grateful navy captain. 'I assume the King will make good my financial loss, Anthony?' Raven asked uneasily.

Mawdsley made an expressive gesture. 'Of course. Do you doubt that?'

Knowing this King, Raven doubted it most sincerely, yet he did not say so. This did not seem like the time for making such unpatriotic pronouncements.

Mawdsley swore under his breath. 'Be God's sonties! How close did that man come to killing the King and his entire council! Not to mention destroying three major ships of the King's navy. And you say Ingledew was working for the Dutch all along?' Mawdsley glanced behind into the dockyard where James Blight, now chained hand and foot, was being bundled into the back of a carriage for transport to the Tower.

Raven noted the man's dreadful bloodless expression as the carriage door was slammed behind him. 'Poor devil! I suppose it will be the rack for him.'

'Ay, and then hanged, drawn and quartered when the torturers are done with him. But it is his own doing...' Mawdsley added grimly.

In the aftermath of these unexpected events at Deptford, most of the King's courtiers and Privy Council members had departed rapidly from this scene of mayhem - this despite having to endure a bumpy and uncomfortable return journey to London Bridge and Whitehall by coach, as the river was still quite impassable upstream for the fleet of Royal barges that would have normally transported the King's retinue in more clement weather. Yet Raven saw that the King, for one, was still here in the dockyard, and even now approaching him and Mawdsley for a word.

Raven tried to bow at his monarch's approach, but the King waved the gesture away impatiently. 'Nay, sir, none of that ceremony. It is I who owe you a most reverential bow. You have saved my life for the second time in a week.' He looked around at the vast dockyard and all the tall ships gathered within its confines. 'In fact *all* our lives...'

'It was not my work alone, sire. In fact it was more *their* doing.' Raven pointed out the captain and crew of the *Anne Raven*, who were talking nearby to some of the men of the *Royal Charles* and exchanging pipe tobacco with them, and, no doubt – from the occasional hearty laugh - some rude and vulgar stories too.

'I will not forget their bravery,' the King said unctuously. 'But *your* bravery must take pride of place because you have also vanquished my enemy.' The King glanced down uneasily at the frigid water, still awash with wreckage and sinister stains. 'Ingledew *is* dead, I assume.'

'He would have to be the Devil himself, sire, to survive such an explosion as that,' Mawdsley assured him. 'I have never witnessed such a scene of destruction before, or the explosion of such enormous forces. It was as well that the *Royal Charles* was at the back of the dry dock, and that the dock wall deflected so much of that destructive force upwards rather than in our direction, or else Ingledew might still have achieved his aim...'

'That explosion would certainly have loosened a few gentlemen's wigs, including my own, if it had gone off inside the dry dock,' the King laughed, before turning his head and staring curiously at Molly and Martin Gibney, who were waiting patiently on their own, also wrapped up heavily in blankets. 'That Quaker girl...' the King began.

Raven was about to say something in response, but Mawdsley cleared his throat and came to his rescue first. 'Yes, sire, what of her?'

The King smiled disarmingly. 'She seems familiar to me.'

Mawdsley lowered his voice discreetly. 'That is because she is a member of the King's company. You saw her perform at the palace last week, if you recall.'

Raven was squirming with discomfort by now as the King made a surprised face. 'An actress? How came she here then?'

'She is a special friend of Mr Raven, sire,' Mawdsley explained knowingly with a long wink.

The King coughed in slight embarrassment. 'Ah, I see. Well, in that case, I shall say no more on the subject, except to note, Mr Raven, that you possess excellent taste in women to add to your many other fine qualities...'

Lady Castlemaine suddenly appeared at the King's side to contribute to Raven's present discomfiture. 'Yes, Mr Raven is a most surprising gentleman on many levels, Charles.'

The King heard this statement with amusement but did not choose to query her precise meaning. The King then took his leave to return to his coach, but Lady Castlemaine lingered for a moment. 'So the rogue who accosted me in the park is lying down there in the frozen mud of the Thames,' she said with indifference. 'It seems a fitting place for him.' She fixed her eye languidly on Raven. 'And you, sir, I shall expect to see you for dinner soon at my apartments where you can explain to me exactly what went on here today. I seem to have missed much in all this mysterious affair.'

Raven bowed, still shivering violently. 'I look forward to it, my lady. But I had better get a change of clothes and some warmth in a nearby inn first, else the only appointment I will be able to keep this week will be with a gravedigger and a parson...'

Lady Castlemaine fluttered her fan artfully, and smiled bewitchingly. 'Not you, sir. Clearly you are indestructible. You will outlive us all...'

*

An hour later, seated in the parlour of the Anchor Inn, Raven warmed himself gratefully by a roaring log fire, in company with Molly and Martin.

Most surprisingly, Raven found that it was still only one o'clock in the afternoon, as announced by the striking of the nearby Deptford church clock. After his considerable exertions this day, both physical and emotional, Raven already felt as fatigued as if he had gone two days without sleep. Now, with a welcome change of clothes brought from his carriage, and finally feeling warm and comfortable again for the first time in many hours, Raven was fighting hard to stay awake.

Yet Molly had suffered no similarly lethargic reaction, it seemed, and was bright and lively in mood. Her only moment of quiet reflection came when she remembered the fate of Mr Raven's beautiful Whitby vessel, the *Anne Raven*.

Raven was less sentimental about the loss of the vessel than Molly, and fought back a yawn even as he considered it. 'I hope the King will recompense me for its loss, of course. In fact I shall insist on it. Yet it was only wood and canvas and nails after all, Molly, and they can always be replaced, whereas a human life can never be recovered. I am grateful that no innocent people died this day. In fact, it seems that Ingledew himself was the only one to give his life in his foolish pursuit of revenge…'

Molly was sitting opposite him, and Raven was suddenly taken by the way the flickering firelight lit up her pretty face. Nay, "pretty" was not the right word: it was truly a beautiful face…

'Do ye think that devil truly is dead?' she asked him doubtfully.

Raven was still admiring the fresh glow in her cheeks, and the sparkle in her blue eyes. '…Ingledew? Yes, I believe so. Even though his body has not been found.'

Martin spoke up from his place on the oak bench next to Molly. 'Perhaps there was not enough of it left to find,' he suggested hopefully. 'But what of Ingledew's men? I did not see what happened to them. What was their fate?'

Raven glanced at the mullioned window and the bleak riverside scene outside. 'They left the madman behind, and made good their own escape upstream. But they cannot get past London Bridge in that boat, I suspect, so the King's men will soon apprehend them. I would wager that all of those "gentlemen" will meet a bloody fate at Tyburn in a week or so.' He had a further thought and turned to Molly again. 'I did not see the man with the feathered hat among those villains, though, so I do wonder what became of him. It would be galling if he was the only one to escape, when he murdered your friend Amy so brutally…'

Molly looked uneasy. 'You mean Parish, sir. I would not worry too much over that rogue's fate, if I were you. Hopefully he is already tasting the full penalty of hellfire and eternal damnation.'

Raven wondered what she meant by that exactly, but was then distracted from a further enquiry on the subject of Parish as another more important thought occurred to him. He clenched his fists in frustration at his lack of attention. 'I am a fool sitting here as if all this is over! What of the woman?'

Molly frowned. 'Which woman do you mean, sir?'

'I mean Ingledew's sister, Carolyn,' Raven snapped impatiently. 'The woman who murdered your actress friends! You said she was with her brother yesterday in that tall storehouse nearby, and that you overheard her admit everything. Yet why did she do it? What were those dead actresses to her?'

Molly had almost forgotten the existence of the woman too for the moment, but now hastily concentrated her attention again. 'I know not, sir. I believe from something that she said that she might have been an actress herself at one time. She said that she bore them no personal ill will, but that they stood in the way of some great reward for her.'

'Reward? Yet neither Sarah nor Anne was wealthy. So how could their deaths possibly benefit Carolyn Ingledew?'

Molly looked bewildered. 'I am at a loss, sir.'

Raven continued in his more persistent vein. 'And where was this woman today? If she was an intimate part of her brother's plot against the King and the dockyard, why was she not here to support him?'

Molly bit her lip. 'From what I overheard, I believe she wanted no part in this desperate plot of her brother's to destroy these ships in the dockyard, even though she had been plotting with him and helping him on other matters.'

'Then where is she now?' Raven asked, greatly puzzled.

'I believe that she returned to London, sir, in company with that other toothless rogue, Wedderburn,' Molly said worriedly. 'I am sorry. I should have mentioned it earlier but quite forgot in all this other confusion.'

Raven was rapidly waking up from his enforced lethargy.

Molly suddenly remembered something else she had not told Raven. 'Forgive me again, sir. I think I might know who this woman's accomplice at the theatre might be. She must have one in the King's company, else she could not have found her way to the tiring room that evening and murdered Sarah so easily. And her helper must be Miles Brammer…'

'Miles Brammer? That pretty actor who played Duke Orsino? Are you sure?' Raven asked uncertainly. 'He does not look the murderous type.'

'I saw him last Sunday morning in a close huddle at a dogfight with the two men who attacked me and killed Amy Leatherbarrow,' Molly insisted. 'That is how I discovered their names are Parish and Wedderburn.' She slapped her own thigh with sudden irritation. 'I have remembered something else I overheard between Ingledew and his sister. There is yet another person in her way that she intends to deal with, someone called Goodricke. Yet I know no one of that name with the King's company…'

Raven leapt to his feet in alarm. 'Goodricke? Are you sure of that name?'

Molly quickly stood up too, with apprehension written on her face. 'Yes, I am. But who is this Goodricke?'

Raven went to fetch his greatcoat. 'I will explain on the way, Molly.' He turned to Martin. 'It is lucky that Bessie is still hitched to the carriage outside because we must make haste to London at once. Another actress of the King's company could be in grave danger…'

*

Sir Thomas Killigrew had a head that was throbbing so much with pain of his hangover that it felt as if it had been cleaved at the back by a blunt axe. He sat on one of the green baize-covered benches in front of the stage in the King's theatre, and rested his sore head against his hand for a moment, to seek some much-needed relief.

It was the end of yet another disappointing rehearsal of the Duke of Buckingham's play *Sir Politic-Would-be*, a play which had gone badly, both in rehearsal and performance, since Molly Titchen's unexplained disappearance on Sunday night. Yesterday's performance of the play had been, if not a disaster, at least a deeply disappointing experience. Perhaps the company was unsettled by Molly's disappearance, although that could not explain all the dismal individual performances last evening. The play was full of bawdy humour yet had hardly drawn a glimmer of a laugh from a sullen and restive audience, who seemed almost as affected by Molly's absence as her fellow players. Sir Thomas realized that he had also made a significant mistake in promoting Christopher Malthouse to play the lead: he was a good workmanlike actor with a fine voice for heroic drama, yet simply not suited to a major comic role like this.

Even Mary Pettican had been poor in performance yesterday, and she was hardly bemoaning Molly's absence, Killigrew was sure - more likely celebrating it, if anything, the unsympathetic punk. So her dull and turgid acting was particularly hard to explain. Only Jane Golightly had played her part yesterday with anything like her usual skill, as the poor downtrodden heroine of the play.

Sir Thomas wondered if it was perhaps the cumulative loss that was taking its toll on the company – first sweet Sarah Lusted, then feisty Anne Carey, and now the lovely Molly too. Although Killigrew had to hope that Molly had merely run off with a man for a few days, and was not already worm's meat like those two other unfortunate girls

Sir Thomas thought about Molly again as this rehearsal came to an uninspiring end. He had hoped to see some improvement over yesterday's performance – some missing spark of fire in the actors that might lift things – yet he had been quickly disillusioned of that sanguine notion. If anything, the rehearsal had plumbed new depths for dismal acting and laboured buffoonery. In an hour or so, the audience would file in for another performance, and all Killigrew had to offer them was this cold turgid stew of a play, masquerading as comedy.

If only Molly would walk through that stage door right now! Her saucy presence would soon heat up the stew again, and re-invigorate this company to produce a more memorable performance...

But what if she never returned? It would be a terrible thing if she never came back - both for Molly herself, and for the King's company - because Sir Thomas had become convinced by now that Molly had a remarkable future in front of her as an actress. Killigrew had seen her perform in several different plays and roles now – as Maria in *Twelfth Night*, in one of the main breeches parts in *The Rival Ladies*, and as a playful strumpet in *Sir Politic-Would-be* - and he knew a prodigious talent when he saw one. That slip of a girl had been utterly believable in each role, which was a considerable achievement for a sixteen-year-old with no formal training at all.

The three actors from the final scene of *Sir Politic-Would-be* were just stepping down from the stage, all in a low mood after that dismal rehearsal, and exhibiting none of their usual banter and boisterousness. In Killigrew's experience, actors were such sensitive and insecure souls that they were rarely able to recognize when they had given a memorable performance, yet always seemed painfully aware when they had given an inept one. Patrick Whelan seemed particularly low in spirits today, but that was perhaps to be expected: he had clearly developed a hot passion for young Molly over the last week and was still ruing his inattention to her on Sunday before her unexplained disappearance. Yet even Jane Golightly and Miles Brammer were in a most subdued frame of mind as they stepped down from the stage, as if deeply apprehensive about this afternoon's performance to come.

Sir Thomas was about to say something conciliatory to the three of them in the hope that it would lift their depressed spirits, when, without warning, a man suddenly burst out from behind one of the tall oak pillars in the pit. The man was poorly dressed in a worn doublet and breeches, and had his face mostly concealed by a wide-brimmed hat pulled low over his sunken cheeks. His venomous appearance distracted Killigrew's attention instantly from mere thoughts of acting, and he had a sudden feeling of impending doom as the man approached the three players. Yet the drama of what followed was much more brutal than Killigrew could ever have imagined: the man simply walked up to Jane Golightly, pulled out a concealed knife from under his cloak, then plunged the full length of the blade into Jane's chest without any compunction or restraint.

Jane collapsed instantly under this wicked and cowardly blow with a scream of pain, while a shocked Miles Brammer, standing just behind her, had to leap forward to catch her and slow her fall.

Patrick Whelan, screaming in disbelief, ran forward and tried to wrest control of the knife from the man, but the attacker used the heavy bone handle of the knife like a club and simply battered young Whelan aside.

Killigrew's mind was still reeling at the nightmarish unreality of what he had witnessed, yet he seemed unable to move or respond. The assailant made no further move to attack anyone, but calmly replaced his bloodied knife beneath his cloak and then turned and walked at an even pace to the main door of the theatre, ignoring all the other scattered people in the hall. No one made any further attempt to stop the man leaving, but then most of those gathered there were merely maidservants and kitchen drudges, who simply stood open-mouthed in shock at what they had seen.

Sir Thomas, to his later shame, did not attempt to stop the man's escape either, but rushed instead to where Brammer sat on the wooden floor, cradling poor Jane in his arms and trying ineffectually to staunch the copious flow of blood. She was still breathing, which was some consolation to Sir Thomas, though not much.

'Stay with her, please, Sir Thomas, and get a physician for her if you can,' Brammer ordered curtly, taking off his coat and making a pillow of it under Jane's head. 'I believe I know that vile man,' he added in a distraught voice, 'and I will make him pay for this infamy with his own life.' With that, he ran for the main door of the theatre too, in pursuit of the villain with the knife.

Killigrew called out, 'But Miles, you are unarmed...!' Yet Brammer paid no heed to his warning and continued running towards the door.

Whelan was groaning with pain from the blow the villain had given him, but did not seem badly hurt, merely stunned. Sir Thomas quickly roused him with a hard slap to the face, and ordered Whelan to stay with Jane and comfort her until he could return with a physician. Killigrew could have ordered Whelan to go in search of medical help, of course, and he would no doubt be considerably fleeter of foot than a lame old man like himself, therefore was perhaps a more sensible choice to go. Yet this was one scene in this theatre that Sir Thomas Killigrew did not care to stay behind for – a sentimental scene with a real dying girl – so preferred to give Whelan that dubious honour instead. It was a cowardly thing to do, yet Killigrew had seen how deep that blade had penetrated Jane's breast, and had no doubt that she was as good as dead. The only wonder was that she was somehow breathing still...

Sir Thomas thought rapidly of where he might find a surgeon as he strapped on his short sword and pulled on his long fur-lined coat. The nearest physician of any sort that he knew resided in Bow Street so he started at once for the main door of the theatre, pausing only for a last regretful look at the sad and bloodied figure of Jane stretched out on the floor of the pit beneath the stage, with young Whelan weeping morbidly over her.

Oh, if only he could get as much emotion into his performances on stage, Sir Thomas thought uncharitably.

Once out in the wintry street, Killigrew immediately turned west towards Bow Street, moving his aged legs as fast as he could.

As he huffed and puffed his way up Bridges Street, Sir Thomas soon became aware of some great commotion ahead of him. Then, nearing the corner of Bridges Street and Bow Street, he realized that the commotion was due to two men writhing and cursing on the ground, and trying their best to gouge each other's eyes out.

Killigrew saw with surprise that Miles must have caught up with that devil with the knife already, and that he was now engaged with him in a life or death struggle on the frozen ground. On such a bitterly cold afternoon as this, there was no one else around on the street to help, so Sir Thomas rushed to the scene of the fight as fast as his laboured breathing could carry him, to try and help Brammer overcome this murderous fiend.

As he drew closer, Sir Thomas was staggered at the degree of violence that these two were inflicting on each other – gouging, punching, head-butting – yet was gratified that Brammer clearly had the upper hand. The villainous man had apparently lost his knife during this titanic struggle, or else could not get his hand to it, and Brammer was making him pay heavily for the loss of that advantage.

Killigrew was surprised at such a fierce display of violence from a sweet young man like Brammer, yet the boy was truly in an uncontrolled rage, pummelling his opponent's bloody face to pulp, and screaming poisonous abuse at him.

Brammer finally pulled the defeated villain to his feet. 'Why did you kill her, Caleb, you filthy cowardly wretch?' he screamed at the man's mutilated face. 'A girl who never did any harm to anyone in her entire life!' It seemed from this philippic that Brammer did indeed know this man as he had claimed, yet the villain seemed an odd acquaintance for an actor like Miles to have - a low and ugly individual without a single functioning tooth left in his jaw. Whatever teeth the villain might have still retained before today had certainly been lost now after Brammer had finished beating him black and blue, Killigrew thought.

Brammer became aware of Sir Thomas standing behind him, and took his eyes off the toothless man for a brief moment to glance back at Killigrew in weary resignation. It was a terrible misjudgement on his part, though, to take his eyes of that other man, and Brammer soon paid an awful price for it.

In a flash, the toothless man pulled out a second small knife from under his bloodied cloak and stabbed Brammer viciously through the belly with it. Aghast, Sir Thomas drew his own short sword and, before the toothless man had a chance to move again, ran him through the heart...

CHAPTER 22

Tuesday, 20th December 1664

At Henry Raven's urging, Martin had driven the tiny carriage at reckless speed from Deptford back to London, so that – remarkably - the clock of St Paul's Church in the nearby piazza of Covent Garden was just striking three as the carriage was turning from Drury Lane into Bridges Street. Raven doubted that Martin had ever driven this fast on such icy and slippery roads before, and certainly not in a carriage as small and unstable as this one, yet providence had looked after them today and brought them safe home to the city.

At Raven's shouted orders, Martin pulled the bespattered carriage to a halt outside the King's theatre. Bessie, the black mare, was blowing hard after her long mad dash from Deptford, while inside the tiny carriage, given the inadequacy of its springs to cope with frozen country roads, Raven and Molly both had many more bruises to add to the considerable number they had already acquired during the last few days.

Despite his aches and pains, Raven leapt out of the carriage as soon as it came to a stop. Yet when he saw the scene of commotion and confusion outside the theatre, his heart fell as he realized that he might be too late...

An equally worried Molly soon joined him on the paved area in front of the theatre, among the clamouring crowd. This was not an audience waiting for the start of the performance, though, but merely a tag and rag crowd of mostly low people, including many obvious beggars, cutpurses and slatternly trulls. Raven used his height and his commanding presence to force a way through this motley assembly, with a subdued Molly following in his wake.

A "Charley" stood at the door of the theatre, in company with two other elderly officers of the Watch armed with lanterns and wooden staffs, all vainly trying to restore some order and to disperse the curious

263

crowd of bystanders, but to little effect. When Raven asked to be allowed through, his gentlemanly dress and manners seemed to carry some weight with these modest officers of the law, and he and Molly were quickly permitted to pass through into the entrance hall of the theatre.

Raven's growing fears of some tragedy were soon confirmed when he found Sir Thomas Killigrew sitting disconsolately just inside the gatekeeper's little waiting chamber to the left of the main entrance hall. Sir Thomas had his head in his hands, and his eyes were red and swollen with weeping.

He looked up eagerly, though, on seeing Raven. 'Thank God you have come, sir. You have heard what has happened, I suppose. Can you go to Jane, and see what can be done for her? Although I doubt that anything can be done for her now...poor sweet Jane...'

'Poor Jane?' Raven repeated bleakly.

Killigrew's face fell. 'Ah, then you have not heard the terrible news. Jane Golightly was stabbed here in the theatre by an evil rogue not half an hour ago.'

'Yet she is still alive?' Raven said hopefully.

'Barely, sir. She was stabbed most cruelly in the breast. Go to her at once, and see what you can do to ease her distress. They have carried her up to my resting chamber, the same place where we laid Sarah just a week or so ago.'

Molly had been standing behind Raven, out of Killigrew's view, but now she stepped forward and took his hand.

Sir Thomas was overjoyed to see her, and stood up to embrace her. 'You are returned, Molly, safe and sound! I am so relieved to see it.'

Molly's face was a picture of misery, though. 'What happened to this villain who stabbed Jane, Sir Thomas?'

'He escaped from the theatre, but Miles and I chased him through the streets.' Sir Thomas uttered a deep sob of regret. 'Then the toothless villain stabbed Miles to death too. I feel a terrible guilt over that, because I may have inadvertently distracted Miles' attention for a moment. But at least I made up for it by running the villain through with my sword. That evil man will murder no more of my actors...'

Molly gasped at this news of Miles Brammer's death, and turned to Raven in sad bewilderment.

But Raven was already on his way up to Sir Thomas's resting chamber, following the trail of sticky blood that led up the stairs at the side of the stage...

*

Most of the members of the King's company were waiting in a concerned line in the narrow corridor outside the chamber, making it difficult to get through. Raven recognized Mary Pettican among them, her face white and grave, and the Irishman Patrick Whelan, fighting back his tears. They all moved quickly aside to let Raven through, when they realized that he had come in his capacity as a physician, to tend to Jane's wounds.

The oak-panelled chamber was warm at least, with the fire burning brightly, and well lit by wall sconces and tall single brass candlesticks. Raven made everyone inside the room leave and closed the door gently behind him. Then he walked over to the bed where Jane lay, as still and white as a marble statue. Someone had already removed her dress to examine her wounds, and she was covered only by a thin muslin sheet marked with an ugly and spreading pool of red.

Raven slowly pulled back the sheet to expose her torso, and bit his lip with anguish when he saw the severity of her wound. He had been forewarned by the quantity of blood he had seen on the floor of the theatre pit, yet this was even worse than he had imagined. The knife thrust through her ribs had narrowly missed her heart, which was still beating weakly, yet must still have caused terrible damage to her major blood vessels. Blood was still pulsing out of the open wound, but with less volume than previously. Yet this was not because the wound was clotting or healing itself, Raven thought, but more likely because she had so little blood left to lose from her slender body. Raven remembered his friend William Croone from the Royal Society, and his experiments at bleeding blood from one dog into another, which had sometimes worked with great success, and at other times had killed the dog receiving the blood within a few minutes. Unlike most physicians, Raven had no faith in the efficacy of letting blood to cure ailments, but rather the exact opposite. What Jane needed now in his opinion was precisely what Croone had been aiming for with his experiments – to transfer a fresh supply of blood from a human donor to a patient who had lost so much of their own supply. Yet until the nature of blood was properly understood, such a perilous experiment could never be attempted on humans...

Raven was so engrossed with trying to imagine the lines of damaged arteries and veins beneath that terrible knife wound that he barely noticed that this was indeed a young woman's body, with no trace of any male characteristics at all. So she had been playing games with him after all, pretending to be a boy, yet he had no idea why she had done such a strange thing...

Her eyes fluttered at the touch of his fingers. ''Tis you, Mr Raven.'

Raven tried to smile reassuringly. 'Excuse my cold fingers, Jane, but I am trying to see the extent of your wound and judge its severity.'

Jane tried to smile back. ''Tis...too late...for that, Mr...Raven. I am...*dead*.' A tear trickled from the corner of her eye. 'But...why me? Why...did that man...murder *me*?'

Raven shook his head numbly. 'I cannot comprehend it.'

Jane's eyes became blank and unseeing. 'It grows...suddenly...dark.'

Raven looked at the dozen candles burning brightly in the chamber. 'Yes, it grows very dark,' he agreed.

'Hold my hand,' Jane pleaded softly. 'Will you please...stay with me? To help me...on my way...'

Raven leaned down and kissed her on the brow as she gave a last wheezing breath and her head lolled abruptly sideways.

The door to the chamber opened slowly, and Sir Thomas came hesitantly over the threshold. He looked at the sad figure on the bed, with Raven still holding her hand. 'Is she gone, sir?' he asked with mock gruffness.

'She is, Sir Thomas. If it is any consolation to you, her wound was so severe that no surgeon on earth could have saved her once that dagger had been plunged so deep into her breast. It amazes me that she lasted half an hour with such a wound. So do not blame yourself for not finding a physician earlier – it would have made no difference, I think.'

Sir Thomas subsided slowly onto the bench by the fire, his worn face hanging in tired folds. He crossed himself. 'And God shall wipe away all tears from their eyes; and there shall be no more death, neither sorrow, nor crying, neither shall there be any more pain: for the former things are passed away...' He paused angrily in mid-sentence. 'Why would anyone kill that poor dear child?'

Raven pulled the sheet back and covered Jane's face, after gently closing her eyelids with his fingers. 'I cannot be sure, but I do know it must be for the same reason that Sarah and Anne were murdered.'

Killigrew blanched. 'When we spoke four days ago, I could not accept your bleak suspicions about the deaths of Sarah and Anne. But we can only ascribe so much to circumstance and ill luck. I know now that what has happened here in my company of players cannot be the result of ill fortune alone, but must be due to the planning of some evil mind.'

'Indeed so,' agreed Raven grimly. He looked at the body under the sheet. 'Tell me, what do you know of Jane's family background? I believe she was an orphan.'

Sir Thomas frowned. 'You could perhaps say that, although her mother died but five years ago when Jane was already fifteen, and full grown. In fact I knew her mother a long time ago as a young woman, which is how I became acquainted with Jane herself this year. She wrote me a letter earlier this year asking to join the company, even though she had no acting experience, but hoping my memories of her late mother would sway my decision in her favour. Which they did, of course, although I hope that I would have been sufficiently swayed by Jane's acting talent and beauty anyway.'

'Who was her mother?' Raven asked curiously.

Sir Thomas sighed as he remembered. 'Her name was Alice Goodricke. She was a most striking looking woman when young. She worked in my company twenty five years ago as a costume maker...though what she truly wanted to be was an actress on stage. Yet that was quite impossible in those more severe times...'

Raven interrupted as a sudden embarrassing suspicion occurred to him. Killigrew was married to a wealthy Dutch woman, and had several children by her, but was also known to have had many lovers, and fathered many bastards, in his active life. 'May I be so bold as to inquire directly – *you* are not Jane's real father, are you, Sir Thomas?'

Sir Thomas shook his head sadly. 'I would be pleased to have been the father of such a beautiful and accomplished girl as Jane, but alas I am not. Alice left my company before the Civil War when she entered into a secret tryst with a wealthy Warwickshire landowner whom she had met while working here in London. Jane was the result of that liaison, together with her twin brother John...

Raven looked up sharply when he heard that name.

Sir Thomas continued. '...I believe that Alice did love this Warwickshire gentleman deeply – it was not just a question of her finding a wealthy patron - though his affection for her was perhaps more questionable. He turned Alice out of his home eventually when he married a wealthy local lady, although – to give him credit - he did continue to support Alice and her children financially, though...'

Raven stopped him again in mid-sentence. 'I only met Jane a few times, but for some reason she played a strange game with me and pretended to be a boy in disguise. Why would she do such a thing...?'

Sir Thomas let out a long breath. 'Ah, that confusion of identity is not so strange perhaps when one considers her personal history. It was all her mother Alice's doing, I believe. I managed to discover some of the details of her childhood from Jane herself when we got to know each other this year, and some more details from another old friend of Alice's, which together was enough to surmise the whole sad family history. My understanding of the story is this: after her lover abandoned her and the children, Alice became a strange and morose creature, even though her former lover did support her with money. This Warwickshire man fathered no other children of his own, it seems – perhaps his wealthy wife was barren - so Alice began to develop the hope that her son John would inherit some considerable fortune from him in time, even though the man never visited her. But then her son

John died of the plague, at the age of only four. I cannot be sure what happened next, but I would guess that a distraught Alice – half mad with grief - tried to pretend to her neighbours that it was *Jane* who had died, while John had survived. Whatever the reason, she took to dressing Jane from that time on as a boy and calling her "John".'

Raven was astonished. 'Could she really hope to get away with such a foolish plan?'

Sir Thomas shrugged. 'Foolish or not, she kept up this pretence for years and Jane was forced to acquiesce. I believe Alice was properly mad by this time so there was little sense to what she did. When her mother died, and Jane was no longer coerced to play a boy, she quickly reverted to her natural female customs and dress, of course. Yet those years of abuse did leave a permanent mark on her character, and she did choose to wear male costume from time to time, and go by the name "John". 'Tis why she made such a convincing Viola in *Twelfth Night*, I believe…she was playing the same part in her real life.' Killigrew wiped away a tear as he remembered her gifted and inspired performance only a few days ago. 'Perhaps it was simply Jane's way of bringing her beloved dead brother John back to life. I do not believe that she was doing it with any deliberate intent of trying to claim her true father's fortune…I doubt that Alice had even told her of her father's true identity.' Sir Thomas paused for breath. 'I do know this gentleman's real name, as it happens, but I decided not to tell Jane as it might only provoke even further sad memories for the poor girl… '

Raven had one last question. 'Then may I be privileged to know what Jane herself never knew? This wealthy Warwickshire landowner who was her true father - *what was his name…?*'

*

Molly found Mr Raven sitting alone in the pit in front of the stage in a deeply distressed mood.

Molly was sad herself at the tragic deaths of Miles Brammer and Jane Golightly, yet she had known neither of them really well so it was less of a personal tragedy to her than a collective tragedy for the company. Yet Mr Raven seemed considerably more affected by the news of Jane's death than she did, which gave her pause for thought. She had seen them conversing together in quite an intimate fashion after the performance of *Twelfth Night* at the palace, yet even then had not got the impression that Mr Raven had formed any deep attachment for Jane Golightly.

Yet how else to explain his defeated air and sombre face? Only this morning he had risked his life to stop that maniac Ingledew from entering the Deptford Dry Dock with his barge full of gunpowder, and yet had seemed remarkably unaffected afterwards by these dramatic events. It seemed strange then that he should be more affected by the death of one actress he had hardly known...

''Tis a sad day,' she said, sitting down beside him.

Mr Raven turned to her. 'Ay, indeed. If only you had thought to mention that name "Goodricke" to me earlier today, we might have left for London a few minutes earlier, and perhaps saved Jane's life.'

Molly stirred resentfully. 'You blame *me* for this tragedy, sir? I made no connection between Jane and the name Goodricke, although I discover now from Sir Thomas that it was her mother's real name.'

Mr Raven touched her hand in apology. 'Forgive me, Molly. No, I do not blame you, of course, after all the courage and resilience you have shown during these last few days. I was simply bemoaning fate, and the evil that lives in the hearts of people like Ingledew and his sister.'

Molly was still upset despite his apology. 'It sounds as if you *do* blame me, sir. Perhaps you are right to do so. I do blame myself most aggrievedly for suspecting poor Miles of being an accomplice of that dark villainess; he proved himself a brave boy in the end.'

'He was no braver than you, Molly. You too performed most bravely today in defeating that villain Ingledew.'

'Yet neither of us behaved as fearlessly as you, sir. You gave your ship to save the King, and you would have given your life too. When Ingledew fired that musket at me, I was most astonished to see you leap across onto his ship and challenge him. Your fame will surely spread throughout this kingdom when the news of this event is made public.'

Raven made a wry face. 'Then 'tis my ill luck that there will be no public report of what happened today,' he said dryly. 'Everyone who witnessed that scene at Deptford today will be sworn to secrecy in order to frustrate the war plans of the Dutch. Lord Clarendon will swiftly arrange for false reports to be spread to the continent through his web of secret agents. In this way we may deceive the Dutch for a short while into believing that Ingledew succeeded in his plans to destroy those three ships, and to kill half the King's war council.'

'Sad for you, though, not to get the credit for your bravery,' Molly said thoughtfully.

'No, 'tis not sad at all. I much prefer my privacy, and would hate to be presented as a great hero of any sort,' Raven declared with apparent honesty.

Molly concurred moodily. 'If that is truly your wish, than I am glad for it.' She brightened up with an effort. 'At least that villain Wedderburn is with his maker now, thanks to Sir Thomas. In fact, all these evil miscreants in Ingledew's gang are either dead or caught.'

Raven coughed. 'With one notable exception.'

Molly nodded. 'Ah yes, the dark lady herself – Ingledew's sister.'

Raven became grim again. 'Indeed so: she is still free to weave her evil spells somewhere. That man Wedderburn may well have struck the blows that killed Jane and Miles, but that evil woman certainly gave the order...'

Molly blinked. 'Do you understand yet why this woman wanted Jane dead? And Sarah and Anne too?'

'No, I do not,' Raven said uneasily.

Hearing that note of unease in his voice, Molly was not sure that he was being completely honest with her for once. Yet she in her turn had not been honest with him about everything – particularly about the death of that man Parish, which was something she still preferred to keep to herself...

'Where do you think the woman is now?' she asked Raven. 'Have you any idea where she might hide?'

Raven glanced around the near empty theatre. 'No, none at all. But wherever her lair is, I trust it is far from here.' He noticed the scenes of increasing activity on stage, and of servants hastily cleaning away the bloody stain on the floor where Jane had been so cruelly attacked just an hour ago. 'What goes on there, Molly? Sir Thomas cannot be thinking to go ahead with this afternoon's performance?'

Molly looked towards the main entrance, her eyes beginning to sparkle in spite of herself. 'There is now a great crowd congregated in front of the theatre – perhaps because of all the rumours on the street about what happened here. So Sir Thomas is determined to make the most of this opportunity of a full house and go ahead with the play that he rehearsed today - *Sir Politic-Would-be*. Even though it will start an hour or two later than usual.'

Raven seemed astonished. 'What? He would perform a play after what has happened here today? With both Jane and Miles Brammer still not cold under their shrouds?'

'Sir Thomas says we owe it to Jane and Miles to continue. It is what they would have wanted...' Molly was not entirely convinced of that herself, but had yielded to Sir Thomas's persuasive tongue.

'How can Sir Thomas possibly manage without Jane? Did she not have the lead role in this production of *Sir Politic-Would-be?*'

'She did, sir,' Molly admitted. 'But I know the lines well enough so I will play Jane's part, and hopefully bring her back to life, for a few hours at least.'

'You!' Raven was even more astonished now. 'Have *you* recovered sufficiently from all the terrors of the last few days to be able to step back instantly onto stage?'

Molly shrugged. 'I believe I am tolerably well recovered, sir. And to perform in a play will help me recover my spirits faster than any other medicine,' she declared honestly.

Raven almost smiled in bewilderment at this answer. 'Then you are truly a member of this company now, Molly, and perhaps even its spiritual leader.'

Molly forced back a smile of her own. 'I hardly think so, sir. But do stay and watch the play from your usual box. It will divert your mind this afternoon from thoughts of bitterness and melancholy.'

Raven stood up sharply. 'Nay, I cannot, Molly. I have other things that I need to attend to.'

'I hope you do not go in search of the dark lady tonight, sir. That would be a foolish thing to do in your black and angry mood,' Molly advised.

Raven shook his head. 'Nay, I have not the heart for such business as that, even if I knew where to find her. Tonight I will find the company of a friend to lift my spirits instead...'

CHAPTER 23

Tuesday, 20th December 1664

Adam Strange put another log on the fire and looked at his friend Henry Raven with concern. 'You look exhausted, Henry.'

Raven was feeling so low that he could barely raise a half-smile in return. Night had fallen and a wintry darkness had descended like a pall on the streets of London. Seated by a roaring fire in Adam Strange's comfortable ground floor parlour in Bow Street, Raven should have felt relaxed and protected in this safe refuge, yet his mind was still deeply troubled, even in turmoil. He had to admire the irrepressible spirit of Molly Titchen who seemed to be able to rise above any adversity, and then simply dust herself down and continue as if nothing had happened. He wondered what sort of calamity it would take to dampen the unquenchable spirit of that unpredictable girl. He was still frankly amazed, though, that she could perform on stage this evening after her terrible trials of the last few days – abducted, imprisoned, and then nearly shot in the head today by a musket ball directed at her by that madman Ingledew...

As for himself, Raven found that he could not recover so quickly from the painful events of today – and particularly from the death of Jane Golightly, which he still felt was something he could have prevented if he had been more diligent. He sighed at his friend. 'It has indeed been a long trying day, Adam. In fact the most trying day that I have ever had to endure...'

Adam seemed fatigued too, Raven noticed, but was still clearly anxious to hear what his friend had been up to today. 'The last I heard of this business, the King had nearly been impaled in Lady Castlemaine's apartments by some strange woman armed with a crossbow. Now I have heard tales of even wilder happenings at Deptford...'

Raven examined his friend's handsome face. Even after a long weary day spent pleading his client's case in court, Adam still looked much the same sweet innocent boy Raven had known at Cambridge. Raven wondered how it was that he had managed to retain his youthful and serene looks, when he must have encountered the corrupting influence of so many evil people and wicked deeds in his professional life.

'From whom did you hear these reports?' Raven asked him warily.

'From a lawyer friend. He regularly visits a married woman in Deptford -' Strange gave a knowing cough – 'the buxom wife of a ship's carpenter, I believe. This willing lady happened to see my friend in the city today and told him of a great explosion that had just taken place at the Royal dockyard. She thought some great arsenal must have gone up in flames.' Strange stretched his long legs in front of the fire. 'As soon as I heard it, I was convinced it must be something to do with you. I hope you will not disappoint me by trying to deny it...'

'I admit to being there, but that is not quite what happened.' Raven quickly went on to tell Strange a truer account of what had happened at the dockyard this morning, though leaving out for the moment Molly Titchen's part in proceedings, and the fact that she had been abducted previously by Ingledew.

Adam listened to the story in astonishment, eyes wide. 'I cannot believe it,' he declared finally. 'It sounds like the mad plot of one of Killigrew's plays. You tell me seriously that this Beelzebub character – whom you have now identified as one Simon Ingledew – tried to blow up half the King's navy at Deptford. And that you stopped him by sacrificing your own fair ship, the *Anne Raven*.'

'I would have preferred to save the dockyard without sacrificing my own vessel,' Raven said dryly, 'but there were not a great number of ready alternatives available.'

'And this madman Ingledew is dead?' Strange asked.

Raven warmed his hands at the fire. 'If he is not, then I am truly afraid of the consequences because he must indeed have sold his soul to the Devil. No mortal man could have survived such a blast as that, I am sure.' He laughed uneasily. 'Yet his body was not found among the debris...'

'It sounds as if there would have been precious little left to find,' Adam said with heavy sarcasm. He clapped his palms together as if in celebration. 'Yet, if all this is true, why are you so glum this evening? You have scored a great triumph, and saved the life of your monarch yet again, as well the valuable ships of the King's navy. Ye should be elated, Henry, and bubbling over with the joy of life, not sunk down in the dumps, so dull and heavy like this.'

Raven twisted his face. 'Perhaps I would be happier if that was all that had happened today. But alas, that was not the end of my troubles. Yet another actress has died at the King's theatre, and I blame myself for not preventing it.'

Strange looked up sharply. '*Another* actress dead? This is beginning to sound sinister, after all. *Three* accidents to the same company of actors must stretch the laws of chance a little too far. So who had died now, Henry?'

Raven examined Adam's reaction as he told him the unfortunate girl's name. 'It was Jane Golightly.'

Strange looked puzzled for a moment. 'Ah, yes, I know the lady you mean - the girl who played Viola in that performance of *Twelfth Night* that we both saw at the palace last Wednesday.'

Raven was still watching his reaction. 'Yes, that is indeed the lady I mean.'

Strange looked uncomfortable. 'Then I forgive you your melancholy mood, Henry, because those are undoubtedly sad tidings. She seemed a sweet and innocent creature. Was the cause of her death as mysterious as those of the first two actresses?'

Raven grimaced. 'Nay, no one could have mistaken today's sad event for an accident. She was stabbed in front of some of her fellow actors by a rogue called Wedderburn.'

Strange raised his eyebrows sharply. 'You know the murderer's name already?'

Raven was sombre. 'One of the actors recognized him.'

Strange was very still. 'And what happened to this Wedderburn?'

Raven narrowed his eyes. 'He ran off, but some of the company gave chase and caught up with him – actually at the corner of this very street. Wedderburn then killed the first actor who had pursued him – Miles Brammer - but then Sir Thomas himself caught up with the man and ran him through with twelve inches of cold steel.'

Adam blinked slowly. 'I did not know that Killigrew had such fire left in his belly any more.' He gazed into the flickering flames. 'But does that not mean that this business is finally over, then?'

Raven conceded that. ''Tis true. I doubt that any more actresses of the King's company will die. The quota in blood has been paid.'

'And how about your strumpet Molly?' Strange asked lightly. 'Is she well?'

Raven bristled slightly at that epithet. 'My "strumpet", as you call her, is well enough. In fact she has taken over Jane Golightly's role in the play this evening - *Sir Politic-Would-be.* '

'Then all is well, even though that play is a very bad one,' Strange said with a thin smile.

Raven grunted in response. 'All is not so well for Jane Golightly, poor creature.'

Strange's smile faded rapidly. 'Nay, I suppose not. Forgive me - it was a foolish thing to say. But at least the man who did this evil thing is caught and punished.'

Raven shook his head. 'Except that Wedderburn was merely the instrument of Jane's death. The person who planned the deaths of these three actresses is very much alive and well. And there is an unexpected connection to the man who was threatening the King.'

'To Ingledew? What connection does he have with the deaths of the actresses?'

Raven came briskly to the point. '*This* connection - the deaths of the actresses were masterminded by Simon Ingledew's sister, Carolyn.'

Strange frowned. 'Ingledew's *sister*?'

Raven nodded. 'Yes, and she is still at large in the city, and probably not that far away from us tonight, I suspect...'

Strange looked up as Mistress Bilby entered the room carrying a tray loaded with food and drink. 'Ah, this is what we need,' he said, clapping his hands together. 'Some good meat and ale. This will take your mind off your dreadful day, Henry.'

Mistress Bilby put the tray on a nearby table, curtsied unsmilingly at the two gentlemen, then withdrew.

Raven glanced at Strange. 'I believe that I begin to see the virtues of your Mistress Bilby more these days, so I can understand now why you employ her.'

'You do?' Strange said, surprised.

Raven's voice took on a steelier tone. 'Yes, although I have to say that I much preferred her in the enticing costume of that odalisque at the palace rather than in the dull servant garb she wears today.'

Strange looked bewildered. 'Have you lost leave of your senses, Henry?'

Suddenly Raven felt something loop around his neck from behind, and then tighten viciously, making it impossible to breathe.

Instantly he felt the blood rushing in his head, and his mind was filled with panic and confusion as he struggled in vain to free himself from this awful hold. He could not see what was tightening around his neck so inexorably but instinct told him that it must be a garrotte, a common instrument of assassination and execution among the Catalans and the Spanish. A black mist descended on him, like a heavy curtain, and he felt as if the veins in his neck would soon explode with the strain, and his eyes would pop out of their sockets.

Far away, almost drowned out by the roaring noise in his head and the sounds of his own weakening struggle, he heard a woman's voice behind him hissing and spitting venom. 'He knows everything, Adam.

We must kill him!'

The hands twisting the garrotte were immensely strong for a woman's, and Raven was growing weaker by the second. He felt the life ebbing out of him, and could barely see now. Yet the most painful thing to bear was the fact that his "friend", Strange, was doing nothing to stop this, but merely regarding his life-or-death struggle with apparent indifference from the seat opposite.

But then, inexplicably, Strange stood up suddenly, and lashed out with his fists at the woman, forcing her to release her grip.

Raven felt an enormous relief as the frightening tension in the garrotte was relieved for a second. He managed to suck in a painful wheezing breath, then loosen the vicious contraption.

The woman hissed again at Adam. 'What are you doing?'

Strange pulled out a dagger from his belt and waved it in her face. 'Enough, Carolyn! There will be no more killing today!'

'I always knew you were a weakling at heart, Adam!' the woman swore.

The commotion in the parlour had attracted attention from the other servants in the house. There was a loud knocking on the door. 'Is everything all right in there, Master?'

'I am all right, Will,' Strange called out, still threatening the woman with his dagger. 'A chair fell over, that is all. Do not trouble yourself.'

Raven heard footsteps receding on the other side of the door, while Strange and the woman still confronted each other, with surprising venom on both sides.

Raven managed finally to loosen the garrotte fully from his neck – a devilish strong piece of leather cord reinforced with metal spikes – and climbed to his feet. His head was still spinning but the world was coming into reassuring focus again, colours and sounds normal.

He kept his wary eyes on Mistress Bilby at the door, though, her face transformed by malevolent anger into a frightening Gorgon vision of a woman. In her uncontrolled rage she looked every inch as intimidating as her mad brother.

'You will regret this betrayal, Adam,' she warned balefully. Yet, with that, she merely opened the door behind her and was gone. In a few seconds more, Raven heard the front door of the house open and then slam shut.

For his part Henry Raven had neither the strength nor the will presently to try and stop her.

And Adam Strange too seemed on the point of collapse, as he sank into his chair in despair. 'What in God's name have I done?' he uttered tearfully.

*

In fifteen minutes, Raven had recovered sufficiently to speak again with relative normality, if still in much pain. He drank a long sip of water, as he took his seat by the fire. 'Thank you for saving my life, Adam,' he said uneasily. 'But why did you do it? Why did you finally turn against that woman?'

'I cannot say. Perhaps I glimpsed a little of the world as I once saw it, and reverted for a moment to my younger and nobler self.' Strange was sunk in a deep depression. 'How did you know the truth anyway?'

Raven breathed out painfully. 'Because – today - I discovered Jane Golightly's real identity. She was the illegitimate child of Sir Oliver Runnalls, *your* wealthy kinsman in Warwickshire. I knew that could not be mere coincidence.' He looked Strange in the eyes. 'I presume that she stood in the way of you inheriting his estate, or something of that sort. What I do not understand is where Sarah Lusted and Anne Carey enter this tale of greed, deception and murder...'

Strange grimaced. 'They entered the story because Carolyn and I could not discover which of those three young women was actually Sir Oliver's child. It could have been any of them...'

Raven felt a chill in his soul at this sombre realization – Adam and his female accomplice had killed three innocent women for nothing. 'How could you do such an evil thing, Adam?' he asked wonderingly. 'How could you put money before your own conscience?'

Strange snorted angrily. 'A rich man like you may be able to afford to take such a high moral position, Henry, but a poor man like me has to be more flexible in his judgements. I could not take the risk of missing out on such an inheritance as that.'

Raven sighed. 'You are not truly poor, Adam. The reality is that evil woman, Carolyn Ingledew, bewitched you.'

Strange acknowledged that fact with a shrug of resignation. 'She did, and showed me a different side of myself.'

Raven glowered at him, seeing that he was still besotted with this woman, despite everything. 'Not a *better* side, that much is certain. Where did you meet this harpy?'

Strange shrugged resentfully. 'It was in Vienna. You remember that I travelled there last winter to try and recover some money after my brother Titus died in that city. Carolyn had been there with him; she had been his lover for several months.'

Raven shook his head cynically. 'A fateful journey for you both, it seems. So she got her hooks into you instead?'

Strange raised his head defiantly. 'I minded not those hooks, which, from her, are capable of delivering both immense pain and immense pleasure. She is a quite extraordinary woman, you know, and one of countless talents,' he boasted. 'She was an accomplished actress and singer at one time, the toast of European theatres. Her fame grew even more when she began performing in magic shows in the courts of Europe under the name Marie-Theresa von Kladowitz.'

Raven touched his aching throat. 'I know well that she is a gifted performer. I saw some of her tricks at the palace last week, including her matchless skill with the crossbow. Yet that was outdone tonight by her skill with the garrotte.' Raven felt the ugly red weals around his neck, which had bitten so deep into the flesh that they would probably leave permanent scars

Strange continued unabashed in his praise of his lover. 'Yet she is much more than a mere performer, Henry. Did you also know that she was an agent of the Holy Roman Emperor, Leopold I, and that she spied for him in his war against the Ottoman Empire? That woman has probably done more than other single person alive to keep the scourge of Islam out of Christian Europe...'

Raven almost exploded. 'Then God help us if we have to rely on such people as her to protect us,' he muttered. 'Yet despite this supposed glittering career in the court of Emperor Leopold, she returned to England with you, did she not?'

'She had many enemies in Europe who wanted to kill her,' Strange explained coolly. 'Returning to England seemed a sensible thing to do.'

Raven let out a long sigh of exasperation. 'Especially when she heard that you might be in line to inherit a vast estate in Warwickshire. Perhaps Carolyn yearned for a quieter life as a lady of the manor, is that it? Her only problem was the existence of an illegitimate child whom Sir Oliver Runnalls might have decided to recognize in place of you...'

'Yes, that is true. In the meantime, Carolyn took up work as an actress again, with the Duke's company in Lincoln's Inn Fields.'

'So that's where the costume of the "dark lady" came from,' Raven realized.

Adam nodded uneasily. 'But I could not bear to be away from her, so eventually she came into my household in the guise of Mistress Bilby. It was a secret pleasure for us both that she could conceal her passionate personality so well in the dreary guise of a stern housekeeper.'

Raven remembered the servants at the door. 'Your other servants Will and Hannah know nothing of Mistress Bilby's real identity?'

'No, nothing. I hired those two deliberately for their complacent and stupid minds. I could have had the Queen of France living here in this house, and those two would not have suspected a thing.'

Raven put his head in his hands for a moment. 'But how came you to devise this wicked plot? And why against Sarah Lusted and Anne Carey, who had no connection with your inheritance?'

Strange became defensive. 'I told you before that I had tried to prise from Sir Oliver's lawyer in Warwick some advance knowledge of what that gentleman's last will and testament might contain. I had high hopes that I would be named as the main beneficiary even if Sir Oliver had fathered an illegitimate child of his own, as many suspected. But this Mr Wadsworth was a scrupulous soul for a lawyer and would tell me nothing of the will, even when I offered him a covert bribe. So, to make sure, Carolyn travelled to Warwick in the guise of a simple country girl and contrived a meeting with Wadsworth's senior clerk, a young man called Joseph Clipper. She used her arts of seduction on this young lawyer's clerk, and found out everything he knew, which unfortunately was limited. Clipper knew of Sir Oliver's illegitimate child, and also that the child had originally had the name Goodricke, and was apparently in line to inherit most of the estate, although he didn't know at the time whether the heir was male or female because of Mr Wadsworth's extreme secrecy over the matter. These were terrible tidings for us, and just what we had feared. Carolyn tried to get him to investigate more, but all Clipper managed to discover from Wadsworth was the present whereabouts of the child. It seemed a stroke of better fortune for us when we learned that the child, now grown up and twenty years old, was working as an actor or actress with the King's company in London.'

Raven finally understood. 'Yet you did not know *which* actor or actress?'

'No, but we could narrow our search down. From her contacts at the Duke's company, Carolyn was able to discover that only three of the King's company could possibly be Sir Oliver's missing child. These three – the young actresses Sarah Lusted, Jane Golightly and Anne Carey - were the only ones who had joined the company recently, and who were of the right age and background to be the missing heir.'

'Orphans, you mean,' Raven interrupted.

Strange nodded. 'It was at this point that Carolyn heard that her brother had returned in secret to England too. She told me that she had met him – that he was now scarred from smallpox and deranged in mind, but that we might be able to make use of him in return for favours of our own. I had no idea that the man was plotting something so serious against this country, and I do not believe that Carolyn knew either. If she did, she kept it from me.'

'Ingledew provided the poison with which she killed Sarah Lusted, did he not?' Raven said.

'It seems you know everything,' Strange admitted. 'It was a poison of extraordinary virulence that he had discovered during his years in the East. One scratch with a thorn covered in this poison will bring death within seconds.'

'You were at the theatre that night, of course, with me and

Mawdsley,' Raven remembered.

'Yes, I left just before the end of the play and went to the side door of the theatre, the one used by actors, for which I had purloined a key from the gatekeeper in advance. Carolyn arrived a few minutes later dressed in a gown borrowed from the Duke's theatre and I let her in. No one would question a young well-dressed woman backstage – they would think her one of the actresses, or one of Sir Thomas Killigrew's many women. I also wore a wig borrowed from the theatre in case anyone should see me waiting in the alley and recognize me. Carolyn was back from the tiring room in a few seconds. Unfortunately she was seen by your interfering orange girl Molly...'

Raven's face fell as he belatedly realized something. '*I* was the one who told you she might have recognized the woman.'

Strange admitted that too. 'You did. Carolyn became worried that the girl might have recognized her as someone from the Duke's company. Particularly as we saw Molly later again that evening when we returned the costumes to the Duke's theatre.'

'So that's why you sent those two men Wedderburn and Parish to murder her?'

Strange held up his hands in protest. 'Carolyn sent them. I did not know, truly, that she had ordered them to kill Molly. I thought they would merely scare her off with some ugly threats.'

Raven was not sure that he believed him. 'How did you come to know a pair of low rogues like Wedderburn and Parish?'

'I knew them from the dogfights in the stable yard at the back of the Cock Inn, which is near here. I own a couple of fighting dogs of my own, and Wedderburn and Parish looked after them for me. Those two would do anything for money, but their intelligence was limited so I was reluctant to use them too much.'

Raven persisted with his questions. 'And the death of Anne Carey? How did that come about? That was *you* who called the page, Thomas Creed, away from the palace chamber where Anne was lying. Did you smother her too?' he asked brutally.

Strange went pale. 'Nay, I could not do such a deed. Carolyn had to do it.'

Raven exclaimed in anger. 'Ah yes, of course. She was already inside the palace in her guise of Madam von Kladowitz, as the secret guest of Lady Castlemaine, who had invited her to stay there while she rehearsed with her maid Henrietta for the coming magic show in her apartments.'

'Her brother had put her up to that mad venture, ' Strange explained, 'but Carolyn was agreeable when she heard that the King's company would be performing in the palace a few days earlier. It seemed a perfect opportunity for us.'

Raven was scathing. 'The loosened chandelier was a clever improvisation.'

Strange stirred moodily. 'As I told you, she is a gifted woman.'

Raven swore under his breath. 'She is also a very evil woman, Adam, who has taken you to Hell with her.'

Strange was unrepentant. 'I care naught for that, provided she is free.'

Raven still had more questions. 'Why did she order Wedderburn to kill Jane today? That death lacked the subtlety of the others, I have to say. You had done your best before today to make these deaths look like mere accidents that no one would investigate too seriously. Yet no one could mistake Jane's death for an accident, could they?'

Strange sighed in exasperated fashion. 'Our hands were forced in the end. Sir Oliver Runnalls died two days ago, and we heard reports that his lawyer Wadsworth was already making plans to come to London to seek out his illegitimate child. So Carolyn said we had to act swiftly, otherwise everything we had done would count for naught.'

Raven felt his anger rising. 'So you took Sarah and Anne's lives for no reason at all! If you had but spoken to Sir Thomas Killigrew, you would have discovered that Jane's real name was Goodricke, and that *she* was the daughter of Sir Oliver Runnalls.'

Strange was uneasy. 'We had discovered the truth already by then – this man Joseph Clipper finally informed us - but too late for Sarah and Anne alas.'

Raven felt his blood boiling. 'And now you have killed Jane for naught too. You can never lay claim to Sir Oliver's estate now. I would certainly prevent that, should you ever try.'

Strange fell quiet. 'No, you are right, Henry. 'Tis too late for everything.'

Raven faced him for an uncomfortable moment.

'What now, then, Henry?' Strange demanded sadly. 'Now that you have heard this sad tale of greed and deceit, what do we do now? Shall I expect to hear the constable and the officers of the Watch banging at my door in the next hour?'

Raven was equally miserable and distraught. 'No, Adam, I do not have the heart to turn you over to the Justice of the Peace. Though you surely deserve to hang for the evil that you did, I cannot be the one to place the noose around your neck, especially since you did relent in the end and save me from your accomplice. Instead I shall leave it to your own conscience to decide what recompense to make, withered though that conscience may be. Permanent exile from these shores may be the best solution for you, Adam – away from the influence of that woman, you may even be able to redeem yourself in time by doing good works.

You had better be gone from this house within a few days, though,' he warned, 'or I may change my mind about reporting you to the authorities.'

Strange said nothing to that, sunk deep in morbid thought.

Raven stood up to go, heavy of heart, but certainly not prepared to offer his hand in farewell to a man with so much blood on his conscience. 'I trust I shall never see you again in this lifetime, Adam.'

Strange remained seating. 'No, indeed, you shall not. You have my word on that. Thank you for your consideration, Henry,' he said finally. 'My conscience may be a withered and desiccated thing, yet – be assured - I will do the right thing this time. If you will excuse me, I will not get up and see you out, but shall sit here for a while to reflect.'

Raven walked over to the door of the parlour, pain pricking at his throat, and tears filling his eyes, as he remembered their good times together. So many good things to recall, yet the memories now forever tainted by the evil his friend had done…

Adam smiled weakly at him. 'A little advice, Henry. You must watch your back from now on. Carolyn will not be forced out of London until she wants to go. And she is an unforgiving soul…'

CHAPTER 24

Saturday, 24th December 1664

On Christmas Eve, at Sir Thomas Killigrew's personal invitation, Henry Raven sat in the pit of the King's theatre and watched a full dress rehearsal of a new play by Mr Dryden called *Secret Love or The Maiden Queen.*

Raven was in an odd mood today that fluctuated between deep morbidity and moments of great pleasure. At the moment the pleasure much outweighed the gloom because Molly was on stage and playing the flirtatious Florimell, wearing a low cut gown that showed off her breasts to great advantage, and with her face painted porcelain white with bright red lips and spots of colour on her cheeks. Although the plot of *The Maiden Queen* was a serious one in solemn rhyme concerning the Queen of Sicily, whose love for a courtier threatened to tear the country apart, there was as usual in Mr Dryden's plays a comic sub-plot in which a couple, in this case Florimell and Celadon, engaged in constant lively verbal and physical jousting. Molly and Patrick Whelan were playing the couple with great verve and humour, and had completely stolen the play from Mary Pettican who was playing the Queen of Sicily. Raven's only complaint about their entertaining playing was that it seemed a little too real for his liking, as if Molly and Whelan truly were lovers…

Raven did feel an undeniable pang of jealousy as he listened to the climax of their lively courtship, when they swore themselves to each other with typically witty Dryden dialogue…

As Celadon, Whelan said, '…*Provided always, that whatever liberties we take with other people, we continue very honest to one another.*'

Molly fluttered her fan seductively as Florimell. '*As far as will consist with a pleasant life.*'

Celadon continued. '*Lastly, whereas the names of husband and wife hold for nothing but clashing and cloying, and dullness and faintness in their signification;*

they shall be abolish'd forever betwixt us.'

Molly as Florimell. *'And instead of those, we will be married by the more agreeable names of Mistress and Gallant...'*

*

After the rehearsal, Molly came and sat beside Raven, still in her full Florimell costume.

He was instantly aroused and bewitched by her in this sensuous guise. 'That was wonderful playing, Molly. You come on in your performances by leaps and bounds. And the play is wonderful too.'

Molly accepted the compliment, but then sighed. 'I agree. Yet for some reason, Mr Dryden is not happy with it yet, and will work on it some more before he will allow us to put it on publicly. So you have been given a rare privilege in seeing it today, a work in progress; Sir Thomas says that Mr Dryden is such a perfectionist that it may be years yet before we can play *Secret Love* on the stage here. '

'Then what play do you put on today instead for the masses?'

Molly looked at the stage. 'We shall do Mr Lacy's comic play *The Old Troop*, which the company all know well. And we can fortunately use the same costumes and set, which will not look too out of place for this other play.'

Raven smiled dryly. 'Yet *The Old Troop* is hardly set in Sicily.'

'No, indeed not,' Molly conceded. 'It is set in a Yorkshire village during the Civil War.'

Raven laughed. 'Yet I am a fool. No one will look at the painted backdrop when you are on stage, Molly, so the scenery matters not one whit.'

'Not in this costume, certainly,' Molly said, glancing down consciously at her bold décolletage.

Raven was even more aroused, though, by the twinkle in her eye. 'Your playing with Mr Whelan seemed very real, Molly.'

'On his part, I believe it is. He says that he is in love with me,' she admitted complacently.

Raven looked over anxiously at the stage where Whelan was talking to a fellow actor. 'And are you in love with him?'

Molly followed the line of his eyes, with a faint smile on her lips. 'Indeed not, sir, although he is an agreeable man.'

Raven tried to hide his jealousy. 'You inspire affection from gentlemen very easily, Molly, do you not?'

Molly shrugged prettily. 'I am merely myself, sir. Whether gentlemen like that or no, is not my doing.'

'And that Puritan farmer, Mr Crabtree, at Deptford?'

Molly looked innocent. 'What of him, sir?'

'He too seemed much enamoured of you, I noticed.'

'He is a nice man – a lonely man who misses a woman's affections. He reminded me of you a little, sir. Although not so young, and not so handsome, of course.'

Raven smiled wryly. 'I am not handsome, Molly. Even my own mother would not have called me a handsome man.'

Molly gazed at him appealingly. 'Indeed you do yourself an injustice. You are a most handsome man, sir.'

Raven could not help smiling even more broadly at her brazen flattery. 'And am I truly lonely too, Molly?'

'You have many companions, and a full and interesting life, I am sure, sir. Yet you seem lonely to me, particularly at present. I suppose the wickedness of your friend Mr Strange must be the major cause of your present melancholy.'

'Indeed.' Raven had visited Madam Hornett's premises on Wednesday and told Molly the unpalatable truth about Adam Strange – that *he* had been the male accomplice of that woman Carolyn Ingledew. It had been a great shock for Molly to hear this, yet she, with surprising sensitivity, had seen how much Raven was affected by his friend's perfidiousness and betrayal, and had not pressed him with too many upsetting questions.

Raven had been called back to Adam's house early on Wednesday morning by his manservant Will Hoskins, and discovered that Strange had not chosen to flee the country after all. Raven still felt badly about the circumstances because it had been Adam's maidservant Hannah who had happened to find her master's body swinging in the frozen yard at the back of the house. And no girl of fifteen should be expected to face such a sight when fetching water first thing in the morning.

Raven also felt badly about the manner of Adam's dying, after examining the body of his friend. Adam had hanged himself from a sturdy iron bracket that projected from the brick wall, and kicked over the stool he had been standing on. Yet the fall had not broken his neck as he had intended, and so he had obviously suffered a long and cruel asphyxiation instead of a quick forgiving snap of his spinal cord. Some might say the manner of his dying was well deserved, but Raven preferred to remember the sweet boy he had once been, who might have lived his life out in blameless and contented circumstances, but for that accursed woman.

Molly became solemn. 'I still cannot believe that your friend had a hand in the deaths of Sarah and Anne, and Jane…'

Raven turned to her. 'Did you know Jane Golightly that well, Molly? Did you understand her character well?'

Molly was puzzled. 'Understand her? In what way do you mean?'

'Did you know that she liked to go around in male dress on the streets sometimes – using her costume as Cesario - and calling herself by the name John Goodricke?'

Molly frowned. 'It was no harm to anyone if she did. But I did not know that, as it happens, although I did see that she was perhaps a troubled soul.'

'That was because of the way she was brought up. Her mother was a woman called Alice Goodricke, who had been a costume maker in Sir Thomas's former company many years ago. Alice became the mistress of a Warwickshire gentleman called Sir Oliver Runnalls. Eventually she gave birth to a twin boy and girl, who were supported by Runnalls, but not recognized officially by him.'

'And why was this of interest to this woman Carolyn Ingledew, and your friend Adam Strange?'

Raven hesitated. 'Runnalls was a distant kinsman of Adam's, who had no close legitimate heirs. So Adam hoped to inherit when Runnalls died...'

'Ah, I understand now,' Molly said.

Raven continued. 'The irony of course is that Adam did not need to kill anyone. I travelled to Warwick on Thursday by coach to speak with Sir Oliver Runnalls' solicitor, a Mr Josiah Wadsworth, and I returned yesterday with the truth. As I told you, Jane had a twin brother at birth. But the boy had actually died many years ago at the age of four, and only Jane had survived. Yet her mother pretended to everyone in the neighbourhood that it was the boy who had survived. She cut Jane's hair, and made her wear boy's clothes from then on, and answer to the name of "John". She could get away with it for a while – up to the age of fifteen anyway - because Jane had looked so much like her dead brother...'

'It was in the hope of inheriting something from Sir Oliver's estate, I suppose,' Molly interrupted.

'Just so. 'Tis no wonder that Jane grew up to be a confused young woman, after such a childhood. Yet her mad mother had actually managed to dupe Sir Oliver into believing that his boy John still lived, and he had made his will accordingly, naming John Goodricke as his principal heir. But the deception had lapsed after Alice's death, and Jane, who had known nothing of the reasons for her mother's odd behaviour, had soon let her hair grow again and reverted to wearing female costume. So Jane Goodricke would never have inherited anything under the terms of Sir Oliver's will, for the simple reason that Sir Oliver believed her to be long dead so had not named her as a beneficiary. He had named her dead brother John only in the will, so Jane could not have made a claim unless she had tried to pretend that she was John. But of course she knew nothing of this anyway, so would never have tried to follow her mad mother's plan...I believe she only dressed as her brother from time to time out of confusion over her identity, which was an unintended consequence of her sad mother's plan...'

'Now I see why Jane was so convincing in her role of Viola in *Twelfth Night,*' Molly exclaimed. 'Jane was in exactly the same situation as Viola in her real life – a girl pretending to be her dead brother, in order to keep his memory alive...' Molly sighed loudly. 'So, if they had done nothing but be patient, Mr Strange and his evil lover would have likely inherited the estate anyway.'

Raven nodded. 'Exactly. Consider the cruel irony of that – that woman's evil plan actually destroyed Adam's hope of the inheritance.'

Molly got slowly to her feet, with much rustling of silk from her ample petticoats. ' 'Tis indeed a sad story of human greed and folly. So I was never truly at danger from those people, was I? They had no interest in me.'

Raven stood up too. 'Except that they feared that you could identify them. That's why they sent Wedderburn and Parish after you.' He took her hand and squeezed it. 'I am most heartily glad that they did not succeed, though.'

Molly smiled at him, clearly liking him holding her hand. 'Will you stay this afternoon and watch this other play too, sir? I am a little nervous of the challenge because I barely know the lines yet, and would appreciate your comforting presence in the audience. And the company is having a Yuletide supper afterwards in Sir Thomas's private chambers, which Sir Thomas has asked me specially to invite you to, if you wish.'

'How can I possibly say no to such a pleasing invitation?' he said affectionately.

*

Raven watched Molly's performance in John Lacy's play *The Old Troop* with even more pleasure than her role of Florimell. Molly played the naughty company whore in this drama of corrupt Civil War soldiers billeted on resentful villagers, and brought the house down with her playful manner and knowing ways. The play was full of bawdy jokes and ludicrous mock French from the company chef 'Monsieur Raggou', played with relish by Christopher Malthouse.

Raven was captivated by Molly each time that she stepped onto the stage, and dispensed her saucy quips and suggestive lines.

Raven had sent word over to Mawdsley at the palace and begged him to join him at the theatre to watch this Christmas Eve performance. Mawdsley had accepted the invitation, even though he was, if anything, even more upset about the untimely death of Adam Strange than Raven was. Both gentlemen were left to reflect that it was but fifteen days since they had sat together with Adam in this same place and watched that performance of *Love in a Tub*. And both were left equally to wonder whether they had always misjudged Adam's true character, or whether he had been simply an innocent seduced by great evil.

Yet Molly's performance distracted both gentlemen completely from their melancholic mood and brought tears of laughter to their eyes. As the cast took their bows at the end, Mawdsley said, 'That truly is a wondrous girl, Henry. If you do not proposition her, then I certainly will,' he promised, only half in jest. 'But I would suggest that you act quickly before she is stolen away from you.'

Raven blinked. 'Stolen away? By whom?'

Mawdsley nodded discreetly at the box opposite. 'In your preoccupation with ogling Molly on the stage, you may not have noticed that the King is in attendance today.'

Raven *had* noticed the Royal presence in the theatre, but had not otherwise paid too much attention to his monarch, who seemed to have quickly lost interest in him in return now that the threat from Ingledew was gone.

Mawdsley went on. 'I noticed that the King was taking much note of Molly's performance today, and that perhaps he recognized her as the "Quaker girl" from Deptford. Therefore please bed that girl quickly before the King steals her away from you –' he smiled wryly – 'or else she dies of boredom from your slow and ponderous approaches.'

Raven cleared his throat uncomfortably. 'We shall see.'

Mawdsley laughed. 'We shall indeed. But I wager that girl will be in your bed before the end of December, Henry. You are quite besotted with her.' He put a cautionary hand on his friend's shoulder. 'I trust that you will not be so silly as to propose marriage to her, though, Henry. Molly is a delightful girl, yet she would never be a fitting wife for a sober man such as you…'

*

A few minutes later, with the audience mostly gone, and while he was waiting for Molly and the cast to change so that he could go backstage and share their Christmas supper, Raven received a message asking him to go to the King's box. But when he knocked at the door, he found only Lady Castlemaine and her maidservant Henrietta seated there.

Lady Castlemaine used some brisk strokes of her fan to freshen the stale smoky air. 'Did you enjoy the play, Mr Raven?'

'I did, my lady.'

Lady Castlemaine gave him a knowing look. 'Yes, I noticed that you did. I wanted to remind you that you did agree to have dinner at my apartments this coming week. Would Wednesday suit you?'

Raven bowed formally. 'It would suit me very well.'

She smiled at him in response, looking very beautiful in the flickering candlelight.

Yet for some reason Raven had a sudden distressing vision of how her life might develop once the King finally tired of her. He saw her, forty years on, perhaps neglected, perhaps a little drunken and blowsy and down on her luck, living in a house in unfashionable Chiswick or Kensington, and flirting shamelessly with boys young enough to be her grandsons while reminiscing about her long gone days as the King's mistress...

Raven hurriedly cleared his mind of these distressing thoughts, and returned his attention to the beautiful woman she was now.

She gave him her hand and he kissed it most gallantly. 'I will look forward to our dinner, my lady.'

*

Later that same Christmas night, Molly lay in bed with Celia. Celia had gotten into the habit of coming up to Molly's garret room and sharing her bed for the last week, which was not something she had done since Molly was little. Yet Molly preferred not to sleep alone, especially on winter nights as cold as this, and had welcomed her mother's company.

Celia's voice was drowsy. 'How went it at the theatre tonight. Molly? There are no more actresses dead, I trust?' she said sarcastically.

Molly smiled sadly to herself. 'None, mother. Those villains have been apprehended.'

'And did you see the King tonight? There have been rumours that he survived an attempt on his life this week.'

Molly had wisely never told Celia anything of what had happened at Deptford, knowing she could never keep her mouth shut. 'Ye should not believe everything you hear, Mother,' she said complacently. 'I did see the King this evening, Mother, and looking most well and handsome. Although, if I am being critical, perhaps he is a little swarthy of complexion, and has a rather large bony nose.'

Celia smiled. 'A large bony nose on a man is a sign of a prodigious horn in my experience.'

Molly stirred. 'Mother...!'

'Did you see Mr Raven at the theatre?' Celia asked, in a more proper tone.

'I did. He joined the company for our Christmas repast.'

'And did you flirt with him?'

Molly laughed. 'A tolerable amount. Yet he is not the most flirtatious man in the world.'

'That may be because he loves you, Molly. True love tends to tie the tongues of men, and smoothes off their rough edges.'

'Mr Raven has no rough edges,' Molly said, 'and he is certainly in love with me, I am sure,' she announced.

Celia sat up sharply in bed. 'That is wonderful news, Molly, if it is true. And has he made any formal approaches to you?'

'Not exactly. Yet he will, I am sure.'

Celia settled back in bed with satisfaction. 'And how did the play go today?'

Molly yawned. 'It went well enough.'

'What part did you play?' Celia inquired, though without much genuine interest.

Molly was still yawning and finding it exceedingly hard to stay awake. 'I played the company whore, Mother.'

Celia was outraged that Sir Thomas should be getting Molly to play a whore.

''Tis gross hypocrisy on your part, then, Mother,' Molly complained. '*You* are a whore, and you have often told me there is no shame in it. So why do you object now when I merely assume the part of one. In any case, I played the part with *your* voice and *your* manners.'

'Oh, I see.' Celia seemed almost touched at discovering that she might be the inspiration for Molly's role. 'Yet I was not always a whore, Molly, you know. I was an innocent girl once, and I did have genuine love affairs when I was young. But men always disappointed me, except perhaps Captain Tommy, who did disappoint me in the end, I suppose, by dying so inconsiderately...'

'So tell me about these great loves of your life, Mother,' Molly asked sleepily.

Celia hesitated. 'I do have something to tell you about the greatest love of my life, Molly, as it happens. Something that affects you directly.'

Molly was wary at the tone of her voice. 'What is it?'

Celia sighed softly. 'You have always thought that you were the child of Samuel Titchen, draper of Bartlett's Passage, and his wife Mary.'

Molly held her breath for a moment. 'What do you mean? Am I not their child, then?'

Celia sounded deeply uneasy. 'No, you are not. In fact you are my own sweet child...'

'What!' It was Molly's turn to sit bolt upright in bed now. 'I thought you could not have children.'

'After *you*, I could not. My womb was much damaged in giving birth to you. It was those damned French doctors, I believe...' Celia still lay on her back, her voice sad. 'I gave birth to you when I was living in Paris nearly seventeen years ago. But I gave you up on my return to London a few months later. I was but twenty, Molly, and with no knowledge of bringing up children, so I thought it for your own good. The Titchens were a modest and sober couple with no children of their own, who I was sure would give you much better care than I ever could.'

Molly felt her heart turn over.

Celia's voice fell to a whisper. 'When the Titchens died in that terrible fire at their shop a few months later, it seemed a miracle of providence that you – a babe of only nine months – should survive. You were thrown to safety at the last minute from an upstairs window by Mary Titchen before she succumbed to the flames.'

Molly could feel her heart racing now. 'You took me back? Why, when you had disowned me so recently?'

Celia took her hand under the bedclothes. 'I could not bear to be parted from you a second time, Molly.'

Molly felt tears pricking her eyes. 'But why did you never tell me the truth before now?'

Celia gave a long sigh. 'Because I knew that you would have wanted to know immediately who your real father was.'

There was a long pause before Molly said determinedly. '*Well...*?

CHAPTER 25

Tuesday, 27th December 1664

Henry Raven stood in the condemned cell at the Tower, and watched his own icy breath rising in dense white clouds around him. This truly was a dank and depressing place, and Raven was not sure why he had come on this cold Tuesday evening.

James Blight was chained to the dripping stonewall opposite by heavy iron manacles. A single candle burned fitfully on the wall by his head, and showed the cruel lines of strain on his face, and his bruised and bleeding features. Despite his obvious injuries, it seemed he had confessed quickly to complicity in the plot to kill the King and destroy the *Royal Charles* in Deptford Dry Dock, although Raven was far from convinced of his full participation in this plot, or even of his absolute guilt. Raven admitted to himself that this was the main reason why he had accepted the request to visit Blight in his cell; it was a last opportunity to discover the real truth about this man. He was uncomfortably aware that he himself had been the first person to link Blight directly to the plot, when he had followed him to Southwark ten days ago, and the thought that he might have helped condemn an innocent man to the gallows was weighing heavily on him.

These were troubling times to live in, Raven reflected, when so high a man as this – a Groom of the Bedchamber, and a long time ally of the King - could be reduced almost overnight to this miserable and wretched state. It meant that no one was safe any more from being denounced and flung into prison on the flimsiest of evidence. And the initial evidence against Blight had been extremely flimsy – merely that one meeting between Blight and Ingledew in Southwark that Raven had reported to Anthony Mawdsley.

Watching this miserable and broken wreck of a man, Raven was consumed with pity for him. There would be no more meetings of the

Royal Society, or genteel evenings of entertainment at Whitehall Palace, for Mr James Blight: he was due to be hanged, drawn and quartered on Tower Hill at first light tomorrow, and seemed anxious to unburden his soul to someone beforehand.

'Why did you ask to see me, Mr Blight?' Raven demanded curtly, keeping any note of pity out of his voice. 'I scarce know you.' It occurred to Raven that Blight's inquisitors must have mentioned his name as one of those who had accused him. Yet if that were so, Blight did not seem to resent him for it, and there was no overt anger in his manner towards his visitor.

Blight had seemed a defeated and cowed man when Raven had first been shown into his cell by the turnkey, yet his eyes now flared into life, and he adopted a surprisingly defiant tone. 'That is true. I do not know you well, Mr Raven. Yet I have heard good reports of you from others, and was sure that *you* would give me a fair hearing, despite you having given evidence against me.'

'It matters not if I am a fair man or no. I am not your judge, sir.' Raven glanced at the cell door, and lowered his voice discreetly. 'But are you truly guilty of these heinous charges, Mr Blight?'

Blight flinched as if in great pain. 'That depends on which charges you mean, sir.'

'Did you truly plot with that madman Ingledew to destroy the Royal dockyard?'

'No, Mr Raven, I knew nothing of that.' Blight winced with pain and lifted his right hand up into the light to examine it. Raven saw with distress that he had no fingernails remaining, and that the fingers themselves were black and swollen with ugly bruises. Blight might have confessed quickly, yet it did not seem to have been quick enough to spare him from the violent acts of his inquisitors.

'But you did know Ingledew well?' Raven pressed him, his eyes transfixed by the savage injuries to Blight's hand.

Blight lowered the shattered remnant of his hand. 'Yes. I knew him as a boy in Bedford, and then later as a comrade during the Civil War.'

Raven paced a little up and down. 'Did you know that he was working as an agent for the Dutch?'

Raven could see that this was clearly a surprise to Blight, as the man blinked slowly in disbelief. 'No, I did not. I merely thought that he wanted to kill the King for personal reasons –' he laughed humourlessly – 'which I suppose is bad enough to justify my interment and punishment here. Ingledew made contact with me only a fortnight ago. I had not seen him before that in near twenty years, but he said that he wanted my help to kill the King. He claimed that he sought revenge for his father, who was one of the regicides, and I had no reason to doubt that.'

This sounded like the honest truth to Raven, and was consistent with what he had seen directly. He watched the candle flame flicker for a second in a brief draught issuing through a crack in the heavy studded oak door. The cold in this cell was truly awful, and he was beginning to shiver uncontrollably, yet for some reason Blight seemed unaffected by it. 'Why would he think that you would give your help in such a venture? You fought on the King's side in the Civil War.'

Blight grimaced. 'We both did. Yet Ingledew gave me no choice in the matter. He knew somehow that I had become a member of the Fifth Monarchy sect, and threatened to expose me if I did not aid him...'

Raven finally understood. 'I see. But what made you turn to such a dangerous non-conformist movement as that?'

Blight was hesitant. 'That was my late wife's doing. She was a woman of great principle.'

Raven nodded resignedly. 'Ah, then I pity you if you were led to this fate by a principled wife. Such women have much to answer for.'

Blight's eyes were like smouldering coals in the light of the candle. 'You misunderstand me, sir. I do not resent my late wife's influence, or my allegiance to the Fifth Monarchy cause. It will lead me to everlasting life...'

'And very soon,' Raven pointed out harshly.

Blight almost smiled through his broken teeth. 'Yes, soon indeed. Yet, despite my meetings with Ingledew, please understand that I took no active measures in support of him, and I certainly knew nothing of the plot at Deptford.'

'I believe you,' Raven conceded. 'Ingledew's primary target was always the dockyard at Deptford, and the ships being refitted there. That was what his Dutch masters had agreed to pay him for. It was not the death of the King that they sought, but only the disabling of his new warships.'

Blight's anger was growing, but the anger was not directed at Henry Raven, only towards his former friend Ingledew. 'I cannot understand it! What did Ingledew want this blood money for? The wretch was finished – he was a miserable and scarred shadow of the noble soldier and Englishman he had once been.'

Raven remembered what Molly had told him of the conversation she had overheard between Ingledew and his sister. 'Even so, I believe that he dreamed of a new life in the Americas.'

Blight frowned. 'But why did he have to involve me in his wretched plan? There was no need of it. I could not have helped him in the plot to destroy the dockyard. I have no knowledge of naval matters that might have been of use to him.'

Raven deliberated. 'I cannot claim to divine the man's twisted mind exactly. But it seems that his actions were designed as much to entrap you as to fulfil his bargain with the Dutch.'

Blight gasped as he realized the truth. 'You think Ingledew *wanted* me to be caught?'

'I can see no other likely explanation. Perhaps he was jealous of your rise at court while he was reduced to this disfigured outcast. Or perhaps he blamed you for not trying to help his father during the trial of the regicides...'

Blight gave a cackling laugh. 'He denied that he felt that way, yet I see now that what you say has to be true. Yet the irony is that I fully deserve this punishment. In my heart I had become a secret enemy of the King.'

'Why? Because of your conversion to the Fifth Monarchy?'

'Partly that. But also because I have come to believe that the rule of Kings will always be arbitrary and unfair. Kings may start off with the best of intentions towards their subjects, yet they all become tyrants in the end. I suspect that you and I, Mr Raven, are much alike in our politics. I believe that you too, in your heart, want England to be a republic eventually. Therefore it is ironic that you have done so much to preserve this particular king's life.'

Raven was uncomfortable with the accusation. 'Charles Stuart is not a bad king.'

'Not when judged against the greatest tyrants of history, perhaps. Yet he is not a good king either. And, mark my words, he is a secret papist at heart, who is determined to place England under the power of the Church of Rome again.'

Raven refused wisely to be drawn on this dangerous subject of the King's true religion. 'Are you in much pain and distress, Mr Blight? Did they put you to the rack?'

'They did, even though I had confessed already.' Blight twisted his face in agony. 'These gaolers wanted their pound of flesh and would not be denied by my ready cowardice.'

'No man could call you a coward, Mr Blight,' Raven said quietly. 'Not with your military record during the War.'

Blight seemed grateful for the compliment. 'I hesitate to ask you, sir. But you are a scientific man, and you have also seen men hanged, drawn and quartered, I have no doubt. I have never seen a hanging as it happens – I have always felt a great distaste for witnessing the misery and suffering of my fellow men. It is perhaps a foolish question, but is there great pain and torment involved? Worse than I have already suffered?'

'Alas, a thousand times worse,' Raven said bleakly. 'The punishment is intended to keep the victim alive as along as possible to suffer continual agonies.'

Blight began to weep pitifully. 'Then God help me through this coming day.'

Raven looked around carefully to check that no one was watching them through the small viewing panel in the door. 'God *will* help you, sir, if you take this beforehand.' With that, Raven took out a small phial of liquid from under his cloak. 'If you prefer to avoid the agony of tomorrow, then this small draught of physic – an extract of monkshood - will ease your passage into the next world in less than one minute.' Raven gently placed the phial into Blight's left hand, which seemed less injured than the right.

Blight took a long grateful breath. 'Thank you, Mr Raven. You have taken a huge risk in bringing me this phial, but you have relieved a great burden from my soul.'

'Thank me not, sir, 'tis little enough that I do for you.' Raven wished indeed that he had thought to offer Adam Strange such an alternative painless route out of this world. But at least this poor man would be spared the agonies of being hanged on Tower Hill tomorrow, then taken down alive to have his bowels removed with red-tongs, his heart ripped from his chest and his severed head to be displayed for a baying crowd to mock...

*

Raven was in a deeply sombre mood as he walked west along Thames Street to return to his waiting carriage. Raven had earlier had some business at the Navy Office in Seething Lane with the Clerk of the Acts there, a Mr Pepys, before keeping his appointment in the Tower, so had asked Martin to wait there with the carriage.

The night was yet one more of penetrating frost, this one without a single breath of wind to even stir the branch of a tree, and with a wonderfully clear sky ablaze with stars. The constellations were so bright and well defined that Raven could make out many stars and nebulae with his naked eye that he would usually require a telescope to see. Foremost among these was the now infamous comet, whose tail now seemed almost to be dividing into a distinct fork.

Yet, as a portent of disaster, this comet had been a poor example for believers of such superstitions in Raven's opinion. While there had no doubt been the usual catalogue of death, disease and human misery during the comet's visitation, these did not seem to have been notably more severe than when there was no comet visible in the sky. Perhaps if the King *had* been murdered in Whitehall Palace, or if the King's dockyard *had* been destroyed by that great explosion a week ago, then the prophets of doom would have had some justification in attributing some dark occult powers to the comet. Yet Raven had to acknowledge that several people of his acquaintance had sadly lost their lives while that comet had been blazing malevolently in the sky – including blameless innocents like Jane Golightly – therefore it might be premature to mock the baleful power of comets entirely…

Raven turned from Thames Street into Seething Lane and, by the light of a wood brazier burning brightly at the door of the new Navy Office building, saw his carriage parked nearby, with a harnessed Bessie waiting patiently, tethered to a tree. Yet there was no one sitting up in the driver's seat, so Raven wondered with slight irritation where Martin had gone. Pulling level with the carriage, and peering inside, Raven saw Martin apparently sleeping inside, his head leaning against the side rest. Raven was more amused by this slight dereliction of duty than anything else: Martin was such an upright and ethical young man that Raven could not remember him ever sleeping on the job before.

Raven thought he would play a childish game with him, though, and rapped loudly on the polished satinwood door of the carriage.

Yet Martin did not even stir at this loud knock, which was odd - he must indeed be sound asleep. Raven leaned in through the open window to give his shoulder a shake, but had hardly made contact with Martin's sleeve before he heard a strange whistling sound behind him.

Then the world went black…

*

Raven awoke to find himself confronted by a face that seemed barely human. He jumped in fright at this dreadful apparition, yet found that he could not move too far, having his hands and feet tightly bound. He realized that he was seated in the back of his own enclosed carriage, but had no idea how long he had been insensible. Of Martin there was worryingly no sign…

'Good evening, Mr Raven,' Simon Ingledew said formally, taking a slow and laboured swig of some liquid from a small flask. 'And how went your visit with Mr Blight? Is he in rude health?' The man sat on the opposite corner of the carriage to him, his right shoulder leaning heavily against the window of the carriage as if he needed it for support. With his immense height, his scarred head was jammed up so close to the roof of the carriage that he only had an inch or so to spare. Because he was wearing all black against the black upholstery of the carriage seat, the illusion that his head was dismembered and floating free in the air was a convincing and frightening one.

Raven remembered with chagrin his own dismissive remark to Adam Strange that Ingledew could not possibly have survived that explosion at Deptford, except with supernatural help. For a moment he felt a thrill of terror at the possibility that this might indeed be some supernatural visitation come back to torment him, like Banquo's ghost. Certainly the figure opposite seemed almost like some resuscitated corpse - no more than a moveable head attached to a seemingly frozen and near immobile body.

Yet this was only a momentary lapse into superstition and irrationality on Henry Raven's part, and he soon recovered his proper sense, convinced again that this man was merely a resilient rogue, and not one gifted with occult powers. 'How did you survive that explosion on the barge, Mr Ingledew?' he asked with bluff confidence. 'I am greatly impressed with your talent for survival.'

Ingledew laughed, although whether such a terrible rattling noise in his throat could really be construed as caused by amusement was difficult to say. 'I could ask you a similar question, sir. How did you survive that explosion in Southwark? Granted that it was much smaller than the one at Deptford, of course, yet its force was also concentrated into a much smaller area. Yet I am glad to see that you remain a rational man like me, Mr Raven, and that you do not yield to unscientific beliefs and superstitions the first time you are tested by some unexplained mystery. Our mutual friend, Mr Hooke, would be proud of your constancy. But as for the details of how I survived the explosion that destroyed my vessel a week ago, I care not to elaborate. 'Tis enough for you to know that I did survive, and have returned to wreak my vengeance on you.'

Raven tried not to panic at the quiet threat in this evil man's voice. 'Did your sister help you rise from the dead perhaps?' he suggested woodenly, surmising that Ingledew could not possibly be acting alone tonight. Someone had struck him hard on the back of the head with fierce force, and Ingledew seemed in no present condition to have done that. In fact Raven could have sworn from a close study of his limited movements that the man was paralysed from the waist down.

Ingledew acknowledged his sister's help with a wry smile. 'I confess that she did help me rise from my watery grave at Deptford. But then she has a score of her own to settle with you, Mr Raven. You destroyed her little plan to obtain a country estate in Warwickshire, and you also turned her lover against her. Carolyn is not likely to forgive and forget such wicked insolence as that...'

'And where is the lady in question?' Raven asked warily, hoping to God that the harpy was now occupied elsewhere and was not here. 'And, more to the point, where is my manservant?'

'Worry not. Our argument is not with your coachman. Luckily for him, he is a handsome young man of pleasing countenance, so Carolyn felt no pressing desire to slit his throat. He is presently lying insensible in the alleyway at the side of the Navy Office, but will eventually wake up, I am sure, even if having a very sore head when he does.'

Raven was relieved to hear that, although not so sure that his own fate would be quite such a happy one. He had no other plan in mind now but to try and keep this man talking somehow, so as to preserve his own life as long as possible. Perhaps Martin might awake earlier than expected and come to his rescue...

'Why did you not kill the King when you had the chance, Mr Ingledew?' Raven asked.

Ingledew spoke in a hoarse whisper, his lips barely moving at all now. 'I believe you know the answer to that question already, sir. I was commissioned by the Dutch States General to destroy the *Royal Charles* and the other ships in the dry dock at Deptford, not to kill the King.'

Raven kept talking. 'So this vengeance you swore against the King was mere smoke and mirrors to disguise your real intentions. But why did you involve Mr Blight when there was no need of it...?'

Ingledew's eyes flashed. 'I had long hated Blight for what he had become. It was him I truly wanted revenge against, not the King.'

Raven gasped at the degree of venom in this evil man's voice. 'For what reason?'

Ingledew sank back slightly in his padded seat, his arms now as rigid and unmoving as his legs. 'For his air of pious hypocrisy. '

'Yet he was your friend once,' Raven said in wonder.

'Once, perhaps, a long time ago. Yet feelings like that mean naught to me now. Human companionship of any sort has meant little to me for years. I despise the world and everything in it. But particularly people like Mr Blight who sacrifice their principles so easily.'

Raven reflected sombrely. 'Mr Blight will face a terrible punishment on the morrow because of your actions.'

Ingledew shrugged. 'I did not make him join the Fifth Monarchy. And I doubt that he will suffer any great agony tomorrow. A soft-hearted visitor to his cell like you, skilled in the apothecary's arts, will no doubt have provided him with an easier passage into the next life. In fact I am sure that Mr Blight is probably already with his maker, is he not?'

Raven was shocked: this man did seem to be able to read his mind as if he truly was the Devil...

Ingledew had trouble even moving his lips properly now. 'Now I need to exact my vengeance against you for foiling my little scheme at Deptford.'

Raven said nothing. The man seemed to be very close to death himself, and incapable of doing him any direct harm. *But where was his evil sister?* She was more of a worry, if she was waiting nearby...

Ingledew tried to smile. 'You seem remarkably unconcerned

considering the many dreadful things that I could be about to inflict on you. I admire such sangfroid in the face of impending disaster.'

'It is not sangfroid that makes me fearless of you, Mr Ingledew. I can see that you have lost the power of movement in your limbs. And the paralysis is spreading even now to your face. Soon you will not be able to turn your head, or move your lips, or even breathe.'

Ingledew attempted a laugh again, but his lips could barely move. 'I was right about you,' he said in a strangled whisper. 'I told my sister that you would not be so easily cowed. '

'So where is the lady?' Raven asked again.

'Gone, to do my bidding elsewhere.'

'Why did she not kill me before she went, if she hates me so much?' Raven was emboldened to ask.

Ingledew's eyes were glazing over. 'I think perhaps she wants to reserve that pleasure for some other time. And I asked her not to kill you tonight, because I wanted you to hear my last will and testament.' He paused. 'I am indeed dying, as you say. It took considerable medical arts on the part of my sister to keep my broken body alive for this last week. And now I have taken a little dose of a compound to ease my own passage into the next life, as you no doubt did for Mr Blight in his cell. In fact you saw me drink it a few minutes ago. I believe I have but five minutes of life left now at most, and so am gazing into the very abyss of infinity.'

Raven stared in horror at the dying man, still wondering what awful fate this man might have planned for him before his own demise. He could not believe that he would be simply left to go free.

Ingledew moved his head weakly. 'You believe that you have won a victory over me, do you not? The victory of good over evil?'

Raven had a terrible feeling of foreboding. 'What have you done?'

'Destroying those ships at Deptford was only part of my plot, Mr Raven. There is another element to the plot all of my own planning, something my Dutch paymasters know nothing about. You see I also intend to revenge myself on the city that butchered my father, by inflicting a great scourge on its people.'

Raven was aghast. 'What scourge?' he demanded, struggling frantically to free himself from his bonds.

Ingledew shrugged, his eyelids seemingly grown heavy as lead. 'Do not concern yourself too much. There is naught you can do to prevent it now, even if you were free.'

'What evil thing have you done?' Raven repeated through gritted teeth.

Ingledew gave a long sigh. 'Ay, 'tis better perhaps that you properly understand your fate. And the fate of this city. You see, I brought a ship load of black rats with me from Constantinople...'

Raven was filled with dread now as he remembered what Molly had told him she had seen in that storehouse at Deptford. He had doubted that part of her story at the time, but no longer. 'Rats? Why would you bring rats here? We have more than enough vermin of our own.'

Ingledew gave a final bitter laugh. 'Not like these...rats. These Eastern vermin of mine are infected with the...*plague*...' He stopped to catch his tortured breath. 'That is why I had decided to keep your orange seller friend alive in that storehouse at Deptford – I was going to leave her in the company of a few of those infected rodents to see if she would indeed catch the plague. But I underestimated her resourcefulness and intelligence. I still do not understand how she contrived to escape from that secure prison. Yet it matters not...tonight I will perform a similar experiment, but on a much larger scale...the whole city of London...'

Raven gasped as he finally understood the depth of this dying man's depravity.

'...My dear sister...is releasing these rats...all over this city even...as we speak. Once released, they will...hopefully...find themselves comfortable burrows...to survive the winter. When the summer comes...this city shall know the full force of my...vengeance. You see, Mr Raven...that comet presently blazing in the sky...truly is a portent of...disaster after all...'

With that Ingledew's head slumped forward against his chest.

CHAPTER 26

Saturday, 31ˢᵗ December 1664

'You seem melancholy, my love. I hope it is not my presence here that makes you so sad,' Molly said teasingly.

Raven smiled at her. 'Of course not. I am not at all melancholy, merely reflective. It is a great pleasure to have you here in my home as my guest. And to see in the end of the Christmas season with you.'

Molly snuggled up to him under the covers. 'Then I am glad of it too, my love.' She laid her head on his naked chest and stretched luxuriously beneath the sheets. Raven could feel her bare legs pressed pleasurably against his, and reflected wryly that Mawdsley had indeed won his wager about Molly ending up in his bed before the end of December.

'Yet something troubles you deeply, Henry, I can see,' Molly went on. 'Of course, you must be remembering your ordeal with that man Ingledew.' She lifted her head to gaze appealingly into his eyes. 'It still perplexes me how that evil man could have survived that explosion at Deptford...'

'It perplexes me greatly too,' Raven said with wry honesty. He recognized that he should perhaps be simply grateful to be alive after that ordeal, yet those hours trapped in the back of his own carriage with the corpse of that madman had been excruciating torture. Most of the torture had been self-inflicted, of course, as he worried himself to death about the consequences of what Ingledew had said. Had the man and his sister really released hordes of plague-infected rats all over the City of London to wreak a terrible vengeance on its people?

When he had spoken to Molly again, the day after his ordeal in Seething Lane, she had – worryingly – confirmed that there had been hundreds of caged rats in that storehouse in Deptford before Christmas, all of which were gone now, so the threat did not seem a hollow one.

Raven had consulted immediately with Mr Hooke at the Royal Society over this threat, and even that ingenious gentleman had no solution to it other than to hope for the healing hand of nature to solve the problem. Mr Hooke believed that the plague was carried not by the bites of the rats themselves, but more likely by the bites of the infected fleas they carried in their fur. Therefore he had some hopes that, even if these rats had been released into London's streets as Ingledew had threatened, the cold winter weather would kill most of the fleas on them.

Yet, Raven reminded himself, it would take the survival of only a few infected fleas to produce an epidemic of the plague…

Raven tried to forget this awful threat, and to enjoy this precious time alone with Molly on the eve of the Feast of Circumcision. They had the house entirely to themselves at the moment because Dora and Kate had returned to Dorset for a few days to visit Dora's ailing sister.

Martin too was still alive and well thankfully – his life had indeed been spared by Ingledew's sister during that incident in Seething Lane, just as Ingledew had said, but for reasons that Raven still did not fully comprehend. Yet it seemed that this lady must be a very strange mixture of evil and gallantry, of wickedness and beauty. Whatever the reason for this woman's mercy, Martin had eventually recovered from the blow she had given him to the head, and had returned to the carriage in Seething Lane to release his master from his unpleasant imprisonment.

Yet Raven had not seen too much of Martin either in the last day or so: it seemed Dora had been right in her judgement of Martin's romantic inclinations, because he was entirely unconcerned about Kate's departure to Dorset, and had spent much of the last three days hanging around the back door of the house at the next corner. But for once Raven did not mind his servant's long absences from the house.

Raven, despite some feeling of regret that Martin had not fallen for sweet young Kate after all, had to confess that the maidservant living in that corner house was a wonderfully pretty maid with sweet pink cheeks and a lovely shy smile, and therefore seemed to be an entirely appropriate choice for a handsome and equally sweet young man like Martin. Raven had still not raised the issue of the mine manager position in Newcastle with him yet, but decided that if Martin chose to marry his beautiful servant girl and start a family, he might consider that job, and the increased social standing and wage it would bring, highly acceptable.

Molly was not working today in the theatre, so had spent the whole day at his home with Raven, which more than compensated him for the temporary loss of his servants. In fact he had enjoyed her company so much, and her playful jokes, and her youthful beauty, that he knew not how he could ever go back to his old solitary ways.

Molly ran her hand through his hair, and then sweetly kissed a strand of it. 'Promise me you shall never cut your hair short, my love, and wear a wig. I will hate you forever if you do such a thing.'

Raven smiled. 'Then of course I promise.'

Molly had an uneasy thought. 'But what do we do when your servants come back, my love? Will they not be shocked at what they find? You in bed with a common strumpet!'

'You are no common strumpet, Molly, but a very special strumpet,' Raven said lightly.

'Ay, you know me well, sir,' Molly said, with a mock show of hurt.

'My servants will accept you, Molly…and respect you,' Raven assured her quickly, though he knew well that she was merely pretending to be hurt. 'If they do not, I will find myself new and more obliging servants. It is not my job to appease the people who work for me.'

'I would not want anyone to lose their position over me,' Molly declared solemnly.

'Then I promise you that no one shall, Molly.'

Molly took a hesitant breath. 'Yet before I make any pledge of loyalty to you, Henry, there is something I should say. Whatever else I do with my life, my love, I want to keep working at the King's theatre for the present. It would not suit me to forego that pleasure in my life.'

'Nor would I want you to simply sit around my house, bored to distraction, and getting up to mischief. I have no wish to clip your wings, Molly, so of course you must keep acting. Yet I have heard that all the actresses in the company must perform favours privately for Sir Thomas from time to time in order to keep their jobs. Is that true?'

'I imagine that it is true,' Molly admitted warily.

'Then such conduct will not be acceptable to me, not as far as you are concerned anyway. In fact, if Sir Thomas lays one more hand on your pretty body, tell him I will come to the theatre and flail his own buttocks alive, even though he be a friend of the King.'

Molly smiled complacently. 'I shall tell him that gladly.' She put her hand to his cheek. 'Do you truly love me, though, Henry?' she asked worriedly. 'Or are you a deceiver like all men, merely spouting honeyed words to get me into your bed?'

Raven put his finger playfully on the tip of her nose. 'I do love thee, Molly. I love every delectable inch of you, and will be as true to you as I possibly can.'

Molly was satisfied. 'Then I will remain true to you in return, to the best of my ability.'

'Then we shall be an eternally happy couple.' Raven suddenly remembered the words of Celadon in The Maiden Queen and quoted them as best he could remember. 'Provided always, that whatever liberties we take with other people, we continue very honest to one another.'

Molly laughed at his unexpected boldness and said her line as Florimell in response. 'Ay, sir, as far as will consist with a pleasant life.'

Raven went on as Celadon. 'Lastly, whereas the names of husband and wife hold for nothing but clashing and cloying, and dullness and faintness in their signification; they shall be abolish'd forever betwixt us.'

Molly kissed him playfully on the lips. 'And instead of those, we will be married by the more agreeable names of Mistress and Gallant...'

*

As Molly heard the bells of St Martin's ringing to welcome in the Feast of Circumcision, she lay back in bed and wondered if she might be dreaming.

Being a girl wise beyond her years, she was fully aware that such contentment could not last, of course, yet for the moment this was a happy life indeed...

She also knew full well that she could never be this man's wife, yet was not pained by that realization. Henry would no doubt marry a sensible and respectable woman in due course, one with no connections at all to the risqué world of the theatre. Perhaps she was being foolish, but she truly preferred, like Florimell, to be a lover and a friend to this man rather than a wife. There were too many things that Molly still wanted to do with her life before she was prepared to accept the constraints and formal rigidity of marriage.

These reflections on life and love made her wonder again about her own origins and whether Celia had finally told her the truth about herself. Molly was convinced by now that Celia was her own true mother, and this was a difficult enough fact for her to cope with by itself.

Yet the identity of her father was an even more challenging thing to accept.

Was she really the daughter of a French count from the court of Louis XIV? It seemed most unlikely to Molly, and was in all probability just another of Celia's strange fantasies about herself.

Yet the fact was that Molly cared less about the possible grandeur of her origins, or even the identity of her real father, than being with a man she truly cared for. Henry Raven was not a handsome man, it was true, yet he had a sweet and patient nature for a wealthy man. And he was a surprisingly proficient lover...

She listened to his steady breathing, and put her hand to his chest, feeling the quiet rhythm of his heart. With that she complacently closed her eyes and drifted off into sleep.

THE END

ABOUT THE AUTHOR

Gordon Thomson is a civil engineer by profession, a Geordie by birth, and Sunderland supporter (and therefore masochist) by inclination.
His professional engineering career took him all over the world - Africa, the Far East, South America, as well as Holland and the UK - and this experience of exotic places and different cultures is what gave him the urge to try writing.
He has a Japanese wife and two grown up sons, one of whom was born in Holland, so he does claim to be a citizen of the world, if a very English one.
Winter of the Comet, which is set in Restoration London, is his second published novel on Amazon. He has previously published the Victorian thriller *Leviathan*.

Printed in Great Britain
by Amazon